RIVAL'S
SON

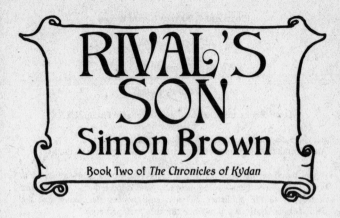

RIVAL'S SON

Simon Brown

Book Two of *The Chronicles of Kydan*

DAW BOOKS, INC.

DONALD A. WOLLHEIM, FOUNDER
375 Hudson Street, New York, NY 10014

ELIZABETH R. WOLLHEIM
SHEILA E. GILBERT
PUBLISHERS
http://www.dawbooks.com

First Printing, March 2006
1 2 3 4 5 6 7 8 9 10

DAW TRADEMARK REGISTERED
U.S. PAT. OFF. AND FOREIGN COUNTRIES
—MARCA REGISTRADA.
HECHO EN U.S.A.

PRINTED IN THE U.S.A.

For Aimee and Georgia, welcome to the fold.
And for Simon Palmer, who showed me Troy.

Acknowledgements

As always, I am indebted to my first victim, Alison Tokley, whose judgment I trust implicitly; and to my patient, patient editors, Cate Paterson, Brianne Tunnicliffe and Julia Stiles, and to my agent Tara Wynne, who leaves no publisher unturned. Thank you all.

240th Year After the Descent

Prologue

THE Empress Lerena Kevleren, having sacrificed those she loved the most so she could Wield the Sefid as it had never been Wielded before, slew all her enemies in the world.

The slaughter was so terrible, the loss of life so great, that the Sefid was whipped into a maelstrom. Lerena, unaware of what she had wrought, thought it would return to its normal placid state when she had finished with it.

But air and earth, fire and water were suffused with it, soaked it up like a desert soaks up rain. It coated every molecule, made everything of metal glow with a blue halo, briefly opened every sentient mind to its own potential. Then it settled out, sinking into the world's recesses. But it was not gone, was not made calm again, and as disease strikes where society is weakest, wherever the fabric of humanity's universe was most worn or under greatest stress, the Sefid made itself manifest.

Lying in her bed, suddenly awake, Lerena could not believe how quiet the palace was. Even her lovely hounds made not a whimper. She should be hearing the servants making ready for the day or, more distantly, the sounds of

merchants' carts making their way to the market near the
royal precinct. There was no birdsong, and that was strangest
of all, for they were one of the few animals the Kevlerens
could not stop entering Omeralt, the capital city of the
Hamilayan empire. Traditionally, the only creatures besides humans tolerated in the city belonged to the
menageries of the Kevleren family, but birds, together with
rats and insects, were always present.

Thinking of birds made Lerena think of her sister, the
Duchess Yunara, and for a moment Yunara was still alive
in Lerena's mind, and so were all the Beloveds and the
Kevlerens in Rivald and all seemed right with the world.
But only for a moment, because then the memory of all the
killing flooded back and she sat up straight in her bed, her
stomach swelling with nausea. Lerena swallowed hard to
keep from vomiting. Her sister's birds even now, surely,
were waking under the dome of Yunara's great aviary,
wondering where she was and why she did not go to them.

But there was no sound anywhere.

Still sitting straight in her bed, Lerena realised it was
not dawn, that darkness still lay over her land, and that it
was bitterly cold. Her first thought was that the sun had not
risen, that her use of the Sefid three days before—beyond
anything ever done before in the history of her family—
had somehow destroyed it or sent the world spinning off its
orbit. There would never be another sunrise.

Her hands were trembling and she pressed them down
in her lap to keep them still.

No, she told herself. Stop behaving like a frightened
child. It is still night, that is why it is so dark.

And yet it was not completely dark. Her room was
filled with a blue glow, and she looked around to find its
source. The gold threading in one of her dresses shone

dully, and the iron support of her dress mirror blazed as if it were on fire. Her breath gushed out as though she had been punched, and it made a cloud in front of her face.

Not daring to believe it was possible, she crept out of her bed and parted the curtains in her room and looked out over the city.

Omeralt was limned in blue flame. The towers sparkled with it. She could almost feel the Sefid humming through brick and stone.

She closed the curtains and sat on the edge of her bed.

It was not possible. She was the only one left in the whole world who could Wield so powerfully. She was sure of it.

Lerena closed her eyes and willed herself to believe it.

The great granite blocks of the central tower and the tall eastern wall of Kydan's Citadel shone as bright as marble in the dawn light, but Strategos Galys Valera did not see them even though she stood on the walkway directly above the wall. She was as still as a statue, and in her mind she was seeing again the writhing mass of black insects that covered the body of Kitayra Albyn, and hearing again the scratching, chirruping sound of thousands of chitinous legs, and smelling again the sour fumes of formic acid.

The memory had no prelude or coda; it comprised just the short few moments that followed Galys's discovery of her dead lover and patron. The memory filled her dreams at night, and much of her waking day. It came unexpected, unbidden, and always brought Galys up short, made her forget whatever it was she had been doing. A part of her mind would try to find a way out of the memory, to bring her back to reality, but often she only broke from it when someone greeted her or asked a question or touched her face or shoulder to make sure she was all right, and then she would shake her head, surprised she was no longer in Kitayra's cold stone room, her lover's corpse, teeming with alien life, lumped in the middle of the floor.

To cover her anguish and to try to forestall the memory, Galys worked every minute she was awake, even eating on the job. She oversaw the repair work on the wall on which she now stood, made sure the dead were cleared away and burned, that the wounded were gathered together in one place for treatment and well cared for, that enemy weapons were gathered, sorted, repaired and stored in the Citadel armory . . .

And still she was not tired enough. Still the memory came as fresh as if it had just happened, and strangely, when her mind finally edged away from it on this occasion she found that although she could move again, the world itself seemed unnaturally quiet, as if she were on the set of an elaborate play and she were the only actor. There was no breeze, no sight or sound of bird. Even the great Frey River seemed to cease its flowing. She breathed out slowly, saw it frost in the air.

It could not be. Not here. Not now.

She turned around to see if someone—anyone—else was around. Below, in the Citadel's courtyard, two workers were mucking out the sentries' latrine. They were moving, but slowly, as if time had slowed down for them. Even as she watched, someone walked under the main gate and into the courtyard, but the gait was odd, limp-jointed, the head lolling too much to one side.

A blue haze drew her gaze to the tower. Light shone from a window. Almost reluctantly, she counted the floors up to the window and realised it looked out from Kitayra's room.

As quickly as it had started the moment passed, and the world surged over Galys like a wave, washing over in a cold rush. She heard the river below, and the workers labouring in the courtyard. A light easterly touched the nape of her neck, sending a shiver down her spine.

She shook her head, confused, and tried to remember what it was she had been doing before. Carefully, Galys made her way down from the wall to look for more work.

Paimer's bare feet slapped on the baked clay floor of the servants' quarters in his alcazar. He opened every door in turn, poked his head in and scanned the room, then ducked out again, leaving doors open as he went. Servants he had roused followed him down the hallway, asking after him, but he ignored their questions until he had inspected the very last room, and then with a perplexed look turned to face the now considerable crowd behind him.

"Has anyone seen my Beloved?" he asked plaintively.

The servants, surprised, threw each other glances. None would meet Paimer's gaze. Eventually one girl, younger and braver than the rest, pointed back to the main house. "One of your own would know best, your Grace."

Paimer frowned.

"I mean one of your Axkevlerens," the girl continued.

"I looked there," he said. His face crumpled, and his servants involuntarily backed away. Their duke, the most patrician, sybaritic and aristocratic of Kevlerens, had never before shown any emotion stronger than selfish satisfaction or any expression beyond a kind of subdued disdain. But then the features straightened, the eyebrow lifted, and he regarded them with a studied indifference.

"What are you all doing out in your nightclothes?" he asked.

The servants as a group mumbled an apology and disappeared back into their rooms. Paimer stopped one by placing his hand on her shoulder and said, "Wine. Red, I think. No. White. In my study."

"Yes, your Grace." She scurried away and the duke, walking stiffly, made his way back to the main residence. Once there he stopped in mid-stride, shivered, and looked around as if he were lost.

"Idalgo?" he called. "I *know* you're here! Where are you hiding?"

This time it was a gaggle of Axkevlerens that came to him, drowsy from sleep, befuddled, startled to see Paimer standing in his nightshirt looking close to panic.

The oldest of them, a bald, hook-nosed fellow with rheumy eyes, came before Paimer and bowed. "My lord? Is there something I can do for you?"

"Who are you?"

The man blinked. "Why, your chamberlain of the house, my lord. I am Dayof Axkevleren. I am the oldest member of your household. I worked for your father as a boy."

"Dayof? Yes, I remember now. I do know you." Paimer leaned towards him and whispered urgently, "Idalgo Axkevleren. Where is he? I have been searching for him all night."

Dayof swallowed. "Why, your Grace, you told us yourself that he is gone. You said he died bloodily at the hands of Rivald."

For a second Paimer did not breathe, and he stared at Dayof as if the Axkevleren must have been a madman. Slowly his expression changed, and Dayof could tell that his master was now wondering about his own sanity.

"I said that?" he said in his old voice.

Dayof could only nod.

There was a sound behind them and both men turned around. The servant stood there holding a brass tray with a flagon of wine and a crystal glass on it. She was trying to hold the tray steady but was so nervous the base of the glass clattered on the brass.

"In my study," Paimer said imperiously, and the servant curtsied and hurried away. He turned back to talk to Dayof but saw that some of his family had gathered behind his people. They were Kevlerens—cousins once, twice, three times removed—who had been shocked almost into insensibility by the deaths of their Beloveds and sent by the empress away from the palace in Omeralt to recover at Paimer's country alcazar; this was the first time they had shown any curiosity at all about the goings-on beyond the confines of their own rooms.

He nodded towards them and said to Dayof, "Make sure they are put to bed. I intend to be up for a while and I do not want to be disturbed."

Dayof bowed and Paimer followed the servant to the study, a long room that ended with a tall window looking northwards out over formal gardens. The gardens were quite extensive, a product of his father's obsession with controlling nature, and although no gardener himself, in daylight Paimer appreciated their beauty. In the dark all he could make out was the silvery outline of trees in the half-distance. The servant put the tray on a table near the window. On her way out Paimer touched her shoulder again and said, "Bring another glass."

"Another glass, your Grace?"

"And my wig," he said, and she hurried off.

He sat by the table. He could feel the warmth in the room leaking out through the glass. The two long walls of the study were lined with shelves filled with books: tall, leather-bound volumes with embossed gold writing on the spine and which smelled of dust and old knowledge. Another inheritance from his father. Paimer never read any of them. Reading was something he always found less interesting than talking, and being a duke he could have a conversation any time he wanted.

It did not take long for the servant to reappear with the second glass and his red wig. She handed him the wig and put the glass on the tray, hesitated to see if Paimer would request anything else of her, and then left when nothing was forthcoming.

When she was gone, the night seemed to fall in around him, making the world smaller. He felt a tendril of something in the back of his brain, something he recognised as his other self, the one who lost control and felt afraid of life. That other Paimer came and went without regard for his feelings or desires, and he was afraid of him. When he returned he could not remember most of what the other Paimer had said or done. He knew he needed help, and tonight he was certain he would get it.

Paimer poured wine into both glasses, took one and sipped on it. His gaze settled on the silvery line of trees. After a while he noticed he could see quite clearly the mottled skin on the back of his hand. The skin was blue. The tall window's metal tracery was glowing, casting shadows back into the room. Cold clung to his thin frame and made him shiver. He carefully placed his red wig on his scalp. He remembered he was famous for his red wig.

The second glass of wine lifted from the table. Paimer looked up to view his guest, and although he was secretly pleased more than words could say, he only allowed himself the thinnest of smiles.

"You've been away for a long time."

"Good evening, your Grace," said Idalgo Axkevleren.

"I was worried."

"Now that I'm back, my lord, everything will be all right again."

Shortly after sunrise the river boat edged towards a bank overgrown with reeds and drooping, long-leaved trees that Quenion Axkevleren did not recognise. The two natives who had sailed and rowed for the three nights since their escape from the disastrous attack on Kydan maneuvered the boat under the trees and threw a rope around one of the white trunks to stop it drifting away, then pulled reeds over it to make sure nothing of the boat could be seen from land or water. The younger of them, Velopay, left to find food while the other, Adulla, stayed behind to guard the boat and, Quenion was certain, to stop her from taking the boat for herself and her charge and leaving the natives stranded. It did not seem to have occurred to either of them that Quenion could not have sailed or rowed the boat by herself, and that her charge, her master Numoya Kevleren, was in no condition to help himself let alone his Beloved.

Numoya had been unconscious for almost the whole journey, only half waking when his injuries roused him enough to make him groan in pain. Quenion cried for him but did not know what else to do except hold him and tell him over and over that he would be whole once more, forcing herself to believe it despite the horrendous burns to his face and neck. She was sure his eyes were so damaged he would never see again, and his scalp was so blackened and swollen that even should he survive he would look like a corpse for the rest of his life. It was small consolation, but at least they were traveling by boat, which made for a smoother journey than would have been possible by land, and the river provided them with fresh, cool water to drink and which Quenion could use to soothe Numoya's burns.

Now, at the start of their third day of escape, she felt Numoya's condition was improving. The heat coming from his injuries was diminishing and his breathing was more even, and she thought he had moved from being near comatose to a deep but troubled sleep. Quenion left him for a short while to stretch her legs on shore, never straying too far in case Numoya should call for her, and always alert for any sign of pursuit from Kydan. When she returned she settled herself as comfortably as she could against the stern thwart and rested Numoya's gory head on her lap.

As the day warmed she started to drowse, but her head lolled too far back and she woke with a jerk. Her arms prickled with goosebumps. Her breath frosted. Adulla looked at her in wonder, then gasped when his breath did the same. His head jerked away, retreated from it as if the puff of air was a live thing.

Quenion next noticed how still and quiet everything was. She looked across the dappled surface of the river, scalloped by a slight northerly breeze. It seemed hazy, as if the rising sun had started a mist, but it was too late in the year for that. She rubbed her eyes to clear them, but the haze did not go away. She thought she was seeing deep into the river, as though the sun were no longer reflecting off its surface but revealing what lay underneath. She saw long, red fish with golden fins gliding through the water, strips of green water weed, spiders carrying their own bubbles of air, and crayfish scuttling along the riverbed looking for tiny snails and worms.

Numoya moaned, but Quenion was so distracted by what she was seeing she did not realise at first that he was muttering words. It was only when Adulla retreated to the bow of the boat that she looked back. Numoya mumbled words again, and she automatically asked, "My lord?" Then two things happened, one after the other. First, she felt her master's skin tighten under her hands and the swelling under his scalp visibly reduce as if it had been drained, and then the native lurched forwards, hand outstretched.

Almost without thinking, Quenion stamped her foot on the firegon resting on the bottom of the boat and Adulla stopped in mid-action. His eyes darted between her and Numoya, and he said shakily, "You gave me the weapon. It is mine."

"Once fired, it cannot be used again," she said evenly, speaking in the patois that had developed over the years between those from the Rivald colony of Sayenna and the natives that had contact with it. "His highness is no threat to you."

Then she moved her foot so the native could retrieve the firegon. He was about to do so but gasped and fell back again. The firegon's metal barrel was glowing blue. "He does his magic," the native accused, nodding towards Numoya.

"He is Wielding," Quenion admitted. "But only to heal himself—"

Even as she spoke, Numoya's mutterings ceased. She inspected his injuries as closely as she could under their canopy of reeds and branches, but it seemed that only the swelling had eased. The burns looked as hideous and dangerous as before. She had hoped his eyes . . .

"Is he finished?" Adulla asked.

"He is no longer using the Sefid," she said.

"What did he sacrifice?"

Quenion's breath caught in her throat. What, indeed,

had Numoya sacrificed to Wield? Sacrificing was the only
way the Sefid could be accessed, and then only by a
Kevleren. And how could Numoya possibly have been
aware enough of his surroundings to find anything to
sacrifice?

"He used demons," Adulla said after a moment.

"There are no demons," Quenion said scornfully.
"There is only the Sefid."

For a moment neither said anything, and Quenion tried
to hide the confusion she felt. She had seen Numoya sacrifice many times, almost always something small, like
one of the lovely cats from his menagerie, and once something much more precious and costly to him. It involved
blood and loss and grief and words. This time there were
only the words, and they barely audible. Something had
happened that she did not understand.

The firegon stopped glowing, and the native, hesitantly,
picked it up. He handled it gingerly, as if it might burn him.
He glanced towards Numoya again but did not cock or aim
the weapon.

In the depths of the Deepening Sea there is no light and
almost no movement. The great current that surges east to
west rushes above the sea floor, barely stirring its muddy
surface. But things long and black and sightless make their
sinuous way below the current, sifting the mud with pin-
cers and tentacles for scraps of food that have drifted down
from the surface. When they are lucky enough to find the
carcass of a large animal they fall on it like flies on an open
wound, taking a mouthful of rotten flesh and twisting and
writhing until they tear it loose. In this way, the remains of
a whale or shark can be reduced to nothing more than a
skeleton in no time at all. But when a group of them fell

upon one new such morsel, the smell of rotting meat permeating the water around it, they encountered something entirely unexpected.

A barrier of metal was between them and their meal, but their hunger was all-consuming. In their jaws the metal came away as easily as bone, great links of chain disappearing under the mud. When the barrier had been almost completely dismantled, the dead thing suddenly jerked. The scavengers automatically pulled back, but the smell of decay was so strong it overcame their natural caution and when it did not move again they lunged in to feed. But they had become the prey instead.

The thing that attacked them exceeded anything in their experience. Strong beyond resistance, vicious and ravenous, it swirled in the mud and water, lashing out, grabbing them around their long bodies and tearing them apart with tooth and claw. They tried to defend themselves, but their bites went unnoticed and the thing's flesh squirmed in their jaws until they spat it out. More and more of their fellows swarmed in to share in what they thought was a feast and found themselves being fed on instead. Eventually, the thing kicked away from the floor to find and destroy more of the scavengers, but instead was found by the current. It was picked up like a leaf in a wild wind and swept away from the slaughter below.

1

IT was almost noon, and what had started as a cool spring morning on the grasslands north of the city of Kydan had developed into a warm, slightly muggy day. Ensign Ames Westaway halted his half-troop of fifty dragoons and sipped water from a leather bottle he retrieved from his saddle. He felt itchy and sweaty under his jacket and was tempted to undo the toggles to let in some air. While considering whether or not that was something he should do, by wondering whether or not it was something his hero Commander Gos Linsedd would do, his gaze settled on the hill to the east that rose above the grasslands. The land north of Kydan and the river Frey had been uniformly flat until now, covered in lush, knee-high grass that grew from a rich alluvial soil.

Good hunting ground, Ames thought grimly but without much satisfaction. Any ideas about earning honour and glory as an officer in the army of the Hamilayan empire had been dispelled for him since the battle for Kydan, when the city's enemies had been bloodily repulsed at great cost to the defenders. He had done things during that struggle that turned his stomach when he thought on them, and now he wondered how he had been capable of such actions. The only excuse he could offer himself was that in the heat of battle whatever humanity he possessed had been repressed, and the only comfort he gained was in the knowledge that every combatant in the battle had committed similar excesses, so his guilt, if not ameliorated, was at least shared.

As well, he would never forget the death of his best friend, fellow ensign Ilver Ward, who had been split from shoulder to rib cage by an axe blow. Ilver had not died immediately but thrashed on the ground like a cut snake, spraying his blood everywhere in a great hissing fan, and Ames had not been able to hold or comfort him.

After the battle he had wandered aimlessly and bewildered, hardly taking in the carnage. Stone and earth were covered in a glaze of blood so thick it took hours to dry. Broken and dismembered bodies were heaped around the Citadel and walls where the fighting had been fiercest; broken and torn, the worst thing for Ames was how inhuman the corpses became: they were carcasses, nothing more, and it was impossible to think of any of them truly ever having been human at all.

Nor had the defeat of the enemy stopped the killing. Ever since the failed assault, Ames had been leading his half-troop in pursuit of the retreating enemy on the north side of the Frey, while his commander, Gos Linsedd, led the other half of the troop on the south side. Ames's orders were to harass the enemy, picking off stragglers and making sure they did not reorganise and turn back to try their luck on the city a second time.

At first Ames had been glad of the chance to get out of the city and its stink of death, but the companion forced on him by Gos Linsedd had killed any relief he felt. Perhaps

the commander had assigned Kadburn Axkevleren to his
force out of consideration for Ames's youth, or perhaps
simply to get the Beloved out of everyone's way, but the
man was haunted by his own hatred, a hatred ignited by the
terrible death of his master, General Third Prince Maddyn
Kevleren.

Ames, grieving himself for what he had lost in the battle for Kydan, could not comprehend grief so great it consumed life like fire consumed paper, and yet Kadburn
seemed like a man shriveled by his loss, made a ghost by
his suffering, only coming truly alive when they came
across the enemy, usually forlorn and desperately afraid
stragglers. Kadburn was always first to attack, and when
the enemy was slaughtered he returned to his near cata-
tonic state, withdrawn and forbidding.

In the three days he had been hunting them, none of the
enemy had so far offered any serious resistance, and in the
grasslands there was no place to hide from the dragoons on
their horses and armed with carbines, short-barrelled firegons, and sabres made from strong Hamilayan steel, but
the day before the dragoons had come across evidence of
a much larger band than any they had yet encountered, although still heading directly away from Kydan.

The decision to follow this band instead of concentrating on smaller groups had been an easy one for Ames: he
reasoned that the larger band offered the greatest threat to
Kydan. He had asked Kadburn's advice, but the Beloved
had only nodded.

The trail they were following suggested they were pur-
suing at least a hundred infantry, well shod and organised,
and it soon became apparent that the enemy were aware
they were being pursued, because evidence of their passing became harder to find. If Ames were the enemy's

leader, he would be looking for a chance to turn the tables on his pursuers, and the hill to the east presented the first real opportunity for an ambush.

Ames took one more swig from the water bottle and put it away. Despite how uncomfortable he felt under the jacket, he decided to leave it done up. He was an officer, not an enlisted man, and he had an example to set. And a job to do. He sighed heavily. He scanned the rim of the hill, searching for any hint of an enemy lookout, knowing as he did so that he was too far away, but hoping he might catch a glint of sunlight off metal or a movement against the clear blue sky.

Two things occurred to Ames: first, if the enemy were waiting for him and his troopers on the other side of the hill, then they would expect him to be following the trail as it curved around the base; second, to make sure the ambush went undetected, they would pull back any lookouts well before they could be seen by the approaching troopers, which would be about a longyard on horseback. Again he sighed heavily; fear and stress were making him breathe more deeply. He could feel his heart pounding behind his ribs, and it occurred to him, briefly, that he should have joined his father as a cloth merchant, traveling the very safe route between Castell and Omeralt, the capital of the great empire of Hamilay. But Hamilay was thousands of miles away, across the Deepening Sea, and the life of a cloth merchant, while largely without risk, had few other compensations.

Ames became aware that his men were looking at him, some with an anxious expression. He wished Kadburn would speak up, offer some words of advice, but the Beloved sat on his horse, eyes cast down, dark and silent. Ames thought then that his men would probably have preferred it if Ames had joined his father's trade, too, and the thought made him smile.

It was the best thing he could have done, and he knew it immediately by the sudden eager interest on some of his troopers' faces. If Ensign Westaway can smile when there were probably a hundred or more of the enemy just over the rise, they were thinking, then everything was going to be fine.

And just then, as if someone had whispered the advice in his ear, Ames knew what to do.

Quardo Sienna was a scared man, and had been since the night he had met the bitch from Hamilay, the self-styled Strategos Galys Valera. Until then he had been an up-and-coming member of the plutocratic government that had usurped power in Kydan, earning the respect of those who sided with the plutocrats, and feared by those who did not. There had been some guilt in his rise since most of his friends—former friends—had been enemies of the usurpers, but not much else to trouble his soul. That is, until the plutocrats' great rival, Poloma Malvara, returned from exile with a Hamilayan army and firegons to back him up. Galys Valera had been one of the Hamilayan leaders, the one who had first made a fool of him in front of his former friends and then taken him prisoner.

In his heart Sienna knew he should be angry and vengeful instead of scared, but he could not help himself. It was easy being brave when your friends were in charge, but out here on the grasslands far from home, pursued by the terrible Hamilayan dragoons, and in the company of desperate, defeated and exhausted soldiers, all he wanted to do was lie down on the ground and become completely invisible. He consoled his conscience with the thought that if he survived the next few days there would be plenty of time to replace the fear inside him with anger and the need for vengeance.

The band he had fallen in with had been chased down by the dragoons over several hours. In that time their collective hopes had been raised and dashed, the dragoons at first losing and then rediscovering their trail. Now the band's leader, the deposed plutocrat Maira Sygni, had decided that their only chance was to turn and fight. Sienna and a few others had argued the point and been told that if they did not like it they could go off on their own. Sienna and the others declined the offer; like small sparrows in a big flock, they instinctively felt their best chance of survival was by staying in the middle of a large group and hoping they went unnoticed when the falcon swooped.

Maira Sygni kept the band moving until they had reached the hill behind which they all now waited in ambush. The plan was simple but should work if the dragoons kept on their merry way, following their trail and not watching where they were going. For the unprepared, even the slightest rise in a flat landscape could hide a big surprise.

As they waited, Sienna's fear started manifesting itself physically. He wanted to throw up. The air was warm and humid, and although he had not had any food for several days his stomach felt as if it were filled with cold, stale porridge.

Ames did not know if the enemy had yet withdrawn their lookouts on the hill, but he could wait no longer; one of the most important lessons Commander Linsedd had drummed into him was that soldiers hated seeing their leaders hesitate. When his half-troop was near the shadow of the hill he called a halt and ordered a scout to dismount and climb to the top and survey the other side. A few minutes later the scout had scrambled back down and confirmed Ames's suspicions about the enemy waiting in ambush on the other side, and their numbers. The ensign surprised himself by receiving the news with something like relief: he had guessed right, after all, and without his commander nearby to give advice.

A slight breeze ruffled his hair, cooled one cheek. He turned and looked out over the plain, and for the first time, and entirely unexpectedly, he realised how beautiful and how rich the land was. The new colony would prosper here, given half a chance. One day, maybe one of his own descendants would settle on these grasslands and grow wheat and raise cattle and horses and breed fat, happy children.

One day.

He turned back to his men, his gaze passing over Kadburn Axkevleren. He wondered, briefly, if he should ask him for advice, since the Beloved seemed so reluctant to offer it, but dismissed the thought almost immediately. The troopers would see it as a sign of self-doubt on his part; anyway, he reasoned, if Kadburn had any advice to give, surely it would have been delivered by now.

Ames ordered nine dragoons to dismount and follow the scout back to the top of the hill. The remaining forty he divided into two equal squadrons, one to move around the hill to the south, the other to go with him as he continued to follow the trail around to the north. He waited until the dismounted troopers finished the ascent, then ordered the first squadron, which had further to go, to move off first, and when these were almost out of sight gave the order to his own squadron to unsheath their sabres and advance at the trot along the trail.

*   *   *

Kadburn did not consciously make the decision to follow the ensign and his twenty dragoons; since being attached to the half-troop by Gos Linsedd—for reasons Kadburn only dimly understood through the haze of his grief and anger—he had followed the young officer like a gosling. He was aware the ensign sometimes talked to him, but the words may as well have been in another language, for Kadburn's mind was occupied with the need for revenge, and nothing else.

The enemy had taken from Kadburn everything that had meaning. His life was mere existence, without purpose or reason. The only thing that gave him hope was the prospect of revenge, the prospect of doing to the enemy what they had done to Maddyn Kevleren, his master and his friend and his only family. Killing the enemy had helped him survive the hours immediately after Maddyn's death, but when the enemy had fled the walls of Kydan he had fallen into a dark, dreadful hole so deep that he could see no light at all.

But now, with the prospect of action, his mind cleared. He was aware of the way the dragoons sat more stiffly in their saddles, and the way the ensign held his saber in his right hand, pointed to the ground, his arm as straight as a rod. There were enemy nearby, and he felt his own senses sharpen in expectation of combat, felt his heart beat faster, felt his limbs loosen and his mouth dry. A part of him marvelled at how easily his body adapted to being on a horse again; it had been so many years since he had ridden to war that he had forgotten how fast the animal could move at a canter and gallop, how quickly the ground raced underneath.

If only, if only, his master were here as well! If only

Maddyn Kevleren could lead the charge, Kadburn's life again would be complete.

The first sign that things were not going according to Maira Sygni's plan was the thwack of something hitting the ground near Sienna's feet, followed closely by the crackling report of firegons. Sienna glanced up at the top of the hill and could just make out the heads of Hamilayan troopers and the gleaming barrels of their carbines. Part of his mind was thinking how strange it was that although he had almost never heard the sound of firegons until the overthrow of the plutocrats, and had never been hit by one of the balls they fired so lethally, his body automatically cringed whenever a shot rang out, making his head duck and his nerves jangle. For a moment he forgot his fear, but it rushed back twice as strong. He did not even think of drawing his sword, but started backing away from the base of the hill to get some distance between him and the enemy.

Then a line of troopers appeared from the south, their sabers held upright by their shoulders. There was another round of fire, and a man in front of Sienna dropped without making a sound. A cloud of black smoke lifted into the sky over the hill.

And just like a flock of sparrows, the band swung north away from the new threat. Many of them were already running, dropping their weapons, and soon the ambush had turned into a rout. Sienna tried staying with the group, but between looking over his shoulder for signs of pursuit and avoiding the feet of others around him, he soon found himself several yards from anyone. He did not even know in what direction he was fleeing. His heart yammered in his chest and his mouth was dry; sweat prickled his skin and tears welled in the corners of his eyes.

Sienna was so intent on running he did not hear the bugle call ring out over the plain, and until it was too late did not see the trooper coming straight for him.

Ames waited until he saw the enemy starting to disperse in panic before letting the bugler sound the charge. Now that the band was not clumped so tightly together the dragoons' horses would not pull up before driving into them. Once the charge started, he knew he had no real control over the course of the battle any more. He had done what he could to deploy his half-troop to best effect, and so far it had worked perfectly. Now came the final test, and it was all up to chance and the skill of his troopers.

He focused on one enemy, a man near the middle of the dispersing band. He held his saber out, and although one hand still held the reins he guided his horse with his knees. As he galloped past enemy he swiped at them, his arm turning like a windmill vane, but his eyes never left the original target he had set himself. Just as he reached him the man turned and saw Ames bearing down on him, and in his last second of life opened his mouth to scream.

Ames did not wait to see what his saber had done—he knew well from the fighting for Kydan what the weapon was capable of—but charged through, using the reins now to help pull the horse north to pursue other enemy.

It took nearly an hour to hunt down every last member of the band, and the dragoons took no prisoners: Ames could not spare any men to supervise their return to Kydan. They heaped the bodies into a mound and set it alight, then kept the blazing pyre behind them as they headed back to the Frey to water their horses. Only Kadburn lingered behind to watch the pyre burn. They reached the river just before nightfall. Exhausted and covered in the gore and sweat and dust of battle, the troopers stripped and washed off the blood that caked uniforms and boots.

Ames, naked to the waist, was last in the line, and watched, hypnotized, as the blood of the dead was carried away, a thick red ribbon that eddied and whirled into the centre of the river and down towards the Deepening Sea miles away.

2

A breeze whispered through the tower window. Papers rustled on the desk and Galys looked up. The sun was high in the sky and she realised with a shock the day was half gone. She must have been staring into space for . . . she tried to calculate the time, but her mind refused to do anything so logical or precise. Kitayra could have done it standing on her head, with her eyes closed.

Galys's heart lurched. It seemed to her that every waking moment of her life was spent either reliving the discovery of Kitayra's body or trying to keep at bay her grief at losing her lover. Although she threw herself into work, some trick of fate, or perhaps simply the wounds of memory, too often made the real world recede away from her and the presence of Kitayra loom in her mind. Sometimes she would hear Kitayra speak to her, never with anything deep or revelatory, but of the everyday and the intimate, and when she automatically turned her head to respond and there was no one there the pain would rush in, raw and vivid and cold, and fill her up.

Galys constantly reminded herself that she was not alone in her suffering. The attack of the plutocrats had resulted in many dead, many wounded. It had taken more than two days to bury all the slain, and some of the wounded would not see out another tenday. At night the wailing of the bereaved lifted into the night sky above Kydan, the sound accompanying Galys's own fitful, disturbed sleep.

She sometimes wondered, but never said to anyone else, whether she would manage better if the prince had survived the battle. Perhaps they all would manage better.

General Third Prince Maddyn Kevleren had been the leader of an expedition from the distant empire of Hamilay to found a colony at Kydan, a city in the mysterious New Land taken over by plutocrats with the connivance and assistance of Hamilay's traditional enemy, the kingdom of Rivald. The expedition had included Galys and Kitayra among its members, and Poloma Malvara, Kydan's former prefect, returning from exile. Maddyn had been given command as a way of disguising his exile from the court of Empress Lerena Kevleren, his cousin. The reason for the exile had been his commoner mistress and their child, and the fact that both had died on the voyage across the Deepening Sea added even greater poignancy to Maddyn's own death during the assault on the city.

Galys stood up from the floor, being careful not to upset the piles of papers she was sorting from the mountains of documents Kitayra had left behind, and went to gaze out the narrow window in the room's north wall. In the afternoon light, the island of Karhay, the most northern of the three that made up the city, looked like a teardrop made from jade. The waters of the river Frey that swept around the island were golden in the sunlight. It was on Karhay that the settlers from Hamilay were making their new home, building huts and fields and byways. From her position in the tower of Kydan's great Citadel, she could also look down along the length of the main island, Herris, where most of the housing for the original inhabitants existed. Nearby was the Long Bridge, straddling the Saddle that bisected Herris, and on it several Kydans were looking north, just as she was, observing the goings-on of the newcomers.

Perhaps they think of us as invaders, Galys thought. We came uninvited, after all, even if we did help free them from the yoke of the plutocrats and their Rivald backers. How would she feel if Kydan had been her home? She thought she might be resentful, and the thought unsettled her in a way she could not yet properly describe. She realised a part of it involved her uncertainty about the future, and not just her own but the future of all the colonists from Hamilay. Galys told herself that the best way to overcome the uncertainty was to plan and work for the future she wanted, but so soon after the battle for the city, so soon after losing everything her heart cared for, she could not help feeling callous about the days and weeks ahead, as if the future were no longer as important as it once was. She understood, with grim resentment, that it was because without Kitayra life for her lost a lot of its meaning and promise.

Galys stared out over the city and told herself she would strive for all the people who even now worked with back-breaking labour to repair the damage from the battle, struggled every time they woke to a new day to find the courage they needed to carry on for the sake of those left behind. She imagined how the city might look in ten or twenty years time, with a proper commercial harbour and bridges between all the city's three islands, and even a track for a steam carriage running from the city and deep into the interior of the New Land. She saw, too, Kydans and Hamilayans working together, no longer separated by their pasts.

I will do this for Kydan, she told herself. And I will do it for poor Maddyn and all the others who died.

I will do it for Kitayra . . .

Galys caught her breath. There she was again, back with Kitayra. She turned away from the view, only to stare into the cold, stone room that had been Kitayra's last home. A beetle scuttled across the floor in front of her and she stepped on it without even thinking. Her lover's papers lay everywhere, kept in place by books and chair legs and goblets, and in one case by Kitayra's traveling chest.

Galys blinked. She had not yet sorted through Kitayra's effects. She closed her eyes and for a moment fervently wished she had not been the grammarian's lover, that she were cleaning up after some anonymous victim of the assault. She breathed out and opened her eyes, so ashamed of the thought, no matter how brief, that she was blushing.

I was her lover, she told herself, and then said it aloud. "I was her lover. She was my life mate, and I hers."

And a cooler, more rational part of her brain reminded her that furthermore Kitayra had not been a victim of the assault. No, her lover had died no ordinary death, and Galys had a good idea the Sefid had been involved, but how and Wielded by whom and for what reasons were questions for which she as yet had no answers and did not know how she would find any. But she would keep on searching because she could not accept that Kitayra had died without reason. Then, unbidden, she clearly remembered the blue glow she had seen coming from this very room when she had stood on the east wall. When had that been? Yesterday? The day before?

And what had caused the glow? That it originated from the Sefid, Galys was sure . . . at least, she had no other explanation for it. But had it been caused by someone in the room at the time, or had it simply been an after-effect of the energy used to kill Kitayra?

Galys's shoulders slumped. So many questions to answer, but no way to answer them. She sighed heavily and knelt down by the chest. The clasps lifted easily and she swung back the lid. On top of everything else was a beautiful red dress, the one Kitayra had worn as a special treat for Galys when they went to meet Empress Lerena, and had never worn again.

"Oh."

Galys touched the dress gently, almost hesitantly, then lifted it out and carefully placed it on the room's single cot bed. She returned her attention to the chest. Boxes, scarves, jewellery. A small jar of henna. A packet of blue dye. More books. Undergarments. Spare brushes, one with a broken tortoiseshell handle. A mirror with the silver flaking off the back. A child's toy, a cloth kitten, tucked in between balls of woollen stockings and a pair of slippers.

Kitayra's oldest possession, Galys guessed, and picked up the toy. She held it to her nose. She could smell Kitayra. At that moment she knew she was going to lose control. She was going to cry, going to wail out her grief . . .

Something in the chest sparkled, something that had been hidden by the cloth kitten. Galys looked down and her grief gave way to surprise.

It was an imperial birth chain.

Poloma Malvara stood outside the basilica of the goddess Kydan, after which his city had been named. He had been on his way to the Great Quadrangle from his family home, dressed in his best and brightest clothes, the white sash of the prefecture hanging from his neck, but he stopped when he came abreast of the basilica's modest stone entrance, a simple archway with a wooden door at the end. Some of his fellow citizens passed him as they entered the basilica. They nodded to him respectfully and he absently returned the gesture. For a long moment he hesitated, then went under the arch, pushed open the door and entered the basilica's atrium. He was caught in a stream of golden light from a tall window in the west wall. Dust motes sparkled in the air before him. The shaft of light crept slowly across the basilica's stone floor as the sun started its long afternoon descent, sharply illuminating depictions of the goddess's life that had been chiselled into the heavy basalt paving.

Poloma raised his hand as if to catch the light and watched it glide across his smooth brown skin.

With this very hand I slew my fellow Kydans, he thought heavily, remembering the battle against the traitorous plutocrats and their followers. And yet the hand was unmarked in any way. Poloma thought that wrong somehow—against nature. There should be some stain from all the blood he himself had shed or had caused to be shed in his name.

Other worshippers bustled around him, some regarding him curiously. The light moved on. Poloma dropped his hand. He looked around, suddenly distracted, not sure what had urged him to enter the basilica. He went through to the chapel, a large square space surmounted by a tall white-plastered dome and with long windows in each wall. In the centre of the room was a tall statue of Kydan herself. Her painted face was both beautiful and alien and altogether real, as if the sculptor had really seen the goddess. Her human head and torso twisted into a crocodilian tail, reflecting the city's own divided nature, between land and sea.

Even as he gazed at the statue, Poloma automatically started mumbling the prayer to Kydan his mother had drummed into him when he was a child, but when he re-alised what he was doing he stopped himself. The goddess had not treated her city so well in the last few years that she deserved worship. He knew the thought was blasphemous, but—with some surprise—realised he felt no guilt over it.

No, Poloma had not come into the basilica to pray. He made to leave, shaking his head at his own wayward mind, wondering what had diverted him from his course to the Great Quadrangle, when he stopped suddenly and turned back to face the statue. He watched others mouthing silent prayers; one or two had children, and they fidgeted impatiently.

He caught a fleeting memory of the first time he had been brought here by his father. To his child's mind the statue had been much more imposing then—terrifying, even—but his simple faith had brought with it certainty and security about the universe and how it worked. He realised he yearned for the simple assurances of the past. He wanted his old life back, the life he had lived before his exile at the hands of the plutocrats, the life forever out of his reach.

The basilica was getting crowded, and Poloma could not remember it ever being this popular before. Obviously others as well yearned for the old certainties.

The light from the windows was now yellowing as the afternoon drew on, and he remembered he was expected. He hurried from the basilica and continued on his way to the Great Quadrangle, arriving slightly out of breath. Around him were gathered other members of the city council, also dressed in their finery, and more were coming. Poloma thought there was little joy in their faces; if anything they looked self-conscious, even embarrassed, to be there.

The last time he had stood like this with his colleagues had been more than two years before. The day had been a festive one, the first of the new term of sitting in the Assembly. The sky had been bright and high and blue, the mood cheerful and generous. Onlookers had gathered to watch them admiringly. Pride had radiated from the councilors, pride in their city and its institutions.

Then the soldiers of Rivald had marched into the quadrangle. Let into the city by the traitor plutocrats led by Maira Sygni, they loosed volley after volley from their firegons into the crowd.

That, Poloma reminded himself, was when the old world had died.

He turned on the spot, looking around the quadrangle. The cobblestones still had bloodstains from that day, in places overlaid with new stains from the more recent battle for the city. The biggest mark was a long, black smudge in the northeast corner. It was from this direction that the Kydan militia had tramped down from the Citadel, their pikes flashing in the sun, ready to take the blue and white uniformed soldiers of Rivald in the flank.

His temples ached as he remembered, and he massaged his forehead with the tips of his fingers.

One among the Rivald had not been dressed in the soldiers' blue and white. He was a tall, pale-skinned and dark-haired man, protected by bodyguards and accompanied by . . .

The prefect grimaced.

Accompanied by a sacrifice.

Poloma had never before seen a Kevleren, let alone seen

a Kevleren Wield. He had heard stories about that remarkable family, of course, as had everyone since traders from across the Deepening Sea had been coming to Kydan, bringing tales and legends as well as their goods. They were a clan mighty in the use of the Sefid, the great well of power that resided in a different plane from the world, and had spread east and west from their original home to take over the fledgling kingdoms of Rivald and Hamilay. The two sides of the family inherited their countries' rivalry and became bitter enemies, ready to take advantage of one another whenever an opportunity presented itself, and as far as the Kevleren who appeared in the Great Quadrangle that day was concerned, Kydan had been one such opportunity.

When he was young Poloma had been told by a trader visiting his family's house that the Kevlerens could only use the Sefid if they sacrificed something they loved. Consequently, each Kevleren was surrounded by a menagerie of pets called familiars and human servants called Axkevlerens, but closest of all was their Beloved, their most trusted aide, confidant and best friend, reserved for only the most powerful Wielding; most Kevlerens got through life without ever considering killing their Beloved.

Poloma's very first experience of the Sefid showed him what happened when a Beloved was sacrificed.

He had seen the Kevleren, behind the screen of soldiers, reach out to grasp the neck of a woman by his side. At first Poloma hadn't realised what was happening, but then he'd seen the woman's eyes pop open, seen the blood flow over the Kevleren's fingers. His whole body had felt a wave of intense cold as invisible energy washed around him. Blue flames had sparked off anything made from metal. The air between the enemy soldiers and the approaching militia had visibly wavered. The cold he'd felt had been blown away by a wall of intense heat. He had gasped for air, seen a mass of flame where the militia had been only a moment before.

Poloma felt light-headed. He looked down at his feet and the memory slowly receded.

Kydan used to be filled with joy. Now it was filled with grief and pain and too much history. And growing division.

Poloma had hoped—had believed—that getting rid of the plutocrats and their supporters would heal Kydan, but already there were signs of a widening gulf between the city's original inhabitants and the colonists from Hamilay. He had also thought that the death of Prince Maddyn Kevleren, although a source of genuine grief for Poloma, would ease the way because it left the Hamilayans without an obvious and overall leader, someone to whom they could give their allegiance.

Instead, since the finish of most of the repair work after the battle, the Hamilayans had largely confined themselves to the island of Karhay, building shelters and planting crops, while the native Kydans largely withdrew to Herris and tried to come to terms with the new world they found themselves living in. Members of the two groups mingled only when they had to, their natural caution and need to be with their own kind reinforcing their separation. And already he was hearing rumours from fellow councilors that there were those among the Kydans who resented the fact that so much blood had been spilled expelling the plutocrats and their Rivald allies, only to find they were yoked to another group of foreigners. Furthermore, this time there were even more and better armed foreigners. As well, the Hamilayans had the only trained soldiers in the city, and it was they who now occupied the Citadel and patrolled its walls and kept lookout, a constant reminder to the original Kydans of their reduced status.

Poloma sighed heavily. He knew he should have expected the division. Neither party had had any choice in the development of the present situation: the colonists had been scrounged from Hamilayan prisons and poorhouses, and the original inhabitants had been attacked, taken over and bullied by a succession of foreigners and power-mad plutocrats.

He heard someone approaching and looked up to see Galys Valera and Gos Linsedd, his two new friends from across the sea. Their friendship, forged through the most severe trials, was one of the few good things to come out of the last two years of his life.

"Thank you for coming," he said quietly.

"It's a special occasion," Galys said simply.

"The first convening of the city's true Great Council since the plutocrats took over," Gos expanded. "This is an important event for both our peoples."

Poloma's chest tightened. He knew Gos meant well—gods, the soldier always *meant* well—but he could have phrased it more delicately. He glanced around to see if any of his fellow councilors had overheard, but they were studiously ignoring him and the colonists, not necessarily a better sign.

"For all our people," Galys said softly to Gos.

The commander looked blankly at Galys. "Isn't that what I . . ." His voice trailed off as he recalled his actual words. "Ah. I should be more careful."

"We are one people now," Galys continued. "If we cannot accept that, then no one else is likely to."

"It is up to us to find a way to overcome the differences," Poloma added, but could not help wondering how much time they had before violence broke out between the two camps. "Unless differences are settled and a genuine start made to creating a new city together, then the situation will deteriorate."

He sighed deeply. So much work to do, so many things to take into consideration, and yet he felt that time was running out, that the breathing space they had earned through their victory over the plutocrats would be short lived.

"We had best get started," he said, trying to be cheerful but hearing himself how forced it sounded.

The Assembly was a plain, single-storey building designed to emphasise the principle that no councilor had precedence over another. Inside, surrounded by a tiered gallery where interested citizens could perch, councilors sat around an elliptical table, no member's chair higher than another. Officially, Poloma's role as prefect was largely ceremonial, its chief political influence arising in a tied vote where the prefect's choice was decisive. Unofficially, the holder of the prefecture was looked upon by fellow Kydans as leader of their city, and thereby had opportunity to influence and even implement policy, change the course of debate and set the flavor for the entire sitting of the council. Within the Assembly itself, the only advantage offered the prefect was a seat directly under the ceiling's largest skylight, a welcome boon during early-morning sessions in the cooler months.

Galys, sitting in the tiers, watched the members of the reconvened council take their seats. They looked magnificent in their colourful pants and tunics, like oversized birds. Their dark, serene faces seemed noble to her, patient and wise. Some of the members had been councilors under the plutocrats, some even during Poloma's time, and Galys thought she could almost read their minds as they sized each other up, judging who among their fellows would

make allies and who would become enemies. She did not
envy Poloma his role as prefect.

Even as she thought of him, Poloma cleared his throat
and started talking. Despite the fact that she knew only a
few words of Kydan, Galys had hoped to understand
something of what was being said by inflection and tone,
but Poloma spoke in a nervous monotone and she found
her attention sliding away. Inevitably, her mind settled on
Kitayra. She absently put her hand in her pocket and handled the birth chain she had found in the chest. Its discovery had been a shock. Birth chains were given to Kevlerens
when they were still children as part of the test of their
power over the Sefid. Although Kitayra, as a grammarian,
had studied the Sefid for most of her life, she had no right
to a birth chain, unless there was something hidden about
her past that Galys had never suspected.

Which, she admitted to herself, was entirely possible.
Their life together had been so intense and had covered
such momentous events that it seemed as if they had been
together for a decade rather than two brief years.

Finding the birth chain had made Galys feel even more
lost than before. There were so many questions about Kitayra's life and death that needed answering, she was not
sure where to start. Who could she talk to about the Sefid?
Who could lead her in the right direction?

She returned her attention to Poloma's speech. Occasionally she caught a word in Hamilayan, and even a handful of Kydan words she knew, but it was like listening to
someone talking in the middle of a storm.

"... Kydan ... thank ... Hamilay ... battle ..."

Kitayra. Galys was sure she had died by the Sefid. But
who had done the Wielding?

"... union ... Kydan stronger ..."

If only Maddyn had survived, she thought. He would be able to help her. He knew about the Sefid, even though he was one of those rare Kevlerens who had never had an ability to Wield. She wondered idly if he had still possessed his birth chain when he died.

Galys's skin goosebumped with an unexpected thought. Could the birth chain in her pocket originally have been Maddyn's? Would he have given it to Kitayra for safekeeping, or so that she could study it?

" . . . Maira Sygni . . . Kevleren . . . Numoya Kevleren . . ."

She looked up. Numoya Kevleren, the Rivald prince she had helped capture when they retook the city from the plutocrats, together with his Beloved . . .

Galys straightened. Of course there was someone she could ask about the Sefid and the birth chain. How could she have forgotten Kadburn Axkevleren, Maddyn's own Beloved? He would help her, if she could find him. With a twinge of guilt she realised she had not seen him since the day of the battle. What had he been doing? Had Gos or Poloma spent any time with him?

She had to fight the sudden urge to run out of the Assembly to find Kadburn. Again she forced herself to concentrate on what was happening. She heard someone other than Poloma talking in a low, grumbly voice, and recognised one word: *canKydan . . . our Kydan.*

She located the speaker, a small, sharp-faced man with a prominent larynx who was leaning over the table, staring hard at Poloma. She did not like the way he had emphasised the word, and sensed trouble. She noticed that several of the councilors were nodding and murmuring their agreement.

Poloma spoke in response. Galys heard the name Kysor Nevri and assumed it was the councilor who had drawn her attention. Then Poloma mentioned the prince, but using his

full title: General Third Prince Maddyn Kevleren. She
guessed Poloma was making a point about what the Hamilayans had done for *our* Kydan, the sacrifices they had
made. He finished with a raising inflexion, and Galys
groaned inside. Never make a point in a debate by asking
a question unless you already know what the answer is; she
wished she could shout it out to Poloma.

The one called Kysor Nevri smiled easily and replied in
an equable voice. There were more sounds of agreement.
Then he held a hand up and complete silence fell in the
Assembly.

Poloma sensed he had been outmaneuvered; this first
meeting of the reinstalled council was going to discuss the
very issue he had wanted to avoid. Worse, the discontented
among the native Kydans already had a champion on the
council, and he was declaring their position only a tenday
after both Kydan and Hamilayan had fought side by side
against a common enemy.

It was too quick, Poloma told himself. He had not had
enough time to make a difference, and the council itself,
in its very first meeting since the plutocrats forced their
bloody coup, was already dividing.

"Now that the emergency is over," Nevri continued, "I
say it is time we made Kydan a city for its true inhabitants.

"Do not let it be said that I, or any of those who agree
with me, wish anything but good fortune for our friends
from across the Deepening Sea, but I put it to them they
would react no differently if several shiploads of Kydans
suddenly appeared in one of their cities, demanding to be
made citizens."

Poloma glanced quickly around the viewing galleries
and saw Nevri had support among at least some of the

people. He returned his gaze to the councilor. He knew almost nothing about him; he had inherited his position from his older brother, once a close supporter of Poloma's—close enough, at least, to have been executed by the plutocrats.

"I will speak," said a gruff voice in a thick Hamilayan accent. Poloma looked sharply up at the gallery. He saw only Galys and Gos, and knew the voice did not belong to either of them. Then someone behind them stood up. At first Poloma did not recognise the pale and gaunt face with shrunken eyes and an expression as hard as stone, then he saw the blond ponytail and the scars. Kadburn Axkevleren! Where had he come from?

Galys and Gos appeared as surprised as he by the man's sudden appearance.

Kadburn came down to stand beside Poloma; the other councilors, including Nevri, looked on shocked, too stunned to say anything.

"Would you translate for me?" Kadburn asked Poloma, and the prefect nodded.

"We came here and died fighting by your side for your freedom," Kadburn said in a voice loud enough to be heard by everyone in the Assembly. "The colonists on Karhay know nothing about Kydan politics, but they know something about standing by their friends." He put a hand on Poloma's shoulder. The prefect studied the man's face, afraid he might be drunk or demented, but Kadburn seemed more like someone on the verge of exhaustion.

"You, sir, are a guest in this great house," Nevri said coldly, Poloma translating. "You have not been granted the right to speak in the presence of—"

"My master died defending *your* city," Kadburn said angrily, his voice rising in volume and power. Poloma could hear the authority in it. "My master died swallowed by fire because of the bloody, cursed, vengeful Numoya Kevleren who wreaked such ruin on *your* people when he first came, and who wreaked such ruin on my poor beloved prince when he made his escape!"

There were cries of horror from many in the gallery, and even some of the councilors looked aghast.

"Undoubtedly what you say is true, sir," Nevri said. Poloma, who continued to translate for Kadburn's sake, thought the councilor's voice no longer projected any confidence. Nevri licked his lips nervously. "Nevertheless, we have customs that should be observed—"

"And you can be sure, Councilor," Kadburn continued, "that the same bloody, cursed, vengeful Numoya Kevleren is even now plotting how to punish Kydan for overthrowing him."

The Beloved cast his gaze around the entire Assembly.

"Do any of you imagine you can hold out against him when he returns if the colonists' soldiers and troopers are not here defending the city by your side?"

For the second time a heavy silence fell in the building. This time it was Poloma who moved to fill the gap.

"Fellow councilors, surely it is inappropriate at this juncture to discuss any matter other than the future security of Kydan?"

Many of the councilors swapped furtive glances, but no one openly disagreed, and no one moved to reintroduce the matter of the Hamilayans, not even Kysor Nevri.

Poloma sighed in relief. He knew the issue had only been forestalled, not forgotten, but between them, he and Kadburn had won the colonists a reprieve.

3

IT was a bright summer morning and Lerena Kevleren had started off in a pleasant mood, or what passed for a pleasant mood for the ruler of a vast empire. She greeted her attendants with a smile, commented favourably on the spatchcocks in honey served for breakfast, and overlooked the messy hair worn by one of the newest Axkevlerens in her household. But her mood changed on her way from her private quarters to the Great Hall and its throne room. The members of her family in attendance at the court only barely responded to her greetings, and their downcast features eroded her goodwill like storm waves eroded a beach. By the time she sat down on the throne and was ready to start the day's business, she had decided she was surrounded by selfish, sour-faced and spiteful subjects.

Lerena was tired of having to cheer everyone up all the time. In the last few days she had filled the court with music, commissioned and staged plays for its sole benefit, conscripted entertainers off the streets, held lavish banquets. But nothing worked. The members of her family refused to dig themselves out of their self-pity, their morose and endless grief at losing their Beloveds.

Worse, she was continually stumbling across reminders of the bad old days, when the palace—indeed, the whole capital city of Omeralt—had been filled with the Beloveds. It had taken a harrowing three days for her to clean out her own Hanimoro's old quarters, with its collection of mementos and sentimental bric-a-brac. One of Lerena's Axkevlerens, who had worked closely under Hanimoro, told her that items such as the clay fish and toy trident had been kept by the Beloved because they reminded her of her childhood before becoming an Axkevleren. Lerena had been scandalized. She had never imagined that Hanimoro, who had been dearer to her than any other human, might yearn for her life before her time as part of the imperial household.

Like all Axkevlerens, Beloveds included, Hanimoro had been recruited at around seven years of age to serve the Kevleren family; her abilities had been detected early and she was chosen to be among those who might reach the highest rank among her kind. Hanimoro was trained every day of her childhood to forget her past and think only of her mistress. For this she was rewarded with security, food, shelter and all the comforts of life and, most importantly of all, the love of a Kevleren.

It confirmed for Lerena—not that any confirmation had been needed, of course—that she had been right in destroying every living Beloved she could reach through the Sefid. The sacrifice for such a Wield had been enormous—her own sister, Yunara—but the empire sometimes demanded such effort, and as empress she was duty-bound to fulfil her responsibilities, no matter the cost to herself or those close to her.

Still.

Still, late at night when she had dismissed her Axkevlerens

and she was left with only her dogs for company, she cried for Hanimoro. She cried for herself, too.

It was all the fault of her distant cousins in Rivald. They had let things get out of hand in their own kingdom, had let the Beloveds usurp their power in a revolution whose end point could only be the overthrow of the family in Hamilay as well. If her uncle, Duke Paimer Kevleren, had not accidentally discovered the truth behind the revolution on a diplomatic mission to Rivald, then the Sefid only knew where they would all be now. As it was, she had had to destroy that side of the family entirely to ensure the canker did not spread.

The loss of the Beloveds, heretofore an essential cog in the great administrative wheels of empire, should be considered a sacrifice for the preservation of the state; after all, in the end that is what all Axkevlerens ultimately had been trained for, including the Beloveds.

In her bleakest moments Lerena would remind herself that was what all of them were trained for, Kevlerens and Axkevlerens alike. Sacrifice and empire.

Why did her family have such trouble accepting what had happened? Why did they have to behave so morosely that her court now resembled a wake and not the center of the civilized world, despite the music and play-acting and performances? Why could they not be more like her, in fact?

Everyone else in her capital city of Omeralt seemed in normal spirits. It did not seem to disturb them that the great and traditional enemy, Rivald, was at last crippled; quite the reverse, in fact. Her family should take a lesson from them.

Lerena got through the morning's official business as quickly as possible. The administrative gap left by the destruction of the Beloveds needed filling, and it was a difficult and laborious process, involving the employment of non-Axkevlerens in important positions for the first time in the history of the empire. Not only did the machinery of government require new blood, but so did the many and various Kevleren households now without major-domos to organise the daily lives of their extended family.

At midday she dismissed most of the court and took a stroll in her private garden, by far the largest in the empire. Her dogs lolled happily behind her and their devotion restored her spirit somewhat.

Well, for the moment her family could take care of itself. Lerena had an empire to run. She tried to remember what it was she had arranged to do in the afternoon, but there was so much going on she could not be certain. She would have to find someone to take Hanimoro's place as a matter of urgency. Someone she could trust without being beholden to, someone she did not have to love. And someone who did not have to keep knick-knacks from a past life in their quarters.

One of her Axkevlerens, a thin sallow-faced girl called Uilder, came to her. Since Hanimoro's death, Uilder increasingly had taken up most of the secretarial duties once done by the Beloved. She told the empress that Chancellor Malus Mycom had arrived for their appointment and was waiting in her chambers.

Lerena closed her eyes. Malus Mycom was not a person she looked forward to seeing. He was the one man in her empire who had a face she thought was perfectly suited to misery, designed to express the pain of the whole world, and yet he was the one man who remained obstinately and perversely cheerful. Why could not her universe be arranged so that everyone except Malus Mycom was happy?

Nonetheless, he had his uses. Given a task that required the application of knowledge shaped by a sharp intelligence, he would worry at it like a terrier at a rat. Mycom had little imagination, but given an objective and all the information he needed to reach that objective, there was no one else in the kingdom quite like him.

Lerena had first discovered this when considering how to deal with two troubling issues that had promised only to get bigger: first, the insubordination of her cousin General Third Prince Maddyn Kevleren in the matter of his horrid, common mistress and their unborn child; and second, the Rivald colony in the New Land, a way for Rivald to expand its influence and power base without coming into direct conflict with the larger and stronger Hamilayan empire.

She had discussed these matters in a roundabout way with the chancellor at one of their irregular encounters during an official event in the palace, and he had almost immediately suggested that both problems might be solved with a single solution. His insight had made her consider the small man in a completely different light; she still found it difficult to be around him, but she held his brain in the highest regard, even if she wished it had been housed in a different body.

She nodded and Uilder hurried off, her message delivered. None of them seemed to enjoy being in her company any more. Perhaps not too surprising, considering the fate of Hanimoro. And Netarger. And about forty other Beloveds she could name.

A round shadow broached the garden wall. She glanced up and for a moment coolly studied the great glass dome

of Yunara's aviary, the only structure in the whole of
Omeralt that rivalled Lerena's palace in size and beauty.
She absently wondered who was looking after the birds
now that Yunara and Netarger, her Beloved, were dead.

She sighed deeply. Yet another matter she would have
to look into.

Quenion, who did not understand a single word of what
was being said, knew perfectly well what the argument
was about. The two natives who had helped her and Numoya escape from Kydan were trying to convince their fellow villagers to spare the lives of the Kevleren and his
Beloved.

Quenion surprised herself by not being afraid. She was
so exhausted and filthy after so many days and nights on
the river that she was as depressed as she had ever been in
her life. It was not that she did not care whether or not she
lived or died, only that dying was no longer the worst thing
that could happen to her. Another tenday on the Frey River
was the worst thing that could happen to her.

She could tell her protectors were having some effect
on their fellows: voices were no longer raised, questions
were being asked, and some of the villagers actually approached the two strangers and studied them as best they
could in the dim light inside the long hut where everyone
was gathered. She heard one or two of the observers mut-
ter "Kevleren," so Quenion knew they were fully aware of
who their guests were. Quenion could not be sure, but she
thought that probably counted in their favour. The
Kevlerens had only been known about in the New Land for
a generation at most—from when Rivald first established
a colony on the continent's south coast—but already they

had acquired a status approaching myth in the communities that had some contact with either Kydan or Sayenna.

Thinking of Sayenna made Quenion long for the sight of it, to see again its turquoise harbor and sunny, white-washed houses. She wished to be there more than anywhere else in the world. She sighed disconsolately. Instead she was here, in a village roughly halfway between Kydan and Sayenna, her future, and that of her master, a subject of debate among strangers.

Not complete strangers, she reminded herself. Rivald administrators at Sayenna had learned very early on that their only trade rival in the New Land was the city of Kydan, and that there was a complex relationship between Kydan and the many settlements and towns that lined the Frey. The river was the main road of commerce to and from Kydan, and the economic life of the entire region depended upon it. As well, river people often migrated to Kydan, making it their home, refreshing the blood lines and over time becoming Kydans themselves. But traditionally the river people were also the persistent enemies of the city, often sending raiding parties to attack it in hope of easy booty, and then themselves being attacked in retaliation. Over time, as Kydan became stronger and built its great Citadel, warfare became less frequent, but the hostility still existed and could be brought back to a blaze if fanned by events or, in the case of Sayenna, an external agency.

On the whole, Sayenna found the river people willing recipients of bribes and gifts, and offered an alternative market that was not entangled by an ambivalent tradition of hate and love and war and peace.

When Kydan opened its doors to trade from the Hami-layan empire, Rivald's colony of Sayenna found willing allies among the river people for their attack and takeover of the city.

Numoya, still unconscious, stirred, his head twisting in Quenion's lap. She automatically brushed his brow and made soothing sounds. Some of the curious locals gingerly stepped back and Quenion smiled mirthlessly. In the dark of the large hut, she could not make out expressions clearly, but she knew if she had been able to she would have seen fear on their faces. They had all heard stories of what a Kevleren could do with the Sefid. Instead, Quenion satisfied herself by gazing out of the hut's single opening; all she could see of the outside world was a muddy patch of ground, and except for the voices of the debating villagers, all she could hear was the sound of rain on the thatch roof above.

The younger of their native escort, Velopay, came to Quenion and said her life and that of her master were safe for the moment.

"It was the promise of the firegons," Velopay added. "They are more desired by us than gold."

"They must know then," Quenion said, "that if anything happens to Numoya Kevleren while he is in their charge, they will not get a single firegon from Rivald."

"They know that," Velopay said solemnly.

"And that if they were to harm him, Rivald would send an army to destroy this village and kill everyone who lives in it."

Velopay smiled slightly. "Adulla is arguing your case. The elders are coming around, I think. But it will not help for you to say to the elders what you have just said to me."

Quenion blushed. She felt like a child caught in the act of lying. "What do you mean?" she blustered.

"If we killed you and your master, how would Rivald

know? It could even be argued that it would be our safest course, and leave us free to choose between Kydan and Sayenna if the two cities go to war."

"Rivald would know because Numoya is a Kevleren—"

"Exactly," Velopay interrupted. "He is a Kevleren, and everything we hear from the traders who come from Sayenna suggests that family no longer rules in Rivald. Indeed, it is possible that Rivald would even thank us for ridding it of your master."

Quenion, blushing only a moment before, felt her body instantly go cold. She had dangerously, and stupidly, assumed the natives would be naive and even ignorant about events in the world at large. She promised herself that if she survived she would never again make that mistake.

"Then why are we still alive?"

Velopay's smile widened. "Because Adulla argues your case with skill and determination, and because we think Rivald will look kindly on those who help its own, even if they happen to be a Kevleren and his Beloved." Then his smile disappeared. "And because the family of Maira Sygni, overthrown by your enemies, came from here."

"Rivald will thank you," Quenion said, trying to sound convincing. The truth was, she had no way of knowing how Rivald would react to their return to Sayenna, and to the removal of Kydan from its sphere of influence. "And your village," she added quickly. "What is its name?"

"Orin," Velopay said. "Orin of the Two Rivers."

"The two rivers?"

"The Frey, upon which we escaped from Kydan, and the Elder, not far from here, which turns south and joins the Younger in The Wash, the river that runs to Sayenna."

"Then we are not far from Sayenna?"

Velopay stood to leave. "Closer than we were yesterday," he said noncommittally.

"Good morning, your Majesty!" Malus Mycom declared cheerfully when Lerena entered her chambers.

"Chancellor," she said, trying hard not to sound as irritated as she felt. Perversely, his good mood shattered the
last remnants of her own. She sat down, ignoring his bow,
and nodded for him to take a seat close enough for them to
talk in private but not so close she could see the dandruff
that always powdered his shoulders.

He beamed at her. He was a short fellow, sharp-faced
with dark hair, and very clever, possibly brilliant, syco-
phantic to a degree that bothered even Lerena. The empress found herself relying more and more on his judgement
and acumen now that Hanimoro was gone and her family
seemed set in its despondency. He reveled in his new-
found influence.

"How may I be of service to my empress?"

"Do you remember our discussions about power?"

Mycom raised an eyebrow. "Your Majesty?"

"Before the . . . recent upheaval . . . we spent time, now
and then, talking about the responsibility of leaders to consolidate power in their hands."

"Ah, yes," he said, his tone vague. In fact he did dimly
remember the subject coming up, but never to the extent he
would have called a discussion. What had taken his attention, however, was the empress's reference to the "recent
upheaval". No one knew precisely what had happened that
night in the palace, a tenday in the past; at least, no one
alive. He would give almost anything to know how Lerena
had managed to destroy not only her sister Yunara—the
only serious rival to the throne—but also every Beloved in

the empire, as far as he could tell. Obviously the Sefid had been the key, but to the best of his learning, and the combined learning of every grammarian—those who could not Wield themselves but spent their lives studying the Sefid—at the University of Omeralt, no Wielding in history had ever been used to such destructive effect.

Lerena was watching the expression on the chancellor's face, and the way his eyes lost their focus. Her imperial upbringing and political training had made her very good at understanding people and what motivated them, and she had some idea of what was going through his brain. That understanding helped her keep him off balance; her subjects were more loyal when they did not know where they stood with her, always striving to win and keep her favor.

The door to the chambers opened slightly and Uilder's head appeared. "He's here, your Majesty," she said.

Lerena nodded and the door opened wide to let in General Second Prince Rodin Kevleren, the head of Hamilay's intelligence service and her first cousin. He was a short man, bald except for a border of gray hair over his ears. His expression, usually dour, was downright miserable.

Mycom jumped to his feet and bowed. Rodin ignored him, went to Lerena and bowed himself. "You requested my presence, your Majesty."

"Take a seat next to the chancellor, cousin. The three of us have important matters to discuss."

Rodin did so, ignoring Mycom. The chancellor and his undisguised sycophancy were unpopular with almost everyone; among the Kevlerens generally he was at best thought of as an academic on the make who had clambered above his station in life. As a rule, they were used to obsequiousness, and in the manner of the rich often sought it, but there was something particularly oleaginous about

Mycom's behavior that made everyone feel ill-disposed towards him.

Mycom looked enquiringly at Lerena, but she put her hand up to forestall any questions. "What have you found out from your people about Rivald?" she asked Rodin.

"The word from our outposts on the border suggests there is no movement that could be construed as preparation for an invasion."

"Invasion!" Mycom squeaked.

"Continue," Lerena ordered Rodin.

"Indeed, the outposts report almost no movement of any kind. Even enemy patrols are hardly ever seen. There have been no raids into our territory for nearly a tenday."

"Is . . . is that unusual?" Mycom ventured.

"At this time of year, yes," Rodin answered. "It is much harder to detect small enemy incursions when the trees provide good cover and the traveling at night is much easier. In winter the snow reveals their tracks, and the deciduous forests, at least, are clear—"

"Go on," Lerena urged.

Rodin glanced sideways at the chancellor.

"He can be trusted," she said. As Mycom opened his mouth to thank her, she added, "For now."

Mycom's jaws snapped shut.

"Reports from the few agents we have left in that kingdom after the overthrow of our family are . . . confusing, to say the least."

"Confusing?"

"The administration seems to have collapsed totally. Accounts are left outstanding. Garrisons at the front that are due for rotation are staying where they are. No work crews have been sent out to clean up after a storm at Bef-

eren damaged part of the capital's harbour. And many that
were in the Safety Committee are no longer seen."

Rodin hesitated.

"Yes?" Lerena prompted impatiently.

"There are stories," Rodin said carefully, as if he did not
want the empress to think he gave them any credit.

Lerena said nothing, but her foot was starting to tap.

Rodin swallowed. "Stories about a terrible massacre at
the palace. Something happened not too many nights ago.
Details are vague, and no one from the palace is talking
openly about what they saw. But rumour and gossip and
hearsay . . . our family . . . has been wiped out entirely."

Rodin said the last words in a hush and Lerena and even
Mycom had to lean forward to hear him properly.

"Entirely?" Lerena echoed.

"Not one survivor. And that's not all. Apparently—as
happened here—all the Beloveds are dead." Rodin scratched
his head. "It seems that several of them had actually been
on the Safety Committee."

"Beloveds?" Mycom said, astonished. "Cooperating
with the usurpers?" He looked aghast. "Your Majesty, I
would give no credence to these reports—"

"Be quiet," Lerena said evenly. Rodin smirked at him.
"Cousin, can we confirm these stories?"

Rodin shrugged. "Not immediately. Our lines of communication with many of our agents in Beferen and other
cities were disrupted after the coup. It will take time to re-
establish contact."

"How long?"

"Months . . ." Lerena was shaking her head. "Several
tenday, at least." His voice held a note of urgent appeal.

"One month," she said.

"Your Majesty—"

"You can have whatever resources you require."

Rodin sighed heavily, accepting the inevitable. "Very well."

"See me again in two days. Let me know then how much it will cost and I will see that you have it immediately from the treasury."

Rodin stood, his expression uncertain, but he bowed and said, "I'll start at once."

"Well?" Lerena asked Mycom after the prince left.

The chancellor stared at her for a moment. He was overwhelmed not only to be privy to what were obviously most secret reports to the empress, but also by the content of those reports.

"I cannot believe it," he said eventually.

"You think Prince Rodin is lying to me?" Lerena asked, the corners of her lips curving into a dangerous smile.

"Oh, no, your Majesty!" Mycom said quickly. "I am sure he is passing on exactly the intelligence he has learned, and even that the reports themselves are genuine, as far as they go, but the story they tell is hardly to be believed, surely? An agent may pass on rumor and gossip with every good intention but still be in error. His highness himself has said he is not in touch with many of his agents in Rivald."

"I have reason to believe the intelligence is accurate," she said levelly. For a moment Mycom caught her gaze, tried to see into her mind, but for all his wisdom he had no wiles.

"You have received information from elsewhere perhaps?" Mycom suggested hopefully. "Traders from across the border? A drunk Rivald diplomat?"

"Think it through, Chancellor. What happened the night my sister died?"

Mycom swallowed. "It is said that every Beloved in Hamilay died that night."

"Take it for granted," Lerena said. "What else have you surmised about that night?"

Mycom struggled with the answer, which told Lerena he had deduced the truth, undoubtedly along with many others.

"That I Wielded the Sefid to accomplish the destruction of the Beloveds," she said for him.

The chancellor nodded.

Lerena waited.

Mycom's face paled to the color of chalk and his usual cheerfulness evaporated altogether. "Because the Beloveds in Rivald had rebelled against the Kevlerens. You killed *all* the Beloveds, in Hamilay and Rivald."

"Very good. Now take the logic one step further."

"The Rivald Kevlerens then had to be dealt with for failing the family."

"Failing the family?" Lerena laughed, the sound uncharacteristically harsh. "And failing their Axkevlerens, their subjects, their kingdom and history! Their incompetence, their lack of regard, was as great a crime as that committed by their Beloveds."

For the first time in his adult life Malus Mycom said something without any regard for its consequences. "You murdered members of your own family."

"Don't look so surprised, Chancellor. It was not the first time."

Mycom's head jerked up sharply and he half stood from his seat as if he had just discovered he was sharing the room with a large and poisonous snake and had to find a way out.

"We even discussed the possibility once in general

terms," she said evenly. "But enough of that. Let us return specifically to the subject of Rivald. What condition do you think the republic will be enduring?"

"Chaos, your Majesty."

"And from that?"

"That it is no threat to the empire," he said slowly, but even as he spoke his eyes widened with sudden understanding. "And if Rivald is no threat to Hamilay," he continued, more excitedly, "it in turn suggests that Hamilay *is* a threat to Rivald. If there are no Kevlerens alive in that kingdom, and the ruling Safety Committee is half gone, then nothing can stop your armies from crossing the border."

"Exactly," Lerena said, and Mycom beamed. "Which brings us back to our discussion, some days ago now, about power and its consolidation."

"You intend to take advantage of Rivald's current crisis to destroy it once and for all . . ."

"Of course not," Lerena said disdainfully. "I am interested in consolidating my power. I don't want to destroy Rivald, I want my empire to absorb it."

Quenion paused before the door, gathering courage and breath. She balanced the supper tray on one hand and knocked. As usual, there was no answer. She turned the knob and slowly opened the door. A thin gray cat escaped from between her legs.

As she entered, an angry voice demanded, "Who's there?"

"It's me, your Grace. You know it's me." Quenion spoke gently, consolingly. "Who else comes to you this time of—"

"Don't you dare presume to speak to me in that fashion!" the man said sternly. He was sitting on the end of his bed, dressed in very rich and fine clothes. The pants were buttoned wrong and the shirt not tucked in properly, and the jacket was askew, but it was a better effort than usual for the blind Prince Numoya Kevleren. The skin on his face looked as if someone had tried to melt it off, and his scalp was patchy with new growth of stubbly hair. It broke Quenion's heart to see him so, and worst of all were the clothes, for he had been such a fastidious master and would be ashamed if he could see himself.

No, she corrected herself. Even *more* ashamed than he already was at his reduced circumstances.

"Forgive me, your Grace, I meant nothing by it—"

"What lunacy inspired me to make you my Beloved is now entirely beyond my ken," he raged. His hands moved up and down as he talked, as if he was making a speech in front of a crowd. "You are insubordinate! You are careless! You speak discourteously . . ."

"I am learning. Slowly, I admit. But I *am* learning." She used her foot to manoeuvre a side table in front of the prince and carefully laid the tray on it. "Sievad, the cook, has made you a fine fish stew for your supper."

She looked around for the tall stool she used when feeding him. Quenion knew Numoya often asked the cleaner to take it away because it made her job difficult. He seemed to delight in spiting her.

She would have to sit next to him to feed him, and edged herself sideways between the side table and the edge of the bed.

"What are you doing? You make more noise than a horse—"

"I am going to sit next to you. The stool seems to have mysteriously disappeared again."

"Nothing mysterious about it. I ask for it to be taken away because I keep on tripping over it." His voice was suddenly sombre. He hesitantly touched his eyes with the tips of his fingers and flinched in pain.

"Does it still hurt badly?"

"Of course . . ." Numoya started angrily, but let his voice fade, and some of his anger with it. He sighed. "Yes. Not as bad as before. But it hurts."

"Is there no sacrifice you can make to heal yourself?"

He shook his head, and said under his breath: "No."

Quenion cursed herself for asking the question, but she had done so from frustration and concern for Numoya's condition. Her master had lost all his Axkevlerens when messengers had arrived in Kydan from Rivald to inform him of the overthrow of his family and the installation of the Safety Committee, and of his own dismissal as governor of Sayenna and Kydan when the committee eventually got around to choosing a successor. When they left they had taken with them all the Axkevlerens except Quenion, his Beloved.

His familiars, the tribe of cats he kept, had been removed by the Hamilayans when they took Kydan. So far he had only adopted a few strays, and did not seem interested in increasing their number. At any rate, a hundred familiars sacrificed would not be enough for Numoya to heal himself, and the emotional cost would be devastating, especially considering his already traumatized state.

There seemed to be no way out for him.

"Eat," Quenion said, lifting a spoon of stew to his lips. "You will feel better."

For the duration of the meal he said nothing, but ate slowly, determinedly, frowning the whole time. When he finished his food, the sullen silence continued and Quenion decided to leave. When he fell into one of these moods there was nothing she could do to reach him. After leaving the tray in the kitchen, she walked to the top of the keep and enjoyed the last part of the day by herself.

Quenion, who came from a cold, windswept farm on the grasslands of south Rivald, thought Sayenna was more beautiful than any other part of the world. From her position on the roof of the town's stone keep, the first permanent structure built by the new settlers several years before, she was able to see over the whole bay where Rivald had established its first overseas colony. It had grown into a thriving trading port of several thousand people; furs, lumber, grain and ore streamed into it from the hinterland and south coast of the New Land, and were bought by merchants in Sayenna's markets and from there taken by deep-drafted ships across the Deepening Sea to Rivald. Those same ships then returned with their holds filled with kingdom goods like cloth and jewelry and household goods made from steel and tin and silver for sale to the towns and villages in the New Land.

Sayenna was a town flush with new money and rough, frontier optimism.

Well, thriving with trade and flush with money until recently, that was. Troubles back home, troubles still ill-defined for those living in Sayenna, had reduced the trade from the kingdom to a trickle. Still, the colony was self-sufficient when it came to food, and was large enough to generate a moderate trade with the inland. Even were it a poor settlement the benevolent climate and fertile seas made it a far more attractive place to live than Quenion's childhood home, or the capital Beferen where she had been indentured as an Axkevleren.

Quenion remembered Beferen as a city that, like

Sayenna, was created originally to take advantage of its
harbor, but it was a gray, miserable place, damp and dismal
and, despite its population, desolate in a way that she
thought eroded hope for most of those who lived there.

A sea breeze stroked Quenion's face, reminding her of
how lucky she was to be here instead of back in Rivald itself. Thanks to Numoya Kevleren.

Or indeed, back in Kydan in the arms of the enemy, or
dead and buried in some pit along the Frey River, saved
thanks to Adulla and Velopay, who between them had not
only convinced their village elders to let Numoya and
Quenion live, but to help them back to Sayenna as well.

Quenion had dreaded another journey by river, but this
time it had been done in more comfort, and without the
constant worry about discovery by enemies. Adulla himself had accompanied them down the Elder River and then
The Wash itself to Sayenna, together with a select band of
warriors marked to protect their guests against any attack.
The temptation of getting their hands on some firegons of
their own had proved too much, especially considering the
advantage it would give them in the interminable raids and
brushfire wars that broke out among the people who lived
along the rivers in the hinterland.

Quenion clearly remembered her first sight of Sayenna
and its harbour as The Wash swept out into the Deepening
Sea, staining the coast brown with the silt it had carried
down from the spring rains in the mountains. The colony,
if not yet a city, was large for a town, and its whitewashed
buildings with red and yellow terracotta tiled roofs were
organized along a grid pattern of streets. It looked so warm,
so orderly, so welcoming. It was civilization, and with its
garrison of several hundred well-trained and well-armed
troops it was security as well.

And for her master it was a chance to recover from his grievous wounds. He had first gained consciousness soon after leaving Orin of the Two Rivers, but it had been a fitful wakefulness that had let him slip back into a deep sleep after only half a day. Two nights later he had roused again, and this time had been able to take stock of his situation, and with Quenion's prompting could even remember much of what had happened back in Kydan.

But he was still not well. Far from it. And consciousness only brought Numoya psychological pain to match his physical torment.

Quenion breathed the sea air again. Life for her would be perfect were it not for her master's pain and despair. She did not know how to help him as she felt she should, not having been properly trained as a Beloved. She loved him the way an Axkevleren was supposed to love their Kevleren, like a dutiful child. She was devoted to him, and yet even before the disaster at Kydan he had shown her little more than contempt, an attitude that his wounds seemed only to deepen. Quenion thought—believed—that his attitude to her was a result of the pain he still felt at having had to sacrifice Thenge, his first—and truly—Beloved. But the knowledge did not ease her own pain at his hostile indifference to her, and she constantly struggled to find ways to change his feelings, to become the Beloved he so desperately wanted and needed. It was her duty as well as her greatest desire.

Quenion looked out to sea, hoping for a glimpse of a sail from home, a ship bearing a new governor who could take responsibility for the administration of Sayenna away from Numoya. But there was no sail. No ship had come from Rivald for many tendays, and rumors for the reason behind it were as common as fleas on a beggar. There was a sense of rising panic in the town, of some cataclysm back home still to make its way across the sea.

The sea breeze held a chill in it now, and she could not help shivering. Numoya's future, and her own, were entirely up to her. The responsibility weighed down on her, making her shoulders slump.

Sounds from below made Quenion look down again. Several wagons, pulled by bullocks, were making their ponderous way into the colony. Judging by the furs heaped in them, she guessed they were from some of the villages located on the rough, whitewater rivers that flowed from the mountains a month's journey inland. She did not know for sure whether or not the merchants were still buying, but she would be surprised if they gave up the chance to procure the furs which only came once a year and brought a high price in Rivald; whatever troubles they were having over there, trade would be re-established eventually.

Everything happens eventually, she reminded herself, and felt a distant consolation from the knowledge.

If Numoya's fate was in her hands, she told herself it meant she had the chance to succeed as his Beloved, had a chance to make him love her . . .

For a moment she felt as if she were back in Beferen. Suffocating in the warren of the palace, ignored and despised, a lackey and servant, running with all the other rabbits. In that place, how could Numoya have noticed her, learned to love her as she wanted? He had always been a private man, reserved, learned, committed to duty, so different from the rest of his family in its outgoing and flamboyant gaucherie, its isolation from the goings-on in their own land. He had volunteered to assume the governorship of Sayenna, to separate himself from his own kind, from his first home, to find something different, to find a home for himself and his lovely Thenge. The only person he had truly loved.

He had sacrificed Thenge two years before during the attack on Kydan, to save the Rivald infantry from the Kydan militia. Duty had made him destroy the one person who was more important to Numoya than himself, and from that time on he had cursed the fate that had taken him away from Beferen, even though it had been a fate of his own choosing. And ever since that time, Quenion was sure, he had been unable to truly love anyone else. He had made her his Beloved merely because she was the Axkevleren in his service he was most familiar with after Thenge, and because she had offered him the most sympathy.

So, Numoya did not love her the way he should. That was why he was always so angry with her, so angry with everyone, and that was why he could not Wield to heal himself: there was no one he could sacrifice whom he loved enough to affect the Sefid with the necessary strength.

It would take time to turn him around, Quenion knew, but one of the most important virtues all Axkevlerens learned was patience.

It was an offhand comment from Prince Rodin that made the empress sit up straight. They were sitting at a high table in the Great Hall, watching an entertainment— a few scenes from Kashell Graythane's latest major work extolling the virtues of the Kevleren family—while being served dinner. Lerena's relatives watched on with morose disinterest, any spark in their heart still quenched by the loss of their Beloveds, while Lerena was morose because of their company. The playwright wilted under the lack of interest her play inspired in its audience. Even her actors could not help noticing the mood and were fluffing lines.

But Lerena had no thought for any of this. She and Rodin were deep in discussion about Rivald, about its defenses and past strategies, and how the new situation in Beferen might influence them. The conversation even went some way to lifting her spirits, until Rodin, almost casually, said, "If Maddyn was here, your Majesty, he could tell you more about the condition of Rivald's frontier defences than I or any of my agents. His years fighting the enemy across our border . . ."

Rodin's voice faded as he saw the effect his words had on the empress. "Your Majesty? Are you feeling well?"

Malus Mycom, sitting on a lower table, also noticed the change in Lerena, and hurried to stand behind her, despite the reproving glances of her relatives. Rodin opened his mouth to tell him to go back to his seat, but in that instant saw the genuine concern on his face for the empress, and he said nothing.

Lerena shook her head slowly. "I cannot believe I have not given him a thought since—"

She stopped abruptly, looked at Rodin and Mycom. "What's wrong?"

"Are you all right, your Majesty?" Mycom asked solicitously. Rodin could see he wanted to reach out to pat her hand. He doubted even the chancellor would get away with that kind of familiarity.

"Given whom a thought?" Rodin asked. He had an idea she had been about to say something important, something he should know.

Lerena drew a deep breath and gave the two men the benefit of a smile. "Why, you know I had not spared a single thought for the prince. He is so far away from the palace." She frowned then. "I must write to him urgently. He will be deeply distressed by the news of my sister's death."

Mycom and Rodin quickly exchanged glances. The antipathy that had existed between the Duchess Yunara Kevleren and her cousin, Prince Maddyn, was known by every member of the court. Rodin even had a fleeting mental image of Maddyn raising a toast to Lerena for destroying her sister.

"You may return to your meal, Chancellor. I assure you I am perfectly well."

Mycom bowed and retreated, but threw the empress a curious look over his shoulder as he went back to his table. Rodin understood Mycom's interest. Something had just happened that had set off a few of his well-developed and virtually subconscious alarms. He was head of Hamilay's security services not only because he was a senior Kevleren—the responsibility could hardly go to someone outside the family—but because he had an uncanny intuition when things were askew and needed investigating. Being a Kevleren he also had a well-developed sense of self-preservation, and knew that if Lerena was behind the alarms he was probably best advised to leave well enough alone.

He turned his attention back to the play-acting. It occurred to him then that he, the empress and Mycom had just indulged in a spot of play-acting themselves, but Lerena was the only one who knew what the story was about.

Damn my curiosity, Rodin cursed silently, and leave well enough alone.

4

THE Citadel of Kydan was made from granite blocks floated down the Frey River from the mountains to the east. Kadburn rested his hands on the strong stone as he leaned over the parapet and gazed down to the slope of the eastern end of Herris. No more than a tenyard to his left was the gap in the wall caused by the exploding ship's longgon that had been mounted there, an explosion caused by the pillar of flame that had once been his master, General Third Prince Maddyn Kevleren.

Some attempt had been made to repair the gap, but the job had been hurried and slapdash, and Kadburn thought he would have no trouble kicking it in if he had been so inclined.

He leaned further over the parapet. A twinge of vertigo made the walls seem to waver, like a flag in a gentle breeze, but he did not pull back. A little more, he told himself, just a little more and all my pain will be over. The cool granite under his hands seemed to leach the warmth from him.

Kadburn, once Axkevleren, once Beloved, no longer knew who he was. He no longer knew what he was. For almost all of his life he had been half of Maddyn Kevleren. Wherever Maddyn had been, so had he been. Whatever danger Maddyn endured, Kadburn had shared it. He had been the prince's companion, brother, shield, friend, advisor. Maddyn had been his mirror, and without him Kadburn had no reflection and could no longer see himself.

A flurry of wind channeled up the wall and blew his hair back. A warm wind. A wind from the east, from the heart of the New Land.

Kadburn wondered if he himself had a heart any more. All he could feel was a cold, knotted anger that roiled inside him, keeping him alive and aware. Without the anger he knew he would simply evaporate into thin air, so he directed it against the world. But the anger had a deeper, greater purpose.

He pulled himself back from the parapet.

Not yet.

He conserved the anger, kept it for the man he was absolutely certain was most to blame for his master's death: the Rivald prince, Numoya Kevleren, who had used the Sefid to kill Maddyn to help cover his escape during the assault on Kydan.

By now Numoya would be safely ensconced in the Rivald colony of Sayenna, somewhere on the southern coast of the New Land. But Kadburn knew the Kevlerens, and he knew Numoya would not be satisfied until he had exacted his revenge upon Kydan for the disgrace it had caused him. That meant Kadburn in turn would have a chance to exact his revenge against the enemy prince, a chance that would only be realised if Kydan was strong enough to resist the Rivald storm when it came.

He had seen the fracture lines appearing between the Hamilayan colonists and the indigenous Kydans, had understood that if the two groups ended up at each other's throats they would do Numoya's work for him, so he made sure he was present at the first meeting of Kydan's reconvened city council, made sure they were aware of what division between them would mean. He owed it to Maddyn to ensure that the city the general had died defending would survive, and that when Numoya came it would be ready so that Kadburn would have his chance to carry out the last thing he would ever do: kill a Kevleren.

Heriot Fleetwood stood and stretched her back, pushing with her hands behind her waist. Some of the kinks disappeared, but there was a knot somewhere at the base of her spine that was not going to go away, and which she knew would give her hell when she went to bed.

A gentle breeze brushed her skin and she automatically turned towards it as she sniffed the air. She smelled river water, and something indescribably exotic. The wind was from the east, which was unusual. This time of day Kydan was usually hit by a sea breeze, coming from the west, cool and refreshing. The easterly, on the other hand, was warm. Warm winds never bring good, she told herself, and smiled when she realised it was the old Heriot thinking that, the young, poorly educated and suspicious inhabitant of Omeralt's poor quarter.

Now look at me, she reminded herself. In a new city in a new land, building my own future instead of inheriting someone else's, with new friends to boot. I've sailed the Deepening Sea and fought a battle and helped create a guild for colonists.

Not bad for a whitesmith's daughter.

"Time for you to change into your dancing clothes, eh?"

an old man beside her said, grinning out the side of his mouth as he kicked the stone block at his feet.

"Mind your own, Carder," she replied, but without rancor. She looked down at the block they had been manouvering to lift into position in the new wall the colonists were constructing on the eastern side of Karhay, and idly wondered how many she and Carder had dragged from the makeshift dock on the north side of the island where the stone was brought from the mainland and shaped by stone masons before being handed over to the laborers. The knot in her spine twinged.

Too many, she told herself.

"My turn to raise it, you lift," she said.

Carder handed her the heavy branch they had been using as a lever and Heriot shoved it under the block. Carder shifted a brick fulcrum under the branch for her and she pushed down. One side of the block raised a full span, enough for the man to get both hands underneath and roll it onto the webbing of the neck brace; he crouched, looped the brace over his head and stood up as straight as he could. The block lifted into the air, and Heriot guided it into position in the wall. As soon as she slipped the block off the webbing, another colonist slapped a layer of mortar on it, ready for the next stone.

"One 'underd 'n ten," Carder said under his breath.

"What?" Heriot asked.

"How many bricks we've shoved." He stood now and stretched. He was short for a man from Hamilay, though still a good deal taller than Heriot. Although he had a long, drawn face, he was quick to smile and worked harder than most men of Heriot's acquaintance, and never raised his voice or lost his temper. The two of them jibed each other now and then, but mostly he showed her more respect than she was used to, and she wondered if it was because she was head of the guild or the friend of Arden or simply because Carder thought she deserved it in her own right.

Thinking of Arden made her look around to see if she could locate him. Although there were a lot of colonists on the island—working on the wall or its great iron entranceway, or preparing plots of land for planting, or building huts—Arden was easy to find. It was possible Heriot was the shortest member of the colony, but it was certain that Arden was the tallest, and biggest. He sometimes seemed more bear than human to Heriot, and unlike Carder he almost never smiled and almost always spoke in a heavy monotone. Other colonists called him Grim Arden, but they respected him just for the sheer amount of work he managed every day, and for his heroic defence of their island during the attack on Kydan by the plutocrats and their allies.

Heriot thought of him as her friend, most of all. He had been her protector on the voyage across the ocean; the Colonists' Guild had been his idea, as was making Heriot its first leader. Although there was a lot about him she did not know or understand—he was close-mouthed about his past and feelings—she felt in her bones that he was someone she could depend upon. Sometimes, especially at night when she was in her cot by herself, she wondered—almost idly—if there would ever be anything more to their relationship. It was not something she actively desired, but Heriot could not help being curious about what it would be like, how their feelings for each other might change or grow.

There he was, his huge black-bearded head well above the crowd around him. He had a length of timber under one arm and his tree axe under the other. She had seen Arden swing the axe during the battle for Kydan, and he was as adept at using it to lop off heads as he was in using it to cut down trees or shape beams.

Carder tapped her on the shoulder. "C'mon, lass," he grumbled, "there's enough light to do one more."

Heriot nodded absently and followed the man to the jetty to collect another stone. It was backbreaking work, building the wall, and plenty more to do yet, but without one the colonists had only barely held off the previous assault on the island, and it had to be done. There would be time to catch up with Arden after the day's work was finished.

Commander Gos Linsedd knew how many times the colony had come close to failing. Even its start, amid the internecine rivalry of the Kevleren court at Omeralt, had almost been stillborn. Then it survived the crossing of the Deepening Sea, including a terrible storm that had claimed many lives despite the expedition's flotilla finding shelter. And at the end of the voyage the colony's small force of soldiers and dragoons ousted the plutocrats and their Rivald supporters from power without laying siege to the city. Then it withstood the following counterattack by said plutocrats and Rivald supporters.

Now it had to survive the antagonism of Kydan's original inhabitants, a task that looked to prove the greatest obstacle of all. Gos did not know how the colonists would react if the Kydans turned against them, but the fact that many of them had died defending the city, and many more had been wounded, made him think they would be reluctant to just give up and sail back to Hamilay. Spilling blood on ground made it sacred to you, and most of the colonists could not have said the empire ever truly gave them a home.

What worried Gos most of all was how quickly the goodwill between the two groups had evaporated after the battle, as if having dealt with one enemy they both immediately needed another to keep their minds busy.

There were curses up ahead at the jetty and Gos brought his mind back to the present. Some of the colonists were abusing a squad of soldiers for taking up so much room on the track to the jetty; the squad was on its way to the ferry that would take it to the mainland for a patrol north along the coast. Gos strode between a colonist and one of his men who were arguing with angry voices.

"All right, soldier, move along," he said.

"But Commander—"

"Don't want to hear," Gos said in a voice that told the man there would be no appeal.

The soldier grumbled something under his breath and moved on; when he was out of earshot Gos turned to the colonist who had been arguing with him.

"A little patience on your part wouldn't have hurt," he said firmly.

"That works both ways," said the colonist, a very short and very young woman, and Gos noticed how quickly the other colonists took half a step back in deference to her.

"These stones are bloody heavy," the woman continued. She spoke in a surprisingly confident and mature tone for someone who looked so young. "Your man was asked to move aside only long enough for us to get past, no more."

"He's going out on patrol—"

"For which we're grateful, Commander Gos Linsedd, being for our common defense and all. But we're also working for the common defense, building the wall around the island, and it's bloody hard work to boot." She hefted the neck brace with its stone cargo to prove her point.

"And you are?" Gos asked.

"My name is Heriot Fleetwood," she said briskly, as if they were discussing business.

"She's head of our guild," said a colonist proudly, as if he was talking about his own daughter.

Gos frowned. "Guild? What guild?"

"*Our* guild," the man said.

"The Colonists' Guild," Heriot said determinedly.

Gos scratched his head. He had heard nothing about any such organization, although he thought it sounded like something Maddyn Kevleren might have dreamed up. "I've never heard of it," he admitted.

"Of what account is that?" the woman asked.

Gos was not sure how to respond. He was accounted one of the expedition's leaders, but as military commander did he have the need, let alone the right, to know everything about the colony? Did this guild they were talking about impact on the colony's defense in any instrumental way?

"Not necessarily of any account," he said, unsure of his ground. "Who founded the guild?"

"We did," Heriot said, her hands on her hips now.

"Well. Good work. Excellent." He drew a deep breath to give him time to think. Say something positive, he told himself. "Let's hope in future your guild and my troopers are more accommodating of each other's needs."

Heriot's eyes narrowed, as if she was appraising him. "Aye," she said eventually, and with a curt nod turned and waddled away, the stone hanging from the neck brace swinging between her legs. He watched her for a moment before catching up with his men.

Gos wished he were going on patrol as well, but he was needed here. The patrols he and Ensign Westaway had led into the surrounding countryside after the battle had ensured there were no concentrations of enemy nearby, and with Maddyn gone and Kadburn in no state to do any good for anyone, all those with any authority had enough administrative and political tasks to keep them busy for months to come.

He looked on with envy as the squad loaded onto the ferry and were transported to the north bank of the Frey.

Work on the wall stopped soon after the sun went down. Tired, hands blistered, neck red raw from where the brace had chafed, Heriot was not interested in her evening meal of porridge and bread. She sat with her back against the incomplete wall, staring east along the course of the Frey. A warm wind still blew from inland, chopping the surface of the river. The moon glinted off the dark waters. Heriot thought it would be fine to sail a boat up the river and see what could be seen. Because there had not been a lot of mixing between colonists and Kydans, rumors abounded about what could be found in the interior of the New Land: man-eating monsters were common, apparently. Heriot was inclined to believe it, because she wanted to believe there was a world more dangerous, more beautiful and more mysterious than the one she had got to know. So far, disappointingly, the New Land seemed much like the old. Admittedly, the Kydans were different: darker skinned, on average taller, and more reserved than the average Hamilayan. But the essentials did not seem to have changed very much; there were still the poor and the rich, the ugly and the beautiful, the venal and the noble.

There was a sound behind her and Arden appeared, carrying a jug of beer as well as his own meal. It was ironic, she thought, that the one person she felt closest to in the world was a Hamilayan who was taller and even more reserved than any Kydan she had met.

Arden sat down next to Heriot and she found she could eat her dinner at last. In silence, they ate their food and shared the beer.

"That from the city?" she asked eventually, wiping her lips with the back of her hand.

"The beer? Aye. Not bad."

"Not bad," she agreed. "Saw you wandering around with an axe today. Could have used your help on the wall. Those stones are bloody heavy."

"They needed braces and framework for the stables."

"What stables?"

"For the dragoons' horses. Kydan's never had any cavalry as such—no need for it, being sited in the middle of a river—so the city doesn't have any place for horses."

"So you've been cutting and splicing all day?"

Arden shrugged. "Mostly."

Heriot regarded him for a moment. "Go on."

"Eh?"

"'Mostly,' you said. What else?"

"Been thinking about all those swords and daggers we took from the dead enemy after the battle."

"They haven't been discovered, have they?" Heriot asked, alarmed.

"No. But if we leave them where they are, in a hastily dug pit covered over by naught better than gorse and bracken, some soldier will stumble across them eventually."

"So what have you been thinking?"

Arden actually offered one of his very rare smiles. "I've been thinking about the stables."

At first Heriot stared at Arden with disbelief. Then her expression changed and she smiled too. "Brilliant. Who would think of looking there for a secret hoard of weapons?"

"Talked to some of our guild members who'll be working on the stables; they reckon they could build spaces in one or more of the walls, and leave a loose stone or two that we could take out if the need arose."

"You're smarter than you look, Grim Arden."

"By the way, I saw you talking with that officer."

"Gos Linsedd," she said. "Heard him called that by soldiers around about. He speaks like us. He ain't no la-de-da officer. Field trained."

Arden shook his head. "Like us? Don't think so, field trained or not. Don't like the army. Could be used against us if the leaders don't like our guild."

Heriot looked sternly at Arden. "It's our job to make sure that don't happen. We're all on the same side here."

"Maybe," Arden said, but did not sound convinced. "But it was your idea to keep and hide the weapons."

"That's being prudent. There's a difference. I'm not consorting with the enemy," she said. "We fought together, remember. Anyhow, I seen you chatterboxing with the Kevleren's whatsit."

"Beloved." Arden said the word almost as a grunt. "He's hurting. Lost his whole life when his master died."

"Whatever. Don't go accusing me of consorting—"

"I did no such thing. Just be careful with this Linsedd fellow, and the others. Particularly the woman. She's smarter than most, and knows what's what."

"Woman?"

"Blonde one. Fought by our side here on Karhay."

"Galys Valera," Heriot said. "Soldiers talk about her as well; they like her. She's the strategos the Kevleren prince brought with him for the colony."

"Strategos, eh?" he said. "That explains a lot."

"Maybe she could be an ally."

"She's one of *them*, Heriot. They're not natural allies for us."

"Same could be said for the Beloved."

Arden looked away from her. "Just be careful. That's all I'm saying."

Heriot placed a hand on his huge arm. "Grim Arden," she said affectionately, "you gotta learn to trust someone."

"I trust you," he said, his voice subdued.

5

THE thing about love, Chierma decided, is that you always want it but are better off without it. Not only did the absence of love simplify life, it eliminated guilt, dependence, fealty and, to a remarkable extent, responsibility. Love was an obstruction to a life truly lived, truly explored.

I am better off, now, he told himself. He was standing at the foot of the grave of Lady Englay Kevleren. Once he was her Beloved. Then he had become her master.

One of his aides had asked him why he had dug a grave for the lady. After all, there was hardly anything left of her to bury after the fire.

Nonetheless, enough of the Axkevleren remained in him to order a grave dug and something of hers placed in it: a blue scarf she had loved, and her gold Kevleren necklace with its triangular pendant. It did not seem enough as the grave was being filled in, so Chierma put some flowers on top of the scarf.

He took a deep breath, turned to go, but something held him back. Every time he visited the grave—daily, if duties allowed—he was reluctant to leave, as if by doing so he was deserting her.

In fact, he had done that many months before, when she was still alive and governor of Hamewald. The revolution had all seemed so straightforward at the start, and the conspiracy beforehand had brought a real element of excitement into his life. He had joined the movement against the Kevlerens because he could never forgive them for taking him away from his family when he was only a child, and could never forgive Englay for not . . .

Well, that was all in the past now. The Rivald Kevlerens were all gone, if the word of Velan Lymok, the young Leader of a Thousand from the Safety Committee in Beferen, could be believed. A bloody massacre, a Wielding of such force that everything in the palace flickered blue light for hours afterwards and left not a single member of that terrible family alive. And not just the Kevlerens gone.

All the Beloveds, too, Velan Lymok had told him. Except Chierma, all alone far away in Hamewald.

He forced himself to take a step back towards the governor's residence where he now resided. Governor in Englay's stead, governor despite Velan Lymok, who had come not just to deliver the news from the Safety Committee but to take his office as well. The shock on Lymok's face when he saw that Chierma was still alive would have been amusing had not the tale he told subsequently been so grim.

Of course, the tale explained what had happened to Englay, caught up in the same Sefid storm as her relations in Beferen. It also left behind a singular mystery, the same one that had caught Lymok by surprise.

Englay had died at the same time as the Kevlerens. As had the Beloveds, all except Chierma. Why had he survived?

He thought he knew, in his heart, but would not voice it. That would be too much pain to bear.

It was ridiculous, he told himself. There was almost nothing of Englay in the ground where her marker lay, and yet Chierma sometimes felt as if she really was buried there, and more, that in some way she was still alive, still conscious of his presence. She did not want him to leave her side, still, despite everything that had happened.

That gave him comfort.

A servant from the residence bowed and scraped and told him that Velan Lymok was ready to depart. He wanted to tell the Safety Committee in person that Chierma was still alive. He did not want to entrust the information to a pigeon or courier, especially not so close to the border with Hamilay.

By the time Chierma returned, Lymok's carriage and escort of a dozen cavalry were ready. Lymok himself was sitting in the carriage, the door open, inspecting his gloves with studied patience. He was a vain young man, and feigned a foppish attitude that may have gone down well in the capital but only irritated everyone in Hamewald where everyone was more used to plain speaking and plain behaviour. It was strange, Chierma thought, because he was sure there was a great deal more to the officer. There was something in the way Lymok constantly appraised his environment, the carefully arch way he phrased his sentences to hide his real intelligence behind superficial words. Chierma allowed that Velan Lymok may have been a better man than Velan Lymok liked to show, and in Chierma's eyes that made the officer dangerous; he would be glad when Lymok was gone.

"I am sorry to keep you waiting," Chierma apologised. "I hope you have a safe and uneventful journey."

"They will not believe me, you know," Lymok said, regarding the governor coolly. "They were certain you were as dead as your ilk." He sighed heavily. "They will not know what to do with me."

I could give them a few suggestions, Chierma thought. "They will think of something, I'm sure. The army will be needed more than ever now that our Kevlerens are gone. Nothing else stands between us and the empire."

Lymok paled a little, and glanced nervously over his shoulder in the direction of the border. "Yes, I'm sure you're right."

"You have the report I've written?"

"Right here." Lymok slapped the case between his feet.

"Give my regards to the Safety Committee." He smiled grimly. "What's left of it."

"Oh, it will be quite changed by the time I return. They are recruiting from the army, of course." He smiled condescendingly. "After all, there is nowhere else any more. Oh! I completely forgot to let you know that an old acquaintance of yours is now on the committee."

"An acquaintance of mine?" Chierma could not think of whom Lymok was speaking. Other than servants and minor officials, almost everyone he knew had been a Kevleren or one of their retinue.

"Leader of a Thousand Marquella Montranto." Lymok pursed his lips. "Don't know him well, of course, but he looks very martial."

Chierma did not know what to say. It did not speak highly of the committee that it would employ someone like Montranto, a man the governor thought of as a showy buffoon.

"Yes, he looks the part," Chierma conceded without elaborating; after all, he might need every acquaintance he could lay claim to. He had no doubt Lymok was disappointed that he was not, after all, to be the new governor of Hamewald, and there might be others with more authority and influence looking at his office now that there were no other Beloveds in the republic, let alone on the Safety Committee, to look after his interests.

After Lymok had gone, Chierma returned to his office at the top of the residence. The windows in the north wall looked out over the mountains that marked the border between Rivald and Hamilay, and the windows to the south looked out over Hamewald and the small park across from the residence where Englay was buried.

For the first time it occurred to him that he may not be just the last Beloved in Rivald, as Velan Lymok had told him, but the last connection with that whole way of life. Only in Hamilay did the Kevlerens still rule, and of that family a group, or one or two particularly powerful individuals, had used the Sefid to eliminate their relations in Beferen. As far as Chierma could see, there was only one reason to do that, and that was to open up Rivald like a ripe melon. The Safety Committee could place all the trust it wanted in the army, but it would do them no good. Without the Kevlerens to protect the republic, nothing would not stop the Hamilayan army from marching south.

Chierma had said as much in the report Lymok had taken with him. "It is not a matter of *if* Hamilay invades," he had written, "but *when*." He hoped the committee agreed with him, and followed his advice.

Beferen was a city that stained the landscape like spilled wine, finding every nook and cranny and filling it, but always spreading out, never building up because of the fierce storms that lashed this part of the coast. It sprawled either side of the Eskelstone River that had given it birth, its newest sections creeping east and west along the coastline. Other than a crumbling stone wall that had once protected the old town near the mouth of the river, there was nothing else that gave the city definition or character, and the gray stone used to build most of the houses only added to the feeling of sameness.

Croft Harker, President of the Safety Committee and Leader of a Thousand in the Rivald army, was standing on a balcony of one of the few buildings that had a second storey: the late Queen Sarra Kevleren's palace, once chief administrative centre of the kingdom, now chief administrative centre of the republic. For a long time Harker had thought that all that the revolution had changed was the name of the government; everything else went on pretty well as it had before. But lately he had discovered that the Rivald he had known and loved was inextricably tied up with the Kevlerens. Without that family, Rivald became like its capital, shapeless and ill defined. The army officers who had united with discontented Beloveds to overthrow the monarchy—and subsequently control the Kevlerens and their Wielding—had believed they would be freeing Rivald to follow its true destiny, unbound by any traditional ties with the rulers of the Hamilayan empire.

Harker laughed bitterly. Destiny? All the revolution had succeeded in doing was to give the Hamilayan Kevlerens the excuse they needed to finish off their Rivald relatives, and without their own Kevlerens, Rivald was utterly helpless. He knew in his bones that his homeland's destiny now was to become nothing more than Hamilay's newest province.

A cold southerly blew in his face. Harker felt the moisture in the wind and knew it meant a storm was coming. The southerly would develop into a howling tempest, driving black clouds over the land and whipping Beferen with rain and sleet.

This was how the Hamilayans would come, Harker

thought. Like an ocean storm, cold and dreadful and irresistible.

The worst thing for Harker was how all the noble sentiments that had inspired him and many others like him to start the revolution against Queen Sarra and her brood were now of no avail. The desire to overthrow tyranny and the terrible slavery of the Kevlerens meant nothing in the face of overwhelming force, and would bring no consolation to all those who would die defending Rivald against the invasion.

Better, he realized with dreadful certainty, that there had been no revolution at all. Rivald would be worse off under the rule of foreign Kevlerens than their own home-grown ones, Kevlerens who felt no emotional tie to his country and his people.

A part of him still wanted to hold onto the dream of the republic, of a nation ruled by the best of its own citizens, a dream he had cherished since old enough to witness and understand the deprivations of the ruling Kevlerens, but his own native intelligence would not let him hold onto a dream that events had made as insubstantial as smoke.

He wondered how many of his fellow members on the Safety Committee had foreseen the republic's destiny. They had all been so confident that they had won not only the revolution but, by securing the royal family, had prevented the Hamilayan Kevlerens from interfering. They had shown off to Duke Paimer Kevleren, Empress Lerena's uncle, all that they had wrought, how they had reduced the Rivald Kevlerens to nothing but servants.

That had been their big mistake, Harker realised. Lerena had not reacted the way they had expected. Not at all.

The province of Rivald . . .

And then Harker remembered Rivald's own province, Sayenna. Not only a part of Rivald far from Hamilay, but maybe—just maybe—with a Kevleren still governing. He stood back from the balcony, back from the coming storm.

A chance yet, he thought. Perhaps a chance to escape subjugation under the Hamilayan heel.

Then, with a tightening of the heart, Harker also remembered that Numoya Kevleren had been commanding in the captured port city of Kydan, and as far as he knew, the Hamilayans had sent an expedition to secure the city for themselves. Had the attack succeeded, and if so, had the Kevleren survived the assault?

Numoya Kevleren had always believed blind people lived in absolute darkness. Now blind himself, his imagination filled his mind with memories of colour and movement and shapes and shadows . . . everything except faces. In a way it was the worst thing about no longer being able to see: memory was no guide to people's faces. He could no longer fix in his mind what he looked like, let alone what anyone else looked like, including Quenion, his Beloved.

Reflecting on this—rather than wallowing in grief over it, which was what a part of him really wanted to do—he realised he had not been able to recall the face of Thenge, his first Beloved, within days of her death at his own hand two years before. Memory was obviously not as reliable as he had once believed, and being blind just exaggerated the condition.

The discovery offered no relief, just revelation, but it offered proof that his mind was still in working order, and for a Kevleren nothing was more important, not even sight. At least, that is what he had always secretly believed, but now he was not so sure. Perhaps his parents and siblings and cousins had been right from the start. Perhaps the capacity for love was the most important faculty for a Kevleren.

Certainly without it he could not imagine a way out of his current predicament, and it was love others held for him that made his current predicament even remotely bearable.

No, blind people did not live in absolute darkness, at least not those who had once had sight. But once sight was gone, he learned that there was an abyss deep inside him which no light touched, and which made him afraid of himself. It was made from emotion, love and hate and desire, and its name was revenge, and its coldness sometimes kept him awake at night. He did not mind. It gave him time to consider how he would punish Kydan, and later, perhaps, Hamilay itself.

Not without help, though. He could do nothing without the support of others, particularly strange Quenion, his Beloved not beloved. That, at least, would have to change, something owed her not simply because of her devotion to him but more importantly because he was a Kevleren, and it was the duty of a Kevleren to love.

Numoya stopped himself. Not duty. That was the wrong word. Duty was what was owed the Kevlerens for the love they gave freely. That was something he had forgotten after Thenge's death.

Her sacrifice, he corrected himself. Even now, although he could no longer clearly recall what she had looked like, he could remember the fear and surprise in her eyes when he had taken her life from her, when her blood ran hot over his hand as he had pierced the artery in her neck. But her death had been necessary, for Rivald. It had been her duty, and he should not be ashamed of what he had done. Or feel guilt, or self-hate, or remorse . . . and he should not let it stop him from loving again.

6

LERENA roused from sleep in the middle of the night, crying for Hanimoro. When she woke fully she stopped, berating herself for being foolishly sentimental, but stared into the darkness for a long time, surprised by the power of her own dreaming. Eventually, unable to return to sleep, she got out of bed and scrabbled for her gown. Once upon a time Hanimoro would have roused as soon as Lerena was awake and found her gown for her.

Lerena stood by her bed and sighed heavily. She refused to let herself cry again. She looked around for something to distract herself, noticed moonlight, silvery hard, coming through her window. She went to it and looked out over the palace grounds, with its Great Hall and Great Courtyard, the family alcazars, the War Office, the buildings holding various other government ministries. Her domain, her entire empire, captured in miniature within the yellow walls of the royal enclosure. If only the real empire were so easily controlled and supervised, she thought wistfully.

Her gaze settled on the huge dome of Yunara's aviary; the light reflecting off its glass surface made it look like a small moon half embedded in the city of Omeralt. Lerena had still not visited her sister's alcazar, and Yunara had been dead now for more than a tenday. The place needed cleaning out, and her familiars and Axkevlerens needed tending, which meant distribution among other family members, given freedom or—in the case of some familiars—put out of their misery.

Lerena sighed heavily. Inevitably some of Yunara's Axkevlerens, voluntarily, would also end their own misery. Often, such was the terrible consequence of being loved by a Kevleren and loving in return.

The empress cast her eyes down. She did not relish this task. She had seen enough death to last her the rest of her life, but she had duties, and she would not shirk them.

Lerena just wished there was an easy way out of the responsibility.

Something caught her attention. She glanced up, but saw nothing untoward; then, after a long moment, she noticed something peculiar in the night air, like a halo. A blue halo. Not everywhere, though. Just around . . .

Lerena jerked back from the window, retreated hurriedly into her room. Part of her mind realized surprise was being overtaken by panic, and she forced herself to stop then slowly return to the window.

It was not possible. After the first time she had convinced herself it had been a dream. No one in the world could Wield so powerfully.

Yet there it was, a blue haze, almost invisible, hovering around one of the metal gates that quartered the palace wall, and ever so faintly around the water pipes in her private garden. In fact, Lerena saw that anything made from metal was haloed. Even the barrels of the firegons carried by patrolling Royal Guards were affected, not that the guards seemed to notice.

Someone was Wielding with enormous energy; it was as if the city had been flooded with it.

Suddenly afraid, Lerena stepped back from her window again and closed it.

Duke Paimer Kevleren was woken by the sweetest singing he had ever heard. He lay in his bed trying to catch the tune, but it faded away with the last remnants of sleep.

"Your Grace?" asked Idalgo Axkevleren. "Are you all right?"

"I thought I heard . . ." Paimer shook his head. "It doesn't matter. Where are you, Idalgo?"

He felt the presence of someone hovering nearby. "Right here. Can I get you something?"

Paimer peered into the dark but could not see his Beloved. "Is there a lamp?"

"I think so. But you should close your eyes. You have an early start tomorrow."

"Do I?"

"Yes, your Grace. Your niece needs you. She is visiting Yunara's home and will want you by her side."

"Ah." Paimer thought for a while. "What can we do about Yunara? She could be the downfall of everything the family has striven for, you know. She is that powerful."

"I think the empress will have her in hand, eventually. But she will need your help."

"I am not done yet, eh? My nieces—one or the other— will always need my help. That's what old age brings you. Respect. And from respect comes security. Security and trust." He lost his concentration for a moment and just at the fringe of his conscious mind heard again the beautiful singing. He cocked his head, trying to remember where he had heard it before. A long time ago, he was sure.

"Get some sleep," Idalgo urged him gently. "I will wake you as soon as it is dawn."

"Yes." Paimer curled on his side, and before all thought left him, remembered to say, "Goodnight, Idalgo."

"Goodnight, your Grace."

Captain of a Thousand Avenel Kendy, only recently made Rivald's ambassador to the court of Empress Lerena Kevleren, was confused and frustrated and frightened. Despite several urgent messages sent by pigeon to Beferen over the last few days, no instructions had come through. The first time he had sent a detailed report of how his secretary, Siness Ardra, while working in his office, had suddenly been consumed by a ball of flame, leaving nothing behind except a charred chair and a terrified note-taker. The second time he had sent a more concise report, stressing the fact that Ardra was no longer around to guide him in any diplomatic deliberations with the Hamilayan empire, and that furthermore his enquiries indicated that every Beloved in the city of Omeralt had died in similar terrible circumstances. Subsequent messages merely pointed out that Siness Ardra, the Axkevleren the Safety Committee had appointed to oversee his mission, was regrettably deceased; repeat and underline: deceased.

As far as Kendy could figure, no one in Beferen gave a damn about the passing of Siness Ardra, which, if the man had been an actual member of the Safety Committee as Kendy suspected, was strange indeed. Although, he admitted to himself, Ardra could hardly have been described as an agreeable sort of person, let alone affable or likeable. Maybe, like Kendy, the Safety Committee was secretly pleased that Ardra had disappeared in a blaze of fire. This last thought made the ambassador feel guilty, which only added to his burden as Rivald's sole representative in the whole of the Hamilayan empire, with all the responsibilities pertaining thereto.

Worst of all, Ardra had been responsible for managing Rivald's spies in Omeralt; the man had even boasted of placing a man in the palace itself. Now how would the Safety Committee get the information it so badly needed about goings-on in Lerena's court? Kendy had no idea who Ardra's contacts and informants were, or even how he had paid them.

The whole thing was a bloody mess, and the deaths of so many Beloveds in the city on the same day had frightened him more than he could say. He did not know what was going on any more. With the death of so many high-ranking Axkevlerens something basic and fundamental had changed in the world, and he was no longer sure of his place in it.

Kendy decided he just wanted to go home. He had been a useless soldier and was proving to be an even more useless diplomat. The only task he thought he had ever performed satisfactorily, and indeed the only one he had enjoyed, was being a clerk in the palace bureaucracy back in Beferen in the old days.

Kendy half ran up to the pigeon house on the roof of the embassy, hoping desperately that a bird from Beferen had flown in overnight; but as usual, the coops were empty.

Kendy sighed. His shoulders sagged. He sat on the edge of one of the coops, feeling desperately sorry for himself. Then he looked up and the city of Omeralt, towered, domed, made from the warm yellow stone of the Vardar Mountains and topped by hundreds of fluttering pennants, lightened his heart. At that moment he realised he was probably luckier than he had thought. He made a conscious effort to look on the bright side and methodically listed the advantages of his current position.

First, he was in Omeralt, a city that in climate and temperament completely outshone the dark, cold and storm-driven city of Beferen. Second, he was in the fortunate position of being head of a diplomatic mission, ensconced in comfortable lodgings with a bounty of servants and clerks to do his every bidding. Third, Siness Ardra was dead; a man he had never warmed to, and indeed one who had seemed as intent on spying on Kendy as on Lerena's court. Fourth, with Ardra gone, he was free to influence and perhaps even shape diplomatic relations between Rivald and the empire free from any interference, at least until further instructions arrived from the Safety Committee.

Looked at in that way, the changed circumstances represented an unlooked-for opportunity, and he immediately decided to grasp it with both hands.

Kendy stood up and straightened his clothes, then straightened his back and shoulders. He had work to do.

Lerena had intended to go to Yunara's alcazar as soon as it was light, but Uilder had gently reminded her that it was a court day. Still suffering from the effects of her interrupted sleep, she let herself be dressed in the formal attire she wore when presiding from the throne in the Great Hall. It was not until she entered the hall and saw members of her family, as disconsolate as usual, milling around waiting for her arrival, that she hesitated.

"Is something wrong, your Majesty?" Uilder asked, noticing the expression that crossed the empress's face.

"Last night . . ." Lerena began, but her voice faltered.

"Last night?" Uilder prompted.

"Did you see? Outside?"

Uilder looked as confused as Lerena was starting to feel. But how could Lerena explain what she had seen? How could she admit to Uilder that someone could Wield so powerfully that everything in the city made of metal glowed blue? Why was her family not mobbing her, terrified out of their minds that some terrible catastrophe was again about to befall them?

Unless they knew beforehand . . .

Lerena almost turned on her heel then, but that deep reserve of courage that had seen her through so much already helped her keep calm. She put a hand on Uilder's shoulder to support herself and paused to gather her thoughts.

Who in her family had that kind of strength with the Sefid? No one except herself now that her sister was dead. Therefore something else was behind what she had seen during the night. Or there was someone in the family who had been keeping their talent secret all these years. The last thought she dismissed almost immediately: such a strong talent with the Sefid would almost certainly have been detected by Yunara while she was alive.

She studied the faces of her family members, now all looking at her expectantly. There was no hint there of conspiracy or smugness. Indeed, they all had the same crestfallen look they had worn since the night they had lost their Beloveds. None of them posed a threat to her.

Her composure regained, Lerena proceeded to the throne and for the next hour tried to focus on the business of the court until what had to be done was done. As matters proceeded, however, she found herself increasingly dwelling on what might have caused the effects she had observed the previous night, until she was constantly asking officials and plaintiffs to repeat what they were saying because she was not really paying them any attention.

Eventually she dismissed her family and the court attendants and asked Uilder to order her sedan brought to the front of the Great Hall. "I wish to visit my late sister's alcazar."

As Lerena left the front of the hall there was a hubbub in the Great Courtyard. Uilder, sitting in the sedan with Lerena, poked her head out of the window to see what was happening.

"It's the duke," Uilder said.

"Paimer?"

Lerena pushed Uilder aside and opened the sedan door. Duke Paimer Kevleren was halfway through the process of getting out of his own chair, but he had one heel caught behind the step and his carriers were obviously finding it hard to keep their balance as he struggled to free himself. A Royal Guard was trying to help him out of his difficulty, but he was slapping him away.

"I'm perfectly fine, thank you very much," he was saying in short, exasperated breaths.

"Uncle? What is the meaning of this?"

Paimer twisted around to face his niece. Just then his heel came unstuck and he jerked forward. Lerena watched with admiration as he turned the stumble into a bow. "Good morning, your Majesty," he said. "I thought I would come with you."

His famous red wig, which did not seem to fit properly any more, sat slightly adrift on top of his head. Lerena felt a surge of pity for the man, a mere shadow of someone who once had been a pillar of strength and wisdom in the family.

"Come with me where?" she asked.

"To Yunara's alcazar."

Lerena blinked. How could he possibly have known . . . ?

"I *need* to come with you," Paimer continued, his voice almost pleading, then he stopped suddenly and blinked. His voice stronger, he said, "*You* need me to come with you."

For a moment Lerena did not know how to reply. There was something vaguely desperate about his manner that warned her off, but the pity she felt for him proved stronger and she opened the sedan door to let him in.

He clambered aboard, this time graciously accepting the help of the guard, and slumped in the seat opposite Lerena's, the position once taken by Hanimoro. The empress felt uncomfortable, as if some social convention was being betrayed. And, she noticed, the duke had not bathed for some time.

As the sedan door closed she moved apart the window's curtains. "Let's enjoy the fresh air while we travel," she said, trying to keep her voice light.

At first there was a tense silence inside the cabin. Lerena made an effort to look out the window but could not help glancing at her uncle every now and then, and every time she did she found him staring at her. The wide, unblinking eyes and the offset red wig made him look inhuman rather than comical, like a blind god's poor attempt to make a man. After a while she could take it no more and decided to glare back, but it was like staring at a rock for all the emotion she could sense behind his eyes. Then, when they were only minutes from their destination, he looked to his left, to the empty space beside him, and said, "Yes, I agree."

Lerena and Uilder exchanged glances.

Paimer faced Lerena again. "Your Majesty, you should let me enter the alcazar first, just in case."

"In case?"

Paimer coughed discreetly into his hand and mumbled, "In case of deceit."

Lerena wished now she had not let Paimer on board. His mind obviously had been far more damaged by the deaths of Yunara and all the Beloveds than she had first thought.

He was staring earnestly at her. "Of course, Uncle, enter first if that is your wish."

The duke nodded and seemed to relax. He looked out of the window instead of resuming his staring at the empress. For her part, Lerena found herself wondering if Paimer's behaviour might have something to do with the flood of Sefid she had witnessed during the night. Or . . . or could he have caused it?

Although it was generally believed that Paimer was one of those rare Kevlerens without any ability with the Sefid, Lerena was now the only person alive who knew that in fact he had always had some capacity to Wield. This secret had made the duke an invaluable tool for Lerena and her mother in any number of tasks, from diplomatic missions to sorting out family squabbles. But his ability had always been a small thing, never more than enough to send a simple message over some distance, or to turn someone's head at exactly the right moment.

Still, who knew what aspects of the Sefid had been unleashed that day when Lerena had sacrificed so mightily? Especially since the sacrifice had included her own sister Yunara, a necessary act to enable Lerena to destroy every Beloved loved by a Kevleren, which in turn had generated the extra energy she needed to destroy every member of the branch of the Kevleren family that had ruled in Rivald. The whole world had been charged with the Sefid for hours afterwards, and Lerena's mind had coursed through it like a fish in a spring river.

Her thoughts were disturbed by a challenge from ahead: Yunara's guards still fulfilling their duty, despite no longer having a mistress to serve.

The challenge was answered by her own guards, and the sedan passed through the alcazar's gate and into the main courtyard unchallenged. Lerena saw Axkevlerens gathering there, with more coming from the main building. Their expressions were a mixture of hope and bewilderment. The guilt she felt was reinforced by pity. One of them rushed forwards to open the sedan door but was rebuffed by a guard.

"No, it's all right," Lerena said, and the guard, reluctantly, stood back. The servant came forward again, opened the door and bowed deeply.

Lerena was about to step out when Paimer put a hand on hers. "I'm first, remember?" He winked at her. "Just in case."

She thought that the obviously demented Paimer would not necessarily make the best impression on those waiting in the forecourt, but before she could say anything he dropped from the sedan, his red wig lurching over his forehead. Lerena watched aghast as he nudged back the wig and glared at those nearest him. People pulled back from him, frightened. Lerena stepped out quickly and went to his side, smiling benignly, using her arm to urge Paimer behind her. He would have none of it.

"Sweet Uncle," she said as calmly as possible, "these are obviously loyal servants who mean no harm to me or those dear to me. Please step back."

Paimer frowned in thought, as if listening to another

voice, then nodded stiffly. "Of course, your Majesty." He moved behind her.

"I have been remiss in my responsibility," she declared magnanimously. "I have neglected cruelly my sister's dependents. You have been waiting patiently for me to come, but I have let the many, and often onerous, duties of the throne divert me from an equally important and far less onerous duty: my care for you. I ask for your forgiveness."

Her words had the desired effect. The gathered Axkevlerens all started crying at once: "No, your Majesty!" and "Not you, your Majesty!" and even "We knew you would come!"

She put as much modest sweetness as she could into a smile. "You are kind, and for that I thank you. But know that you will be neglected no longer. I accept all of you into my own household. As well, I intend to take my late sister's alcazar as one of my own residences and wish you to continue to work in the home you have known almost all your lives."

Scattered cheering broke out, uncertain, followed by a clatter of applause. Lerena, who had expected a greater show of gratitude, thought the assembled Axkevlerens had not yet comprehended their good fortune. She would let it go for the moment.

She looked up at the imposing edifice that comprised Yunara's main residence, almost as large as her own royal quarters, and behind it a glimpse of the even more imposing dome that housed her late sister's aviary. Lerena thought the residence, dark and vertical, had something of the mausoleum about it, and for a moment felt, absurdly, she would be committing sacrilege by entering it. She felt herself quail a little, but then told herself she was being ridiculous.

Yunara may once have been a great power in the empire, but Lerena had taken care of that, as was her right and responsibility. For the good of the empire.

"*For the good of the empire*," she breathed between her teeth, and went to enter.

Paimer suddenly interposed himself again. "Your Majesty, I insist you—"

"Oh, for the Sefid's sake, Uncle," she said crossly, moving him aside with little grace, and entered the building.

Paimer stood by as people streamed past him. The empress was followed by most of her guards and Uilder, and then by most of the Axkevlerens who had assembled in the forecourt, leaving behind only a few.

He felt confusion and humiliation in equal measure. He noticed the two guards who stayed behind with Lerena's sedan were looking at him, although they averted their eyes quickly enough.

Paimer was not sure what had just happened. He thought Lerena had agreed to let him go first. He had only wanted to protect her, as was his duty and right. He loved her, the daughter of his sister, the previous empress. His niece. He wanted to protect her from his other niece, the terrible Yunara . . .

The duke frowned. Where was Yunara? Why had she not been here to greet Lerena? He turned to ask Idalgo if he had any idea what was going on, but his Beloved was not there either. Maybe he had gone in with the others.

A cold wind, straight from the Vardar Mountains, licked around his feet. He felt cold and foolish standing there by himself. Perhaps he should go back to the chair. He glanced over to the guards. They were looking at him again. No, he would stay where he was. He felt his wig slip a little, so he adjusted it carefully.

Oh, why had Lerena treated him so shamefully? He was a duke and her uncle and deserved better from her. He deserved better from everyone. Well, he would show them. He did not need any of them. He would walk home by himself.

Paimer, his mind made up, left the forecourt, ignoring the guards who called after him. He found himself on a busy street. People bustled around him but none of them was staring at him. Indeed, they ignored him completely, and in a strange way that gave him some comfort. Now, which way was it to the city gate? Straight ahead. Yes . . .

"Best return to the Great Hall, your Grace," Idalgo said.

"Ah, there you are. I was wondering where you had got to. Why the Great Hall?"

"That's where you left your sedan."

Paimer stopped in the street. Passers-by swore as they swerved to avoid colliding with him. He ignored them.

"Of course that's where I left it. Silly of me to have forgotten that."

"You have a lot on your mind," Idalgo said, and Paimer could taste the humor in his voice.

"I'm a duke," Paimer said. "Dukes always have a lot on their minds. Did you see the way Lerena treated me?"

"Her majesty was in a hurry."

"She should slow down then. People in a hurry make mistakes, you know." Paimer resumed walking. "I did not see Yunara at all, by the way."

"She is a dangerous woman, your Grace."

"I've decided that all women are dangerous. My life is a series of misadventures, all because of women. First my sister, the Empress Hetha. Then both my nieces. Then all my . . ." He could not think of the appropriate word. He glanced at Idalgo and raised his eyebrows. It was a signal his Beloved knew very well.

"Dalliances?" Idalgo suggested.

"Then all my dalliances. Oh, Sefid, I'm tired of women."

"That is not entirely true. We must turn down here."

Paimer turned from the street onto a much wider avenue. There were many officials hurrying to and from offices, and some soldiers. Human-drawn carts and sedans hefted by sweating carriers occupied the middle of the way, and Paimer had to dodge to avoid them. Still no one paid him any attention.

"You are forgetting your place, Idalgo. Of course it is true. I tell you I am cutting myself off from women."

"My apologies, your Grace. I should not doubt you. At least, not until you see the next pretty face that will make you forget your self-imposed exile."

Paimer harrumphed. His Beloved knew him too well. He frowned. No, that was not true. It was not possible for a Beloved to know his master too well.

Someone collided with the duke and he was spun around. His wig fell to the ground. He bent to retrieve it, and when he was standing straight again he was looking directly into a round face with a big nose and two glaring blue eyes.

"Sir!" shouted the face. "You were in my way!"

Paimer stood back to better view his assailant. The man was a little shorter than the duke but more solidly built. He wore the black jacket and breeches with the red stockings that was almost a uniform for clerks in the palace administration.

"If I had more time I would teach you a lesson—"

The man's angry voice cut off the moment Paimer

swung his wig back on his head, and his face paled to a sickening shade of white.

"Your Grace! I am *so* sorry! I don't know what over-came me . . ."

Paimer ignored him and continued down the avenue. This was the last time he would go anywhere with Lerena. He would use his own chair from now on. Up ahead he could see the roof of the Great Hall. Not far, then.

"Idalgo, you may kick my royal arse if I ever fall for an-other pretty face . . ."

Even before he finished the sentence he felt instinc-tively that he was talking to himself. He glanced around. Idalgo was nowhere to be seen. He must have gone ahead to warn Paimer's carriers the duke was coming. But a Beloved does not leave the side of his master. Paimer was starting to feel confused again.

"Your Grace?" someone to his left asked. The accent was not local.

Paimer turned and saw a short balding man in fancy dress. A servant standing behind him looked on curiously. "Who are you?" he demanded.

"I am Captain of a Thousand Avenel Kendy," the man said. "I am ambassador to the court of her majesty, the Em-press Lerena, from the Republic of Rivald."

"Ah. Have you see my Beloved?"

Kendy blinked. He did not seem to know what to say.

"Idalgo Axkevleren," Paimer went on, looking down his nose at the ambassador.

Kendy shifted uncomfortably.

"By the Sefid, man, you have them in your kingdom, don't you?"

Kendy swallowed and looked around uncertainly. "You have no guards with you, your Grace?"

"Guards? I don't need any guards. I need my damn Beloved!"

"Perhaps he is waiting for you at the Great Hall. You were going there yourself, were you not?"

"Yes. Yes, maybe you are right. But I will have a word with Idalgo about this. He should not leave my side."

Kendy looked concerned. "May I accompany you?"

Paimer looked surprised at the suggestion.

"Only until the Great Hall," Kendy added hurriedly. "I am sure we will find your Beloved there. Anyway, I am heading there myself."

"As you wish," Paimer said, not sure if it was appropriate for an ambassador from Rivald to escort a duke of the empire anywhere let alone to the Great Hall.

After a few moments of strained silence, Kendy said, "It is a beautiful day, is it not?"

"You said you were captain of a thousand?"

"That's right, your Grace."

Paimer's forehead creased in thought. "I think I have met one of you before. A long time ago. Somewhere."

Kendy swallowed. "Perhaps my predecessor as ambassador?"

Paimer slowly shook his head. "No, no I don't think so . . . Why don't you have a sedan? Surely your kingdom can afford one."

"Republic, your Grace," Kendy said carefully. "We are a republic now, not a kingdom. And it was such a lovely day for walking, I thought I might visit the empress under my own power."

"A republic? Really?" Paimer stopped and grabbed Kendy's arm. "What happened to Queen Sarra?"

Paimer thought Kendy looked perplexed, but then his face brightened. "Ah, we are here!" the ambassador declared, easing his arm out of Paimer's grip. "Is this perhaps your sedan?"

The duke glanced over his shoulder. There was the Great Hall, and in front of it, waiting patiently, his carriers and chair.

"Yes." He turned back to Kendy, but the question in his head was gone. "Well. Well, thank you."

Kendy nodded, and he and his servant hurriedly made their way to the hall. Absently, Paimer went to his people and was helped into the sedan. As soon as they were off he frowned at Idalgo and said, "You should not have gone on ahead."

Idalgo smiled quizzically as he watched the retreating Kendy. "Strange fellow," he said.

"But helpful," Paimer said.

"Yes, very."

"You know, I should have told him that Lerena was not there." Paimer sighed. "I daresay he will find that out for himself."

Lerena's first impression of Yunara's alcazar was that she did not know how her sister could have lived in such a dark, winding warren. Yet as she made her way through the edifice, led by a nervous and overly obsequious servant who stopped every tenyard to scrape and bow, her impression slowly changed. Narrow passageways barely wide enough for one of her Royal Guards and lined with unpolished beams of wood became proper corridors with smooth walls and finally hallways with tapestries and windows and carpets underfoot. Rooms changed from cold, bare boxes and storage bins into comfortable living quarters and eventually proper chambers with more than one door and lighting and fireplaces and tables and chairs and shelves and shelves of books.

After passing a long single window that gave a panoramic view of Omeralt nestling under the white-capped Vardars, she remembered something her Beloved, Hanimoro, had told her after visiting the alcazar. It was a trap. At the start you are sure you have entered a termites' nest not a home, but gradually you are brought deeper and deeper into a personal domain that slowly reveals its secrets and the wealth and confidence behind its construction.

When the imperial party finally reached the glass-enclosed skyway that led to Yunara's aviary, the full import of what her sister had designed and built was revealed. From the skyway Lerena could look down not only on the whole city but on the palace enclosure as well, including Lerena's own quarters. The view was a reminder to visitors about who the real power was in Hamilay.

The empress stopped, took in the sight and smiled. Of course, no one now doubted who was the real power in the land.

The obsequious servant was smiling toothily, his hand showing the way forward, even though there was no other way to go. Lerena groaned inside and followed the servant to a wire door which he opened to let the party pass through into a short corridor. At the other end of the corridor was an iron gate with decorated glass panels. The servant squeezed by the empress, almost tittering he was so nervous, and opened the gate on its sprung hinges.

Lerena stepped into the aviary and, without thinking, stopped short, making the line behind her concertina. She stood on a gallery with thin iron lace railing that circled the huge dome halfway up its circumference. Looking out over the complex of woods and reed beds and lawns, waterways and even a lake with its own island, she felt as if she were a god looking down on the whole world, on all creation. There did not seem to be many birds, though. A few could be seen swooping between trees and over grass, catching insects on the fly, and she saw a pair of cranes fishing by the edge of the lake.

The air was warm, and soft breezes, faintly aromatic, caressed her cheeks.

"Excuse me, your Majesty," the servant was whining, obviously wanting to get past so he could continue being of service.

"Stay back," she said in her most imperious voice.

Without another sound the servant left, a ripple in the line of people behind the empress the only indication of his passing.

"All of you stay back," she said distractedly over her shoulder to the rest of the party. "I want to go on alone. Wait for me here."

The guards seemed unsure, but she repeated her injunction and made sure everyone moved back far enough for the gate to close behind her.

She looked up to the top of the dome, a glass hemisphere that arced so high above her that the tracery which kept it together was invisible. A twinge of vertigo made her look down again, but that only seemed to make it worse. She closed her eyes briefly, set her gaze on the iron lace railing and followed it to a set of spiral steps that descended to ground level.

Lerena tested the mat of grass she finally landed on. It was springy but firm, and her vertigo left her completely. She sniffed the air, smelled the water and dark rich earth. The air was cooler down here than on the gallery, but there was no breeze. A grass parrot skipped over her feet, landed not far from her. She could hear a raven calling from among the woods that seemed to fill the small island in the middle of the lake. She decided to go there, to the center of things. The journey did not take as long as she thought it would: distances were deceptive under the artificial sky. When she reached the small bridge that led to the island she saw it was bisected by a trail made from crushed stone, and following it she stepped through a ring of trees to find herself in a hideaway, a glade cut off from prying eyes. There was a plain bench seat offset to one side. Yunara must have spent a large part of her life just here, Lerena thought, and understood why. Although of course she had known of the aviary's existence, Lerena had never known it was such a perfect place: a small ideal world within a world.

Distantly she heard a clatter and a bang. She left the glade to see what was happening. Up on the gallery her guards and some of Yunara's Axkevlerens appeared, searching anxiously for her.

"For the Sefid's sake!" she shouted at them, angry her tranquility had been disturbed. "Get out! All of you get—"

Her words were cut off by a sudden storm of feathers and whistles and rushing as whole flocks, startled by her shouting, leaped into the air. The dome was filled with an eruption of unexpected life. Blues and greens, reds and yellows, oil-sheen rainbows, small pattering hearts and round eyes. Thousands of beating wings made the air whir and blur, kaleidoscoped the glass dome into sparkling fragments.

After what seemed a very long time Lerena started breathing again, but her mind was still elsewhere: skimming over grass, gliding over water, cutting between trees, soaring to the highest point of the dome and diving back to earth.

Then she noticed the soft blue glow of the Sefid, picking out the metal tracery that ran through the dome and the gallery with its iron lace railing and the spiral steps. This time she was not afraid. This time she understood, and the revelation was a wonder to her. She started laughing, and it seemed to her the birds sang to keep her company.

7

THE birth chain sparkled in the sunlight, and not just the gems: even the stones reflected pinpoints of light, as if they were coated with gold dust. Galys carefully studied the stones but could find nothing that would explain the phenomenon. It was another mystery to add to the long list of mysteries she already had to deal with.

Hardly an important one, however, she thought, then stopped herself. How did she know? The birth chain, and whatever properties it held, could be behind Kitayra's death.

"You're sure this did not belong to Maddyn?" she asked.

Kadburn shook his head. "He did not look at his own chain very often, but I don't recognise any of the pieces." He took the chain from Galys and held it up. The reflected light was almost too bright to look at. "And I'm certain none of them ever shone like these."

"Who would give Kitayra something like this?"

"Only a Kevleren. No one else could have given it to her."

Galys held Kadburn's gaze. "Which Kevleren? Did Maddyn . . . ?"

"He only had the one that I ever saw, and if he had another there would be no reason for him to hide it from me."

"Of course," she said, disappointed.

"How many Kevlerens did she know?" Kadburn prompted.

Galys snorted. "That's just it. Before she met the prince I don't think she had ever actually met a Kevleren before."

"She was a grammarian! She studied the Sefid!"

"Grammarians have never been endeared to the Kevlerens." She patted Kadburn's shoulder. "I'm afraid that Maddyn's lack of ability with the Sefid made him more open-minded than most of his family."

He did not argue the point. He handed back the birth chain, then moved away from the window, slumped against the stone wall and grimly surveyed the contents of the room they were in. "Is it like this with Kitayra?" he asked, waving at all the cases and leather bags that took up most of the floor space and the single cot in one corner. "I don't know how I'll sort through all of Maddyn's possessions. What should I do with them?"

"Yes, it is just like this," Galys said. She pocketed the birth chain. "It is hard to let go of anything, no matter how incidental it may have been when your prince was alive. But I know there are colonists who could do with some of his clothes. We can donate his books to Kydan's library, if they have one. I'll help you organise it if you like."

"Thanks anyway, but you have Kitayra's possessions to clear through."

There was an uncomfortable silence for a moment. Galys took a deep breath. "I have to ask this. What exactly happened when Maddyn died?"

"I don't want to talk ab—" Kadburn hesitated. He swallowed and started again. "It's not because I can't remember. It's because I can't forget."

"I know. I think every second thought I have is about Kitayra. Every dream I have, every pause in my life, is taken up with remembering her and the way she was when I found her."

"Stop," Kadburn said reproachfully.

"But I think that's how I'm learning to live with it. Kadburn, I don't have to forget but I do have to understand, and I can't do that without help." She licked her lips. "When you made your announcement in the Assembly about Numoya Kevleren killing the prince, I realised he must also have been responsible for killing Kitayra. But I still don't understand how. Most importantly, I don't understand *why*."

Galys waited but Kadburn remained resolutely silent. She nodded her acquiescence, but as she started to leave he said, "Wait. Please."

It was his turn to take a deep breath and his body shuddered with it. He closed his eyes and slowly the words came.

"Maddyn was standing next to me and suddenly he pulled his hands away from the stone," he said slowly, pulling his own hands up in demonstration. "He blew on his palm to cool it. I remember thinking the Citadel wall must have been hot."

"Your Highness?" Kadburn asked, looking at General Third Prince Maddyn Kevleren with sudden concern.

"It's nothing . . ." Maddyn said too abruptly and looked out towards the river where he had been directing the fire of the longgons against the enemy in their boats.

Kadburn heard him say "No" quite clearly, as if

answering a question he had asked himself. But then he saw light poured from Maddyn's chest; he could even see the individual stones in the birth chain around his master's neck shining like miniature stars through his shirt.

"Kadburn," the prince muttered, and then shouted in pain. He started falling. "Kadburn . . ."

Kadburn reached out to steady him, but every part of his master's body burst into fire.

"There was a wall of heat, or something. I could feel my hair and skin singeing. I fell down the stone stairs. Then my head hit something." Kadburn rubbed the back of his head and grunted. "The lump's still there. Size of a quail's egg."

"Go on," Galys urged.

"When I recovered I was at the bottom of the wall. I looked up and saw Maddyn on fire." He shook his head. "No. I didn't see Maddyn himself, but it *was* him. A ball of flame in the night. He made no sound, but the fire was breathing like . . ."

Kadburn's voice trailed off.

"Was there anyone else on the wall?"

"There must have been someone up there. I heard them shouting that the longgons' canvas cartridges would go up. Then the whole wall exploded. I was knocked out." He looked up wearily at Galys. "That's all I remember."

"I'm told that when the Sefid is used, there are signs. A feeling of cold. A blue haze around metal."

"It was night. I saw no haze around the longgons. Can't say I was looking, though. Don't remember much before his highness died, except that we were shooting at the enemy boats, hoping we'd get enough before they reached Karhay or Herris. Karhay especially, because the defenses weren't finished. We were worried about the colonists."

He looked at Galys and attempted to smile. "But we knew you were there, Strategos. Maddyn knew you'd hold it for us, no matter what."

Galys blushed and did not know what to say. That level of trust scared her. She was glad for the sake of the prince's memory that she and the colonists had managed to hold the island, that his trust had not been misplaced.

"Anyway," Kadburn continued, "maybe when it's a powerful Wield there is no warning. Maybe it just happens."

"How do you know it was the Sefid?"

"I told you, Maddyn's birth chain was glowing, like it was burning its way to his heart! It was the Sefid, there is no doubt in my mind. No doubt at all." Galys could hear Kadburn's voice grow stronger with anger. "And I've no doubt it was Numoya Kevleren who Wielded it."

He lurched to his feet and pointed east, upriver from Kydan. "That's the way he will come back for his revenge, and I'll be waiting for him."

Galys nodded. She completely understood his driving anger, even shared it. If Numoya Kevleren returned, she would help Kadburn gut the Rivald prince. But something in the back of her mind was keeping her a lot cooler than the Axkevleren, who was now pacing up and down a narrow channel between Maddyn's possessions.

"A lot of people died in the plutocrats' assault on Kydan."

"You think I don't know that?"

"Many of them mutilated beyond recognition. Some were burned to death. Some had buildings fall on them. Some were butchered. Many bodies were dragged from the river for days after the battle."

Kadburn eyed her suspiciously. "What are you suggesting? That this Numoya may have been among the dead?"

"Is that impossible?"

Kadburn's laugh was a bark, but when he spoke his voice was almost a whisper. "Yes, it is absolutely impossible," he said.

"How *can* you be so positive?"

"Because I saw him escape."

Galys's eyes widened in surprise. "Why didn't you say so before?"

"No one doubted my word before," he said ruefully.

Galys stood, angry. She felt her cheeks flush with blood. "I was not doubting your word, Kadburn, and you know it. I am just making sure."

Kadburn stepped back and swallowed. "I'm sorry. Maybe I should have mentioned it but I just didn't think it was important. Not compared to what it means: that he will be back."

Galys breathed through her nose and looked away from Kadburn, allowing herself to calm down. "What did you see, exactly?"

"It was near the end of the battle. I was helping defend the wall where it had been destroyed by the exploding longgons. The enemy was making its last charge. I saw him fleeing just then, when we were too preoccupied to stop him."

"Was he unhurt? Was he by himself?"

"I think so . . . no, wait . . ." Kadburn rubbed his eyes with the fingers of one hand. "He was being helped. One person. She helped him get to one of the enemy's boats. That's the last I saw of them."

"She?"

"His Beloved. I can't remember her name."

"Quenion," Galys said absently. Her mind was already chasing down something important.

"Yes, I think that was it."

Galys caught the thought. Her head snapped up and she captured Kadburn's gaze. "I have to ask one more time. This is important. Are you sure it was Numoya Kevleren you saw escaping, and are you sure he was being helped by Quenion, his Beloved?"

"Yes to the first. Reasonably sure to the second. You're not going to suggest that just because he needed help to the boat he later died of his wounds?"

Galys shook her head. "Think, Kadburn. Think what it means."

"Think about *what* means?"

"Numoya left *with* his Beloved."

"So?"

"She was still alive. Don't you understand?"

"Of course I see that she was alive," Kadburn said irritably. "That's what I've been telling you."

They stared at each other for a long moment, and then Galys saw the annoyed expression on Kadburn's face evaporate, to be replaced by one of understanding.

"And if she was still alive," he said slowly, speaking as his thoughts coalesced, "then Numoya did not use her as a sacrifice. And if he did not sacrifice Quenion, the only Axkevleren he had access to, he could not have Wielded with the strength to kill Maddyn."

"Or even Kitayra," Galys added.

"Not even Yunara could have managed to access the Sefid at that level without destroying Netarger or someone almost as close."

Galys's eyes widened. "Could Yunara have—?"

Kadburn waved his hands. "No. Not over that distance. Not even Ember the first Kevleren could have done that."

Galys could not help the groan escaping from her lips.

"Are you all right?" Kadburn asked, concerned. He put a hand on her shoulder.

"I thought I understood something of what happened that night. How those we loved died. But now I'm even more in the dark than before. If Numoya did not access the Sefid that night, and the distance was too great for Yunara, the most powerful Wielder for generations, then who did? And how did they do it?"

Gos Linsedd and Ames Westaway were standing on the site where the stables were being built. There was some dispute about the quantity of stone Gos had specified to be used for the buildings, and they had come to talk to someone about it. As soon as they appeared, one of the laborers left to get someone who would talk for them. With nothing to do for the moment, Gos relaxed as best he could in the warm weather, wondering if he would ever get used to the hotter and more humid climate of the New Land. He noticed that Ames was imitating his pose. He was flattered, in a self-conscious way, and amused. He remembered the way he used to imitate his hero, Maddyn Kevleren.

He smiled at the memory. Way back then the prince had only been Master of Horse Third Prince Maddyn Kevleren, a name and title almost as long as the column he led on raids across the border with Rivald. Maddyn had been Gos's big brother, hero, sage and patron all rolled into one. He had wanted so much to be like the prince, all the time aware he never could be because he was not Kevleren born. Still, being in his company was near enough to being an actual Kevleren for the young Gos, and he was proud of the way Maddyn would sometimes ask his counsel, especially as they both gained combat experience. As they served together, he, Maddyn and Kadburn Axkevleren became close-knit as only soldiers on the field can be. More to each other than brothers, friendship could not begin to describe their relationship, the intuitive understanding that existed between them when they fought.

And now . . .

Gos sighed. Now the prince was dead and Kadburn was a stranger.

A party of colonists was approaching him, led by a woman he recognized from an earlier encounter. Behind her ambled a big, dark man Gos had seen working around the island. A bodyguard? For protection against whom? Not he and Ames, surely.

"Madam Fleetwood?"

The woman smiled tightly. "You remember, Commander. I'm flattered."

That manner, confident and experienced. He remembered it from their first conversation and was still surprised it came from someone who seemed so young and fragile. He glanced at her large companion, received an equally appraising look in return. A gaggle of other colonists had accompanied the pair, but they hung back.

"Now I remember," Gos said. "You're head of their guild."

"That's right. The Colonists' Guild."

"And your position in this guild?" Gos asked the big man.

"Member," the man replied in a monotone.

"Of course," Gos said evenly, and returned his attention to the woman. "I believe there are concerns about the amount of stone needed to build the stables."

"Too many," she said. "Too many by far."

Out of the corner of his eye Gos could see Ames fidgeting. His second-in-command was not comfortable with the relaxed manner in which Heriot Fleetwood was addressing his superior officer. Some of the colonists were watching the young ensign nervously.

"What are you suggesting?" Gos asked.

"A third the amount, enough for the base and columns. Then timber to the roof, and thatch for that."

Gos shook his head. "No. A thatched roof invites fire. Too risky."

"And hauling several thousand bricks up this slope for a herd of horses is too much work for my members. We suffered enough injuries putting up the walls, many of which cannot be healed. A back damaged once is damaged forever."

"But the walls were needed to defend all of us."

"Which is why we built them, and without complaint," the woman returned.

"And the stables will protect the horses which allow my dragoons to patrol far and wide from Kydan, keeping our enemies at bay."

"Horses don't need stables any more than we colonists need proper shelter. Why should your beasts get brick walls and proper roofs when all we get is mud and straw?"

There was a murmur of agreement from the colonists behind her.

"It's a matter of necessity," Gos said.

"Exactly," Heriot Fleetwood said. "It's necessary for us now to build proper houses for our own people."

"I repeat, we need the horses to help protect all of us—"

"Protect what? A bunch of colonists dying from sickness and cold?"

The colonists laughed. They were obviously enjoying the debate and knew they were on the winning side so far.

Ames moved forwards, his mouth open to say something. Gos put a hand out to stop him. "It's fine, Ensign."

Some on the other side smirked at Ames then, but Gos noticed that neither Heriot Fleetwood nor the big man joined in. He understood then that this issue was not merely a device for the colonists to shirk work. These two at least were very serious about the whole matter. Instead of being put off by the thought, however, Gos felt it put him on firmer ground. He had learned as soldier and bureaucrat that people interested in getting real results were usually prepared to compromise.

"I understand your reluctance to haul so many bricks," Gos said. "But your proposal is not good enough."

He was not sure if he imagined it or not, but his words seemed to make the woman less tense. She smiled again, and this time it was genuine.

"You gave in quickly enough," Arden said solemnly as he and Heriot made their way down from the meeting with the dragoon officers.

"I did not give in," Heriot said cheerily. "I got what we wanted."

"You could have got more from them."

"Maybe, but if this Commander Gos Linsedd remembers we deal fair and straight, he will do the same with us. No point in squeezing a lemon dry: there'll be no juice left. Besides, we want stone walls, remember? To hide our store of captured weapons."

Arden considered her words. "He may not be the one

we always negotiate with. He's only in charge of the soldiers. The blonde woman—"

"Strategos Galys Valera."

"Aye. She's in charge, right? At least, she took charge on the *Hannemah*, remember, and in the fight for this island. Will you give her the benefit of the doubt too?"

"I remember her on the *Hannemah*. She gave *us* the benefit of the doubt on that occasion. Let us up on deck when the captain preferred we stayed below and guarded." Heriot shook her head. "Anyway, in the end she won't be in charge. This Kydan has its own council."

"We have the firegons."

"So did Rivald; in the end it made no difference. Firegons won't keep us here."

Arden grunted. "You think the Kydans will force us out?"

"Not if we're Kydans too."

"Them over on Herris won't accept that," he said, nodding to the big middle island that housed the main part of the city and most of the original inhabitants.

"That's not what I meant. *We* have to accept it. We have to learn to think of ourselves as Kydans and not as Hamilayans. After all, we don't owe the empire anything: it cared so much for us it chucked us in grain ships without our permission and sent us across the Deepening Sea."

Arden's black-bearded face broke into one of his rare smiles. "You came of your own accord, Heriot Fleetwood. You wanted this new life."

"That's beside the point," Heriot sniffed. "I thought I was going to Kael, anyway, not halfway round the world.

"The point is we have to start believing this is our home and that we have as much right to be here as them soldiers or the strategos or those on the other island. This is where we belong, because if we don't belong here, Grim Arden, we don't belong anywhere."

There was a long silence. Eventually Arden said, "I'm not that grim."

"You're as dark and serious and dangerous as a storm at sea."

"Oh, aye," Arden conceded. "But not *grim*."

If he had not visited the basilica of Kydan only the day before, he would never have given its entrance a second glance. He stopped, trying to see what made it look different, but nothing stood out. He turned to continue on his way to the Assembly when something caught his eye again, and this time he kept track of it as he strode up to the stone archway. About head height on the right pillar were three vertical marks, each about as long and wide as a finger. The marks had been gouged out recently, the newly exposed stone clean and bright, but not with any skill. The middle stroke was chiseled deeper than the other two and was slightly longer and wider. He wondered briefly if it had any meaning or was just a random act of vandalism. He hoped that if it was vandalism that it had not been done by a sightseeing colonist; that was all his opponents on the council would need to resurrect their separatist philosophy: one of the interlopers from across the sea defacing the city's most holy shrine.

Then, halfway to the Assembly, he saw the sign again, engraved on one of the stones of the Long Bridge. It was almost exactly the same size and fashion as the one he had seen at the basilica, and with the same lack of expertise. This one, too, judging from the fresh colour of the marks, was only recently made.

Not random vandalism, then.

As soon as he was on the other side of the Saddle, the steep valley that divided the two halves of the island of Herris, he forgot about it. The council was meeting again today, and although he was sure Kysor Nevri and his allies would not raise the subject of forcing the colonists to leave Kydan before Numoya Kevleren's plans were known, he was politically experienced enough to know they would try to outmaneuver him in other ways. The difficulty was that he had so few allies himself. During his two years of exile, most of his old friends on the council had been murdered by the plutocrats, and although many of the surviving councilors were grateful for the part he had played in freeing Kydan from the grip of Rivald, it did not necessarily translate into support in the Assembly. Given time, he was sure he could recruit enough councilors to his way of thinking, especially regarding the colonists from Hamilay, but he knew time was something he did not have enough of. Ironically, it was the threat of an assault by another foreign power—that of Rivald through its colony of Sayenna— that made the position of the Hamilayans temporarily secure. But what would happen after the attack, assuming it came and they all survived it?

As he entered the Assembly people greeted him warmly, even those whom he knew sided with Nevri. Although opponents, Poloma thought, we are not yet enemies. He took his place at the elliptical table, directly under the skylight, and waited for the rest of the councilors to seat themselves while he quickly read the agenda the Assembly secretaries had prepared and placed before every chair. The agenda was filled with relatively minor matters, and he knew the rest of the day would be taken up with arguments and counterarguments over ridiculous details. But that was the way the council worked and had always worked. Nothing that affected the city, no matter how minor, was beneath its attention. He scanned the list of items to see what were most likely to give his opponents a wedge to use against him. Nothing leaped out at him, and he fervently hoped the day would go without any ambushes.

Councilors were still filing in. Poloma studied each carefully, trying to pick up some hint to their character and attitude by their appearance and mannerisms. Some he recognized from the old days, or were younger siblings of those he had known. A few were completely new to him, from families on the rise, taking positions left vacant by the fallen or exiled, much as saplings move up to replace fallen trees.

Then, to his surprise, he saw the three stroke design on the sleeves of some of the councilors' tunics; in these cases, the middle stroke was not only slightly longer and wider than the two on the flanks, it was colored green, while the others were black. All of those he recognized who carried the sign he was sure were aligned with Nevri.

Then he understood what the sign meant. Three strokes for the three islands of Kydan: Kayned, Herris and Karhay. The middle island, Herris, where lay the heart of the city, was represented by the larger, green stroke. Those who carried the symbol were marking themselves as true Kydans, as opposed to those who lived on Herris.

Nevri had found a way to raise his divisive philosophy without making an issue of it within the Assembly. They would wait until after the Rivald attack, if it came, was repulsed with the help of the colonists from Hamilay, and then when the city was safe they would make their move to expel them. For now they were just preparing the groundwork.

                         *   *   *

Galys was thinking about how to organize the Hamilayan soldiers and dragoons within the established Kydan
administrative structure. Physically, she was striding the
circumference of Karhay, oblivious to everyone she
passed. Mentally, she was running into a lot of walls and
finding very few doorways.

Old Kydan had depended on a militia for its security
and defense, a part-time army with little professionalism
and almost no experience, and led by councilors who took
turns to be commander and gatekeeper of the Citadel—the
only truly military structure in the whole city. That kind of
lackadaisical approach would not work with the professional soldiers from Hamilay. The trouble was, they were
a product of empire, a political system with the population,
administration and resources necessary to create and maintain a full-time army. Kydan was a single city, and not a
large one at that . . . at least not by Hamilayan standards.

The truth was, the companies Maddyn had brought with
him across the Deepening Sea had been meant for one job
and one job only: to defeat the Rivald forces occupying
Kydan. Galys did not know what Maddyn had planned for
them after that, but she suspected if he had lived his thinking would have echoed her own.

The companies would have to be broken up.

Some of the companies, she corrected herself. It would
be stupid and dangerous to disband the best of them: Maddyn's household guards and the dragoons gave the city an
immense advantage over any native threat it was likely to
face. And the engineers should be kept together for the difficult building projects and military defenses that would be
needed in the future. But it was not going to be possible to
properly maintain the other three companies of infantry. As

well, Galys thought, dissolving half the Hamilayan formations would ease tensions between the colonists and the original Kydans. If an unforeseen emergency arose they could always be reformed, like a militia . . .

. . . like a militia, Galys thought. Like the Kydans once had. In fact, why not resurrect the part-time militia, mixing colonists and Kydans together? And if Gos and Poloma agreed they could be armed with firegons instead of spears. That could do more for union than any number of political speeches in the Assembly. Actually get them working together again, like they had when preparing for the attack of the plutocrats. And the city administration already had experience of running militia. That way Kydan would only have to bear the cost of two full-time companies.

"Excuse me," said a female voice.

And if by the very fact of their existence those companies could help secure the alliance of nearby towns, especially those that had once been enemies or rivals of Kydan, then they just might recoup the cost of maintaining them.

"Strategos Galys Valera?"

Hearing her name broke her from her reverie. She stopped striding and looked up. Then down. It was the little colonist with the strong voice she had met once or twice before. On the ship, she thought. And then? She couldn't remember the other time.

"Yes?"

"My name is Heriot Fleetwood. We've met before."

"I recall," Galys said. Vaguely, she added silently.

"I am the elected leader of the Colonists' Guild."

Galys blinked. "The what?"

"The Colonists' Guild. Formed to protect the interests

of us colonists. Most of us are members now. Several hundred of us, in fact."

Galys was finding it hard to catch up with the conversation, moving from soldiers to guilds.

"We're worried," the woman said.

"*You're* worried," Galys said dryly, but Heriot Fleetwood gazed steadily at her, without the slightest hint of a smile. She cleared her throat. "Worried about what in particular?"

"If you come with me, I'll show you."

Galys did not want to go with her. She wanted to continue her walk and decide how to organize the military. Ah, the engineers, she thought. I forgot about the engineers . . .

"Strategos, is this city's council in charge of all of us?"

That got Galys's attention. Up until now she and Gos had avoided the delicate issue of leadership. It was a problem both had been willing to leave in Maddyn's more than capable hands. What his long-term plans had been regarding the governance of the colony, especially concerning its relationship with the city's original ruling council, was something he had not confided in anyone. When she had given it any thought since Maddyn's death she had more or less considered Poloma would take up the reins for both polities; after all, he was the rightful ruler that Hamilay had sent an expedition across the Deepening Sea to reinstate. She assumed that any critical problems would arise from native Kydans wanting to "purify" their city of all interlopers, and had never seriously considered that the colonists might have other plans.

Galys felt as if someone had tipped a basin of cold water over her. Her skin goosebumped as she realised she and Gos had let things go dangerously. This woman claimed to be head of a guild for colonists. They were making the first moves to taking political power for themselves. This was not good, she told herself, especially if the colonists wanted to make an issue of governance.

"Strategos?" Heriot Fleetwood asked again. She waited calmly for an answer but was apparently in no hurry to leave without one.

"This is a delicate issue," Galys said slowly.

"Yes," the woman agreed. "Which I think is why you should come with me."

Kadburn knew he had been a fool. Grief-struck, exhausted, bewildered, but still a fool. He had been so overwhelmed by Maddyn's terrible death from the Sefid he had automatically assumed it had been caused by Numoya Kevleren. He had never considered any other possibility, even though he had seen with his own eyes Numoya and his Beloved escaping. Now what worth was his own existence? He did not know against whom he could direct his vengeance. He wondered if there may have been another Rivald Kevleren involved in the attack, but dismissed the possibility almost right away. Such a pale, dark-haired creature would stand out among the golden-skinned Kydans like the moon in a clear sky, and if one had been among the attackers, how could the attack against Maddyn and Kitayra Albyn have been so specific?

And yet no Kevleren in Hamilay or Rivald had the power to reach across continents. Yunara must have pushed herself to the limit when she used the Sefid to slay Alway Selford and her baby when the expedition was only a few days journey out to sea.

Kadburn wanted to rage and slay and scream, but there was no one to direct his hatred against and it left him feeling useless and, despite the burning inside of him, enervated and listless as well. He had always known what to do because either Maddyn had told him or he had done what was necessary to secure his master's safety. He had been an Axkevleren for so long he had no memory of what had come before, of his family or where he had come from.

He had become like a bird without wings, a spirit without body, and now that the target of his revenge had proven to be a mirage, he was an Axkevleren without purpose.

Deep in his heart he knew he had to find some reason to exist outside of his past, some reason to survive long enough to discover what had happened to Maddyn. Once he knew that he would move the universe itself to wreak his revenge, and then be able to lie down and die himself, to find whatever peace death could bring. But until then he had to attach himself to some other cause, something worthy of his talents and skills.

Heriot led the blonde strategos to the wall on the south side of Karhay which the colonists and engineers had finished building only a few days before. It was strongly, if roughly constructed. Over time the wall would be rebuilt properly, with properly set stones, debris in between and capping blocks on top, but as it stood it would deter any casual raid. Of better quality was the gateway, its pillars sunk deep into the earth, its rough-hewn heavy wooden doors reinforced and bordered with iron. Several colonists were gathered around the right-hand door, talking excitedly among themselves.

"What's going on?" the strategos asked.

For an answer, Heriot gently pushed aside the gathering, pulling Galys Valera after her, and pointed to a strange device of three strokes that had been carved on the right-hand door during the night.

The strategos went to the gate and studied the engraving closely, then turned to Heriot and shrugged. "Is this supposed to mean something?"

"I was hoping you could tell me," Heriot replied.

"Who did it?"

"I was hoping you could tell me that as well."

Heriot watched Galys closely, interested in how she would deal with this.

"You would not be showing me this unless you thought it was serious," she said. "Why don't you tell me what *you* know?"

Heriot searched among the colonists still gathered nearby. "Belwyth, come here," she said.

An old man ambled over. He had thin white hair, a large nose in the center of a spray of wrinkles. He smiled broadly at both Heriot and Galys, showing lots of gum.

"Miss Fleetwood, ma'am," he said, and even tugged what passed for a wispy forelock.

"Please tell Strategos Valera what you saw on Herris today."

Belwyth stood a little straighter and cleared his throat. "Well, it was like this. Looking for timber to work on some gables we're doing for the commander's stable—that'd be Commander Linsedd, you understand—and my being a carpenter, you understand—I got myself rowed across to the middle island to find a timber store that might hold a suitable piece—the stables being quite large structures, you understand—"

"And on that island you saw?" Heriot prompted, without any sign of impatience.

"Well, that," Belwyth said plainly, nodding to the marking on the door. "All over the place. On wood and stone. Always the same, three up-and-down strokes with the middle 'un a wee bigger. An' all newly made." He shook his head. "Clumsy work, too, but that's just my opinion."

"Thank you, Belwyth," Heriot said, and with another tug of the forelock he rejoined the other colonists, still talking animatedly among themselves.

Galys looked blankly at Heriot. "Be patient with me, Heriot Fleetwood, but I don't see what this is all about."

"Three strokes," Heriot said. "Three islands. Only the middle stroke is given any prominence."

Galys looked surprised. She started laughing, but the expression on Heriot's face made her cut it short.

"You're a hero for both sides," Heriot explained. "You're known by them on Herris as well as us colonists. You're a good soldier, a friend of the dead Kevleren and the commander and the foreign prince."

"Foreign prince?"

"The Poloma fellow. Point is, no one on their side would do anything to spite you yet. But we colonists who go to Herris now and then, or who watch Kydans when they come across here, we notice things. We notice how they stay away from us, don't look at us except out of the corners of their eyes. They don't like us, Strategos, and they don't want us here." She pointed to the markings on the door. "And I'm betting that's their sign."

Galys was obviously skeptical, but Heriot could see she was still thinking on it.

"So I ask you again," Heriot continued, "who's in charge? Who do we go to about this?"

Sunsets were undeniably beautiful in this part of the world, Gos thought.

From his position at the western end of the island of Karhay, the Bay of Kydan shone like gold plate. The bloated rim of the sun still capped the horizon, its light resisting the dark blue of early evening sliding across the eastern sky. Back home in Omeralt, or the farm where he had grown up near the southern city of Bowtell, sunrise was the special time; in the summer the sun rose like a flaming bird and set early behind the Vardar Mountains, sending purple shadows across fields and streams.

Gos felt a twinge of homesickness, but searching deeper realized it was his receding youth he missed the most. He had enjoyed being responsible to no one but himself and his comrades in the field, and his prince. He thought Maddyn would have liked the sunsets here.

He heard footsteps behind him, and Galys joined him. Then to his surprise, Kadburn as well. The Beloved stared westwards, his eyes unblinking, the scars in his face looking like runnels in old leather.

The three companions watched the sun finally disappear under the sea, then turned together to go back to the settlement.

"We cannot count on Poloma holding back Councilor Nevri and his supporters," Galys said. "We must do something to help him or we may lose everything."

"Even before the Kevleren attacks?"

"If he attacks," Kadburn said, which surprised Gos. When he had heard Kadburn talking about Numoya in the Assembly he had sounded certain that there would be an assault from Sayenna.

"Nevri will wait long enough for us to help defend Kydan, if necessary," Galys said. "But he has already started a campaign against us. It is underhanded—"

"Unworthy," Kadburn interrupted.

"—but very clever. He intends to garner popular support for his cause, and antagonize the colonists at the same time."

"You two have already discussed this," Gos said, feeling a little left out. "I haven't a clue what you're talking about."

"We only talked about it on the way to find you," Galys said. "And I only found out this afternoon, thanks to a strange little woman who claims to represent all the colonists."

"Heriot Fleetwood," Gos said matter-of-factly. "She does. And what have you and Kadburn decided to do about the problem?"

"Nothing yet," Kadburn said.

"But we have an idea," Galys added.

8

CHIERMA had been staring at the paper in front of him for what seemed like hours. It was a list of those army units at his disposal for distribution along the frontier. As seemed to be the case of late, the frontier was very long and the list very short. Some decisions were automatic: a unit to garrison here at Hamewald, the largest city in northern Rivald and the republic's second capital, administering a vast territory; a company of infantry at the main border crossing, the halfway point between Hamewald and Kuttle, the most southern of the empire's cities; and a roving regiment of light cavalry to patrol the barren ground west of the crossing. That only left about four hundred miles of border with scarcely two thousand soldiers to cover it.

There was no solution to the problem, of course, but in the desperate hope that something—*anything*—would reveal itself if he stared at the figures for long enough, he let his mind chew over it whenever he had a spare moment, not that there were many of them any more. Which was the way he wanted it. Too much time meant he would think about his late mistress, the Lady Englay Kevleren, and far too much pain resided there for him to want to resurrect it.

He put away the paper in the top drawer of his working desk, the same one he had used as a faithful Beloved, and locked it. His secretary saw him clearing the desk and started standing from her own desk to hand over more work, but Chierma put up his hand.

"Later, Feruna," Chierma said.

"Time for your walk, sir?" Feruna asked. Then, sympathetically, added, "You haven't done that for a while. I worry about you."

Chierma smiled tightly. "We will talk about that collection of papers on your desk when I get back."

Guards saluted him as he left the governor's residence and ambled across to the little park south of the road. It was an uncharacteristically bright spring day, the season that usually brought storms and high winds. That, together with the cold winters the city endured, made Hamewald a place not many visited for pleasure, although once upon a time a regular flow of Rivald Kevlerens and their households would visit because it was meant to be the place where the great family had its origins. It was from Hamewald that the rebel Ember moved north and started the dynasty that eventually created the Hamilayan empire, may his memory be forever cursed.

But no visitors came now that there were no more Kevlerens south of the mountains, Chierma mused sadly. He brought himself up short. Did he genuinely miss those days? He had revolted against the family because of its cruelty and arrogance, the way it had stolen generations of children from their homes to supply its insatiable demand for potential sacrifices. That was why he had turned against the only person he had ever truly, deeply loved.

And there he was, by her grave. He squatted down and

removed a few weeds and strips of bark. Grass was growing nicely over the mound.

He remembered her screams of pain coming from her private suite, which he had allowed her to keep after the coup; he had rushed there, suddenly a loyal Beloved again, ready to risk everything, even his own life, to protect her. The door had been locked. With the help of another servant and a bench seat taken from the kitchen he had attacked her door, her frantic screams driving him to greater and greater efforts. At last the door had given way, but not before the screams had died away in a sigh, and too late for Chierma to do anything but watch in horror as the thin, blazing torch in the middle of her bedroom slowly consumed itself. When the last flickering fire had withered and disappeared, nothing had been left but a deep dark stain on the wooden floor and the triangular Kevleren medallion on its chain, curiously untouched by the blaze, as was everything else in the room except some singed papers on a nearby set of drawers.

He screwed shut his eyes, not from the memory—that was burned into his brain forever—but to keep back tears. He felt foolish. He was middle-aged, a governor, a man of importance and not a little influence, probably the last Beloved left alive in all of Rivald, and here he was crying next to the grave of a Sefid-blasted woman who had never loved him the way he deserved . . .

He let the thought evaporate and stood up jerkily. This was no way to behave, he told himself. In her way, Englay had loved him. The same way Kevlerens always loved their Beloveds—like a particularly intelligent dog, a best friend who demanded nothing more than food, shelter, affection and something to love above itself.

Enough.

He walked back to the office. He would go through some outstanding matters with Feruna, then look at the military disposition again. He would find an answer.

Croft Harker left while the other members of the Safety Committee were still arguing over Chierma's terse report, brought back to Beferen by Velan Lymok. Harker allowed himself to smile thinly. The very disappointed Velan Lymok. Although he had always had little time for the Beloveds, and had always felt uncomfortable sharing power with them in the Safety Committee after the coup against their Kevleren rulers, he admitted to himself that he disliked the young Velan Lymok even more. Unfortunately, to compensate him for missing out on the governorship of Hamewald, he had got a seat on the committee, and this knowledge wiped away Harker's thin smile. A nonvoting seat for the moment, but Lymok's supporters would see his position improved in time, and then they would have the strength to move against Harker's presidency.

Although, Harker reminded himself, and in Lymok's favor, the officer had not argued that Chierma was exaggerating the threat posed by Hamilay to keep his governorship secure. Others had made the point, however, and argued that the best course of action was to summarily dismiss Chierma, which would have the double benefit of removing a fear-mongerer and an irritant from the current tender relationships between Rivald and the empire. The fact that such an action would then open up the governorship for someone like Lymok was mentioned in passing, but Lymok had refrained from making any comment. A clever man, Harker thought, and therefore exceedingly dangerous. He would have to find a way to neutralize the officer.

Harker swept into his office and closed the door behind him, sat on the edge of his desk and from his jacket's inside pocket retrieved the private letter from Chierma that had been in the sealed portfolio of documents Lymok had brought back with the public report.

President Croft Harker, felicitations. Undoubtedly Velan Lymok will provide his own slant on my report to the Safety Committee. He is a very perceptive young man with an inquiring mind and, I suspect, with enough ambition to have done a Kevleren proud. I am writing to reinforce my main point. Hamilay will invade Rivald. I do not know when. I do not know what the Safety Committee can do about it. Resist, naturally, but I fear for the result. Without our own Kevlerens to protect us, we are like a child abandoned to the wolves of winter.

If you can convince the committee to send me more troops, especially infantry, I can promise we will delay the enemy advance for some time in the mountains, but make no mistake—in the end Hamilay will get through.

By the way, if Lymok angles for my job as governor of this province and all its problems, he is welcome to it. Indeed, I considered offering my resignation to him directly, but my pride would not allow it.

Kind regards, Governor Chierma Axkevleren.

Harker was tempted to accept Chierma's offer of resignation; it would get Lymok off the committee again and swing the power balance back towards himself. But not for long. No one could hold such high office and keep it in such catastrophic times. The people would want someone to blame for their troubles, and as president he would be the natural focus for such resentment. The committee, including his supporters, would throw him out if it served to protect their own hides.

No, Chierma was worth more where he was.

Harker folded the letter and put it back inside his pocket. He gathered his thoughts before returning to the committee meeting with his news that Rivald had one more chance because it had one more Kevleren, and that the mission to recruit the Kevleren should be undertaken by a member of the committee itself—and who better than its newest member?

For Numoya, living in his blind world, the past was as real in his imagination as the present. He relived his life with his first Beloved, Thenge, from when they were first matched at the age of seven, to her death at his own hand. He knew he did this partly from self-pity, but mainly he did it because he wanted to understand how he had loved Thenge from the very beginning to the very end of their relationship, and why he did not feel the same way towards Quenion.

When Thenge died, he naturally turned to the Axkevleren who responded most deeply and consolingly to his grief, and most honestly to his guilt. That was how he had chosen her, because emotionally they were so in accord, just as once he had been with Thenge. Numoya had thought that was enough to fire his love for her, but he had been wrong. Now the guilt he still felt over Thenge's death was compounded by the guilt he felt for the way he behaved towards Quenion, and this drove his anger beyond reason. Not only could he not find a way to love Quenion, he was quickly losing any love he had for himself.

Every day he resolved to do better, for both their benefit. Frustration sometimes fouled his mood and stoked his temper, but all the time Quenion was patient and caring and understanding, and though in a perverse way that sometimes only made it worse, at other times it helped reaffirm his faith in his own capacity to love. Why else would Quenion be so dedicated, so loyal, so trusting? Surely she saw in him those very virtues which, at the worst of times, he doubted he had ever possessed?

Such acknowledgement was a small step, he knew, but from such small steps, one at a time, longer journeys were made. And, he thought, perhaps with more faith than reason, his feelings towards Quenion were changing, were evolving into something that might be equated with love, or at least the kind of emotional devotion that hinted at the feelings he had once held for Thenge.

It was something, Numoya was sure, something that promised more and better to come.

Quenion's footsteps clicked outside. He had come to know them better than he knew his own heartbeat. He counted them along the corridor. Five. Ten. Fifteen. Now the door. He heard Quenion using her elbows to open the door and then close it. She was carrying a tray. He heard an earthenware jug clunk against a glazed plate. So, beer tonight instead of wine.

"Your Highness, I'm sorry I'm late."

"What was it this time?" he asked, his voice automatically becoming terse. He cleared his throat and forced himself to say more evenly, "I lose all track of time, you see."

"That's because the days are getting longer."

"What have you brought?"

"Beer—"

"I know that," he said brusquely.

"And flat bread with cheese and meat. You asked for it last night."

Numoya mentally squinted. He could remember small details about his life from twenty years ago, but could not remember a single word he had said a day before. "Give me the bread."

He felt Quenion's hands turn up his palms and give him some bread, still warm from the oven. He hungrily took a bite.

"Your appetite is returning," Quenion said. "That is a good sign. It means you are getting better."

He had not realized it before, but now that she had mentioned it he knew it was true. He was *genuinely* hungry, as if he had not eaten properly for weeks. He greedily finished the bread and asked for more, then some with cheese and meat on it. When he had finished all the food, Quenion helped him with the jug of beer. Her hands covered his and he was surprised by how warm they felt.

"Thank you," he said when the beer was gone. "I feel almost . . ." He stopped, honestly not sure how he felt. Being at rest came closest to it. For the first time in a long, long time, he felt at rest.

"I feel I am beginning to cope," he said.

He could not see Quenion, but he got the distinct impression she was not moving at all, that she was entirely focused on him.

"Thank you," he said again, more sincerely.

Chierma had thought it the strangest thing.

On the way home to Hamewald from inspecting a barracks near the border post with Hamilay he had seen a metal gate glow with faint blue fire. He had blinked but the glow was still there.

"Do you see that?" he had asked Feruna, but she had looked at the gate he pointed to and shrugged at him. "You see nothing unexpected at all?"

"I am sorry, your Grace, but no. What is it?"

Chierma had ignored her and asked the young ensign in charge of his cavalry escort if he could see anything untoward about the gate. The ensign had looked long and carefully at the gate, and then at Chierma. "No, your Grace. Do you wish me to send one of my men to investigate further? If you tell me what he should look for—"

Chierma had cut him off by shaking his head.

"Maybe you are overtired," Feruna had suggested. "It has been a long day for you."

Now, even later at night, he had to admit he had been tired then, just as he was bloody exhausted now. But he could not sleep. He had not been seeing things, or imagining them. He had seen that glow before, but only when the Sefid had been used.

Perhaps he should have allowed the ensign to send someone to investigate further. Perhaps it had been a Hamilayan Kevleren sent to spy . . .

He shouted with exasperation. Now his mind was creating fantasies. There would be no reason for a Kevleren to come all the way over the mountains to spy on Hamewald and then give away the whole game by Wielding.

It must have been something else. He rubbed his eyes with forefinger and thumb and climbed between the sheets in his bed. It *must* have been.

For what seemed hours he tossed and turned. A hundred urgent tasks bounced around inside his mind begging for attention, but uppermost was that blue shining gate.

"If Lady Englay were here she could tell me what was going on," he muttered to himself, and felt very lonely.

Even though spring was more than half over, the nights were still bitter in Beferen. A sea mist had rolled in shortly before nightfall, and Croft Harker's oilskin coat was covered in fine droplets of water. He shivered and admitted to himself it was not just from the cold.

Two men stood in front of him. The first was a tall, wizened sailor with one arm and a sorrowful expression; the cold and mist did not seem to affect him at all. The second was Velan Lymok, who managed to look uncomfortable, dreary and apprehensive all at the same time. Lymok took the package offered by the president and slipped it inside his own oilskin coat.

"You will not fail the committee," Harker said flatly.

"Absolutely," Lymok replied lightly. He blinked, and added quickly, "Absolutely not."

Harker turned to the sailor. "And you, Captain Roward, will make sure Leader of a Thousand Lymok reaches his destination."

"I haven't failed Rivald yet," the man said gruffly, "and I have no intention of starting now."

Harker nodded, felt foolish for making his statement. Captain Roward did not deserve to be doubted. He was the best officer in the republic's small navy, and its most experienced. If anyone could make the journey to Sayenna and back in time to save Rivald, it was he.

"All of our fates lie in your hands," he said. "I know they are safe."

Roward nodded brief thanks for the compliment. "If we're to make the tide I must go now. There are no further instructions?"

Harker shook his head, but as the captain and Lymok turned to leave, he grabbed Lymok by the arm and said, "Promise anything to Numoya Kevleren. Anything at all. But bring him back to Rivald."

*　　*　　*

Chierma woke just before dawn, dressed quickly and left the residence. The metal tips of the spears held by the tired guards shone blue. He made his way to Englay's grave, and saw her waiting for him. He knew he should have felt shock, or at least surprise, but instead he felt a kind of relief, as if part of him had all the time been expecting her to reappear.

"I am still angry with you," she said in the calm, almost indifferent way that had once infuriated him.

"I suppose it could be said, your Highness, that you have good reason to be."

"You are not in a dream, you know. It's the Sefid. There is so much of it now that things are happening which have never happened before."

"What does it mean?" He held his hands in front of him, pressing his nails hard against the bones in his fingers. He felt pain. She was right, he was not dreaming. This gave him no comfort.

"Sometimes I think I know, but most of the time . . ." Englay shook her head slightly.

"I am sorry for what happened," he said.

She tilted her head to look at him. "Yes, I know. At least you didn't kill me."

"I wanted to, at first."

"But you loved me too much."

"That's why I wanted to kill you. I just wasn't brave enough."

She lay down on top of her grave. "You know she's coming, don't you?"

It took Chierma a moment to figure it out, but then he said, "The empress."

"She doesn't know it for sure herself, yet. But yes. There will be nothing you can do. I wanted to warn you."

"I must try."

She laughed lightly. "You were always so *bitterly* loyal. You resented it but could not avoid your duty, until the very end when it was all too much and you joined the other traitorous Beloveds. Now you are back where you started, but with the army instead of the Kevlerens."

She was irritating him again, knowingly, as she once used to. "I know why I survived the fire," he said, making his voice as cold as possible.

"Ironic, isn't it? You visit my grave all the time because you still want my love, and yet if you'd had it you would have died with all the other Beloveds who were truly loved by their Kevlerens. You should be thankful."

He remembered something she had said before. "Why do you want to warn me? Why do you care one way or the other what happens to me?"

"Because of all the living things in the universe, my lonely, confused Chierma, you are the only one who truly misses me."

"We need an army," Numoya said.

"An army?" Quenion asked.

Numoya was surprised to get an answer. He had been involved so much in his own thoughts that he had forgotten Quenion was still there. He wondered what she did at night between feeding him and taking away his tray. Maybe she looked out at the stars. He would like to be able to do that again.

"Eventually the Safety Committee will send for me to come home, where I'll be locked up with my relatives. They were happy to leave me be while I kept Kydan under Rivald's thumb, but when they learn Hamilay has taken it from us they will waste no more time on me. Unless I

make them see sense, make them realise how valuable I
am over here in the New Land, I will become nothing but
a pet for a herd of soldiers and traitor Axkevlerens."

"When you say make them realise how valuable you
are, you mean by retaking Kydan?"

"Yes. And all the territory in between." He heard Quenion's gasp of surprise. "And why not? Those barbarians
who brought us back here to Sayenna pose no threat to a
properly equipped modern army. In fact, we'll recruit
them. They have no reason to love Kydan. If Maira Sygni
could buy them, then so can we.

"Rivald may not be a match for Hamilay back in the old
land, but out here it can forge a new kingdom. Even a new
empire, one to rival the Hamilayans."

The bed creaked as Quenion sat near him. "How do we
start?"

"Find out everything you can for me. Find out the location of the tribes the plutocrats recruited for their attack,
and the names of their leaders."

"I will do it tomorrow."

"Good," he said, and reached out a hand. Quenion took
it, held it between her own. "I know I can depend on you."

He felt her lean closer, and then felt her lips brush
across his broken eyes. Before he could react or say anything she was gone, leaving him breathless and feeling—
absurdly! for he was a Kevleren!—privileged, as if her
love was a gift he had earned instead of something owed
to him. Numoya was confused by it, and also strangely, be-
wilderingly, confused by the flush of emotions he was feeling towards Quenion.

9

LANNEL Thorey had nightmares. All the time. He slept maybe three or four hours at a stretch, then he would wake up pale as a worm and slimy with sweat and breathing like he had run a longmile. His difficulty sleeping made him view the world with something less than charity. It was not a natural character trait, but grown like a dark flower from his chronic insomnia.

It was not an illness, although if the subject came up in a conversation with friends he would say it was an illness. Truth was, when he was barely eight years old, his only sibling, an older sister, had died in her sleep. Ever since then he had believed that one night sleep would kill him, too, believed it so deeply it became the single central tenet of his life, replacing all religion, all superstition.

Until he had met Kysor Nevri, the councilor with a cause, a cause Lannel Thorey latched onto like a child to a parent. For the first time in memory there was something in his life bigger than his fear of sleep. He had never known hate could be so powerful, so overwhelmingly satisfying.

Five of them met on the hill where the stables were being made. Heriot Fleetwood and Arden were already there, waiting for Gos, Kadburn and Galys. The strategos, who had asked for the meeting but left it up to Heriot to organize the place, did not know how much forethought had gone into selecting the site, but she would be surprised if the fact that a large number of colonists were building stable walls at the time was merely coincidence. She was sure Heriot, or maybe her giant companion, had thought it out very carefully. Ostensibly a meeting to discuss the sign that was appearing all over Kydan and its possible implications for the newcomers, Galys understood that for Heriot and Arden it was a show of their authority. The colonists working nearby would see their representatives meeting the three remaining Hamilayan expedition leaders on an equal footing, if not in equal numbers (although some might allow that Arden was worth two of anyone else).

Not just recognizing their authority, Galys realized, her respect for the two unlikely companions growing every time she met them, but also recognizing their *right* to authority as representatives of the colonists.

The realization jolted her, made her remember that her original role in the expedition had been strategos, someone who was supposed to have the necessary training, intelligence, imagination and insight to thread a safe way through all the future's possibilities. In that she had failed so far, succeeding only in dealing with each crisis as it occurred rather than in finding ways to avoid the crisis in the first place. She knew this meeting presented a chance to set that aright.

When all five had gathered, Heriot started without preamble, announcing that she and all the other colonists knew what the sign of the three strokes represented. "The Kydans don't want us here, that's what the sign's saying."

"That isn't fair," Galys said. "Certainly some don't want us here, and they've stated their case in the Assembly—"

"Already?" Arden asked darkly. "They barely gave us time to bury our fallen, who died defending their city."

"*Some* of them," Galys stressed. "Many, including the council prefect, Poloma Malvara, are pleased to have us here. They don't pretend Kydan's future will be easy, but they see all of us facing it together, come what may."

"Arguing in the Assembly is all well and good," Heriot said, "but this sign that's appearing everywhere is not one or two Kydans going their own way. The fact that so many appeared so quickly means it was organized. It means there are those on the middle island willing to take action apart from the council. If we're not ready to show them we won't be pushed around, what will they do next? Engrave their sign on our foreheads?"

"I agree," Galys said mildly. Heriot and Arden looked nonplussed. "But let's take the right action."

She picked up a stick and drew three long strokes on the ground, long enough and deep enough for everyone to see, and making the middle mark the longest.

"The three islands of Kydan. Karhay, Herris and Kayned, with Herris emphasized."

She lengthened the two side marks and then drew bars across the top and bottom, joining all three strokes at head and base. "We use this symbol. It means everyone living on the islands, natives and colonists, are joined together as Kydans one and all."

For a moment no one said anything. Galys watched Heriot and Arden's reactions closely because she was sure the colonists would follow their lead.

Arden nodded. "Clever," he admitted. "And we can go around adapting all the signs our enemies have done to make them look like this, turning the symbol against its makers."

Heriot smiled. "Arden is right. That *is* clever, Strategos."

Heriot used her title as a sign of respect. Galys surprised herself by blushing slightly. "It also suggests that instead of setting ourselves in opposition to those who are against us being here, we become the voice of cooperation."

"We become the voice of reason," Heriot expanded.

"Could we convince Poloma to wear the symbol?" Gos asked Galys. "It might encourage those among his people who sympathise with us to openly declare their support."

"I think he'd agree to that," Galys said.

"If he doesn't, what next?" Heriot asked.

"What do you mean?" Kadburn asked suspiciously.

"I mean, if Poloma Malvara does not take the lead, who among us will?"

Kadburn and Gos exchanged glances, then both turned to Heriot. "What's this about?" Gos asked warily.

Galys sighed. "Heriot Fleetwood has raised a perplexing issue. It hasn't come up before because we've all been so busy doing what we knew had to be done—securing Kydan, building shelter for the colonists. But Maddyn never appointed a successor, as such. If Poloma does not support our cause—"

"He will," Kadburn said firmly.

"—if he does not," Galys persisted, "then who will be leader of our contingent? What action do we take? Can we return to Hamilay?"

"We won't do that," Heriot said sharply. "Hamilay did not want us. We will not let ourselves be exiled a second time. As Arden pointed out, some of us died helping to defend this city, and we have something owing us. We stay here."

"Are you sure you speak for all the colonists?" Gos asked.

Heriot smiled, pointed to those building the stables.

"Why don't you go over and ask them, Commander? I won't interfere."

Gos had been outmaneuvered, and he knew it. Galys could not help matching Heriot's smile.

"Let us agree for the moment that leadership naturally falls to Poloma," Galys suggested. "He is already prefect of the council, and since we all want to be considered as Kydans, we should respect that."

"Fine," Heriot said. "In that case, two things. First, let the Kydans know we colonists put our weight behind the prefect; if you say he has already supported our presence, then it cannot hurt his position to know we support him in turn; it may well help."

"Good idea," Galys said, and both Gos and Kadburn nodded their agreement. "And second?"

"Second, since we seem to have agreed that we are all Kydans together, the colonists should have members on the council."

When Poloma Malvara strode into the next meeting of the council no one could miss the modified design he wore on his prefect's tunic, nor what it was based on. As well, the badge was worn by all those councilors who supported his position on the colonists. The message was not lost on anyone, least of all Kysor Nevri, who seemed glum for the whole meeting and said not a word, although his face fairly glowered when Poloma suggested the council discuss the possibility of allowing one or two colonists to sit with it. There was an agreement for further discussion; nothing on the table, Poloma knew, but at least it was a start and would show the colonists he was serious in wanting to include them in the political life of the city.

When the day's business was done, Poloma and his supporters gathered in the Great Quadrangle, joined by Galys, Gos, Kadburn and Heriot and Arden with half-a-dozen colonists, all prominently wearing their badge, all hearty and in a good mood. They were careful not to flaunt themselves, but it was apparent to all that they did not lack confidence. The same could not be said for Kysor and his supporters, who seemed almost to slink away from the Assembly.

After the quadrangle had mostly cleared, Gos said with some satisfaction that it had gone well. As soon as it was apparent they were no longer being closely observed by his fellow citizens, Poloma lost much of his gaiety and assuredness. "We won today but cannot depend on our opponents not finding some other way to make their point."

"In fact," Arden said, "we can depend on them finding another way."

"But if we are observant and keep our wits about us, we may find a way to counter that too," Galys pointed out.

"And the first victory is often the most important," one of Poloma's fellow councilors said.

"No," Gos said plainly. "The last victory is always the most important."

Lannel Thorey had a smooth round face on top of a tall, gangly body that made those who saw him for the first time think he was an oversized youth, but his voice had the resonance of old wood and a too-eager friendliness that sounded hollow and warned off the cautious.

"Do we meet now, Councilor Nevri?" he asked his smaller, more dour companion. A troop of Kydans followed behind them, looking depressed after the council meeting.

"Yes," Kysor said curtly.

"We are going the wrong way to my home," Lannel said, licking his lips nervously.

"That is because we are not meeting in your home any longer."

"But all will see who we are . . ."

Kysor stopped suddenly and grasped the surprised Lannel by the arm. "You saw what happened outside the Assembly?"

Lannel frowned in thought. "I saw Prefect Malvara and some of his friends. They had a badge."

Kysor shook Lannel's arm. "*Our* badge, which they have made their own. Now that our opponents are openly declaring their allegiance, there is no longer any need for us to keep ours secret. We will meet publicly; there must be many who agree with us but were afraid to declare before they knew where everyone else stood. We will go to the inn near the basilica of Kydan." He smiled to himself. "Yes, that would be best." He turned to some of those following him. "Find the others. Tell them where we are going. Tell everyone whom you know is sympathetic to our cause."

Several hurried off and Kysor resumed his walking, Lannel still by his side.

When the group in the quadrangle broke up, Galys kept Heriot behind. Arden stayed of his own accord; not that Galys minded, she was almost used to his presence now.

"What plan is there of construction on Karhay?" she asked.

"What do you mean?" Heriot asked.

"What the colonists are building. Who instructed them to do so, and in what order?"

"First it was the prince."

"That and common sense," Arden added. "Shelter to protect us from the weather, walls to protect us from the enemy, sturdy roads to connect the island."

"And now stables," Heriot added, "for the dragoons. That was at the commander's request."

"Next should be mangers and sties for cattle and pigs," Arden cut in again. "The Kydans are used to letting them roam free on the island, but that must change now we are living there."

"Where are they kept now?" Galys asked, realizing she had not seen any livestock on the island.

"All the animals were moved to temporary pens on the mainland before the last attack," Heriot said. "We didn't want them blundering around behind us in the fight. They've been there ever since."

"Best to keep them there, maybe," Galys said.

"Why these questions?" Arden asked.

"Because there has to be some structure to our work on Karhay. What must be built first? What will we need in summer? And I have one or two ideas that will benefit both the colonists and the original Kydans."

"Such as?" Heriot asked.

"A bridge between Karhay and Herris, for example. And a regular ferry before that, to help move goods and people between the islands and the mainland. And I know that Maddyn Kevleren planned to construct a steam carriage eventually."

Arden grunted sceptically. "Useless waste of iron and . . ."

"Kydan may be able to face off Sayenna," Galys interrupted. "But not Rivald, should that kingdom decide to invest seriously in the New Land. We have not the numbers or resources, not yet at least. Industry will eventually give us an advantage, though. With mills and smelters needed to construct a steam carriage, we can also build firegons, longgons, ships and products for trade, and trade will help us build alliances with the tribes and villages inland. This city is in a perfect position to become a center of commerce." She stared Arden down. "I'm thinking of the future. Our future."

Arden did not seem willing to argue the point, but Heriot said simply, "There are problems to overcome first. Like stopping a civil war, for example, and like surviving an attack from Sayenna, if it ever comes . . ."

"Kadburn Axkevleren thinks it will," Galys said. "And this time with a Kevleren to lead the assault." She breathed deeply. "Nevertheless, that should not stop us planning what future to build, a future that is only possible if the colonists agree to help create it."

Kysor sat near the front of the inn, watching each person who came in. When it was someone he knew supported his cause he smiled a welcome; when it was someone he did not know, he ordered Lannel to discover where their sympathies lay. If the newcomers agreed the colonists from Hamilay had overstayed their welcome, Lannel would buy them a drink and introduce them to Kysor. Inevitably they were flattered to find such a prominent member of the council interested in their opinions, and stayed to find out more. On the other hand, if the newcomer was reluctant to discuss an opinion, or was obviously a supporter of the prefect and his new friends, they were asked politely to leave the inn, and if they showed any reluctance to do so, a few of Kysor's larger supporters would suddenly loom behind Lannel and offer to help them on their way. The innkeeper objected the first time this happened, but many coins passed his hand and from that point he retreated behind the serving bar and minded his own business. In the end, business turned out much better than it usually did so early in the afternoon, so the innkeeper had no real objection, and even a commercial interest in seeing that more meetings took place, as long as it was in the afternoon and did not interfere with his night trade. Besides, some of what they were saying rang true with him, and he lent more than half an ear to the conversations of his guests.

When the inn was near to full and a reasonable amount of drink had been consumed—but not too much to make anyone insensible—Kysor banged his mug on the wooden table and yelled, "To Kydan!"

All conversation stopped and many looked around to see who was interrupting their drinking time.

"To Kydan!" he repeated, hitting the table again. "And to its true children!"

With that, Lannel and the other members of Kysor's entourage started banging their mugs as well, and soon after everyone was beating the tattoo and shouting the toast. Before it got too disorganized, Kysor stood up. Gradually the noise subsided as everyone looked towards him.

"The Hamilayans are our friends," he started lowly. "They came from far away to free us from the yoke of Rivald and Kevleren." He was nodding with the rhythm of his own words, and some in the audience picked it up and started nodding too.

"They are good people, I am sure," he continued, "with their own homes to go back to."

There were murmurs of approval.

"Back home with their own husbands and wives and children."

More murmurs of approval.

"Instead of being with ours," Kysor said.

The murmur became a rumble and Kysor's voice gained volume.

"Yet here they stay. Uninvited. Occupying. Looking at us from their conquered island."

One or two shouted in anger but were quickly shushed by neighbors who wanted to hear out the councilor, but Kysor's own tone was now colored by anger and deep resentment. Lannel and others started tapping their mugs to capture the beat.

"First we are taken by Rivald, then we are taken by Hamilay! Once we were free, and we must be free again!"

On the last word he slammed his mug down on the table. For a moment a strange and threatening silence rang out, and on the tail of it, Kysor, his voice softly menacing, said, "Aye, the Hamilayans are our friends . . . when they are back in Hamilay."

Since Kitayra's death in the Citadel, Galys did not like being there. However, since the only troops really capable of using the Citadel to best effect were Hamilayan, it was decided that Gos, she or Kadburn should be on station there at any one time.

On this day she was inspecting the repairs to the wall that had been destroyed by exploding longgons during the attack of Maira Sygni and his fellow plutocrats; the first try at it had been quick and piecemeal, purely for show, but on Kadburn's advice she had ordered the engineers to repair it, and with Heriot's cooperation had arranged for extra labour provided by shifts of colonists. When Poloma had seen what was happening he had immediately ordered a working party of original Kydans to help as well. Galys was pleased to see the three groups working together so efficiently. To some degree, the engineers lording it over the workers had united the colonists and Kydans, at least temporarily.

Poloma watched with her for a while, deeply interested in the work, and especially the expert assistance of the engineers.

"Do you know what most impressed me in Omeralt during my time as an exile?" he asked Galys.

She shook her head, not really interested in conversation.

"The university."

This grabbed her attention. Memories of Kitayra flooded in, as well as less welcome ones of Chancellor Malus Mycom. "The university?"

"I saw it as one of the engines of your nation's power. It produced grammarians and strategoi, physics and administrators." He nodded to the work being done on the wall. "And the engineers. The Kevlerens gave Hamilay predominance but the university trained the soldiers and clerks and scientists who have since kept it. The university is the difference between Rivald and Hamilay."

"Rivald is much smaller—" Galys began.

"So, once, was Hamilay. The Empress Lerena's grandfather oversaw much of the empire's expansion and, not coincidentally, also founded the University of Omeralt. A clever man. He knew what he was doing."

"Yes, I suppose he did."

"And I am a clever man," Poloma said without pride. "Indeed, you and Gos and I are all clever people. No match for Lerena's grandfather, perhaps, but together might we not establish something similar here in Kydan?"

Galys's mind absorbed the suggestion. "That's a wonderful idea," she said, suddenly seeing a future for herself that went beyond the current demands of establishing the colonists in Kydan and defending the city from further attacks. She saw herself teaching new strategoi until her old age, helping to create and consolidate Kydan's status as a great city . . .

Then, like a cloud blocking the sun, reality set in. "It's a nice dream, Poloma, but such a university needs capital, buildings, teachers and students."

Poloma smiled. "But we have plenty here among our people who would be eager to learn or to change career, and some who could teach, at least enough to get things started. We can use buildings that already exist. The houses of the plutocrats have been impounded by the council: we could use those. And the Assembly is used only when the council is in session."

"And capital? I know Kydan is a city of merchants, but compared with the great trading cities of Hamilay and even Rivald, you have a long way to go."

"You forget the *Hannemah*, the *Grayling*, the *Zarim* and the *Laxton*," Poloma said.

"I have not forgotten them," Galys said defensively. In fact, she had not thought of them for a long time, not since Captain Avier in the sloop *Annglaf* had agreed to escort them back to Hamilay stuffed with New Land goods and raw material with the hope they could trade them for empire products Kydan would find useful, such as firegons.

"They already form the core of a merchant fleet," Poloma continued. "There is no reason they cannot be used for trade up and down this coastline as well as across the Deepening Sea. They can also be models to help our boat-builders become shipbuilders. After all, they're not going to be used to transport the colonists back to Hamilay, are they?"

Galys smiled. "No, my friend, they are not."

Poloma slapped the strategos on the shoulder. "And besides, if we use the ships for trade, it will appeal to the Kydans' sense of acquisitiveness. As you said, we are a city of merchants."

Galys accompanied him part of the way back to the Citadel's gate. "I have been thinking that another way to bond our peoples is for many of the soldiers Maddyn brought across to disband, to join the labor pool. They could still be used as militia, and if we matched each of them with a Kydan, whom we could train in the use of the firegon, then in an emergency they would create six companies instead of three."

Poloma seemed pleased by the idea and thought it would go down well with the council. When he had gone, Galys climbed to the inner wall and looked out over the city. There were doubts and misgivings in her heart, but now there was also a feeling that a new city of Kydan could be made from the struggles of the past, that the stone and mortar was there in the people and their determination to succeed. This was the New Land, after all, and what better home for new hopes?

Lannel Thorey had adapted to the dark. He found some solace in being awake when most everyone else was asleep, of being alert when everyone else's guard was down. He napped during the day, snatching an hour here, an hour there. He knew it was no way for a man to live, and he struggled to prove to himself that he was a man. Now that he was a follower of Kysor Nevri, he would prove it to him as well.

Even before he met the councilor, Lannel had felt instinctively that it was wrong for his city to be home to so many strangers. He had hated the Rivald soldiers who had behaved as if Kydan was their personal whorehouse, and

hated the pale Kevleren of whom he had occasionally
caught glimpses. When the expedition had come from
across the sea with Poloma Malvara returned from exile,
Lannel had been exultant, even if the expedition had been
led by another of the terrible Kevlerens. Then after the battle when the plutocrats, Rivald's servants, had finally been
repelled, he had celebrated with the rest of the city. The
next day the Hamilayans were still there. And the next day.
And then they had started building homes for themselves.

Lannel felt violated, as if the body of the city were his
own. The Hamilayans were parasites, pestilence, plague.
They had to be scoured from Kydan, and he had known as
soon as he heard Kysor Nevri talk that he was the one to
do it. Certainly the small, ineffectual Prefect Poloma Malvara would never see off the Hamilayans. Like the plutocrats before him, his power was derived from foreign
soldiers and firegons and the threat of the Sefid, even if, as
some said, the Hamilayan Kevleren was dead and gone; it
was rumored that the empress across the sea was a terrible
sorceress who could blast a soul into nothingness anywhere in the world just by thinking about it.

Not that he believed everything he was told . . .

Raised voices from the inn near the basilica drew his
attention. Raised Hamilayan voices. He slunk out of the
shadows and peeped into one of the inn's street-front windows. The place was filled mainly with Kydans, but there
were some Hamilayans among them. The lot, Kydans and
Hamilayans alike, appeared dirty and disheveled, as if they
had been working together in the fields. It was almost too
much for his stomach to bear: not only were Kydans frat-
ernizing willingly with Hamilayans, but they were doing it
in the very inn where Kysor Nevri had so inspired the nativists only hours before.

Nativists, he thought. That's what we are. The true native Kydans.

There were salutations and farewells from inside. Lannel ducked back into shadows. The inn door opened and yellow lantern light splashed across the road. A group of revelers strode out, looking very pleased with themselves. They walked east a short way before splitting, most of them heading south, two continuing to move east. Lannel assumed the first group was mostly Kydans heading home, the latter Hamilayans heading towards the Saddle and a boat back to Karhay. Curiosity, or perhaps the inkling of some future action stirring deep inside him, made Lannel follow the Hamilayans. Since there was no moon, and he knew the road very well, there was little chance of his being seen.

When the two foreigners reached the Long Bridge, one farewelled his companion and continued on, perhaps looking for another drinking hole, while the other used the ramp descending to the Saddle, followed by Lannel. Here it was truly dark, unlit by any nearby homes. The Hamilayan kept close to the cliff face on his left, brushing his fingertips along its stone surface. He started singing a ribald Kydan song in his appalling accent, humming where he did not know the words. Disgust and anger roiled inside Lannel, and almost without thinking he surged forwards and grabbed the man by his shoulders, yanking him off his feet.

The Hamilayan did not have time to yell before he hit the ground, all the breath whooshing out of him. Before he could get up, Lannel kicked him in the ribs, and again. The man tried to crawl away from his attacker, making begging sounds.

"Singing a different song now, eh?" Lannel sneered, and kicked again, this time striking his victim in the head. The Hamilayan shuddered terribly and was still.

Lannel froze, his right leg swung back for another blow, but as quickly as his blood had rushed to his brain it now seemed to drain out completely. He slowly put down his right leg and squatted next to the Hamilayan, touching his face tentatively. The skin and flesh underneath was as pliable as cloth, as clammy as boiled cabbage. He put his hand over the man's mouth but felt no breath. His fingers touched something wet, and Lannel smelled the iron of blood. He stood up quickly, his stomach heaving. It seemed to Lannel that the cooling night air sucked the heat from him, and with it any resolve. He did not know what to do. He had not meant to . . .

He stopped the lie. Of course he had meant to hurt the Hamilayan. Not to kill him, maybe, but to hurt him, yes.

There were voices from above, near the start of the Long Bridge. His breath caught and he waited for discovery, but the voices continued on and faded away.

Lannel found he could move again. He reached down and grabbed the dead man's hands and with some effort, for all his strength had fled with his anger, pulled him to the edge of the ramp. He laid the man out along the rim and then pushed him over. It was a long way to the bottom of the Saddle, and the sound the body made when it hit the ground was no more than a soft crump.

Lannel stood unsteadily. He was a murderer now. He tried wiping his hands on his pants, but they shook so much he had to press them against his thighs. He waited until the shaking subsided, then climbed to the main road and disappeared once more into the shadows.

10

O N his second attempt to pay his respects to the Empress Lerena, anxious to take advantage of the absence of anyone from Rivald's Safety Committee, Ambassador Avenel Kendy found himself stopped by two guards and an officious-looking clerk at the entrance to the Great Hall.

"Her Majesty is no longer in residence," the clerk sniffed. "Perhaps you should have made an appointment."

Kendy wanted to bop the clerk on the nose. He made sure he never patronized anyone, and he expected the favour in return.

"I have made an appointment. For this day. At this hour. Here, at the Great Hall."

The clerk's eyebrows climbed his forehead. "Really?" He unrolled a scroll he held in his right hand. "Ah, yes. You did not get the empress's reply, I gather."

"If a reply had been sent, assuredly I would have received it." Avenel was determined not to retreat, and the clerk was starting to get the message.

"I am not sure what I can do—"

"Check," Avenel said bluntly. "Someone in the palace must know what's going on."

"Wait here, if you please," the clerk said stiffly, and withdrew.

Avenel, feeling more influential than he knew he deserved, started whistling. The servant he had brought along for company studied his feet. The guards stared straight ahead. Other people, mostly officials of one description or another, bustled around them. He saw a different clerk poke his head around the entrance, sight Avenel, and disappear again. It was this man who eventually ventured out and bowed almost indecently low.

"Your Eminence, I am the empress's chief of correspondence."

"Very nice, I'm sure," Avenel said. "The other fellow said I was supposed to get a reply from her majesty. Regarding my appointment. On this day. At this hour."

The new clerk cleared his throat and held out an expensive-looking envelope decorated with gold curlicues and tracery. "This would be the reply. I apologise for its tardy delivery, but things have been . . . well, a little disorganized of late."

Avenel worked hard to stop his face showing his curiosity. He took the envelope and retrieved the letter inside. The clerk quickly turned to go, but Avenel called out without looking up from the letter, "Wait, please. I may have an answer."

He had to read the empress's reply twice.

"The aviary of Duchess Yunara?" Avenel asked.

The clerk looked pensively at the ambassador. "The aviary, your Eminence?"

"It says here I am to present myself to Empress Lerena at Duchess Yunara's alcazar; the aviary to be precise." He folded the letter back in its envelope, tucked it inside his jacket and faced the clerk. "What is going on here? Does the empress usually hold court in a birdcage?"

The clerk swallowed. "I'm not sure I can explain the current situation. Perhaps it would be best if your Eminence proceeded to the duchess's alcazar to see for himself." He looked around Avenel. "You have not brought your sedan?"

"I enjoy walking," Avenel replied shortly.

"I will organize one for you. You won't want to be late, I'm sure."

"I'm already late—" Avenel started to say, but the clerk was gone.

Lerena had one dog left; all the other hounds had died. The aviary had not agreed with them. The survivor had been the runt of the pack, and Lerena wondered if its size had something to do with it. It was not the fault of the birds, she was sure; except for the occasional swooping magpie, none of the dogs had been attacked. Her familiars had simply . . .

Well, Lerena told herself, simply not adjusted.

They had cringed and whined from the first day they had been brought into the aviary. Lerena had thought she would have a problem controlling them, stopping them from chasing all the birds, but instead they had lain on the ground, their heads flat against the earth, and stopped eating.

She studied the officials and family members who were gathered nearby and thought some of them were not adjusting either. They looked pale and drawn and haggard, as if they were being wasted by some disease.

Perhaps the problem with the dogs and her family was that the Sefid did not agree with them. Lerena found this an amusing idea.

It was hard to move and hard to think beyond the present. The aviary was the world contained. It was always warm and green. The birds were like her own thoughts, filled with colour and beauty and energy. And here, too, the Sefid seemed strongest.

Imagine all that energy left over, infusing the world. She no longer had to sacrifice anything to Wield, not for little things anyway. Just as well with all but one of the dogs dying.

Lerena made sure no one was looking and chose a leaf hanging precariously from a tree not far from her throne. She thought for a moment, and the leaf went from green to red, from summer to autumn in a blink of the eye. Then it fell to the ground. As usual, she felt a thrill of pleasure at the effortless ease of it all.

Lerena had spent a great deal of mental effort on trying to understand why the Sefid was suddenly—and painlessly—so accessible, and why no one else seemed to notice it. In the end, the solution was so obvious she did not know why she had not immediately realized the truth.

After destroying every Beloved on the continent, as well as every member of the Rivald branch of the Kevlerens and Maddyn far away in the New Land, she initially assumed she had used up entirely the store of Sefid she had created by sacrificing Yunara and Hanimoro, the two people she loved most in the universe. But then Lerena realised the deaths of her cousins in Rivald were the equivalent of an even greater sacrifice; true, she had not loved them the way she had loved Yunara or even Hanimoro, but they were Kevlerens, and like every member of the family she was raised from childhood to love and respect her own. The deaths of so many Kevlerens was a sacrifice without a Wielding, and the excess Sefid was still available, still waiting to be used. A continent of the stuff! An ocean! And all for her! Lerena might never run out again.

Having solved that puzzle, she was then left with an even more curious one—why was she the only one able to sense the excess Sefid? For a long while Lerena thought the problem intractable, and then one day she noticed a servant carrying a tray of drinks for guests in the aviary. The servant looked up at exactly the right time, and got an eyeful of sunlight. Dazed and temporary blinded, the servant barged into one of the guests and dropped the tray. It occurred to the empress that when she had used the Sefid that day and slain across land and sea, the effect on every other Kevleren had been like staring straight at the sun. It had overwhelmed them completely, which explained their current mordant behavior and blinded them to the Sefid at the same time.

The only thing was, Lerena was not sure if the effect was permanent, and if it was only temporary, how long would it last?

A bird warbled prettily somewhere behind her, bringing her back to the present.

She took in a deep breath of air, smelling grass and plant and water.

She liked the place. She liked it a lot; certainly more than the old palace. This is where she wanted to spend the rest of her life. Alas, she had responsibilities beyond her own pleasure.

She sighed heavily. The family for example. What to do with them if they never recovered?

The court sergeant, looking too formal and stiff for the aviary, came before her and bowed.

"Your Majesty, the Rivald ambassador, Captain of a Thousand Avenel Kendy, begs an audience."

Lerena frowned, trying to remember if he had an

appointment. The sergeant must have been reading her mind, because he cleared his throat and added, "As already arranged with your office."

"Yes, all right," she conceded, and noticed him use a finger to widen his collar as he left. She would have to design new uniforms for everyone if she intended to re-establish the court permanently in the aviary; it was much warmer here than in the old court. And she would have to redesign the alcazar. And find some other use for the Great Hall and her old quarters. In fact, she would start now . . .

The sergeant returned with an uneasy Avenel Kendy in tow, disturbing her train of thought. As the sergeant eagerly withdrew, she looked crossly at the ambassador.

"I was thinking of rearranging the whole palace," she said to him as if it was part of a conversation they were already having.

"Excellent idea, your Majesty," Avenel said, bowing so low his nose almost touched the grass.

"Yes, it is. Perhaps as part of it we could move your embassy inside the palace grounds."

Avenel could not hold his surprise. "The *Rivald* embassy inside the imperial enclosure, you mean?"

Lerena nodded. "Yes. Close by. Then we could see each other as much as we needed."

Avenel tried to read some clue to her mood by studying her face, but it was as guarded as always, and those around her seemed as surprised and confused as he, so they were no help. He remembered to say something. "That would indeed be a great honor. The Safety Committee would be . . . speechless . . . with joy."

Lerena's guarded expression suddenly evaporated, and in its place was one of utmost curiosity. "Have you heard from your committee recently?"

Avenel wondered how much to say. Of course, that depended on how much the empress knew; he had an uneasy feeling she knew a great deal more about the situation back home than he did. That possibility convinced him to be honest.

"Not recently, your Majesty." He swallowed. "Have you . . . enjoyed any correspondence with them?"

Lerena laughed, but it was not a pleasant sound to Avenel's ears. "You might say that."

"I have been considering asking for your leave from court."

"Leave?"

"To absent myself from the capital so I might cross the border. Perhaps I would have more luck communicating with the committee if I were closer—"

"That will be unnecessary," Lerena said simply.

Avenel bowed again. "Of course, your Majesty."

A smile crossed Lerena's face. "Entirely unnecessary," she added.

Paimer was dithering and he knew it. The captain of Royal Guards watched him impatiently, constantly checking the course of the sun across the quarter of sky he could see through the tall windows in the duke's reception hall.

"Her majesty would like to see you some time today," the captain said. It occurred to him that only a few weeks before he would never have dared to speak to Paimer like that—or any Kevleren, for that matter—but things had changed at court, and the duke had changed most of all. Once patrician, imperial and aloof, he now behaved more like one of the clowns that sometimes led parades in spring festivals. It was hard to respect someone like that.

In fact, the captain thought, the duke's entire household

was a shambles. His servants, Axkevlerens and otherwise, were scrabbling around looking for something Paimer had lost. Even one or two Kevlerens, looking as bewildered as Paimer, had joined in the search.

The captain's disdain for the lot of them was visible in his expression.

"Have him shot," Idalgo said to Paimer.

"He's only doing his duty," Paimer said under his voice. He did not want the captain to be embarrassed by his Beloved. "It's my red wig!" he said out loud. "Can't find it anywhere. Never go outside without it."

"Yes, your Grace," the captain said. "Perhaps in your chambers?"

Paimer paused to consider the suggestion.

"Stay here," Idalgo said. "I'll check for you."

Paimer hated it when Idalgo did this, leaving him behind with nothing to do except look thoughtful. He faintly recollected he once knew how to do that, and chitchat too, but these days both seemed beyond him, like so many other things. He tried to look thoughtful anyway; judging by the captain's expression, he was failing miserably.

Idalgo reappeared. "Yes, it's in your chambers."

"Then why didn't you bring it?" Paimer said crossly.

"Your Grace?" the captain asked.

Paimer shook his head and went to his bedroom. No wig there. He checked the privy. Yes, on the floor. A mess. He must have left it there in the evening. He faintly remembered getting up for a piss about halfway through the night, although he had no idea why he took his wig with him. He picked it up, plopped it on and returned to the reception hall.

"Right, Captain, ready when you are."

"About bloody time," the captain muttered, but still stood to attention as the duke passed him on the way out.

*   *   *

Yes, small things seemed to do well these days, Lerena thought. Her runty dog, the Rivald ambassador, Chancellor Malus Mycom. Herself, of course. Everything and everyone else was doing it hard. Her uncle, for example—and what was delaying him, by the way?—had never been the same since that wonderful, terrible day.

She gazed up to the top of the dome. The metal skeleton hummed with a soft blue light. As usual, no one except her noticed it. She wondered, briefly, if she was the only one left alive who could Wield any more. That might be another reason no other member of the family seemed able to detect the Sefid's presence.

As if she needed another theory for it all. She sighed heavily. The truth was she was guessing; she did not know the real answer, which irritated her somewhat. Although not nearly as irritating as trying to keep her mind in order. It got harder and harder to remember what it was she was meant to be doing. She felt adrift, like a ship at sea without a breeze. Everything was in working order, sails and rudder and whatnot, but there was no direction. Life had become like that too. Out of sorts. Out of focus. No Yunara to plot against, no Maddyn to hate to death, no ambitious family members to put in their place, no officials wasting her time. No army from Rivald banging on the frontier.

No Beloved to love.

Stop it, she told herself. No remorse. The empire was safe. That's what counted. And then she caught one of her thoughts.

No army from Rivald. That's right. Of course there was something she could do; how could she have forgotten *that*?

Lerena looked around for the ambassador, the short fellow with very little hair and a tummy. He was standing apart from everyone else, still waiting to be dismissed. Should she tell him that all the Beloveds in his country were dead now, all shrivelled up and blown away? What a surprise it would be for him.

Wait. She was not supposed to know about that yet; at least, not for certain. Not until her spies had got word back to her. She wished they would hurry up.

"Do you come from Beferen?" Lerena asked the ambassador.

He looked startled for a moment. His mind had been a thousand miles away. He drew nearer. "I'm sorry, your Majesty. I didn't quite hear."

"Where in Rivald do you come from?"

"Lately, the capital. Before that—"

"What is Beferen like?"

"Dark and cold in winter, your Majesty. More pleasant in summer, but never as warm as here. It rains a lot all year round. The seas are gray."

"Sounds miserable," she said.

"It often is," he conceded with a slight smile. "But it has its good points. In summer it is soft with rain, and the seabirds always call—"

"It still sounds miserable."

"It was home for many years," Avenel said gently, almost to himself.

"Do you like Omeralt, your Eminence?"

"Very much," he said, his tone cheering up. "It is a handsome city."

"Do you know how long your commission lasts?"

"No, your Majesty. I wait upon the pleasure of the Safety Committee, as do all loyal servants of Rivald."

"Well said," she said, not meaning it. "Could you send your committee a message for me?"

"Anything, your Majesty."

"You know, I've never been to Beferen. For that matter, I've never been to Rivald. My uncle, the Duke Paimer Kevleren, speaks highly of his time there."

"I am glad of it," Avenel said slowly, having guessed where the conversation was heading but not knowing how to avoid it.

"Do you think your Safety Committee would consider issuing an invitation?"

Avenel licked his lips. "An invitation?"

Lerena regarded him coolly. "Don't be obtuse, man."

The words spilled out, although later Avenel was not sure how they came into his head. "I am confident the Republic of Rivald would be overjoyed to issue an invitation to her majesty the Empress Lerena to visit their humble capital." He drew in a deep breath, the pause enough for him to gather some wit. "Subject to my despatching to the committee your inclination for such a visit." That should give me some time, he thought. Especially since as far as I can tell no message of mine has yet been answered.

It then occurred to Avenel that the committee might not be getting his messages. All it would take was a pair of falcons and a handler with keen eyes positioned on one of the first peaks of the Vardar Mountains not more than a mile or two from Omeralt. Lots of dead pigeons, no communication between Beferen and their ambassador in Omeralt. If that was the case, he had no doubt that the next pigeon, carrying the empress's guarded request for an invitation, would be allowed through.

Lerena brightened. "Then get to it, your Eminence. Despatch away."

*　　*　　*

Paimer was carried from his estate to Omeralt's main gate in a military carriage, built for speed, not comfort. The only relief was Idalgo making wisecracks about the captain, which had Paimer alternately blushing and giggling. The captain pretended not to hear, but often cast sideways glances at the duke, which would only make Paimer laugh the harder. He was met at the gate by a royal sedan, and Paimer made the captain go by foot, desiring no company other than his Beloved's.

"The captain thinks I am punishing him, when I am only trying to protect him. You were heartless when he was in the carriage," he told Idalgo. "The captain was only—"

"Doing his duty," Idalgo finished for him. He stared hard at Paimer then, and the duke shivered under that gaze. "We all do our duty."

Paimer had to look away. Spring was warming up now, but there seemed to be no sign of any of the usual festivals. He wondered what Lerena thought she was doing. The people enjoyed their festivals. It kept them in touch with the Kevlerens, let them see the family's benevolent side.

The sedan reached the imperial enclosure. Instead of making for the Great Hall or Lerena's quarters, the carriers cantered northwest.

"Where are we going?" Paimer asked Idalgo.

His Beloved poked his head out the window and looked around. "I think we're making for Yunara's alcazar."

"That's not good," Paimer said. He had not forgotten his humiliation at Lerena's hands the last time he was there.

"Where the empress commands, so we go," Idalgo said offhandedly, resting back in his seat.

Paimer harrumphed. He did not think Lerena should be treating her sister so generously; she should be making Yunara come to her. Well, he was largely out of it now, he knew. Let Lerena decide her own course. She *was* empress, after all, and he nothing but a lowly duke. And Yunara nothing but a lowly duchess.

"A lowly duchess indeed," Idalgo commented.

Lerena had not noticed before the similarity between the Rivald ambassador and her first cousin, General Second Prince Rodin Kevleren. Like Avenel, Rodin was balding, a little dumpy, and—delight!—short. A good sign, she hoped. And then, she sighed, there was the chancellor. Malus Mycom, also present, and also short. Malus, like the ambassador, was inevitably cheerful, which was not always a good thing, but at least it balanced the grim Rodin, whose expression seemed to predict doom and disaster. She hoped Rodin's spies had been hard at work.

"Any word, cousin?"

Rodin spread his hands. "Alas, I cannot yet confirm any of the rumors about the destruction of our family in the republic, or what part the Beloveds may have played in it."

"Rodin, when will your agents be able to tell me the exact situation in Rivald?"

"When last we met you said I could have a month," he pleaded.

Lerena sighed. She tried not to let herself slip into a bad mood. She did not think she was asking a great deal.

"What is happening there?" she demanded loudly. All the birds in nearby trees took off in a flurry of beating wings. Rodin and Malus cringed and glanced up nervously at the explosion of life.

"What is the state of that nation? Is it disorganized? Are its armies in revolt or leaderless? Have the common people risen up against the Safety Committee for the massacre in Beferen? I need to know."

Rodin spread his hands. "I have not had time—"

"Do not tell me you have not had time!" She took a deep breath and said more calmly, "I have reason to believe the Safety Committee will soon invite me to visit."

Rodin and Malus were too surprised to respond at first, then Rodin asked hesitantly, "And you would accept?"

"Why not?"

"No ruler of the empire has ever visited Rivald," Rodin pointed out.

"They are our enemy," Malus added. "They have always been our enemy."

"Then it is time we changed the relationship," Lerena said, smiling thinly.

The court sergeant appeared and told Lerena that Duke Paimer Kevleren had arrived.

"You will excuse me, gentlemen," she told Rodin and Malus, "but there are matters I must discuss with my uncle." As they bowed she said to her cousin, "And don't forget about Rivald. I need to know as soon as possible."

Maybe it was the time of day, or maybe it was the interview with Lerena, but when he went to the embassy roof to despatch to Beferen the empress's request for an invitation, Avenel Kendy felt less generous about Omeralt than he had in the morning. There was something about the city that reflected the unease he felt in the presence of Lerena, as if the city was in some way a manifestation of the empress herself.

Avenel mentally shrugged. He was not sure how to describe the impression Lerena had made on him in their second meeting. He considered himself to be a reasonable judge of character—no, a good judge of character—and he was sure the woman he met this afternoon was not the same woman he'd first met all those tendays ago when presenting his credentials as Rivald's new ambassador to Hamilay. Something about who she was, what she was, had altered. Something that had been a part of her had metamorphosed or died or been twisted out of shape.

He shook his head at his feeble attempts to explain in a rational way what he felt empathetically, almost emotionally.

He let the pigeon go with its message, silently wishing it better luck than its predecessors in getting across the mountains, then looked out again over Omeralt. Its thousands of buildings, almost all constructed from the same butter-colored stone, stretched lazily across the foothills of the Vardars. It was a beautiful city, especially when compared to the dark Beferen spilled around its cold bay, but now it seemed to Avenel to be less seductive than corrupting. Something was wrong in Omeralt, and it was centred on the empress.

"I want you to stay here with me."

Paimer was watching a swan glide down to the lake from among some reeds on the far side of the island. It looked so clumsy as it struck the water he was sure it would sink, but somehow it all came right. Its wings, so wide in flight, arced briefly, beautifully, then folded as crisply as paper. The smallest of ripples spread away from where it landed. The duke thought it was a wonderful thing. No wonder Yunara liked it so much here in the aviary.

"Uncle?"

He faced the empress.

"Won't Yunara mind?" he asked, trying not to look perplexed. What was wrong with his own estate away from the capital and his two nieces?

He was not sure if it was a smile that crossed Lerena's face, but it was gone as quickly as it came.

"No. She is very accommodating. She loves us both."

"I have no doubt," he said in a tone that suggested he had every doubt.

"You can send for your possessions. At least those you need the most. I will give you one of the wings here." She reached out and took his hand. "Exciting things are happening, Uncle, and I want you near me."

"Tell her the truth," Idalgo said, suddenly appearing behind the empress.

"You don't trust me, do you?"

Lerena laughed softly. "Is that so new? Since when did the ruler of Hamilay ever trust her family?"

He knew that there was a time when he would have agreed, and yet, to his surprise, her comment hurt his feelings. Lerena must have read his expression because she gently squeezed his hand. "But some I trust more than others. You have always served me well."

"I have served you best," he said without pride. "But I understand, your Majesty. There are things we know, you and I, that no one else must learn."

"Yes, that is it exactly. The wind is changing, and things cannot be the same as they once were. I want to make sure that when the storm comes, it blows for us and not against us. For that I need your help. I need you by my side."

"I take comfort in that," he said, and squeezed her hand in turn. He hoped Lerena did not hear his Beloved snickering behind her back.

Captain Avier thought it was almost as if he had never left. The port of Somah looked exactly the same, even down to the experimental steamship *Hetha* being anchored in the middle of the harbour, wallowing like a pig every time it was struck by a wave. The docks were crammed and busy, the smell atrocious, the skyline broken by a forest of masts.

He sighed. After a lifetime of sailing first warships and then his lovely sloop the *Annglaf*, he should be used to it, he knew, but somehow he always expected the world to change as much as he did after every voyage. Just on this journey, for example, he had seen war and death, hopes raised and dashed, lives spent gallantly and foolishly, enemies thwarted . . .

And Somah just carried on, the same port city it had been all his working life, and would continue to be, he supposed, long after he was dead and buried at sea. Perhaps he should have been thankful that Somah provided a constant in his life, a sort of lighthouse for his own wayward existence that brought him safely back to land and the mundane.

And bureaucracy, he told himself. That never changed either.

"These vessels you bring back with you are registered?" the governor of Somah asked. She was a harassed-looking woman dressed in expensive clothes and the sash of her office.

"Directly to her majesty, the empress herself," Avier said with some satisfaction, pointing to the green parchments.

The governor blinked. "Yes, I see. And in their holds?"

"Goods and materials from Kydan in the New Land."

"And your own sloop?"

"Also carries such goods."

The governor smiled slightly, which Avier was not sure was a good sign, and rested back in her seat. "Ah, foreign goods. That will mean custom duty." She tapped his papers with a long nail. "That will be expensive."

Avier smiled back and produced the last of his documents. "A copy of the empress's charter to General Third Prince Maddyn Kevleren," he said. "Ordering him to secure Kydan as the empire's first colony in the New Land."

"I don't see what this has to do—"

"I don't carry foreign goods, your Excellency. I carry domestic goods from one empire port to another. This is internal trade and therefore excused from duty."

The governor took the charter and studied it carefully. Her smile disappeared, replaced by a pained, pinched expression.

Avier knew better than to gloat.

"I have a special cargo," he said. "From the prince to the governor of Somah."

She looked up then, all interest. "A special cargo?"

"A ton of New Land hardwood, to be disposed of at your discretion. In recognition of your part in ensuring the expedition's success."

Avier smiled convivially to hide all the lies. The prince was dead, and the governor's contribution to the expedition had, by all accounts, been nonexistent. But gifts in the right places would grease much of the bureaucracy he would have to squeeze through to complete his business here.

"That is very generous!" she said, and both knew it was true. A ton of New Land hardwood would be worth more than her annual salary. That was a lot of grease.

"My ships need to be unloaded for you to get your gift," he said.

"I will make sure they receive urgent berthing."

"And supplies for the return journey."

"I will let the port master know that you are here on the empress's business . . ." The governor's voice trailed off and she licked her lips.

"Is there a problem?"

"The government in Omeralt has been behaving . . . erratically . . . of late. You may find that it hurries things up if you carry out your business directly through my office rather than through the empress's own representatives in Somah."

She was good, Avier thought. And greedy.

"I am sure the prince would not forget such a favor."

"Then we understand each other," the governor said.

"Completely."

They both reached across her table to shake hands. He gathered up his papers and documents and made to leave.

"One word of caution," the governor said.

Avier looked up, his expression guarded. He hoped, after all the delicate bargaining, that she was not going to put a rider on the whole thing.

"I meant what I said about the government in Omeralt. Even if you have to deal with her majesty's officers in an official capacity, there are some things you must know. Things that have happened while you have been away. Things that may affect your prince and his colony in the New Land."

After carrying it halfway around the world, the ocean currents left the creature stranded on a rocky outcrop made sharp and slippery by the tides. With what consciousness it had, it made its way slowly and painfully to more level ground, and from there climbed up until it was far away from the ocean that had been both its prisoner and its saviour. It found a shallow cave to call its own and to shelter it from the burning sun, and there fell asleep to gather its strength.

11

"ELTREE!" the farmer cried, trying to hide his exasperation. He removed his wide-brimmed grass hat and wiped his brow. It was too hot and still. He looked north and saw huge black clouds moving down the coast towards Kydan. The rains were coming, which was good. A little late maybe, but they were on their way now. And maybe some hail, which was not so good. He sighed heavily and put his hat back on, slapped the donkey's rump. "Move along!"

The donkey reluctantly moved a few paces, then stopped again.

"Oh, by Frey and Kydan, I'll have you hammered when we get back, and I'll use your hide for boots if you don't move your sodden bloody—"

The donkey, unexpectedly, moved back, forcing the farmer off the trail and into an irrigation ditch.

"You bastard excuse for an animal!" the farmer shouted, but the donkey ignored him and took another step back.

The farmer opened his mouth to curse some more, but he was not a crude man by nature, nor so cruel he made a habit of striking dumb animals, so he forced himself to calm down and stepped back up to the trail. The green stubble of growing wheat surrounded him in fields that stretched all the way along the bottom of the ramp to the Sayeff Channel between the islands of Karhay and Herris. He and his beast were on their way to the shoreline, where he had set up a hand pump to pull water from the channel and distribute it along the irrigation ditches to all his fields. The donkey was carrying two heavy baskets filled with chicken poo he wanted to mix with the water to help enrich the fields; it was an unpleasant job, and the baskets stank as high as the sky. The farmer was sure the donkey did not like it any more than he did, so something other than sheer stubbornness was holding him up.

The farmer grunted, edged past the donkey on the trail, holding his breath as he nudged around the baskets of poo, and finally made it to the front. Something was lying across the trail about four yards ahead of him. At first the farmer was not sure what he was looking at, but he only took one step closer before he saw the bloody head of a man lying at the wrong angle to the rest of the body, a man in the clothes of one of those from across the great ocean.

After the initial surprise, the first things that came into the farmer's head were that the poor bugger must have fallen off the ramp, and that he had died an awful long way from home.

Kysor Nevri was woken before dawn by a noise from outside, but such was the discontinuity between being asleep and being awake that he forgot about it as he opened his eyes. Instead, he sat up in his simple bed and wished, for a moment, that he was someone else. He had not wanted the responsibility of being a leader, of being someone others looked to for example and inspiration. When he had decided to follow in his brother's footsteps and become a councilor and had gathered the support he needed to enter the Assembly, his mild ambition had been to contribute to the wellbeing of the city and its citizens. And, too, he remembered now, to work under the guidance of the young prefect Poloma Malvara, a man of much promise and from a respectable merchant family.

Then the Rivald had come with their disgusting firegons and their disgusting Kevleren sorcerer and violently destroyed the city's peace and prosperity. The only hope he had rested in the exiled prefect, far away gathering support to free Kydan from the yoke of foreign domination.

But when he'd returned, Poloma had come with the Hamilayans, and more firegons and yet another Kevleren.

No, Kysor had not wanted the responsibility of leadership, but no other Kydan seemed willing to provide it, especially not the young prefect he had once admired so much.

He laid back on his bed and tried to sleep, but it was no good. His mind was filled with a hundred different tasks, and flittered from one to the other. Sighing heavily, he left his bed, being careful not to disturb his wife and, dressed only in his nightshirt, went downstairs to the kitchen. He found some stale bread and a pot of drying preserve and was about to make a meal out of it when he heard something outside. A whimpering sound, like a hurt dog, and he remembered then it was the sound that had woken him.

He opened the back door to his house and found Lannel Thorey squatting there, a long thread of saliva suspended from one corner of his mouth, whining.

"Lannel?"

Kysor did not know what to do. He had never seen a

fully grown man behaving like this before and he felt faintly disgusted.

"Pick yourself up, man. What's wrong with you?"

Lannel looked up, still whimpering, and held out a hand.

Kysor reached out automatically, realised then he was still holding the bread, and drew back.

"Get up," he whispered fiercely.

"I've done something terrible," Lannel said, the words coming out in a moan. "Oh, sweet Kydan, it's murder . . ." His voice drained off like water down a gutter.

"Murder?" Kysor stared stupidly at the man, then threw away the bread and helped him stand. "Get inside," he ordered.

"It's terrible—" Lannel started again, the moan rising to a dirge.

"Shut up," Kysor ordered, pushing him into the house and shutting the door behind them. He pulled a stool out from underneath the work bench. "Sit, and keep your damn voice down."

"Kysor?" came his wife's voice from upstairs. "Who is it? What are you doing?"

"Stay upstairs, Zole. It's Lannel Thorey, on council business."

"At this time? It's not even daylight."

Kysor heard her getting out of bed.

"Urgent business," he called upstairs. "Secret business. We won't be long."

He held his breath until he heard his wife getting back into bed, then closed the kitchen's internal door.

"Right," he said, turning to Lannel, "what's all this about?"

He used the kitchen flint and steel to light a lantern and

placed it on the bench. Lannel's features seemed even more drawn and haggard in the flickering light, like a mask, and he drew back.

Lannel reached out and took his hand before he could pull it away. "Councilor Nevri, I've killed a man."

"Do you really think the council will let us sit on it?" Arden asked Heriot. "I didn't see many that seemed happy about the idea of sharing the Assembly. Not even among the prefect's supporters."

"I suppose some support Poloma Malvara for other reasons," Heriot said. "They don't all have to like us."

"Do you think *he* likes us?"

They were standing slightly below the rise where the stables were being built, looking out over the new settlement that occupied most of the eastern end of Karhay. The sun was still below the horizon, but the sky was blushed with rosy light and the newly built huts looked almost homely.

"We will need to make a better job of the main east-west road," Heriot continued. "One heavy downpour will wash it all away. Gutters might do the trick. We should get one of those engineers to help us."

"Whenever I mention that man you change the subject," Arden said.

"Once that's done, we should think about permanent shelter. These huts we've got up now won't last more'n two years, thereabouts."

They stood together in silence for a little while, absorbed in their own thoughts, before Arden decided to try again. "About the prefect—"

"And then we'll be wanting a proper dock. And you should talk."

"This isn't about me, Heriot, it's about the prefect."

She turned then, hands on hips, and glared up at her giant companion. "Well, Arden, let's make it about you. I don't know how many times I've asked you about your past, about what you did before we met or before the expedition left Hamilay, but every time I do, you talk about something else, or stuff your mouth with food, or just look grim and stormy and plain ignore me."

Silence, through which Heriot maintained her glaring.

Then, quietly, "I don't ignore you, no matter what you think."

Heriot had to blink. "I don't understand you," she said, almost pleading.

"Ah."

"Which puts you up a peg, because I think you understand a lot about me."

"But I don't ignore you."

Heriot's arms dropped by her sides in resignation and exasperation. "No."

"Can I ask about him now?"

"And not just a dock," she said, turning back to the view. "A warehouse would be good too."

Arden took a deep breath. "You remember after the battle?"

Heriot grunted. "I won't forget that, no matter how long I live."

"I mean, afterwards, when I talked with the prince's man."

"Kadburn."

"Yes. I knew how he was feeling."

"Of course you did. You were once an Axkevleren." She felt Arden stare down at her.

"How did you—?"

"I overheard you talking with him."

"Then why did you pretend you didn't know anything about me?"

Heriot heard frustration in his voice, and felt some pleasure in returning the favor. "Because," she said between gritted teeth, "I heard it while you were talking to *him*. I asked you about your past so many times I nearly gave up, then you just sit down next to him and right off recount your whole life."

"It wasn't like that."

"It seemed like that to me," she said. "And we're supposed to be . . . at least I thought we were . . . well . . . friends."

For a long moment Arden did not reply, but then said in a subdued voice, "What do you want to know?"

"You learned to write when you were an Axkevleren?"

"Yes."

"And fight?"

"Especially that. Because of my size."

"Your master must have been pretty important then."

"Mistress." Heriot heard him swallow. "Yes, she was important."

"You loved her?"

"Axkevlerens always love the one who owns them. That's how the family controls us."

Heriot reached out to touch his hand. "That isn't love, Arden."

"I know that now. But I did *love* her. She was mistress and mother and goddess for us. We felt a part of her family. We were loved in turn by her, I'm sure of it."

They both saw the young woman at the same time, running up the main street towards them. As she got closer, they saw she was wide-eyed and pale. She stopped right before them, out of breath.

"Hamly," Heriot said. "I thought you were working at the Citadel today. What are you doing here?"

"It's Carder," Hamly gasped. "He's dead, Heriot! Murdered, they say!"

Galys put Kitayra's possessions on the bunk and went through them one by one, putting each back in her dead lover's sea trunk. She was not sure what she was looking for, or if indeed it was only an expression of her grief. At first Galys thought holding Kitayra's things was a way of holding onto Kitayra herself, but she soon realised all she was holding onto were memories. Kitayra was gone; what was left of her buried with the hundreds of other bodies quickly disposed of to avoid disease spreading throughout the city after the plutocrats' attack had been so bloodily repulsed. There had been no time to say goodbye, or to say how much she had been loved. There was just a hole in Galys's life and nothing but work and duty to fill it.

As she was packing, Galys wondered what she should ultimately do with it all. Kitayra never really spoke about her own family, but Galys supposed her parents or siblings should get it. She could send it care of the university and they would pass it on. But she would not pack everything: she would keep the birth chain, something she thought might be central to the mystery that had been Kitayra's death. And the research?

Galys picked up the papers Kitayra had been working on up to the day of her death and went to the window to read them. A lot of the writing seemed rushed, as if Kitayra knew she had little time left and wanted to get everything down. Almost all of it was beyond Galys, dealing with what seemed obscure and arcane aspects of the Sefid. It occurred to her then that perhaps her death had been a result of her work on the Sefid, and not caused by some Kevleren Wielding from far away. If true, would it explain Maddyn's death as well? It was an idea she would have to discuss with Kadburn.

Perhaps because she had thought of the prince, her eye picked out his name on one of the lines.

Maddyn Kevleren has told me he wants eventually to introduce the steam carriage to the new colony. He has even employed what he calls "boil makers" for just this purpose; I note, too, that for the number of horses we are bringing with us, there is an unusual number of fettlers. These may be for the making of the steam carriage's track. Certainly, the prince's well-known inability with the Sefid and his intention to spread the use of the steam carriage coincides with my supposition on his family's general attitude towards technology. See Dis Misc, n 3.

Curious, Galys riffled through the pages in her hand, checking headings, then the papers left on the desk. She found a dozen pages headed *Discussions, Miscellaneous* joined together with a pin. On the last page the third note read:

Possible topic for submission to Board of Grammarians, but how to phrase without incurring censure? Esp from his majesty Malus Mycom.

The Kevlerens and Technology, an unresolved tension.

Example, opposition last century to improved horse harness and rig, and carriage manufacture. Mercantile pressure. Compromise—carriages allowed outside of capital.

Example, opposition last century to introduction of

gonblack weapons. Military pressure. Compromise—state control of armaments.

Example, opposition last decade to construction of steam carriage between Omeralt and Somah. Mercantile pressure. Compromise—state control of carriage way.

Reasons: centralization of power, reduce technology's ability to rival Sefid as source of political and military power, reduce influence of technologists, incl physics, engineers. And grammarians?

Galys did not know how Kitayra could have held out any hope of seeing such a paper published. If the Board of Grammarians did not stamp it out, then the Kevlerens would, and the board with it.

It made sense, though, and the connection with General Third Prince Maddyn Kevleren was compelling. Forced into exile by his own family, without any ability with the Sefid, accomplished as a soldier. The evidence seemed to indicate someone who was determined to make a point of his difference within the family and at the same time find some other source of security. It was possible he even found being forced to accept command of the colony the perfect opportunity to exercise all the power and authority usually associated with a Kevleren who could Wield.

A sound from the city below distracted Galys from her thoughts and she looked out the window. Over the walls of the Citadel she could see little except the tops of buildings and the large statues that marked each corner of the Long Bridge. She gazed north towards Karhay, but it was too far away to make out any detail. There did seem to be a lot of boats in the Sayeff Channel, however; a lot more than usually demanded by the ferry traffic between the two islands. The sound, whatever it had been, did not repeat itself, and she went back to Kitayra's notes, but her chain of thoughts had been broken and she put down the papers. She glanced once more around the room, glad most of the packing was finished but at the same time wishing there was more to be done, more reasons to indulge her grief and self-pity.

Galys shook her head. Enough, she told herself curtly. There is enough work to be done for the colony to last ten years. Mourn all you want after that.

"Good morning, Wisdom of Malvara. The rains are coming." Through the window Poloma could see a horizon that was as black as night. The air was humid, too, as the rains driven south by the monsoons further north swept their way down the coast and brought water to thirsty fields, cleaning the air before summer started with its skies so intensely blue they were as hard as diamond. Kydan sometimes suffered badly from these storms, buffeted by terrible winds and lashing rains and occasionally floods that washed livestock and careless citizens into the sea, and although he knew the rains were important, Poloma liked it hot and dry; something he had missed terribly when he had been in exile in high, cold Omeralt across the Deepening Sea.

His mother, Sorkro, joined him at the window. Although she was blind, Poloma sometimes got the feeling she was observing things he would never see. "Is the council meeting today?"

"No, but I need to talk with Galys Valera."

Sorkro opened and closed her hands. "Talk, talk, talk. You should do more with her."

Poloma blushed. "Mama, that is not right."

"Psh. I am sorry her lover died so horribly, but she is free now and needs a companion. You are eligible—none more in Kydan. And she is a good woman. Strong. Smart.

Brave. Not so handsome, I hear from Hattie, but healthy and that will count for more when you—"

"Mama!" Poloma said, more sharply than he intended. "There is too much to do already without complicating matters."

Sorkro shrugged and, followed by Poloma, made her way to the dining room. Once it had held a long table for all the members of the Malvara family and their friends, but when Poloma and his mother sat down the empty chairs reminded him of all the family members murdered by the Rivald-backed Maira Sygni and his fellow pluto-crats. Now there was just a small round table for the two of them. As soon as they sat down, Hattie served them breakfast, smiling at Poloma in the wide, generous way she had done since she had been his nanny.

"Hattie agrees with me," Sorkro said.

Poloma was on the verge of asking about what, but re-membered his mother's earlier hints just in time. "Thank you, Hattie," he said firmly, and she returned to the kitchen.

"There's only us two left, Poloma," Sorkro said, her voice suddenly frail. "I don't want our family, a First Fam-ily, to die out. It would be like Maira Sygni defeating us after all."

Poloma froze, food halfway to his mouth. He had never once since his return thought of his family's trial in that light. His mother was right: if he died without children, the Malvara clan would be extinguished with no hope of res-urrection. The thought threatened to overwhelm him and he fought against it.

"There is no need to be so grim," he said without con-viction, and forced himself to eat.

The rest of the meal passed in silence, but later, when

Poloma was about to leave, his mother was waiting for him at the door. "I am coming with you," she said.

Immediately suspicious, he said, "I am going to the Citadel, Mother. It is a long walk and I have told you the rain is coming."

"It is a long walk, hot or cold, dry or wet," she said matter-of-factly. "Nevertheless, I am coming with you."

"Galys might not even be there. She may have gone to Karhay for some reason."

"Who said anything about Galys?" Sorkro asked innocently. "I am a citizen of Kydan and feel the need occasionally to walk its length."

Poloma knew from her tone he would not be able to dissuade her, so they set off together, taking their time, content to be silent in each other's company until they got to the Long Bridge. Poloma saw a crowd of people at the northern end of the Saddle and stopped.

"What is wrong?" Sorkro asked.

"I can see a large group of people in the Saddle."

"Can you see who they are?" Sorkro asked.

"Yes. They all seem to be colonists. There are many boats pulled up on the shore behind them." His skin felt cold. "I wonder what they could be doing?"

Very faintly he heard a noise coming from the crowd, a constant hum as if he was listening to a beehive in a tree hollow. Poloma watched them for a long moment before saying, "They are coming this way, and I don't think they are very happy."

For his life to have reached its current and unsatisfying state, Kysor Nevri believed he had missed many of the opportunities that come the way of most people, either because he had not recognised them at the time or because circumstance or another's machinations had deprived him. The result was that his personal life was often sabotaged by a dangerous mixture of simmering anger and refined self-pity that bordered on loathing, a mixture that could — given the right circumstances — provide him with the drive and energy to achieve much.

When Lannel Thorey had confessed to murdering one of the colonists, Kysor realised one of those rare opportunities in life had come charging his way, and he would not let it escape him. It had been a strange moment, standing cold-footed in the kitchen with the whimpering Lannel slouched on the stool, seeing the future laid out before him as clearly as if he was looking at a map.

He was standing outside the inn where just yesterday he had inspired so many of his fellow citizens. "Are they all gathered?" he asked Lannel.

The man, red-eyed, as pale and thin as straw, nodded weakly. "As many as we could find, Councilor." Lannel looked around him, feeling safer surrounded by so many Kydans whose sympathy was entirely on his side. But the councilor himself would not look around, as if his gaze was fixed on some distant point and he dare not lose sight of it.

"And the colonists?"

"As you predicted, they are gathering below the Long Bridge." His guilt made him bow his head. "And they are very angry."

Kysor nodded. The first step. It was harder to take than he had thought. For a horrifying moment he imagined the future slipping away from him because he did not have the courage to face it.

"Lead us," Lannel urged him. "Lead us and we will follow."

Yes, Kysor said to himself. Lead.

He moved out into the middle of the street and slowly walked towards the Long Bridge.

Gos led his favourite mare from the temporary stables on the north side of Karhay. She stamped and blew in the cool morning air. He stroked her nose, scratched her behind the ears and led her westwards along the island shore, stepping carefully around newly planted vegetable gardens. He saw two boats out already, the colonists on board throwing lines into the Kareem tributary; by the way they rested back along the thwarts, they did not look concerned about whether or not they caught anything. Away from the boats, a flying fish skipped along the water and disappeared again. Some birds near the mainland shore opposite were diving on a shoal of fish, picking out the slow ones and winging away north to feed chicks.

Once the main settlement was behind him, Gos mounted and set off at a fast walk, quickly easing into a trot and then a canter. The ground ahead sloped upwards slightly, but the mare did not seem to notice it, her pace not altering at all. The ground evened beneath them. Ahead the island sunk into the mangroves that bordered the western edge of all three of Kydan's islands. Gos kept a sharp lookout for crocodiles, which sometimes crawled out of the swamp and onto firmer land, especially to build their mound-like nests. When the swamp was a hundred paces away, Gos pulled the mare south and tapped her into a gallop, enjoying the sound of the horse's hoofs thrumming on the ground and the feel of the wind on his cheeks. Soon he knew the Kydan spring would warm to its summer and riding would become a chore for both horse and rider if the temperature and humidity got as high as Poloma said it always did, so he revelled in the sheer pleasure of it while he could.

So intent was he on the ride, it was not until he reached the other side of Karhay and let the mare slow to a walk that he paid any attention to the rest of the world. He saw right away there was a sizeable crowd of colonists gathering on the Saddle on the opposite shore. He wondered briefly if there was some event he had forgotten about, but he could not make out Galys or Poloma or Kadburn . . .

Wait, that could only be the big fellow, Arden, and sure enough, by his side was Heriot Fleetwood. Gos could not help feeling worried. It was not as if the colonists had no right to be on Herris instead of Karhay, but in such unexpected numbers, and with those two leading, he did not think any good would come of it. Even as he considered what to do next, he saw a crowd of Kydans appear at the top of the western ramp near the Long Bridge, about halfway across the width of the Saddle. It was too far away for him to make out any individuals or read their expressions, but the way everyone among both parties held themselves did not bode well.

He kicked the mare into a gallop again, this time heading diagonally across the island and straight for the temporary barracks. Ames Westaway was out on patrol with half the dragoons, but that still left nearly fifty troopers, and on the flat ground of the Saddle that would be enough to handle any violence, Gos was sure.

Galys reached the Long Bridge from the north about the same time Kysor Nevri and his band reached it from the south. In between she noticed Poloma Malvara and his mother; the two were arguing. She joined them hurriedly and saw that Sorkro was actually holding Poloma back while he was gently trying to disengage himself. Galys did not understand their words but got the general drift from Poloma's gesticulations towards the Kydans gathered at the top of the ramp and obviously preparing to go down.

"Your mother's right," she said loudly enough to be heard by both of them despite their argument.

Poloma stopped struggling with his mother, his face momentarily puzzled by Galys's miraculous ability to understand the Kydan language.

"It's too dangerous for you single-handedly to go up against Kysor Nevri."

Poloma shook his head in frustration and pointed north to the Saddle. "Look down there, Strategos Valera, and tell me again not to interfere."

Galys went to the edge of the bridge and looked over. She swore under her breath. How did all this happen? What the hell did Heriot and Arden think they were doing? She thought they had more sense than to start a riot or worse against the original Kydans. Without another word she headed back the way she had come, her first intention to alert the Hamilayan soldier in the Citadel, but when she reached the eastern ramp down to the Saddle she stopped suddenly. The situation was bad as it was, but to send in troops whose sympathies would obviously lie with the colonists could start a conflagration. Heriot and Arden would just have to see reason.

Galys ran down the ramp as quickly as safety allowed.

Galys's sudden departure distracted Sorkro long enough for Poloma to pull free without hurting her. He told her to stay where she was and quickly made towards the Kydans still gathering at the top of the western ramp. Some saw him coming and automatically backed away, still respectful of his moral authority as prefect and liberator, others stiffened with determination. Kysor Nevri saw him and smiled easily, which Poloma took as a poor sign.

"Citizens!" he cried out. "What are you doing here? Why do you gather so angrily?"

"You ask us that?" Kysor demanded, his voice filled with indignation. "That question is better put to your friends from overseas, surely?" His words were greeted by ragged cheers. "Why else would they come in such numbers if not to force concessions from us?"

"I don't know why they are here, my friends," Poloma said loudly, trying to address the whole crowd and not just Kysor. "Give me a chance to find out before anything happens that we will all regret!"

"The only ones who will regret this day are the interlopers," Kysor said, his voice rising.

"But we have friends among the newcomers," Poloma pleaded. "You all know that—"

"Aye, friends like the soldier-woman who even now hurries to join her compatriots!" Kysor shouted, pointing to Galys Valera running towards the group of colonists.

"She only goes to see what concerns them!" Poloma said angrily. "It is not right for you to invent motives for someone who has risked and sacrificed so much for this city!"

The crowd's temper seemed to calm a little with Poloma's words, and the prefect could see one or two among them nodding in agreement. Then, to his surprise, Kysor said, "The prefect speaks reason! Let us see what these Hamilayans are about before we take any action ourselves. Let it not be said that we were so ungrateful to our rescuers that we did not give them a chance to explain themselves."

Poloma felt both relieved and suspicious, and could not help suspect he was being outflanked by his opponent.

"Why don't we go down, then, and find out?" Kysor continued.

"Perhaps only one or two of us should go down," Poloma suggested.

"The Hamilayans are here in great number," Kysor said reasonably. "They cannot object to us meeting them on equal terms."

Poloma could not think of a ready reply to this, so reluctantly led the whole group down the ramp, keeping a slow and even pace. Kysor walked by his side, far too smug for Poloma's liking.

Heriot and Arden had their hands full with the colonists and did not need Galys to storm in demanding what it was they thought they were doing.

"Trying to stop a civil war from breaking out!" Heriot answered shortly, and resisted the temptation to add angrily, "And whose side will you be on if it happens?" The strategos did not deserve that, and it would not help calm the situation.

For the hundredth time that morning, Heriot thanked the Sefid that Arden was with her. Once he was in the lead none of the colonists wanted to move in front of him, so his steady presence acted like an anchor, slowing everything down. But Arden or no, the angry colonists wanted to know what had happened to Carder, and seeing Councilor Nevri with his supporters waiting for them at the top of the west ramp did not ease their suspicions. Heriot ground her teeth; for that matter, *she* wanted to know what had happened to the jovial old man who had worked with her on building the wall and who had been a keen supporter of the guild.

Heriot quickly explained to Galys the discovery of Carder's corpse, and that by the time they had heard about it word had already spread among the colonists. It was the most both she and Arden could do to convince them not to start pillaging the main city right away in revenge.

"It could just have been an accident!" Galys declared. "He could have fallen from the ramp!"

"That's what I argued," Heriot explained, then nodded towards the Kydans waiting above the Saddle. "But in that case, how did they know we'd be coming? How did they organize so fast?"

Galys looked back at Nevri and his supporters and saw Poloma talking to them. Galys did not know what the prefect could do, but Heriot's suspicions were correct. If Carder's death was an accident, there was no way Nevri could have known the colonists were coming until they had reached the city, at least not in time to organize such a large group of supporters. Even as she watched, Poloma started leading the group down the ramp. Some of the colonists were pointing and raising angry voices.

Arden turned to face them. "Enough!" he shouted. "They're not attacking us! Let's wait and see what's ado-ing before we start something we might not be able to finish."

"We could finish it if soldiers came down!" a voice cried out.

Heriot and Arden both instinctively glanced at Galys. The strategos shook her head. "The soldiers stay out of it. They have to remain neutral in this."

Heriot breathed through her nose, but she understood the logic behind Galys's decision. Still, she could not help feeling that with a few score Hamilayan soldiers by their side they would all feel considerably safer.

But we're here for answers, not a fight, she reminded herself.

"We're not calling on the soldiers," Heriot said firmly. "We're just here to find out what happened to Carder."

"Damn right," said a grim voice. "We'll call on the soldiers after we've found out what happened to him."

The whole group of colonists seemed to stiffen with that, as if it had been a call to attention, and Heriot could see in their faces that they all realised at that moment just what it might mean if fighting did break out between the colonists and original Kydans.

Poloma had stopped the other party about a hundred paces beyond the ramp. He and Kysor Nevri walked on forward alone. Heriot and Arden automatically started out to meet them halfway.

Galys put a hand on Arden's arm. "You should wait here," she said earnestly. "I'll go with Heriot."

Arden said nothing but glanced at Heriot, who nodded her approval. He merely grunted, but he stayed where he was.

"We'll need him to keep our side under control," Galys said under her breath to Heriot.

"*Our* side, eh?"

"Kydan's side," Galys said without missing a beat. "This city is the future for all of us, or none of us has a future."

Heriot could not help hoping Galys was wrong, for she was not sure the city held a future for her and her people. Not yet anyway. Before her thoughts led anywhere concrete they were standing opposite Poloma and Kysor.

"The Hamilayans will always be welcome on Herris," Kysor said easily. "But in such numbers only serves to make us nativists nervous."

Poloma translated hesitantly.

It was an insult hidden behind an apparently harmless,

even gracious concession; he was attempting to enforce the division between the two groups, even calling his own supporters "nativists", but Galys refused to accept it. "Kydans should never be nervous about other Kydans, no matter their number."

Poloma translated again, and Kysor accepted the riposte with what he must have thought was a disarming smile. "Or their intention?"

Poloma now looked enquiringly at Heriot. He, too, wanted to know what was going on.

"One of the colonists was found dead this morning." Heriot pointed to the fields at the bottom of the west ramp. "There. It looks as if he fell."

Poloma looked over his shoulder to where Heriot had pointed. Kysor did not, and that was not lost on either of the women.

Galys spoke first. "How did Councilor Nevri know the colonists were coming soon enough to gather his supporters in exactly the right spot?"

Poloma started translating but faltered when he understood what the question implied. At that moment Galys saw that Poloma knew, as she and Heriot knew, that Carder's death was not an accident.

Before anything more could be said there was a great cry from both camps. The four looked around, trying to see what the disturbance was, then Kysor, with a sound of self-righteous triumph, glared towards the island's northern shore. Galys groaned inside as she saw Gos Linsedd with half a company of dragoons quickly disembarking from barges with military efficiency.

"Poloma, Heriot, stop your groups from starting anything, no matter the provocation!" she told them, and ran for the shore as fast as she could, hoping to reach Gos before he could do anything rash. She knew he was a good commander of soldiers, but politically he could be as naive as a newborn baby. She knew even as she ran past the group of colonists, watched by a bemused Arden, that she would not reach the dragoons in time. Gos was already ordering them into two lines. She called out his name but he did not seem to hear. The half-troop broke into a trot and then a canter, moving determinedly towards·the ramp. She stopped and waved at Gos to go no further. He glanced at her, reproachfully, she thought. The stirrups and butts of the carbines jangled prettily as they streamed past her.

"Oh, Sefid curse all officers!" she swore, and turned on her heel to run all the way back again, hoping desperately that Gos would not order his troopers into action. As she returned the sun disappeared overhead, and she glanced up to see dark, roiling clouds pile overhead on their way south.

She reached Heriot and Arden, panting, with the cheers of the colonists in her ears. The group under Kysor Nevri was starting to retreat up the ramp in some disorder, and she saw Poloma trying to calm them down.

Then, against her expectations, the dragoons turned halfway between the groups, their two lines then turning away from each other so that they faced both north and south, against both colonists and nativists. It was not as bad as she had feared, but nor was it any better than it had been before Gos arrived: indeed, it was even more complicated. At least both sides could now see that the soldiers, under the command of officers who had once been Hamilayan, were determined to keep the peace for the sake of both sides.

"Here's a turnabout," Arden said gruffly.

The nativists by now had regained some order and gradually drifted down from the ramp. Again, Poloma and Kysor moved forwards, this time towards Gos, who had dismounted and was looking pretty smug about things. Galys sighed heavily, turned to Heriot and said, "Now we start all over again."

"I did the right thing," Gos said without any hint of apology as soon as he saw the expression on Galys's face.

"We were coping," she said.

"That's not how it looked from Karhay." He turned to Poloma and Kysor. "It is my duty to see that no harm comes to any citizen of Kydan."

Poloma translated and Kysor harrumphed.

But, Galys thought to herself, Kysor had no reply other than indignation. The same indignation I displayed, she silently admitted. Perhaps Gos had done the right thing after all, although she suspected he had won few friends among the nativists and probably a few enemies among the colonists.

"What now?" Heriot demanded. "There's still the matter of poor Carder, dead by someone's hand."

Gos blinked. "What's this about someone being dead?"

Galys quickly explained and Gos's smugness disappeared. He said, without hesitation, "This is a matter for the Assembly."

After Poloma had translated, Kysor opened his mouth to disagree, but Poloma talked over him, "As prefect of the council, I could not agree more." He repeated it in Kydan for Kysor's benefit. The councilor's face darkened, but he said nothing; instead, he turned on his heel and stomped back to the crowd below the ramp.

"I must make sure he does not try to lie to his followers," Poloma said quickly, and followed Kysor.

With some trepidation, Galys, Gos, Heriot and Arden

watched to see what happened next. They heard Kysor speak, without interruption from Poloma, standing beside him. Some of the nativists, although obviously displeased with the way things had gone, made their way back up the ramp. There were some cheers from the colonists, although they sounded more confused and desultory than victorious. Most of the nativists, however, stayed where they were. Poloma talked then, more animated than Galys had ever seen him before, but only a few more deserted the group. It was Kysor's turn to look smug now.

Poloma rejoined Galys and the others. "Those remaining are still concerned by the number of colonists here. They are afraid they might try some move against them."

"What could a handful of colonists do?" Heriot demanded. "And what about poor bloody Carder?"

"I've already said I'd bring that matter up at the Assembly. At this time I can deliver no more. But now you have to take the colonists back across to Karhay. Peacefully."

"We'll want someone from our guild present at the Assembly when the matter of Carder is discussed," Heriot said.

"We'll want someone on the Council itself," Arden added.

"I guarantee the first," Poloma said. "The second, so soon, is impossible."

"What am I supposed to tell my colonists?" Heriot asked. "One of our number is slain, almost certainly murdered—"

"You can't know that," Galys said quickly.

"—and a council that has shown us little favor so far is to decide on the right and wrong of it."

"The fact that Kysor and his people knew of Carder's death does not mean they were the cause of it," Galys insisted.

"*That* isn't the point," Heriot snapped. "It's what the colonists think and what the nativists think that matters, whatever the truth. If you want the colonists to feel a part of this city, then get them involved in the Assembly."

"In time," Poloma said, "that will happen."

"Not in time," Heriot said. "*Now.*"

"I will not make any promises I cannot keep, Heriot Fleetwood," Poloma said gravely.

Heriot turned on her heel and, followed by Arden, returned to the waiting group of colonists, many of whom were loudly demanding to know what was going on.

As Poloma, Galys and Gos stood together unhappily in the middle, a heavy thrumming came from the north. All three looked up and saw a gray veil sweeping across the channel between Herris and Karhay, potting the dark water, then flow across the Saddle towards them. Seconds later the rain was falling on all those assembled, big fat warm drops that stung their faces and slid down inside their tunics and down their boots. The rain fell so hard it sounded like they had been surrounded by a company of drummers.

The first to scatter were the nativists, scurrying back up the ramp to find shelter. Some of the colonists started to jeer, but their voices were largely drowned out by the storm and the fact that most of their compatriots had made a similar decision and were withdrawing to the boats.

"Thank Kydan and Frey," Poloma prayed under his breath.

Then he remembered his mother. He searched for her on the bridge and saw her frail white form buffeted by sheets of rain, drenching her to the skin.

12

QUENION first saw the ship during the twilight that breathed so briefly in the New Land. She had been standing in her favorite place, atop Sayenna's stone keep with its view of the whole town and its magnificent bay, when she caught the white flash on the western horizon. It could only have been the sun, still high enough that far west, reflecting off a sail. She peered into the growing dimness for many minutes until she was sure she could make out at least two masts, and possibly more. The ship would not make the bay before morning, and even if she underestimated its speed, its captain would almost certainly not try navigating his way into Sayenna in the dark. The town was a growing one, but not so large it could yet afford a lighthouse to ward off ships from the bay's rocky west head. Still, Quenion was certain it came from Rivald. Hamilay did not know the whereabouts of Sayenna (yet! she reminded herself), so any vessel from the west had to be from the republic. She wondered, briefly, if she should tell Numoya, but knew she must. After all, the ship would almost certainly be carrying word of her master's fate, either to endure as governor of this distant colony, or to return home in disgrace to share imprisonment with the rest of his family. He would need a night to prepare himself to receive the news as a Kevleren must.

Quenion waited until after Numoya had finished eating before telling him her news. If she had not known his mannerisms fairly well by then she might have missed the slight inclination of his head that meant the news had diverted him from whatever train of thought he had been following to that point.

"From the west? You're sure?"

"Yes, your Highness. At least two masts."

"So, a navy or merchant ship?"

"Either way," Quenion said, finishing the thought, "it brings tidings."

She did not know what to expect from Numoya, but not the calm indifference that seemed to settle on him. In a way she was angry with her master: it was not fair that she should endure the burden so heavily and he without any effort at all. But that is why he is a Kevleren, she reminded herself, and I am nothing.

When he had finished his dinner, she picked up the tray to take it to the kitchen. He held her by the wrist to stop her. "You must not worry about tomorrow," he said gently. "There is nothing either of us can do to change whatever news the morning tide will bring. Do not forget you are a Beloved."

Quenion blushed with happiness. In his way, Numoya was reminding her that she was loved, and regarded.

"I will never forget, your Highness," she said. He did not let go right away, and Quenion felt awkward bending over him like that, trying to keep the tray level. She saw him smile, something still as rare as a singing bird in a

Beferen winter, and the blush extended to her arms and throat.

That night, sleeping in her own cot at the end of his bed, she wondered if anything in the world could be as pure and white-hot as love.

Leader of a Thousand Velan Lymok had been at sea before, but never for such an extended period of time. It presented problems he had not foreseen, such as the difficulty of maintaining proper personal hygiene, and maintaining some kind of privacy among so many densely packed and unpleasant-smelling sailors. He had never got on with the navy, saw little reason for its traditions and haughty attitudes to landsmen such as himself. Being almost unbearably honest, he admitted to himself he enjoyed delivering snobbery but not receiving it, a vice which he had noticed was common amongst those who, like him, had worked or fought or studied their way up from relative obscurity to some kind of prominence. In Rivald, as in Hamilay, the army provided the quickest—if not safest—means of advancement, at least up to the bottom rung of higher society; once there, newcomers avidly adopted and fiercely maintained the privileges of rank. Snobbery and a love of tradition for tradition's sake were the symptoms of the social climber.

Although his progress up the ranks had been smooth, the cost had been high: wounded twice in border clashes with Hamilayan troops, and guilt from leaving behind the family and friends of his decidedly middle-class upbringing. Velan Lymok's problem was that he had always hated being outside the circle of the wealthy and powerful and had done everything he could to break in. Now, as a Leader of a Thousand and the newest member of the republic's

Safety Committee, he had discovered there were circles within circles. In a way he was more of an outsider than ever before. And now, to cap it all off, he was an outsider in a small, wood-bound universe that made no allowances at all for outsiders, and it was an experience he never wanted to endure again. Knowing that eventually he would have to if he ever returned to Beferen made him feel almost as glum as the black clouds that had seemed to pick them up soon after they left Rivald and had stayed with them for most of their voyage across the Deepening Sea. It had only been in the last few days that the sun had shone and the weather warmed; although this meant the smells on board markedly worsened, it also gave him a glimpse of what it was about life at sea that so entranced and captured others. Technically he was meant to stay on the quarterdeck whenever he went topside, the platform reserved for officers and officials, but the foredeck, really nothing more than a slightly raised extension to the main deck, allowed him to stand near the jib and look down at the dolphins playing in the ship's wake, and to receive the freshest winds untainted by the several bodies and two goats that inhabited the space between foredeck and quarterdeck. He found it easy to be hypnotized by the play of sunlight on the sea and the repeating but never precisely similar pattern of waves. When the wind got up the sea would swell and the waves get choppy and white, and spray would wash over the bow dousing him; he found it exhilarating in a way he could not explain, and for a moment—the briefest of moments—considered looking into exchanging the army for the navy.

But in the end he always roused himself from his foredeck reveries and realised he would never make a sailor. There was something fine about being a soldier with your feet on solid ground, surrounded by a topography that did not move with the whims of wind and current, and without risk of drowning every time a storm broke. He shivered whenever he thought of drowning. On his first night aboard, one of the lieutenants had enjoyed telling him the story of the frigate that had been built from too-green timber and over the years had simply rotted away. One day, in harbor, it was entire one moment, and the next without a keel and sinking so quickly not one of those on board got away with his life. Or her life, the lieutenant had added quickly, since the ship was in harbor and probably had as many women as rats between the decks. Captain Roward, wizened and reserved, growled his displeasure at this elaboration, although he had grunted well enough when it was just a cautionary tale, and the lieutenant shut up, but not before infesting Velan with a nightmare that he was sure would haunt him for the rest of his days. He had already woken on two occasions in a sweating fit, sure that his lungs were filled with water.

Towards the end of the previous day, Velan had heard that shore birds had been seen near the eastern horizon, their wings catching the sun's last rays. He had thought it the best news he had ever received, and the next morning he was on deck early, dressed in his finest uniform, looking eagerly eastwards for the first sign of Sayenna. He was surprised to see the town right in front of him as if some giant set had been fixed across the sea while he was asleep, sharp and white and strangely quiet under the light of a new day, and for a moment he could not believe it was real. Then, unexpectedly, he was afraid. He remembered he had come to deal with the last of the Rivald Kevlerens, and the first task at hand was to let Numoya know his family was dead: mother and father, every sibling, every connection with the old life, gone completely. He wondered for a moment how Numoya would take such news, and although the thought was not entirely incomprehensible to him, who had after all ignored his own family to the extent they may as well have never existed, who knew how a Kevleren might react? Who knew anything for sure about that terrible family?

Sailors bustled around the yards and deck, reefing in some sails, dropping others, taking every advantage of the wind to manouver carefully around the south head and into the bay.

For a strange moment Velan thought he was seeing Beferen in an earlier, happier age. Sayenna spread around its bay in a similar, if slightly more organized fashion, its houses built low and wide in the Rivald manner, but here everything was whitewashed and sunny and new and seemingly untouched by the moss that attached itself to the south side of every structure in Beferen. He assumed it was too warm here for moss to grow happily, and indeed he was beginning to feel the heat in his dress uniform, and an uncomfortable salty, sweaty dampness around his collar.

The town possessed only one major dock, with two smaller traders already attached to it, and since it ran to deep water his own vessel would tie to it instead of anchoring in the middle of the bay. He saw several people on the dock, most working cargo but one standing motionless and erect, as stiff as . . .

Velan blinked. Of course. As stiff as a Beloved.

She was tall and round, with long dark hair, and even from this distance he could sense her imperiousness, her easy connection with power and authority. He thought she was like him, which Velan realised was gross vanity on his part, and wondered if he would have made a good Axkevleren.

Only if I could have been a Beloved, he thought, and faintly regretted that he would never have the opportunity to find out.

The woman waited, unmoving, until the ship was tied, the gangplank lowered and Velan in the process of disembarking. She was drawn to him by their common nature, authority to authority. The dock workers quickly got out of her way.

"You will forgive us," were her first words, "but we do not extend to a carriage here. All that was lost in Kydan."

Too late, Velan tried to hide his surprise. She matched his expression, realizing he had not known, and for a moment they shared the experience of the axis of the world shifting under their feet.

"We have lost Kydan?" was all Velan could manage at first.

"We sent reports . . ." the woman started to say. "Obviously the Hamilayans have been intercepting our ships.

"And the Safety Committee?" she asked, changing the subject. "All is well in Beferen?"

"Your master is alive?" Velan asked tightly.

"Yes. Injured, but recovering."

Velan let out a long breath. "Then they did not reach this far," he said. "Of course, you being alive was evidence."

Velan saw that Quenion did not know what he was referring to, but could see in her expression that she had some inkling of impending tragedy. He wondered if she and Numoya were ready for his news.

Neither had moved since Velan reached the bottom of the gangplank, although several sailors were now queuing behind the officer. One of them cleared his throat and Velan absently moved aside.

"I have a feeling that although we are discussing the same subject," the woman said, "we are actually speaking at cross-purposes. We should start at the beginning."

"Agreed."

"My name is Quenion Axkevleren. I am Beloved to Numoya Kevleren, Governor of the Republic of Rivald's colonies in the New Land." She swallowed. "Colony in the New Land."

"And I am Leader of a Thousand Velan Lymok, member of the Safety Committee, and come to deliver felicitations and instructions to your master."

Quenion nodded to the modest-looking keep perched on the end of the south head. "It is a little steep, but a pleasant walk." She looked around the bay. "Especially on a day like this."

"I find it uncommonly warm," Velan said.

"This is nothing. Wait until summer proper starts. It gets hot enough to swim in the sea."

Velan looked horrified at the idea but said nothing. As they moved into the town he could not help noticing that people seemed whole and healthy and set about their tasks with an enthusiasm he had not seen in Beferen for many months. The clean white buildings and warm air made him feel light-hearted, as if his responsibilities were frivolous rather than serious. He reminded himself he was about to meet a Kevleren; more, he, a representative of a committee that had overthrown his family, was coming to beg for help from this Kevleren. He should be experiencing some anxiety, or at least trepidation.

Velan eagerly smelled the clean air and caught at the back of his throat the scent of strange vegetation and, alluringly, a hint of unknown spices from some kitchen they passed.

The ground rose gently from the shore until they reached the road that led to the keep, when it became noticeably steeper. Lack of exercise for several tendays—and a natural inclination to avoid it whenever possible anyway—made the last few hundred paces something of a chore for Velan, and when they finally reached the shade of the main gate he stopped to catch his breath, pretending merely to admire the view for a moment. In fact, the view was startling. The brown foreshore was met by the turquoise waters of Sayenna's bay, waters that turned into an intense blue as they deepened further out to sea. Inland, surrounding the colony, were a series of low hills and shallow valleys the colour of ancient lichen, and the occasional wood of tall, thin-leafed trees carrying explosions of red flowers. Up here, away from the shelter of the bay, he could feel a light breeze, and again the tingling, tantalizing smells of an unknown land.

Velan had been afraid he would not like Sayenna, so far away from the centre of his own civilization. But at that moment he felt a connection form between him and the New Land, and the tether to his old life start to fray.

Croft Harker was surprised when told a message had arrived for him from Rivald's ambassador to Hamilay. The committee had received nothing from him for so long he knew that either Avenel Kendy had died, had betrayed Rivald, or his messages were being intercepted. Under normal circumstances he would have expected some word to get back from Siness Ardra, either by pigeon or one of his spy couriers, but since the ambassador's attaché had once been a Beloved, Croft Harker assumed he had suffered the fate of all other Beloveds.

Except, he thought curiously, Chierma in Hamewald.

As he unrolled the message from Kendy, Harker pondered again on the fact that Chierma had survived the great dying. He read the message, not knowing what to expect, and laughed despite himself.

So this is how the invasion starts, Harker thought. With an invitation from the Safety Committee. Kendy agreed, too, judging by his laconic comments at the end of the message; but as the ambassador pointed out, Lerena might just be genuine, in which case to refuse her might provoke the invasion Rivald wanted to avoid.

"Oh, how low we've sunk," Harker said to his empty office, "and how much further yet we can go."

His mind wandered to Leader of a Thousand Velan Lymok, and what he knew was a desperate gamble. He almost hoped Numoya Kevleren rejected the plea; to end his days under the heel of any Kevleren was a bitter thought, but to end it under the reign of a reinstated Rivald Kevleren would take irony to an insulting level. But he was president of Rivald's Safety Committee, and he took that responsibility with utmost seriousness. Whatever he could do to secure the safety of the nation, he would do, even if it meant the Republic of Rivald becoming a kingdom again.

Ridiculously, Velan Lymok did not know which way to look. It was not as if Numoya Kevleren would have known Velan was staring at him, but good manners and an almost atavistic certainty that the Kevleren could read his mind made him think constantly about where to set his gaze. At first he tried staring at a point about a hand's width above

Numoya's right shoulder, and then down at his own feet, and then at Quenion, but somehow he always ended up fixed on those terrible scars and the lacerated pits where the eyes used to be. Numoya looked as if his face had actually melted, something Velan did not think was possible. But where the Sefid was concerned, surely anything was possible, even this.

The three of them had deduced very early in their conversation that what had happened to Numoya was related in some way to what had happened to his family back in Beferen, but obviously not a result of the same Wielding, since Numoya was still alive. Velan suggested the distance between Omeralt, where the Safety Committee believed the Wielding had originated, and Kydan would explain Numoya's escape, but the Kevleren said he was sure other factors were at play, although he did not elaborate. Velan assumed that the fact that Quenion was still alive had something to do with it, but did not say as much; as soon as he was in the room with Numoya and Quenion he felt there was something odd between them, a history he was curious about but would not pry into. For one thing, Velan was not yet sure of Numoya's sanity, but he did not know if his doubts stemmed from the Kevleren's appearance or simply the bitterness in his voice when he spoke of the events which had left him in this pitiable condition and destroyed the entire branch of his family.

The first question Numoya asked after being told of the death of his family was, "Not one survived?"

Velan shook his head, and then said hurriedly as the thought occurred to him, "Except your distant relations in the empire . . ."

Velan realised too late that the knowledge would bring this Kevleren little consolation.

"All my immediate family?" Numoya said bitterly. "They were all in the palace?"

Velan swallowed. "As far as I know."

Then Numoya asked the question Velan had been dreading.

"Leader of a Thousand, why are you here, exactly? I am sure the Safety Committee did not send you across the Deepening Sea to deliver the news of my family's extinction. There is something else."

Velan, unable to meet the terrible gaze of blind Numoya, looked instead at Quenion, but he discovered that her attention was no easier to bear. He should not have expected it to be; after all, she was Numoya's Beloved, his representative in every thought and belief and feeling.

"Rivald needs you," Velan began. "The Safety Committee has reason to believe Hamilay will invade the republic before another year is out. We are defenceless against them now that . . ."

Velan's voice petered out, not because he was reluctant to admit that without the Kevlerens the republic was nothing but a sham—something he had been steeling himself to say since leaving Beferen all those tendays before—but because Numoya had started laughing: full belly laughs, bordering on the manic.

Velan, bewildered, looked to Quenion for an explanation, but she seemed as surprised as he. There was nothing to do but wait until Numoya calmed down, which he did only after some time.

"This is a joke," he said eventually, wheezing the words.

"I can assure you, your Highness—"

"Your Majesty," Numoya said sharply, all hint of humor

gone. The change in tone was dramatic, and Velan felt a stab of fear.

"I beg your pardon?"

"You don't think for a moment, do you, that I would return to Rivald to *serve* the Safety Committee?"

Velan's breath caught in his throat. He *had* assumed that, but as soon as Numoya had posed the question he understood the full implications of his mission, and at the same time understood that President Croft Harker had known what the cost inevitably would be. That was why the president had said Velan was to agree to *any* demand. He did not think anyone in the history of Rivald had been as callow as he had just proven to be, and felt a mixture of burning shame and resentful anger.

"If I decided to return to Rivald, it would be as king, with all the power and authority pertaining to that title, the same that my poor aunt, Queen Sarra, enjoyed before she was murdered."

"I don't know that the Safety Committee would agree—"

"Of course they would agree," Numoya interrupted, "otherwise they would not have sent you to ask. And since all the traitor Beloveds on the Safety Committee have been killed, I will ask very few executions in retribution for the revolution."

"Naturally," Velan said weakly, still coming to terms with what Numoya's acceptance of the committee's offer would mean. That the republic, so young, could be snuffed out so easily, was something he had never imagined. For a short while he, like the other military members of the coup against the Kevlerens, had actually believed they had won, that they had found a way to prevail against the Sefid. They actually believed that Rivald had been set free. Now it was a choice between reinstating the native Kevleren dynasty, represented by its sole survivor, or accepting rule by a foreign Kevleren dynasty. Something as simple and idealistic as patriotism had to give way to something as complex and repulsive as political pragmatism.

What shocked Velan most of all was that freedom had been nothing more than an illusion. He felt like he had just woken up from a lovely dream to discover he was only a bit player in one of the staged dramas of which the Kevlerens were so fond.

"But, of course, it all depends on whether or not I decide to return at all," Numoya said almost langorously, as if the choice was nothing more important than what to have for dinner.

"You would not desert Rivald!" Velan declared.

Numoya's voice became harsh. "Rivald deserted me."

There seemed little else to say at that point, and Quenion took Velan to his room in the keep. It was a sunlit space, small but tidy, with a comfortable-looking cot and a desk and chair.

"I will leave you here," Quenion told him. "I am sure you have much to write in your report to the Safety Committee. I will come for you when dinner is ready."

Before she could go, Velan grabbed her arm. She pulled away automatically and he apologized. "I need to ask you . . ." He licked his lips. "I have never had to deal with a Beloved before." He laughed nervously.

"Ask your question," Quenion said flatly.

"How serious is your master about not returning to Rivald?"

Quenion smiled thinly. She nodded to the room's single window and the view it showed over the bay and the sea beyond, with the sunlight playing on the waves and the seagulls dipping and circling on ocean thermals. A light breeze rippled the water.

"Given this, and the opportunity the New Land offers, would you want to return to Beferen?" she asked in turn, then shrugged and added, "He is a Kevleren. Even a Beloved would not dare predict which way a Kevleren will turn."

After reading the letter from President Croft Harker, delivered by rider so late at night he had to be woken to receive it, Chierma stood in his office in his nightshirt, alone and cold and betrayed.

So the Safety Committee was going to beg for a Kevleren. The world had gone topsy-turvy once again, and all the bloodshed and bitterness and hatred that had accompanied the overthrow of Queen Sarra and her brood had been for nothing.

Chierma's whole mind focused on the three paragraphs of the letter, going over them repeatedly, trying to find some word or phrase he might have missed that gave lie to the message. He did not see the blue halo shine around the doorknob and the poker by the fire, and at first he thought Englay's voice was nothing but a memory.

"It is all too late," she repeated, and this time he glanced up at her, almost disinterested. "My family is a fact of nature, like clouds in the sky and fish in the sea and trees in the forest. We cannot be extinguished, not entirely, and we grow back."

"Like moss," he said in a dead voice.

Englay laughed lightly. It sounded like falling water. "Like moss on a Beferen wall."

He frowned in sudden thought and asked, "Tell me, my lady, which came first, the Sefid or the Kevlerens?"

"Do you know, I am not quite sure. Does it matter?"

"I am tempted to ask in turn, 'Does anything matter any more?' But I won't. I need to believe in something. Even a traitorous Beloved, love-lost, alone, needs to believe in *something*."

"This is your bitter loyalty speaking," Englay observed, but not unkindly, and Chierma held onto that.

"My bitter loyalty. I still have it, do you think?"

"Oh, yes. But you must decide where it belongs."

"Many of the communities between here and Kydan are inclined towards us," Quenion told Numoya. "We offer competition with Kydan."

"Where did you get this information?"

"Our friends from Orin of the Two Rivers."

"Adulla and Velopay? Our friends as long as we supply them with firegons."

"At least we have something they want."

The two were speaking at the top of the tower so no one might overhear them. Numoya liked to feel the breeze on his face, but imagination was a powerful thing and he could not help feeling vertigo despite his blindness, so Quenion had to hold one of his hands.

"We don't have enough firegons to go around. We've barely enough to arm the garrison here."

"Enough for the most important chieftains and their biggest supporters, perhaps?"

Numoya nodded. "Perhaps. We should look into the possibility of making more ourselves."

"I will investigate," Quenion said.

"What else have you been able to find out?"

"The area between here and Kydan is densely popu-lated, considering there are no other cities as such. There are some cities further north of Kydan, but not as advanced, nor as developed in trade. The main trade lanes seem to be between the agricultural hinterland and the mountains behind, all the way down to Kydan, using the Frey River for transport. Once Sayenna was established, some of the trade inevitably came our way."

"Necessitating Kydan to open up trade with Hamilay to make up for the shortfall."

"And in turn necessitating our taking of Kydan to stop Hamilay getting a foothold in the New Land."

"Which policy demonstrably failed," Numoya grunted, touching his scars. "And the allegiance of the population between Orin and Kydan?"

"To the highest bidder. They will happily attach themselves to any cause which promises profit and gives them a break from farming, particularly in summer before harvest. Once harvest starts, their loyalty will become as short as their patience."

"Then we must tempt and succor them, Beloved," Numoya said. "We will need their loyalty before all this is over. And when it is all done and Kydan is ours, they will find themselves caught between two cities under one rule and their loyalty will become a given."

There was something in her master's tone which made her think he had made his decision about the future. She hesitated to ask, but her curiosity overcame her reluctance. "Then you do not intend to return to Rivald, your Highness?"

Numoya did not answer for a long while, and when he did his voice was low and filled with pain. "I can do nothing for Rivald. By myself I could never stand up to Lerena and the other Hamilayan Kevlerens. I think President Croft Harker of the Safety Committee is aware of this, but he

must grasp any phantom in his efforts to save the kingdom.
Or, indeed, the republic.

"No, Quenion, my future—" he grasped her hand a little tighter "—our future—is here in the New Land. Together, we will forge a new kingdom, with Sayenna as its
capital and Kydan its first conquest."

Quenion caught her breath and her heart swelled inside
her. *Our future*, he had said, and she could almost see it
then, stretching out before them.

Englay had given Chierma the key to solving his little
military problem. It had to do with loyalty and where it
should lie. He was a Beloved, and always would be, despite trying desperately to be something more, something
different. Something loved. The only chance he had for
that was to attach himself once more to a Kevleren.

That was the crux of the matter. The only honorable
source of Kevlerens these days was in Hamilay, especially
since Rivald itself had fallen to begging ousted princes for
salvation. He, who had betrayed his first mistress, had in
turn been betrayed by his new mistress, the republic for
which he had sacrificed so much to bring about.

Chierma looked once again at the paper that listed those
military units under his command as governor of the
Hamewald province. Too few to defend the border effectively. So why even try?

He smiled to himself, picked up his pen and made some
notations.

13

GOS and his dragoons were left alone with possession of the Saddle. In the downpour they were starting to feel like drowned mice. The fields around them were becoming vast stretches of mud, and the rain gave no indication of letting up.

Gos ordered most of his troopers to return to barracks, but decided he should stay behind with a small escort in the unlikely case some of the nativists or colonists changed their mind and returned for a confrontation.

It was very wet and cold, and increasingly dark. Gos wrapped his cloak tightly around himself and tried to hide under his helmet. Most of the time he liked being a soldier. Sometimes he did not.

For most of the journey back to Karhay, Heriot said nothing; the rain was so heavy that any conversation was out of the question. She sat with Arden on a mid-thwart of their boat, neither allowed to row: Heriot was too small and Arden so strong he would pull the other rowers off their beat and the boat would spin in circles mid-channel.

When they reached the shore, she pulled Arden aside

under the shelter of a temporary grain store. Their feet kicked up husks of wheat.

"Our side controls the Citadel?" she asked urgently.

Arden grunted. "Well, Galys Valera, Gos Linsedd, Kadburn Axkevleren and the soldiers control it, if that's our side."

"Our side, anyway, before the side of that councilor who led the nativists."

"Kysor Nevri, I heard him called. What are you thinking?"

"Being cautious, that's all. We weren't prepared for what happened this morning."

"No one expected anything to happen so soon. Certainly not before word on whether or not the Rivald were returning for a second run."

"But feelings are running high, on both sides of the channel. We can't depend on violence not breaking out next time. We have to stay in control of this or we could lose everything. The strategos and the others have to be on both sides, and that won't do us any good."

Arden was silent for a moment. "Are you suggesting—?"

"I'm not suggesting anything," Heriot said fiercely. "Just be ready."

When Poloma reached his mother and put his hand on hers, she jumped a little with fright, and he realised guiltily that she could not hear a thing in the rain. She was soaked through, and she must have spent a terrifying time standing alone on top of the Long Bridge, straining to hear any sound that would let her know her son—her last remaining child—was safe. He wished he had been better prepared for the rain. He put his arm around her and guided her off the bridge, there to be met by Galys.

"I will help you," the strategos said, and also put an arm around Sorkro. Poloma felt her hand touch his and was surprised by the electric thrill it gave him. His mother snuggled into them and made a sound that was suspiciously like a sigh.

"We will find an inn to shelter in," Poloma said.

"Would the Citadel be closer?" Galys asked.

"Take me home," Sorkro said strongly. Galys looked questioningly at Poloma and he translated for her.

"Wisdom of Malvara, you are already far too wet. Let us find shelter—"

"Do what your mother tells you to do," Sorkro said.

They were near the end of the main road when the hailstones started falling. At first it was only small pinheads that stung the skin like tiny biting insects, but then larger stones fell, cracking on the ground and on the roofs. Poloma grunted in pain when one smacked into the back of his skull. Worried for Sorkro, he and Galys guided her under the canvas awning of a stall selling sunhats. The owner looked miserably at them, and Poloma smiled sympathetically in return. The awning started to bow under the weight of hail, but it held, and for the next while all they could do was shiver together and listen to the sound of stones ricocheting off tile and beam and occasionally the head of someone running by.

When the hail eased the air seemed clearer, easier to breathe. Poloma poked his head out from underneath the awning and studied the sky. The cloud cover had thinned, but obviously more rain was coming from the north. He could see long gray sheets descending across the plains to the north of the Frey River.

"Mother, we must go now. We are not far from home."

"I will manage," she said, and without waiting for her

assistants to guide her took the first step back onto the street.

When they finally reached the Malvara estate, Hattie made a fuss of the old woman and stared reprovingly at Poloma for keeping her out. Poloma could only shrug and ask servants to ready hot baths for Galys and himself. Galys refused, saying she had to return to the Citadel.

"Don't be silly," Poloma said brusquely. "You're dripping. Besides, there are things we need to discuss."

Galys looked down and saw the small lake she was creating around her feet. She shivered involuntarily.

"And my people will dry your clothes for you," Poloma added, more solicitously.

Galys nodded her surrender, and Poloma left to visit his mother.

Lannel Thorey had not meant to kill the colonist, but he felt no shame in the action. Not any more. Not since Kysor Nevri had made things clear for him. Colonists were the enemy. They had to go, either of their own accord or . . .

Or of *our* accord, he told himself. He found it hard to believe he had experienced any doubt and self-hate at all after the death. He had felt guilt when the guilt properly belonged to those who had brought the foreigners to his soil, like the Kevleren prince—dead, thank Kydan and Frey!—and his Beloved and the blonde strategos and the commander of the dreadful dragoons. And Poloma Malvara. Most of all, Prefect Poloma Malvara.

It was a problem, this good man, this brave prefect, being the instrument of a great wrong. There seemed no cause for it, no explanation, but Lannel's mind gnawed on the problem the way a rat gnawed on canvas to get to seed.

Simon Brown

Nothing would stop him. In a strange way he felt his life depended on it, that the life of Kydan itself depended on it.

Barely sheltered from the rain under the canopy of a small copse of trees on the outskirts of the Malvara estate, Lannel's mind worried and dug, and absently registered the arrival of the prefect, the strategos and an old woman between them he assumed was Sorkro Malvara.

The rain eased for a while and then built up again, the clouds darkening the land all around so that shadows disappeared altogether. The trees offered increasingly less protection, but Lannel did not pay any heed, did not notice his clothes sticking to him like a second skin. He felt no cold.

And then he felt no doubt. The solution he had been seeking lay hard and steely in Lannel's brain, like a polished blade.

Galys's clothes had been dried and pressed while she bathed, and she stood in them a little self-consciously, waiting in the entrance hall for Poloma. She was not sure what it was she had to be self-conscious about, but more than ever she felt like an interloper, or someone come to the lord of the manor to plead a case. A suitor, came the word, unexpectedly, and she could not help reddening, as much in surprise as embarrassment. She had never thought of Poloma in that way before; but she was a single woman in the house of a single man, and despite the battles they had fought together, despite their common aim in finding a future for the city that involved both native and colonist, she was aware that another dimension in their relationship may have opened up.

A potential dimension, she warned herself, still not clear in her own mind whether or not it was something she wanted. Since the death of Kitayra the idea of companion-ship—physical or otherwise—had not entered her mind. She had been too busy working, grieving, trying to forget, to consider her own future in any personal way.

"I thought the threat of Sayenna would keep them at bay," Poloma said.

He seemed to appear in front of her suddenly. He was dressed in less formal clothes, and he smelled good, she thought.

"Kysor Nevri's hand was pushed, I suspect," Galys said.

"It was an opportunity he could have refused," Poloma replied evenly.

Galys pursed her lips. "I'm assuming, then, that you agree with me that he had no hand in the death of the colonist called Carder."

"I have no reason to think the councilor is a murderer. However, he knows who did it. Furthermore, and to his severe discredit, he decided to take advantage of the situation."

"Heriot Fleetwood is right, you know."

"About membership on the council for some of the colonists?"

Galys nodded. "And the sooner the better."

"If I nominated you the council would accept it."

He said it without emphasis, his gaze steady, but Galys had the strange idea it was a proposition of sorts, and not a political one.

This is all wrong, she thought, feeling uncomfortable. "And why not Gos? Or even Kadburn?"

"Gos is a soldier. A soldier, what's more, from Hamilay. Allowing him to sit as a member in the Assembly would be tantamount to surrender in the eyes of most nativists."

"And Kadburn is a Beloved," Galys said, providing her own objection.

"Exactly. That leaves you."

"And that would be seen as a cheat's way out by the colonists, since they do not regard me as one of their own. Why not Heriot Fleetwood herself?"

"Possibly. But not the big fellow. Arden. It would be like having a bear sitting at the table."

"Heriot, then," Galys persisted.

Poloma sighed heavily. "I will be honest with you, Galys Valera. I am afraid that if I force the issue with the council at this time I will lose the motion, and that may prejudice any future possibility of the colonists getting seats in the Assembly. It may also lead to me being forced out of the prefecture."

Galys shook her head, more in frustration than in denial of Poloma's words. If only he could be more daring, she told herself. If only he could show a little more courage.

She swallowed. She had no right to question the man's courage. Not after what he had been through.

"Are you all right?" Poloma asked.

A long breath rattled out of her. "I have to go back to the Citadel."

Poloma seemed disappointed. He nodded slowly. "Of course. You have your duties and I've kept you from them."

"It's not—" she started to say, but did not finish. She did not know how to say what she was thinking without hurting him. Instead, she made for the main door.

When the hailstorm hit, Gos sent his cadre of troopers against the Saddle's west wall. It did not stop all the hailstones from hitting them or their horses, but it was manageable: none of the dragoons was hurt seriously and the mounts were too well trained to panic. When the rain replaced the hail, he ordered the troopers back to Karhay. He wanted to join them but thought it more important to discuss with Galys what had happened on the Saddle. He was surprised the colonists and nativists had come so close to violence, and wondered if he should instead have been expecting it. If only the prince had not died, then maybe the future would be a lot clearer for all of them. He wished . . .

Stop it, Gos, he told himself. Just get through the current mess and get ready for the next one. That was a soldier's job.

He made his way up the east ramp and went to the Citadel. One of the engineers on guard duty told him that the strategos had left more than an hour before and was not yet returned. Gos grunted in frustration and turned his horse to go back the way he had come. If anything, the rain seemed even heavier than before.

He stopped, dismounted and handed the reins of his mount to the guard. "See to the horse. I'll wait inside for her return."

As Galys was about to open the door, Poloma said, "I find myself in a perpetual state of worry."

"About what in particular?" she asked.

Poloma had not intended to say anything and was surprised when the words came out of his mouth. "Umm." He swallowed, glanced shyly at his feet, tried to think of something else to say. Anything.

"Everything," he said weakly. His heart yammered in his chest. Why was he doing this?

Galys stopped and watched him, waiting for him to go on.

"The council, the division between the old Kydans and the new, what is happening in the empire, the threat from Sayenna, wherever it is."

"I like that," Galys said.

Poloma frowned, wondering what it was in his litany of troubles that had appealed to her.

"New Kydans and old Kydans," she said. "The only distinction it makes between us is how long we've been here, not anyone's right to be here."

He smiled, a kind of lopsided, sickly thing, grateful to have something onto which he could latch a real conversation. He understood then, with some amazement, that he wanted Galys to stay.

But she's not even pretty, he heard a part of himself say. Not like Kitayra had been, or what Heriot Fleetwood was like in a girlish way.

Yes, another part said, but she is smart, she is brave, she is worth . . .

His thoughts trailed off. Worth what from him?

"It is a question of making both sides understand that," he offered. "We are like two sides of the same coin, forever united but with different faces."

As he was saying it the metaphor seemed fine to him, but hearing the words in his own ears he wished he had not tried to explain it.

Galys smiled, and to Poloma it seemed slightly indulgent, as if she was staying only to make him feel better and not from any real desire to join in the conversation. "Two sides of the same coin," she said, giving the metaphor its proper length.

Poloma had decided to try one more time for a proper engagement, when Hattie appeared and cleared her throat.

"Sir, you should come with me," she said softly and earnestly.

"Hattie?"

"It is important or I would not disturb you."

Although she could not speak Kydan, Galys politely looked away, and Poloma was suddenly acutely aware of her presence in a way he had not been before. She was an outsider, a foreigner, and with dismay he wondered why he was suddenly feeling this way. He felt like a traitor to his own cause. "I am sorry," he said to her. "Family business."

"I understand," Galys said, and left. When the door was closed behind her he turned back to Hattie, and saw that she was on the verge of crying.

"By Kydan and Frey, my sweet Hattie, what is wrong?"

"It is your mother, little Poloma, she is very ill."

Lannel recognised the blonde strategos as she left. Galys Valera, he remembered. A fierce fighter. A strong champion for the colonists. Her death would damage their cause, maybe fatally. The thought made up his mind and he started following her.

How to do this? he thought to himself. He had a long knife under his tunic, the same one he had brought to the gathering earlier in the day. That would do the trick. Slip the blade cleanly between her ribs, from behind. It would be like stabbing a piece of fruit. Or use the sharp edge to cut her throat, see her paper-white neck spread bloody red, blossom like a flower in spring.

Unsurprisingly there were very few of his fellow Kydans on the street, but they kept their heads down to avoid the drenching rain and he weaved between them to keep the strategos in sight. Merchants. A priest. People with baskets filled with food. A young couple talking earnestly about love.

Or one quick jab through the eye, straight into the brain. That way it would be quick. She would see the fine point, flash, a spasm of pain so intense it would almost be beautiful, then consciousness would shrink and disappear and . . .

. . . Lannel found himself wondering what death would be like. When he died, would he meet his father again? Or his mother, whom he never knew because she died when he was minutes old? Would his mother even recognize him, grown tall and angry and devoted to Kydan, even unto death?

Would he meet the colonist he had already killed?

Or nothing. Perhaps death was nothing at all except night without end, a world without a horizon. Winter without summer.

Despite the rain, Lannel thought the streets were very colorful now that spring was moving into summer. All the trees were fully dressed, like women at a marriage ceremony. Ivory and blue flowers for the insects, ones as yellow and radiant as the sun or the crimson of spilled wine for the birds. When it was not raining, birds sang from every branch. At night the crickets were so loud it was as if the air itself vibrated in sympathy. He looked forward to summer proper. He liked the skin-balming warmth, the heavy storms just like this one that rumbled down the coast and spread dark shadows inland.

Lannel shook his head to stop dreaming. He followed Galys Valera's blonde head. He assumed she was heading for the ramp. Perhaps the act could be done there, as it had been last time.

But then it had been an accident, he told himself. And

at night. And now the number of Kydans on the street seemed to be many despite the rain. It was not even dark yet. The foreigner would get to Karhay long before sunset. Should he do it in daylight? Did it matter if others saw him? Would they sympathize with Lannel and his cause? Or with her, with a slain foreigner? At that moment he looked up and saw her looking in his direction. Seeing him?

Lannel hesitated. The strategos had turned again and was drawing well ahead. Not *should* he do it, he realized. But could he? Could he slay her in daylight? Did he have the courage? Before it had been an accident, this time it would be . . .

He stopped that train of thought, and physically stopped himself as well.

He turned around with a vague idea of going back to the prefect's estate.

Now *he* was a different case, Lannel thought. Poloma Malvara had brought the foreigners to Kydan. He had betrayed his own city: under the pretence of freeing Kydan from foreign domination, he had placed it even more firmly under the heel of strangers. Betrayer. Traitor.

Lannel grunted to himself and quickly retraced his steps. Yes, he knew he could finish the prefect. He *would* finish him. He would kill Poloma Malvara.

Sorkro was sitting on the edge of her bed, pale and shaken.

"Mama?" Poloma knelt on the floor so his head was at her height. He took her hands in his. "Hattie said—"

"Oh, Hattie, what does she know," Sorkro said dismissively. Hattie, hanging at the doorway to Sorkro's room, rolled her eyes. "I was tired, that's all. It's been a long day."

"She said you passed out," Poloma said accusingly, obviously not doubting Hattie's word at all.

"Don't use that tone of voice with me. Keep it for the council. Now, help me to my feet. Has our guest gone?"

Poloma helped her stand up. She seemed unsteady at first, but she made him let go and she stood without falling. "Yes, Mama, she is gone."

"Well, I hope my turn didn't chase her away." Sorkro frowned slightly.

"No, Mama, you didn't chase her away. I don't think we had much to talk about, really."

Still frowning, she said, "I think she is a good woman."

"How are you? I'll get a physic, if you like. I'll send Hattie."

Sorkro shook her head, but absently, as if she was listening to a voice that was far away. "No. That will do no good. Help me sit down again. I'm afraid I can't make my knees work." Poloma, fighting a tide of nauseous fear that filled his stomach, took his mother's elbows in his hands and eased her down to the bed. "Isn't that strange? They wouldn't do what I told them." She clasped his hand for a moment and smiled quickly. "Like you won't do what I tell you."

"I'm prefect of all of Kydan, Mama. No one tells me what to do. Not even you."

"You can let go of my elbows. Bending over like that is bad for your back. You are always older than you think, did you know that? I am thirsty. Get me some water. Or wine. Wine would be nice."

He turned to ask Hattie to get some wine, when Sorkro

gently slapped his hand. "No, you go. I want to talk to Hattie."

Poloma did not want to go. He was overwhelmed by the need to stay by her side, but he nodded and let Hattie take his place. When he was in the kitchen he heard the main door open.

"Galys?"

No answer. One of the servants, he thought, although they rarely used the main door. He found a half-bottle of wine. He took it and a cup—Sorkro's favourite, with raised figures dancing around it—and had turned to go back to his mother's side when he saw a man blocking his way. For a moment Poloma assumed it was one of the servants, and wondered why he was carrying a knife around inside the house. Then Poloma realised the man was a stranger, and his gut flip-flopped.

"You are a traitor, Prefect Poloma Malvara," the man said. He was tall and gangly with a boyish face, and his deep voice had a haunted quality.

Poloma squinted. In fact, the intruder was not a total stranger. He had seen him before; indeed, only that morning, with Kysor Nevri.

"You're one of the nativists," Poloma said, more curious than afraid. "What are you doing here?"

"Traitor," the man said again, and took a step forwards, the knife held out in front of him.

Poloma noted in a detached way how his mind made everything go slowly, as if time was stretching out, and remembered this had happened in the fight for Kydan. He absently wondered if this was true fear, a fear of death. If so, it came with amazing clarity of thought.

"You're not holding that the right way," Poloma told the

man. "Not if you want to gut me. You've never actually fought with a knife before, have you?"

"Shut up!" the man spat, suddenly and unexpectedly angry.

Poloma licked his lips. He was not sure how to deal with this, after all. This was no battlefield, it was his home. And his mother was sick. And he was still completely in the dark about *why* this was happening.

"What are you doing here?" he asked, and even before the man could reply he understood, as if the last piece in a small puzzle had just fallen into place. "You murdered the colonist."

The stranger blanched, actually recoiled. "No, not murdered," he said. "I didn't mean to kill him."

"Oh, hello, Galys," Poloma said conversationally, looking over the man's shoulder. "I thought you had gone . . ."

The stranger spun around and Poloma hit him over the head with the bottle half-filled with wine. The man collapsed, unconscious.

Poloma breathed through his nose, not believing he had got away with it. His knees wanted to give way, but he concentrated on staying erect. "Idiot," he said to the man.

14

PAIMER was absorbed by the glowing blue main gate to Yunara's alcazar. Idalgo had to wave his hand in front of his master's face to get his attention.

"What is it?" Paimer asked, reluctantly drawing his gaze away from the gate. As soon as he did it was as if the rest of the world rose up around him. He had an odd feeling he had been in a dream. A nearby guard looked askance at the duke, but Paimer ignored him.

"That will do you no good, you know," Idalgo said. "You cannot Wield."

"I am a Kevleren. I am drawn to it like a bee to honey."

"Like a crow to carcass. Anyway, what you are seeing belongs to the Empress Lerena."

"Why?"

"She created it. There was some excess at first, but that's been used up." Idalgo winked at him. "By you, for one."

Paimer turned to see Empress Lerena staring at the gate and realised she could see it as well.

"Who else can see it?"

Idalgo shrugged. "No one in Omeralt, at least."

"Stop it, Uncle," declared Lerena, looking at him sternly. "I have tried to ignore your little ramblings, but when you draw the attention of my entire court, I can overlook it no longer."

Paimer glanced around, saw that everyone within earshot was staring at him. Idalgo shrugged but kept his mouth shut. The duke bowed to the empress. "Your Majesty," he said.

"And fix your wig."

"Your Majesty." He fixed his wig.

For a long time then, no one spoke. They stood in the courtyard of Yunara's alcazar waiting. For what, no one except Lerena knew. Although it was almost summer, in the shadow of the Vardars the air was still cold this early in the morning, and little puffs of breath escaped from everyone's mouth. We look like little steam carriages, Paimer thought, and then ridiculously imagined everyone standing in line behind Lerena and choo-chooing through the streets of Omeralt. He could not help a chuckle escaping from his lips.

This time the look that Lerena threw him actually made his skin goosebump. For a moment he did not recognize her face, so changed were the emotions running behind her eyes. She was no longer his niece, no longer . . .

He had to turn away from her, and dreaded what she might do, but just then the guards at the gate snapped to attention and one of them opened it. Two men entered the courtyard. Paimer recognised the Rivald ambassador and his servant. The pair stopped, obviously amazed to be confronted by the empress and her entire entourage.

"We have been waiting for you, Ambassador," Lerena said imperiously.

"So I see, your Majesty," Avenel Kendy said. He hesitantly went to her, waving one hand at the servant to make sure he kept pace. Paimer got the impression he was watching a bit of theater—a farce, maybe, like the ones put on by small groups on market days—and tried not to be so self-important he thought it was for his benefit. Ah, but it was still spring, a voice in his head remarkably like Idalgo's reminded him. So maybe this was *all* a farce.

"I did not know I was expected," Kendy said, bowing deeply to the empress. "Or I would have come sooner."

"Obviously," Lerena said without humour, and put out her hand.

Kendy blushed, as if he had been caught doing rude drawings by a teacher.

"Give it to me," Lerena ordered.

With interest, Paimer watched the expression on Kendy's face almost evolve to defiance, and found a part of himself cheering for the round little man from cold Rivald. Go on, the duke thought, tell her to run off and play with one of Yunara's parrots. It will only cost you your head, and it would hearten everyone no end.

But instead the ambassador reached inside his jacket and pulled out an official-looking letter which he gave to the empress. Without looking at it, in fact her gaze never left Kendy, she handed the letter to the man standing to her left, the weasely chancellor, Malus Mycom.

With officious pretension, Malus opened the letter, read it to himself quickly then said to Lerena, "Your Majesty, you are cordially and graciously invited by the Safety Committee of the Republic of Rivald to visit their capital so that peaceful ties between the republic and the Hamilayan empire may be formally and forever established."

It was quite extraordinary, Paimer thought, but at the moment Malus finished reading a great hush fell over the courtyard, and unless it was his imagination, it fell over the entire city. The world seemed to hold its breath for a moment, waiting to see what would happen next, and any impression that what he had been watching was a farce immediately evaporated. This was history. This was crisis.

"This is the end," Idalgo said in his ear.

"I accept the invitation," Lerena said, sounding magnanimous. She turned to Prince Rodin. "You will govern in my absence, Cousin. Chancellor Mycom will assist you." Rodin, who had actually started smiling, became all dour again when Mycom's name was mentioned; he bowed to Lerena anyway.

Kendy tried to look pleased. "When would your Majesty like to commence her journey? If you let me know within the next week or so, I can send off a message and get preparations started in Beferen—"

"Why, Ambassador, no delay," Lerena said, laughing lightly. She clapped her hands and the gate was opened again. "We start now!"

Kendy did not know what to say or do. He knew he could not say, "No, your Majesty, you cannot yet go to Rivald," and he knew he could not stand in the gate to block her progress. In the end he smiled thinly, bowed, and moved aside while Lerena swept past, a small, slightly stocky woman with a heart-shaped face and eyes filled with what seemed to him to be a terrible power that froze the marrow in his bones. When she was gone he put it down to his imagination, or the sheer presence of her authority.

The entire court, except Prince Rodin and Malus Mycom, followed the empress in single file. At the very end came Duke Paimer Kevleren, and he motioned the ambassador to join him. Kendy bowed slightly for the consideration, and as he came abreast, Paimer asked him, "Does the Safety Committee know what it's done?"

Kendy, in the hope it would forestall any conversation, was tempted to say he did not doubt the committee knew what it had done. In fact, when Paimer asked the question it occurred to him that the committee may have been infected by the hypnotic optimism of the doomed, the belief that while evil deeds were constantly delivered upon others, somehow they would miraculously escape the same fate. With gloomy appreciation, he saw that he himself had been infected by just such optimism for most of his time in Omeralt. In that case, perhaps as punishment he deserved conversation with the mad duke.

"I only ask," Paimer continued convivially, "because otherwise they must be accused of sheer idiocy. But my impression of President Croft Harker, the few times we met, was that he certainly was not an idiot."

"I believe the committee is aware of what it has done," Kendy lied, then more truthfully added in a slightly puzzled voice, "I, too, always thought the president no fool."

"And yet he was one of those who so blithely overthrew my relatives."

Kendy searched the duke's face for any sign of sarcasm but saw only genuine curiosity.

"Not every journey starts with a destination," Kendy said. "Sometimes you just have to get out of the house."

"Ah, that was how it was," Paimer said as if it confirmed his own suspicions.

"Since we are being so candid with each other, your Grace . . ."

"It would seem so."

". . . may I ask what your honest opinion is of the revolution?"

"At first I was shocked. Then my feelings were mixed. I was glad the empire was rid of its most determined and dangerous foe, but concerned that fellow Kevlerens could be so easily overthrown."

"A concern shared by the empress, no doubt. Hence your trip to Rivald."

Paimer cocked his head as if listening to someone on his opposite side. "Which, as Idalgo so rightly points out, in turn led to the discovery that the revolution occurred with the connivance, and perhaps even at the instigation, of the Beloveds." Paimer's chin drooped and his voice lost some of its timbre. "An intolerable situation."

Kendy's whole body felt suddenly charged with enormous energy. His mind, until then focused so clearly on the conversation with Paimer, seemed to expand with alarming speed until he saw the whole recent history of both Rivald and Hamilay set out before him like a map.

"That's what happened," he muttered to himself, so shocked his depression lifted away, and the knowledge he now owned, the certainty it brought, unexpectedly renewed and freed him. Despite the tragedy about to befall his country, he experienced a kind of light-headedness.

He thought of Siness Ardra then, and felt the ex-Beloved had deserved his terrible death. Ardra had betrayed his master or mistress, had helped set the course of events that led to his own immolation, and ultimately the invasion of Rivald itself.

"Now it is your turn," Paimer said, completely ignorant of the change in Kendy.

"Your Grace?" Kendy asked absently, wondering how the world had come to this. Ahead the line turned into the royal precinct's main avenue, and he caught a glimpse of

Lerena. *She* had done it, all of it. The world was turned upside down for her sake.

"From your point of view, what was the revolution like?"

"Bloody," Kendy said. "Far too bloody. And so was its resolution."

Paimer fell silent and Kendy stared at him. The duke knew, Kendy was sure. Paimer Kevleren knew what had happened because it was his report to Lerena on his travels to Rivald that had set everything off. Paimer had discovered the truth, somehow, and Lerena had acted on it. No wonder the poor man was unhinged. Despite his antipathy towards the Kevlerens, Kendy felt pity for the man in the silly red wig.

The sheer unlikely concatenation of events made Kendy doubt not his own sanity but the logic he always assumed underpinned the world. To think that the emotionally and intellectually incestuous relationship between Kevlerens and Axkevlerens that had driven the Rivald Beloveds to revolt should ultimately result in the extermination of both. But that is not where it would end. Rivald was about to be invaded, Kendy was aware, but even that would not be the end. His light-headedness dispersed, together with some of the clarity with which he had momentarily understood the past and present, leaving him with a detached dread of the future.

The procession reached the Great Hall where Lerena used to hold court. Sedans were already waiting there, and a full battalion of the Royal Guards. Kendy wondered how many more troops were waiting outside the city gates.

Avenel Kendy decided he would go no further. He did not know if the empress desired his company all the way to Rivald, but he had no intention of joining an invasion of his own country. His servant hung by him, obviously relieved they were going no further.

"I must warn the Safety Committee," Kendy said to himself. He knew the chances of any messages getting through were slim—Lerena had undoubtedly put up the barrier again—but he had to try.

There was a moment as the parade left Yunara's alcazar, and just before it reached the old palace, when the Empress Lerena Kevleren did not know what she was doing. In Yunara's courtyard, in the shade of her aviary and the looming Vardars, a cold purpose had taken hold of her, but marching in the sun, followed by her entourage and surrounded by the low, cheerful yellow buildings of the royal precinct, purpose gave way to confusion. As if in compensation, a cloud lifted from her mind and the world around her seemed to leap into focus. For the first time in a long time she heard people talking with each other, the sounds of footsteps and wind and, distantly, the puffing steam carriage making its way through Omeralt. She smelled food and sweat and sewage, tasted spice and humanity and smoke from a thousand hearths at the back of her throat. Most strangely, she heard birdsong and recognised it as a distinct sound, something apart from her own thoughts and musings and dreams. In that instant she was almost overwhelmed by the need to retreat to her aviary, but the procession turned into the precinct's main avenue and there ahead was the old Great Hall and an assembled multitude of sedans and their carriers, soldiers and their spears and swords, and servants and, most important of all, Axkevlerens.

And Lerena remembered. She was going to war. By invitation, of course, which added a delicious irony to the whole affair, but war nonetheless, and it would be a terrible, terrifying and thrilling thing. She had never before gone to war, although she had indulged in slaughter and did not think it would be too different. As if beckoned, the smell of blood filled her throat and she almost gagged on it.

She reached her own sedan. Uilder stood there, looking slightly downcast but attentive.

"Is everything ready?" Lerena asked.

"As you instructed," Uilder replied, opening the sedan door.

Lerena eased herself in, and just as she sat down she saw the glinting curve of her aviary. As if farewelling her, the tracery momentarily glowed Sefid-blue, then the sun took over again and the dome was just a dome once more and Lerena knew it was time to go. She nodded to Uilder, the sedan door closed and the carriers lifted the empress into the air.

"The empress has thought of everything," Paimer noted, regarding the supply wagons that waited just outside the city gates with their horses lazily grazing on spring grass.

"She has been planning this for several months," Idalgo said.

"I would not be surprised if she had been planning it for several years," Paimer said, stretching his neck outside of the sedan so he could count the soldiers who were coming with them. There did not seem to be enough for an invasion. Perhaps Lerena had arranged to rendezvous with regiments along the way; he wondered if there would be cavalry among them. He did not like cavalry; he thought the troopers were arrogant and overdressed.

"Do you remember that terrible Leader of a Thousand

Marquella Montranto?" he asked Idalgo. "We met him in
Hamewald. Popinjay."

"Yes, I do."

"Brutish, puffed-up cavalryman."

"Yes, I remember."

"Swaggered like a drunk all the time. Rode like a cast
from a bronze statue. All swagger and leather and puffed-
up popinjay—"

"I *remember*," Idalgo repeated.

"Anyway," Paimer huffed, "I wonder if we will meet
him."

"We will meet Chierma Axkevleren before we meet
Leader of a Thousand Marquella Montranto," Idalgo said.
"He lives in Hamewald. Do you remember him, your
Grace? He started it all."

Paimer collapsed back in his seat with a heavy thump.
The carriers almost lost the sedan then, but righted adroitly
enough to save the situation.

"I—had—forgotten—that—man," Paimer said heavily.

"No you hadn't," Idalgo said. "You were being considerate of me, that's all. Yes, everything started with
Chierma. The whole thing. The slaughter and sacrifice,
this invasion." Idalgo studied his nails with the kind of attention some applied to a piece of art. "And we'll soon be
coming to that border post where you—"

"Perhaps Chierma will not be there any more," Paimer
said hurriedly. "After all, we know Lerena killed all the
Beloveds."

Paimer's mouth shut with a snap when he realised what
he had said.

"All the Beloveds except one," Idalgo said dryly, but
without rancour. He lifted his chin slightly so Paimer could

see the puncture mark he had made in Idalgo's jugular. He sighed heavily. "Love has much to answer for."

Paimer did not want to remember what he had done to his Beloved: it had been for the good of the empire, the first act in the cleansing of Hamilay, the first step towards making the Kevlerens safe from their own creation. And it had been the beginning of Paimer's own personal nightmare. He peered out of the sedan. Many members of his family were coming too, apparently, judging from the number of sedans he could see from his little window. Their Axkevlerens followed behind their masters and mistresses, chin-drooping, bent-shouldered, brow-furrowed, as glum as mourners at a funeral.

Paimer would have been interested to know that President Croft Harker's opinion of Leader of a Thousand Marquella Montranto was similar to his own. It differed, however, in that Harker saw a use for the cavalryman: filling a seat in the Safety Committee which he controlled. Harker never let Montranto forget his rise was due to the president's efforts, and in turn Montranto never failed in his duty to the president.

The arrangement had one major disadvantage for Croft Harker, however, in that it required regular meetings between the two men, meetings where Harker was compelled to flatter the officer mercilessly, and Montranto was compelled to receive it. Montranto had the easier task.

"I am not so certain this empress will accept the invitation," Montranto was saying, flicking a finger at the first item on the agenda for the next committee meeting. "She is a silly young thing. Heard as much from that duke fellow I escorted here earlier in the year. Strange man, that duke. But honest, I'm sure. Liked my company, you know. Well, didn't get much of a challenge from that idiot

Beloved of his. Nor from the silly young empress. Tried to keep his spirit up. The duke, I mean. Depressive nature. Comes from the country. Brightened up while he was here. But she won't come. Likes to dilly-dally with her servants, the duke fellow said. Dicky-dally, more like." Montranto barked at his own joke. "Anyway, what would be the point? The republic, alas, is no longer a threat, and she has no Kevlerens here to worry about, not since that terrible business in the palace. Do we know what caused that yet? Terrible. At least they got to see the duke fellow before they died. Apparently they all caught fire, like piles of dry kindling. Terrible. I don't suppose you actually saw what happened, eh? What a mess. What a bloody, stinking mess, I'm sure."

"She will come," Harker said. "Soon."

Montranto swallowed. "Yes, I can see your point," he said weakly. "Impress the natives, that's her show."

For a moment Harker considered telling Montranto exactly what the empress was coming for, but he did not want to frighten him, and men like Montranto, all uniform and polish and bravado, were like high-strung stallions, ready to rear with a puff of wind.

"That must be it," Harker conceded. "But she is coming, Leader, make no mistake about that, and so it must be discussed. Which leads us to item two, an issue on which I'm sure I can count on your support."

Montranto read the second item: The Approach to His Highness Fourth Prince Numoya Kevleren, Governor of the Republic's Colonies of Sayenna and Kydan.

The officer cleared his throat. "Of course, you have my support on every issue. But, ah, bringing back the Kevlerens, I'm not so sure, you know."

"Kevleren, singular. He has no spouse, and no Kevleren to mate with."

"There's always that herd on the other side of the mountains," Montranto said dismally. "They have plenty of brood mares."

"I firmly believe he will be our salvation."

Montranto stared guardedly at the president and, for one of the very few times, Harker saw a spark of genuine intelligence behind those eyes. "He will want to be king, y'know."

"Yes, I expect he will. But the rest of the committee need not know."

Montranto looked away, and Harker followed his gaze out of his office window. It was a tolerable day outside, with sun and little wind. The sea looked almost green instead of slate gray. Harker sighed with a surge of patriotism. He loved his country with all its bleakness and rain and cold-to-the-bone gales. It was his, not that witch Lerena's, no matter how much she desired it, and if he had to restore the monarchy to save it, that is what he would do. He knew it would cost him his own life, and probably Montranto's. He glanced at the officer with something like sympathy.

"You have sent someone to discuss the issue with Prince Numoya?" Montranto asked.

"Yes. One of your own. Velan Lymok."

Montranto's face stiffened. "Yes. We have met."

"He was on the committee briefly, and is still a member, of course. I couldn't send an emissary without some authority."

"I remember. You hardly know him then?"

Harker saw where the conversation was leading and quickly headed it off. "Enough to know he did not have the

integrity and strength of character to sit full-time with the
rest of us," Harker lied. "Not mature or experienced
enough, but possessing the native intelligence and naivety
that will endear him to Numoya Kevleren."

"Ah." Montranto sat more easily in his chair, and
Harker could almost see how his mind was working: Yes,
he saw what the president meant. Did not quite see eye-to-
eye with him on the matter, but with so little real talent on
the committee he had to keep someone like Montranto by
his side. Undoubtedly this Lymok was the most expend-
able. Besides, with any luck, neither he nor this Kevleren
would return from across the Deepening Sea—from all accounts they were dangerous waters these days.

"So I can count on your support on this issue, Leader of
a Thousand?"

"Naturally."

When she was a small girl, no more than six years old,
Lerena was taken by her mother the Empress Hetha on a
royal trip to the port city of Bowtell. Her sister, Yunara,
came as well, but she was no more than a bawling, shitting
squib then, and Lerena had almost everyone's attention to
herself. It was the happiest she had ever been in her whole
life. It was also the only time she had ever been more than
ten miles from Omeralt. And now, just outside her sedan,
the procession was passing the longmile marker on the
road south towards Rivald. Perhaps they could stop at
Bowtell on the way. It would not be much of a diversion.

Lerena had been afraid she would be nervous and tense
about leaving the capital, but instead she was feeling remarkably relaxed. She was glad she had halted work on the
construction of the steam carriage from Omeralt to
the south of the empire; it was an unpleasant way to travel

she was sure, with all that smoke and machinery. And all that velocity; she thought going that fast would feel like being an iron ball shot from a firegon.

She looked up to a clear sky. Summer would be hot this year, so better to head south to colder climes. Some cavalry trotted by, the officers saluting with their sabers, looking dashing and . . .

Lerena could not think of the word. Something to do with animals. Except for dogs and birds, she had never had much to do with animals. She had been excited to see cows grazing in fields not more than two hours after they left the city walls. Imagine something that big and horned being so close to civilization. She had never imagined. Maybe she should take a greater interest in agriculture. After all, it was the source of her empire's wealth, the engine of its progress and greatness. After her family, of course, but she would be the first to admit that even the Sefid could not feed the millions of her subjects.

"Did your family come from a farm?" she suddenly asked Uilder, sitting in the opposite corner of the sedan from her.

"Your Majesty?" Uilder seemed startled by the question.

"Before you became an Axkevleren."

"I don't really remember, your Majesty."

"Surely you'd remember if you came from a farm."

Uilder shrugged. "I do not remember a farm. I think I was from a city."

"Bowtell? We might be going there. Or Somah? Koegrah?"

"I don't think so . . ."

"Ferberin? Castell? High Alt?"

"Castell," Uilder said suddenly. "I think . . . something about the name . . ."

"But not a farm then." Lerena sighed, not entirely happy. She wanted to know what it was like living on a farm. With cows. And, she thought, with pigs and sheep and a horse or two. And dogs to herd the sheep and cows. She frowned slightly, remembering her own dogs. Not farm dogs, but hunters, tall dogs with long legs and gentle eyes. She missed her dogs.

She cocked an ear to hear some birds. She was sure that was a raven or crow. And in the distance, definitely the magpie's wattle-wattle. Beneath the foot of the Vardars there was still some forest, ancient, uncoppiced, with canopies filled with parrots and herons and flamingoes. Or maybe they needed rivers, she thought, not forests. Or grasslands.

Suddenly discontented because she did not know what kind of birds would be in the forest, and feeling she should, Lerena poked her head out the window. The whole wide world, she told herself in consolation, and it was all hers. Maybe she would make her own farm. She would set it up near Bowtell, and put that nice, short round Avenel Kendy in charge of it, since he would soon be out of a job. The farm would be her summer retreat, and she could have any animal she wanted on it.

15

IT was several days since Leader of a Thousand Velan Lymok had first spoken to Numoya Kevleren, although he had enjoyed a few small conversations with Quenion Axkevleren.

Well, perhaps not enjoyed, he admitted to himself. He had not met many Beloveds before Quenion, but in many ways she seemed typical of the class.

Typical, except . . .

Velan drummed his fingertips on the windowsill in his room. He looked out on a bright Sayenna day. Quite enchanting. The women around here were very beautiful, with golden skin and dark hair and shining brown eyes.

He stopped his drumming. Except that Quenion was different in some way he could not define. Not shaped by the Kevlerens, perhaps. He remembered Numoya had sacrificed his original Beloved to win the first battle for Kydan, so Quenion had only been promoted to the status of Beloved since then. She was a novice.

Did that make her a weak link Velan might exploit on behalf of the republic and the Safety Committee?

The sun warmed his skin through the glass, and as if in

response his brain dredged up memories of Beferen, terrible in winter and not much happier in summer. The difference was between sapphire and lead. Between life and death.

Did he want to exploit Quenion on behalf of the republic and the Safety Committee?

Numoya Kevleren was not going to return to Rivald. Why leave all this, and the promise of a brighter, warmer future, for the uncertainty of war and cold and a confrontation with the witch empress from Hamilay?

So where does that leave me? Velan wondered. Stranded or saved? I still have a choice. I can make my future, too.

There was a knock on his door and Quenion entered. "His highness has a message ready for you to take back to the committee." She joined him by the window and pointed to a brigantine in the harbour below. "There's your ship. The captain has said he'll carry you as supercargo."

"Charming."

"You leave tomorrow morning."

"Of course," Velan said carefully, "if the message is written down, there is no need for a messenger as such."

Quenion pursed her lips, considered the statement. "What about your responsibility to the committee?"

Velan breathed deeply. "As I see it, what his highness stated in our only meeting so far made immediate sense."

"In particular?"

"That the committee in making the offer to your master was conceding his right to the throne of Rivald, fully restored and with all the power and authority, umm, pertaining, umm . . ."

". . . thereto," Quenion finished for him.

"Thereto. From which it follows that, as an officer in Rivald's army, I am his highness's servant to command."

"His majesty's," she corrected him. "And if he commands you to return to Beferen?"

Velan swallowed. He had taken the bait before he realised Quenion was fishing. "Then, of course, I will return."

Quenion turned to face him squarely. "Well. I will inform his majesty of your, shall we say, change of heart. He will let you know his decision."

"I am your servant," Velan said and bowed. Quenion stood back in surprise, nodded sharply and left.

She was definitely not used to being a Beloved, Velan thought.

"You will need an officer, one trained in leadership," Quenion said.

"He is not trained in anything except putting on airs," Numoya said. "I know his type from my own days in the army and at court. His kind littered the palace like puppies, looking for favours and an easy life."

"He has no value at all? Shall I order him back to Beferen then?"

"I did not say he had no value. If he can sit a horse prettily, and if he looks good in his uniform, then others will follow him until he shows just how incompetent he is. You are right when you say I need officers. We will be collecting a menagerie of native troops not used to fighting together or under another's command."

"They will obey you," Quenion said matter-of-factly.

"Or anyone from Rivald who looks as if he deserves to be obeyed. Tell me, how does this Lymok look all dressed up?"

"Very fine. He is not a big man, but his uniform makes him look quite martial."

"Should I accept his service then?"

"Perhaps not accept it," Quenion said slowly. "After all, by rights you already have it. You are the sole surviving Rivald Kevleren. You *are* king."

Numoya laughed humourlessly. "Oh, how my family has fallen." He put his palms against his scarred cheeks. "Behold his royal majesty, King Numoya of Rivald."

"Don't laugh," Quenion said sternly, surprising herself. "You are king. And you will have your own kingdom here in the New Land."

Numoya stood, reached out for Quenion. She gave him her hand. "Yes, my Beloved. We will carve it ourselves, despite the carcass of the old world."

It was harder to imagine the future in the dark, Quenion thought, lying still in her cot at the end of Numoya's bed. Earlier in the evening, when she and Numoya talked with excitement about the days and months to come, it had seemed that the future was ready to fall into her lap. But now it was as remote as the stars in the night sky. In the dark, when the keep was silent except for the single watch on the tower above, and the town of Sayenna itself was as calm as a sleeping cat, she could hear her lovely Numoya breathing raggedly through the broken gap that had once been his mouth. His lungs rattled with phlegm, and when he moved in bed his damaged skin sounded like paper against the linen sheets.

She suffered as he suffered, her nerves jangling at the slightest touch, her memory crowded by fire and pain, and at night the world revolved around the suffering of Numoya Kevleren, and Quenion wished fervently it had a broader orbit.

But the very remoteness of any future meant that without that distraction it was possible for Quenion to see the present in greater relief, to explore and analyze it with greater determination and effect. Again and again everything came down to the fact that Numoya needed to be well again. First, she was his Beloved and fervently desired only the best for him. Second, Sayenna needed Numoya to be whole, needed a ruler who was fit and complete and in every sense a Kevleren.

And, Quenion realised, there might now be a way to bring that about if, as she sometimes thought, he felt something like love for her.

Quenion wanted to believe his feelings for her had changed. His gentler, more considerate manner suggested this had happened, and he now openly called her Beloved.

It was not until they reached the deep water dock and the brigantine getting ready to sail that Velan Lymok knew his fate. Instead of giving Numoya Kevleren's message to him to take to Beferen, she asked him only to sign its cover for the committee's sake, then handed the message to the ship's captain with the injunction to hand it personally to President Croft Harker of the Safety Committee.

Velan could not help breathing a sigh of relief, and the world immediately seemed brighter and warmer to him.

"May I ask what the message contains?" he asked Quenion.

"I think you can guess, Leader of a Thousand."

"What will my duties be?"

"To serve his majesty King Numoya Kevleren to the best of your ability."

"Of course. But specifically?"

"Specifically, have you ever been to war?"

Velan blinked in surprise and quickly looked away to hide the fact from Quenion, pretending to study the goings-on around them. A few stalls and shops were opening, almost all dealing with food and everyday things. Very few luxury items, such as carpets and plate and fancy clothing, were for sale; almost all such goods brought better prices inland or back in Rivald. In fact, for all its sunny simplicity and exuberance, Sayenna itself still had the soul of a frontier town, and like all frontier towns was most eager for three things—security, population and trade. But, Velan thought, it had the setting and access to resources needed for a great city. It would come in time, and perhaps he was one of those who would help it happen.

"Leader?" Quenion prompted.

"Not as such. I have fought on the frontier, of course."

"Excellent. For we are going to war."

"We?"

"His majesty and all those loyal to him."

"I thought . . . I mean, from our discussions earlier, I received the clear impression that his majesty was not interested in fighting for Rivald."

"*In* Rivald, Leader," Quenion said carefully. "My master has every intention of fighting *for* Rivald, as he outlines in his message to the Safety Committee."

Velan shook his head. "The distinction is lost on me."

They had reached the top of the town and paused to look back down on the harbour. The brigantine had slipped its ropes and let down some sail, and was slowly edging away from shore.

I am committed, Velan thought, realizing he was cut off from his old home, possibly forever. He had thrown in his lot with a strange female Beloved and her master, the last, and possibly quite insane, member of the Rivald Kevlerens.

Panic struggled to surface in his brain, but he kept it down by concentrating on the sun-dappled sea, the breeze blowing gently across his cheek, the glimpse of the future he had imagined for Sayenna and the New Land. He had always wanted to be part of the inner circle, to be in the middle looking out. This was his chance, he realised, if only he had the courage to grasp the opportunity with both hands.

"His majesty has decided to retake Kydan," Quenion said. "We have a small treasury, and a secure base. Alas, few Rivald soldiers, since the committee saw fit to transport most of them back to Rivald after we first took Kydan, but many potential allies."

"You don't have an army," Velan summarised.

"Yes, but it's not as serious a problem as you think, since except for a small unit or two of Hamilayan infantry, and possibly a small troop of dragoons, neither has Kydan."

"A small unit or two and cavalry," Velan said, seeing clouds already gathering on his future's horizon.

"But we know many of those natives our infantry trained before they left these shores survived the battles for Kydan and returned to their homes along the river. All they need is encouragement. Encouragement and an officer to whip them back into shape." For the first time Velan saw Quenion smile. "Specifically, that's where you come in."

On the whole, Quenion thought Velan took the news of his future employment as she had expected, with apprehension but without any overt displays of cowardice, although he could not hide his expression when the word "war" was first voiced. Numoya might be right about his abilities then; but if Velan was a creature of court, the only court going for a Rivald officer these days was right here in Sayenna, so he would feel at home soon enough.

Anyway, there was something self-contained about the

officer that made her think there might be more to him than
Numoya allowed. He had seen combat, after all, and progressed quickly enough through the ranks for someone so
young, although the revolution against her master's family
had probably eased the way for any number of young soldiers as old officers, stubbornly loyal to Queen Sarra, were
removed or eliminated. But even so, to take advantage in
such a dangerous time suggested initiative, determination
and confidence.

As well, Quenion had seen the way Velan Lymok had
looked at Sayenna and its harbor, the way he seemed to
stare at the landscape for hours, as if it was the first true
geography he had ever seen, and that made her feel there
was a connection, an understanding, between them that
made her more sympathetic towards him.

After several years in the New Land, she herself had
only dim memories of Rivald and Beferen, and most of
those were bleak and charcoal gray. In her memory, Beferen was a mood, not a city, and a dark mood at that. She
wondered if that meant she was without patriotism, and
almost immediately decided that patriotism was for repub-
licans. She was an Axkevleren, and her duty lay with Numoya, not some fanciful idea of nationhood based on the
decisions of a so-called Safety Committee which, in a matter of months, had gone from disposing of its royal family
to disposing of its own republic.

She went to the kitchen house in the grounds outside the
keep. Its chimneys were already smoking, and the cook
was checking loaves of bread in one of the ovens, at the
same time giving instructions to the workers around the
table. One was kneading a dark brown dough, two were
stirring food in large copper kettles, one was trimming fat
off pork, and another slicing dried fruit.

"Sievad," Quenion said. The cook looked up impatiently; she was a short, round woman who looked older than her real age. Her hair and cheeks were white with flour.

Sievad said something under her breath about being too busy to chat.

"His majesty would like only a light lunch. He did not sleep well last night and breakfast was so heavy it has made him tired."

Sievad started muttering something about the master keeping up his strength, then stopped and looked up with large, watery gray eyes. "What'd you say?" she said clearly.

"I said his majesty wanted only a light—"

"His *majesty*?"

"Numoya Kevleren has accepted the title and authority of King of Rivald."

Quenion noticed the servant kneading the dough. She was about Quenion's age, height and build. Not exact, but close enough. "Send her up with the tray," she told Sievad, pointing to the servant.

The cook looked up briefly, noticed who Quenion meant, and nodded.

"She's the prettiest one of the lot, that's for sure. His majesty needs some exercise this afternoon?"

Quenion did not reply, but as she left the kitchen she heard Sievad add, "Then he can't be that tired."

Well, Velan thought, best to give the uniform a once-over.

He laid it out on the bed, admiring the blue and white combination, which he had always liked; certainly a lot more than the rather dull green and yellow uniforms of

Hamilay, which reminded him of hostlers' aprons and those aniseed sticks loved by Beferen children. And children's snot, too, come to think of it. Rivald's uniform was sky and clouds, sea and sun. He straightened the arms. Stood back and imagined going to war. Not some border skirmish on the frontier with Hamilay, but an out-and-out conflict with conquest the ultimate objective. He saw himself dressed in the uniform with longgon smoke washing around him and the crackle of firegons in the background.

I am a fool, Velan thought. I should have gone back with the brigantine.

"Yes, your Majesty, I greatly desire to take back your message to the Safety Committee. Personally. As soon as possible."

He sat on the edge of the bed, trying hard not to feel sorry for himself. That was too much like sulking. Soldiers did not sulk, and those with power and authority definitely did not sulk.

Besides, even if he had gone back to Rivald, it was no guarantee he would not be sent into battle against the Hamilayan invaders, and they had a lot of Kevlerens on their side.

Yes, better to be here, perhaps, on the other side of the world, with a friendly Kevleren behind him rather than an angry one in front. And another besides: war might not be so bad. It was not combat he was afraid of, but the responsibility of leadership. Ironically, he thought, for someone who so badly wanted to be a leader, he had never enjoyed taking men into battle. He sighed heavily. Who knows? He might prove to be halfway decent at it.

He patted the uniform.

Yes. All in all, he had chosen the wisest course. He was sure.

*   *   *

While Numoya ate his lunch, Quenion asked the servant what her name was.

"Boruna, y'greatness," the woman said, trying so hard to whisper it sounded too obvious. She could not look at Numoya, so disgusted was she by his scars. Quenion took her elbow and guided her out of the room, staying in the doorway herself so she could keep an eye on her master.

"I am no one's greatness," Quenion said flatly. "You call me Quenion Axkevleren, or Beloved, or mistress."

"Aye, then." Boruna said. "Mistress."

Quenion regarded her carefully. The woman was a little taller than she, but no wider, and her hair was a similar thickness and length. The skin was more brown, perhaps drier, but she was still young and supple.

"You have a family?"

"Aye. Many sisters, two brothers. Mama and Papa are gone, passed away to join the great sea."

"A family of your own?"

"No, Mistress."

"No children?"

"No, Mistress," Boruna said, trying to sound offended but failing.

"My master needs more helpers. He needs Axkevlerens."

Boruna looked frightened.

"It is a position of much authority," Quenion added. "It would place you in charge of many of your own people."

"But *they* kill Axkevlerens," Boruna hissed.

Quenion arched her eyebrows. "Really? And how many Axkevlerens do you know?"

"None. Well, you, Mistress."

"An Axkevleren is not a servant, keep in mind," Quenion said over her. "We are a chosen few, and have greater respect in the world than any except the Kevlerens themselves. Of course, you can refuse service. I will not force you to become an Axkevleren."

Boruna nodded to Numoya, carefully picking the meat of a chicken wing with his teeth. "But he can."

"He knows nothing of the offer. I have a free hand in this." Quenion sighed, looked bored with Boruna. "Very well, thank you."

"Mistress?"

"You can go now."

"But . . ."

Quenion stared down Boruna. The native blushed so deeply Quenion could see it under her golden skin.

"Thank you. Go back to the kitchen. I will bring back the tray myself."

Numoya turned his head in their direction. "Quenion? What's all that chittering?"

"Nothing, your Majesty," she said, using her most patronizing voice. "Just one of the servants." She threw Boruna a deprecatory glance and returned to Numoya's side. Boruna quickly left.

"Don't tell me 'nothing,' Beloved," Numoya chided.

"It was one of the servants from the kitchen. I thought she might make a good Axkevleren, even though she's well past childhood."

Numoya put his food down and frowned in thought. "I suppose eventually we'll have to recruit Axkevlerens locally. It's not something I've given any consideration, but we're not likely to get them from Rivald any more."

"I agree. Was the food all right?"

"There wasn't a lot of it."

"You have been tired all day, and you were restless last night. I thought it best if you did not eat too much."

"I see. What was her name?"

"Your Majesty?"

"The servant."

"I'm not sure. Nothing like a proper Rivald name."

Numoya sat up straighter and pushed the tray a short distance away. Quenion picked it up and put it on a side table.

"Some wine, please." As Quenion poured it into a wooden cup, he asked, "Do you miss Rivald?"

"Not at all." She gave him the cup and he sipped it slowly. "It is too cold there."

"It is too warm here."

"Even warmer in Kydan."

"It is *hot* in Kydan. I am not looking forward to returning there, but return we must. How did Velan take the news, by the way?"

"With equanimity."

"We must leave soon. I cannot wait much longer. I want to be in Kydan before the end of summer." He drank more deeply from the cup. "This is nice wine."

"It is from a shipment that arrived from Rivald with Velan. A gift from the Safety Committee."

Numoya snorted. "They have taken so much from me, and in return give me wine from my own family's cellars, and a puppy from the army. With this I am supposed to be grateful enough to save them from the wrath of Hamilay." He sighed heavily. "I am tired, you know. Very tired. But there is so much work to do."

Quenion took the cup from him. "Rest. I will be back later when it is dark and the keep is quieter. We can work some more then."

"Yes, I will rest just a little. I am so tired." He lifted his head towards her. "Come back soon. I am used to you, Quenion, and find it hard to be alone now."

Just before dark Boruna went to the Beloved's room and knocked gently on the door.

"Come in, Boruna," Quenion called, startling the girl. She almost decided there and then to turn around and never come back to work at the keep, but before she could make up her mind the door opened.

"Don't be afraid," Quenion said gently, and took Boruna by the sleeve.

"How did you know it was me?" the girl asked nervously.

Quenion smiled. "That was not magic. I knew you would come back. You are not the type to pass up a chance to do better. You have courage and you work hard."

"Yes," Boruna said, accepting the compliments even if she did not quite believe them. Some of her fear melted away.

"You wish to reconsider my offer," Quenion told her. Boruna, who did want to say as much, nodded hesitantly. "Then sit down and I will explain to you what is involved in becoming an Axkevleren, and the responsibilities and advantages that come with belonging to the family of a Kevleren."

"I will belong to his family?" Boruna asked, wide-eyed, taking the seat Quenion moved away from the desk for her. Quenion herself perched on the edge of the desk.

"That is what it means to be an Axkevleren. Some will tell you we are slaves, but that is not true. We are family. We belong to our master the same way children belong to their father."

"I did not know that."

"And did you know that Axkevlerens, once they have proven themselves in service, can reach positions of great authority and power? I have known Axkevlerens who were almost as powerful as kings."

"No, I did not know that."

Quenion regarded her for a moment, and Boruna could not help swallowing. "Would you like some wine?"

Without waiting for a reply, Quenion poured some into a cup from a flask on the desk. Boruna took the cup, her hand shaking so much she almost spilled it. She sipped it cautiously. She thought it tasted wonderful. Much better than the crude stuff fermented locally.

"From my home," Quenion said. "I come from Rivald. You know where that is?"

"Far away. Across the ocean."

Quenion started describing her home, its cold lands and bleak weather, using a lilting tone that slowly degraded into a drone. A few minutes later, Boruna's chin drooped to her chest and her hands fell to her side. The cup clattered on the stone floor.

Quenion waited an hour, until she was sure everyone had either left the keep or, if resident, were in their rooms. She then put her hands under Boruna's arms and slowly, carefully and laboriously dragged her up the stairs to Numoya's quarters on the level above. She rested her back for a short while and checked that Numoya was still sound asleep, affected by the same drug she had given Boruna, then finished dragging the servant to Numoya's bed.

Outside was dark and still. Not even a breeze stirred, as if the night itself was waiting for what would happen next.

Velan knew he was not going to get any sleep. He lay on his bed, staring up at the slice of sky he could see through his window. He tried to think about the stars, hard diamond points, and wondered what they really were, but inevitably his mind would wander back to his future, and it seemed to him a bloody and terrible thing. He told himself it was ridiculous to worry about it. What would come, would come. There was nothing he could do about it. So. Look at the stars.

Were they distant fires? Could a bird reach them? Or were they proof of a heaven that his ancestors had once, absurdly, believed in. Although heaven was not such an absurd construct if you were about to fight your way across a whole continent and all you really wanted to do was sit on the warm shore of a sunny harbor drinking wine and eating pastries.

Stop it, he told himself.

The stars. Again.

Someone, and he had completely forgotten whom, had once told him that the stars were a result of the Kevlerens using the Sefid. Extra magic or something, or a reaction in the sky like his skin sometimes reacted to eating too much fruit, although thinking of the stars as blemishes would stretch anyone's imagination. At the time the statement had seemed reasonable to him, but shortly after he remembered poetry he had read that mentioned stars and had been written long before the Kevlerens stormed south from their mountain home. But maybe the Kevlerens had been playing with the Sefid for millennia before they emerged to conquer all the peoples around them.

He wondered if the Kevlerens died off, would the stars disappear?

Died off? *Them?* Not that he would live long enough to find out.

*   *   *

When Numoya started slowly to rouse himself from the first effects of the drug, Quenion knew she had not long before Boruna would start to come out of it as well. She had to make her choice; the decision could not be put off any longer.

"It is now or never," she said softly, hoping the words would move her to take action, but she lacked the courage.

No, not the courage. The certainty. She lacked the certainty that her plan would work, and so much depended on it. Numoya's whole future, and her own. The future for Rivald in the New Land.

Her master shifted in his bed, and the sound of his skin was like dried leaves rustling together. She took a step towards him, moved by pity. Then another, and soon she was by his bed looking down on him, almost swallowed by her pity it was so dark and enormous. Then she glanced at Boruna and felt something similar for her as well.

But a sacrifice was needed, and Boruna's passing would hurt very few in this world, and perhaps ensure a brighter future for her whole people.

It was not a decision Quenion wanted to take, but she reminded herself that with her actions she had already taken it. She was a Beloved, and a Beloved could not avoid her responsibility to her master.

Quenion knelt down next to the bed and lifted Boruna onto it. Numoya stirred again, moaning softly. The drug was wearing off but still exerted enough of an effect to keep him in the twilight world between sleep and full wakefulness, a world where dreams took on real shape and colour, where the mind surrendered to its most fervent desires without the conscious mind to rein it back.

"My lord?" Quenion whispered, close to his ear. "I have come as you asked. All is ready."

She touched his forehead, stroked the few wisps of hair that were growing back.

"I am ready for the sacrifice."

"No-o-o-o," he moaned, still in his dream world, but a world being shaped partly by Quenion now. "Not again."

"I am ready for it," she said into his ear, and leaned over him to kiss the brow above the empty eye sockets. "I love you more than my own life."

"Ah, Quenion," he said softly, his voice still coming from a thousand miles away. She wondered what he was seeing with his mind's eye, then blushed with the realization that he had called her name and not Thenge, that of his first Beloved. She had truly taken her place by his side.

"I cannot live with you like this, your Maj—" She stopped, afraid that calling him "majesty," a recent salutation, would bring him back to the present and rouse him fully from his sleep. "Your Highness, I have no life when your own life is only half what it should be."

"No-o-o-o."

"I am ready." She held her breath for the lie and hoped it would seem to him like the truth. "As we agreed. The time has come. Rivald needs you. Your family needs you. Heal yourself. Use the Sefid."

"No." The voice was stronger, deeper. "No."

She took his right hand and placed it by Boruna's warm neck.

"I love you, your Highness. I cannot live if you stay like this. Let me prove my love to you."

He shook his head. His left hand curled and pulled at the bedclothes. He tried to pull back his right hand.

Then Boruna moaned as well.

Now! Quenion ordered herself.

"Now," she repeated aloud for Numoya's sake. "Do it now!"

She took his right hand and found the stylus under the nail of his little finger.

"Wield, my lord!"

She stuck the point of the stylus into Boruna's jugular. A drop of blood formed around its end; when she withdrew the stylus it turned into a thin red stream that arched into the air and fell onto the sheets, pooling, spreading.

"Yes," Numoya groaned. "Now."

Quenion's skin goosebumped and her breath frosted in the air.

At first Velan did not notice how cold the air had become.

"If I'm honest about it," he muttered into the darkness, "my prospects here in the New Land are better than they would be back in Rivald."

He ticked the points off on the finger of one hand.

"First, the chances of surviving a Hamilayan onslaught are no greater—and possibly considerably worse—than surviving Numoya's private war.

"Second, if I had returned to Rivald and survived the war, my position in an occupied country would hardly be favorable.

"Third, if I survive conflict here in the New Land, my prospects are promising indeed. For example:

"Four, I will be the third most powerful person in the colony, after Numoya and Quenion."

He waved his thumb, trying to think of a fifth point, but all he came up with was that the New Land was warmer.

Velan had almost convinced himself that everything that had happened was for the better when he noticed the brass buttons on his coat were glowing blue. His thoughts stopped so quickly his mind wandered in a vacuum for a moment before he recalled what the blue glow signified.

Which could only mean . . .

He sat up in bed, feeling the hairs rise on the back of his neck, panic suffocating him.

And then he heard the scream. The sound of it vibrated through stone and flesh, rising and rising into the air, and then slowly passed away like a tempest at sea, leaving everything behind suddenly becalmed.

It had been a man's voice. Numoya Kevleren's voice.

Velan stood to stop his knees from shaking, and put on pants and shirt to stop his hands from doing the same. There were anxious voices from below. The servants who lived in the keep.

"What is the matter? What is going on?" a watch called out tremulously.

Velan surprised himself by opening his door and calling down, "Everyone stay below!" His voice fluttered but no one came up the keep's stairs.

Tucking his shirt in, breathing deeply to steady himself, he climbed to the top floor and knocked on Numoya's door. He heard flapping sounds, like paper picked up by a wind. No one answered. He swallowed, tapped again, called out to the Kevleren. No one answered.

Velan opened the door wide and stepped under the lintel, not quite brave enough to go all the way in. It was dark. There were shapes on the bed, more than one body. And blood in the air. Oily. Coppery.

"Your Majesty?"

"He is safe," said a voice weakly, but he did not recognise it. "Wait."

A match flared. Velan saw pale faces, slick, heard panting now. Something flickered in the corner of his eye, and he turned to the window. The iron bars hummed with a blue flame.

A lantern swelled the room with light. Velan turned his gaze back to the bed and saw Quenion. She was wide-eyed, breathing in shuddering gasps.

"What?" he mumbled. It was all he could say.

"It's all right," she said, and pushed herself off the bed. As she did so the lantern light swept over her front, so thickly painted with blood Velan thought she must really be dead.

16

POLOMA had the servants tie up the unconscious intruder. When the servants realized the man had come to kill their master, they handled him roughly, binding his hands tightly with thin rope; as he roused, they knocked him unconscious again.

Poloma saw none of this; as soon as the intruder no longer presented a threat, he returned to his mother. She was lying down again, on top of the bedclothes, fully dressed, her eyelids fluttering like butterfly wings. Hattie sat on the edge of the bed, stroking Sorkro's hand and frowning in concentration, as if listening for Sorkro's last words.

He joined Hattie and rested his wrist against his mother's forehead, remembering this was exactly how she had measured his temperature when he was only a boy. He was surprised she was so cold. It was not merely the absence of heat, he knew.

He stood straight, unable to sit any more. Absurdly, he remembered the wine he had been sent to the kitchen to get. He was embarrassed he had forgotten all about it and apologised to Sorkro for the oversight.

Hattie misunderstood and smiled at him sympathetically. "She is very proud of you."

Which meant Hattie knew Sorkro was dying.

"A physic," he said. "I will send for a physic."

"A physic will not help," Hattie said gently. Her frown
disappeared, as if by saying it she confirmed it for herself
and her own conscience eased. "There is nothing more any
of us can do. It is up to your mother now."

Poloma felt detached from what was happening, as if he
were watching someone else's mother die. He wanted to be
roused by emotion or filled with understanding or something, but in the end, after all Sorkro had done for him, all
he could do was stand mute and helpless. He might as well
not have been there.

As if reading his mind, Hattie said, "She knows you are
here. When you speak she can still hear your words. I
know. I can tell."

It was not what he wanted to hear. Poloma wanted his
mother to die completely unaware, to be as unconscious as
the bastard who had snuck into his house to kill him. He
wanted his mother to know nothing of her own death. It
was not right. Anger flamed inside him and he gritted his
teeth, his hands balled into fists.

"She doesn't care," Hattie continued. "She feels
nothing."

"How can you know?" Poloma demanded, his voice
sounding from far away.

"Because your mother is not being ripped from her life.
She has not been shot or stabbed. She is dying of old age.
She is worn out. Wearied beyond caring."

Galys returned to the Citadel dripping from head to
foot. A room on the first floor of the keep with views over

the city from one window and east along the Frey River from its opposite had been set aside for whoever was on duty as castellan, and when she got to it she found a fire set for her in the hearth, and a flask of rough red wine and a mug on a map table not far from the blaze. She went straight to the wine and swallowed a whole mug of it in one long draft, then started stripping off her wet clothes, wishing she could have another bath like the one she had enjoyed at Poloma's house.

"I wouldn't go any further just yet," Gos Linsedd said.

Galys spun on her heel. Gos was reclining easily in a chair near a shelf filled with map rolls and bound papers; he looked as if he was just waking from a nap.

"I hope you like the fire. I asked for it to be made ready for you."

"I wasn't expecting anyone to be here," she said. She heard how querulous her voice sounded, and added as evenly as possible, "Why aren't you back on Karhay, stabling horses or trooping the dragoons or something?"

Gos smiled uncertainly. "I thought we needed to talk about what happened today."

Galys let out a long breath. "That's what Poloma said."

"Is that where you've been?" His voice sounded more tense.

She regarded the commander for a moment before answering. "Yes, but his mother fell ill before we could discuss anything in detail."

"Is she all right?" Gos seemed genuinely concerned, and also a little relieved. "Does she need a physic?"

"I don't know; I think it might be serious. I'm sure Poloma will get a physic if he thinks it will do any good."

Gos nodded, looked down at his hands. "You think I did

wrong to bring the dragoons across to the Saddle today. You think I made the situation worse."

"Look, Gos, I need time to dry off and to think before we can talk about what happened."

He stood up quickly. "Of course. Why don't you . . . umm . . . finish what you were doing. Maybe we can talk tomorrow."

"I think that's a good idea."

As he opened the door to leave he stopped and asked over his shoulder, "Have you seen Kadburn about?"

Galys blinked. She realised she had not seen him for two days or more. "No."

Gos shrugged. "He'll turn up, I expect."

Galys, more concerned than she expected by the absence of the Beloved, said vaguely, "I'm sure you're right." But Gos had already closed the door behind him.

The rain continued on into the night, falling so heavily that for the colonists in their huts it sounded like a waterfall was falling across the thatch. Recently made, the roofs held, but some of the walls, made out of mud brick and not yet whitewashed, sagged in places. The watch scrunched their cloaks tight around themselves and looked down and not out to keep the water from their eyes, not worried particularly about anyone trying to sneak onto the island in this weather, or off it for that matter. Those that saw Arden go to Heriot's hut nodded to him miserably, but otherwise made sure to pay him no mind. Heriot was fast asleep, snoring lightly, as tiny as a doll compared to her visitor. He leaned over her, reached out to tap her shoulder, but water dripping from his hair splashed onto her face and her eyes blinked open. They widened in surprise, but she did not call out.

"It's me," Arden said, trying to keep his low voice to a quiet rumble.

Heriot swallowed. "Of course it's you," she said, and sat up, keeping her blanket around her. Arden was her closest acquaintance in the world, and they had bathed in the river with all the other colonists without being embarrassed by each other's nakedness, but in the middle of the night, in her own hut, this was different.

"It's raining outside," Arden continued.

Heriot sighed. "Surprise me," she said, then pointed to a mass of clothing on a rough-made stool. "Pass me my shirt." Arden did so. She slipped it on quickly. "And now my dress." She stared at him. She could not see him clearly in the dark, but she could feel his mass nearby, bearing down on her. It made her resentful suddenly. "Turn around," she snapped.

She heard him shuffle, and stood up quickly and slipped on the dress.

"What's this about?"

"The weapons."

"What?"

"You were wondering about the weapons before. I figure now is a good time to get them together and put them in their new hiding place. The stable walls are ready."

She listened to the rain for a moment. It sounded heavy enough to wash her away if she ventured outside.

"*Now* is a good time?"

"The rain will help hide us, and dull any sound we make."

"Just us two?"

"I've already arranged for others to gather the weapons together. They'll meet us at the stables. Everyone on the watch tonight is one of ours, except for a dragoon on duty at the stables, and in this weather he'll be inside keeping dry with the horses."

Arden seemed to have it all figured out. Heriot nodded resignedly.

Leadership, Poloma thought, was part inspiration and intuition, part tradition and symbolism, part bravado. So far in his term as prefect, he thought, he had failed to provide much inspiration, no intuition, a break with tradition, little symbolism and bugger-all bravado.

But that was going to change.

"What did you say your name was?" he asked the gangly man tied into a stiff-backed chair. One of the bulkier servants of the Malvara household hovered behind the chair, looking as menacing as possible. The prisoner's face was bruised in several places, and Poloma knew the back of his head, where he had been struck with the wine bottle, must have been pounding.

Good, the prefect thought. All pain to him.

"I didn't hear you," he continued.

The man shook his head. "I have no name. I have no history. I am nothing."

Poloma pursed his lips. "I won't argue the point. In fact, I would go as far as to say you are not even a Kydan. Did you slip into the city from one of the settlements along the river?"

The man glared at Poloma. "I am a Kydan!" he hissed.

"You don't behave like one," Poloma said nonchalantly. "In fact, you behave like one of Maira Sygni's thugs. You're not a plutocrat, are you?"

"I fought for a free Kydan!"

"What? By attempting to assassinate members of the council and getting rid of old drunk colonists? The man you murdered fought for a free Kydan, too, by the way. Little good it did him."

For the first time the prisoner actually looked abashed, but he said nothing. With some surprise, Poloma realized the man may have committed manslaughter, but not murder. Not yet, anyway.

"Maybe Councilor Kysor Nevri knows you. I will ask him to come here and identify you." Poloma paused to consider his nails. "Or does he already know you're here?"

At first the prisoner looked puzzled by the question, then realized it was a veiled accusation.

"The councilor knows nothing of my being here," he said, so blankly that Poloma believed him instantly.

Still, Poloma reminded himself, don't forget bravado. "That's something for the Assembly to decide."

The prisoner looked aghast. "You would slander an innocent man for gain in the Assembly? You are a worse man than I ever imagined . . ."

"Worse than someone who would order an assassin to creep into the home of an innocent man and kill him?"

"I already told you, Kysor Nevri knew nothing of this."

Poloma looked noncommittally at him. "If you are not protecting someone, you can have no reason not to tell me your name."

The man now appeared dejected, not defiant. He mumbled something under his breath.

"I did not hear you," Poloma said.

"Lannel Thorey," the prisoner said. "My name is Lannel Thorey."

Galys woke knowing she had been dreaming about Kitayra, but not knowing what the dream had been about; all she could remember was that love had not been a part of it, which disturbed her. She wanted to know what it meant, but was afraid of what the answer might be. She searched her feelings and found the echo of the love she had felt for Kitayra when she was still alive, but the emotion that dominated all others was grief, the sharp end of self-pity.

Galys stared at the fire, wondering why she did not feel more shame at her discovery. Perhaps it meant she had at last accepted the need to leave behind her lost lover, or perhaps accepted the truth that behind Kitayra were great secrets, possibly dark secrets, she did not really want to discover, and the only way to protect herself was to break from the past.

She stood up from her seat and absently stoked the fire. Sparks flew up the chimney. She heard a bird outside whistle half-heartedly and looked out the east window. The horizon was lightening. She wished a dawn would come when she was not afraid of what the day might bring, although a part of her admitted she relished the uncertainty, the danger, the challenge of life in Kydan.

Galys heard the door open behind her, and she turned, expecting to see one of the guards with a report of the night's activities, or possibly someone from the kitchens with breakfast. Thinking about food made her stomach rumble.

It was Kadburn. He looked bedraggled, and even from the window Galys could smell earth and leaves and river water in his hair and on his clothes. He smiled thinly and said, "He's coming, Strategos. I don't know exactly when he'll get here, but Numoya Kevleren will this summer return to Kydan."

The colonists, under the supervision of Heriot and Arden, hid their store of weapons, mainly swords and dag-

gers, in the cavity especially prepared for them in the south
wall of the new stables. It was cold, wet and tense work,
but they worked quietly enough in the heavy rain that only
once did the dragoon on sentry duty hear anything, and
when he reluctantly came out to investigate he did not look
carefully enough to find the colonists, hiding behind
nearby huts and the closed, west end of the stable. When
the last weapon was stored and the stones replaced in the
wall to cover the cavity, the colonists disappeared into the
night to find what sleep they could, drenched to the skin
and shivering with cold as they were.

Heriot and Arden did not even try to find sleep. As
morning approached the rain eased off and the clouds
above started to break up. They took some bread and salt
from the communal kitchen and waited for the sun to rise.

"I've been thinking," Heriot said, munching on bread.

"As head of the Colonists' Guild, that's what you're
paid to do," Arden said solemnly.

"I get paid for this?" Heriot asked.

"In respect," Arden said. "You get lots of respect."

Heriot looked a little crestfallen. "Oh."

"You were saying?"

"That maybe we shouldn't be hoarding weapons."

Arden stared at Heriot for a moment. "But it was your
idea."

"I think knowing we have them, that we're prepared to
use them, may influence our people into thinking we will
not find common cause with the nativists."

"Maybe we won't."

"I've said it before, Arden, but I think unless we all accept ourselves as Kydans, then we will fall. The weapons
may not help us get to that point, that's all I'm saying."

"On the other hand, if the nativists do attack, we'll need

the weapons to defend ourselves. If we're dead, we've got no chance to become Kydans. Or anything else for that matter."

Heriot sighed deeply. "I don't know what the answer is."

"Maybe there is no answer. Maybe we just stumble from day to day, hoping for the best, hoping we survive."

"There must be more to it than that," Heriot said in a small voice.

"You are a dreamer," Arden said, but softly, and with affection.

"And you're not, Grim Arden?"

Before he could answer they heard one of the watch on the south of Karhay call out. Both stood and looked towards the channel. In the still dim light, they could make out a small boat being rowed across from Herris. "Who is it?" Heriot asked.

Arden shrugged. "Let's go down and find out."

They met the boat on the shore, together with half-a-dozen other colonists roused by the watch's call. An old man got out of the boat, peered among the faces in front of him, then craned his neck to look at Arden.

"You must be the grim one," the man said in hesitant Hamilayan.

Arden breathed through his nose. "I'm not grim."

"Just dour," Heriot said, smiling.

The man was obviously measuring Heriot against Arden. "And you are Heriot Fleetwood, if the description I was given was correct."

"It was. Who are you? And how do you come to speak our language?"

"I am a servant of the Malvaras, and they are a trading family; I often carried out business for them with merchants from Rivald and Hamilay. I was sent by the prefect,

Poloma Malvara, to ask you, Heriot Fleetwood, and your big friend here, to come to the Saddle this morning, just as you did yesterday morning. Bring as many colonists as you see fit."

Heriot frowned. "The prefect wants us to come in force to Herris?"

The servant shrugged. "Apparently. He says it has to do with justice and resolution."

Heriot and Arden exchanged puzzled glances, then she said to the man, "Tell the prefect we will do as he asks."

"Come across when the sun is a handspan above the eastern horizon," the servant said, and got back into his boat and rowed off. .

It occurred to Poloma as he was on his way to the meeting in the Saddle that his arrangements were taking on the form of one of those plays he occasionally saw in Omeralt during his exile in the Hamilayan capital. The complex political maneuvers resembled the complex plots of a Kevleren drama, full of dramatic turns, surprise twists and—he fervently hoped—a happy resolution. But unlike in a play, the last could not be guaranteed.

He intentionally reached the top of the west ramp that descended to the Saddle at a later time than he told his servants to ask the other players to arrive. A considerable number of nativists had already gathered, with Kysor Nevri at their head, watching apprehensively as a group of colonists arrived by boat from Karhay. Between them, as yesterday, was a half-troop of dragoons, mounted, with Gos Linsedd at their head. And descending down the opposite ramp was Galys Valera; he was pleased to see Kadburn Axkevleren was with her. Good. The entire cast was present.

Poloma swallowed. All except Sorkro, bedridden, hanging onto life like the last leaf on a tree in autumn despite the wind tying to blow her away. He did not think Hattie was right. Sorkro was not slipping away from life, she was being dragged.

He took a deep breath. "And now for the show," he muttered. The three servants he had brought with him to control Lannel Thorey looked askance at him, while their prisoner stared at the horizon, trying to hold his body erect despite the ropes that bound him. As they started together down the ramp, someone among the nativists saw them and called out to Kysor Nevri. An angry murmur rippled through them and Poloma tried to swallow his growing fear. He saw that Kysor Nevri, having seen who the prefect held captive, was trying to calm down his followers, not rile them into action.

Without looking left or right, without answering any questions, Poloma and his servants marched Thorey, who remained as silent as his captors, through the nativists and stopped under the protection of the dragoons.

"What is all this about?" Gos asked Poloma.

"You will see," the prefect said, not looking at him. He beckoned for the nativists and colonists to come closer. The dragoons shifted uncomfortably on their horses, but people were wary enough to leave a wide circle around them. Poloma waited until Galys and Kadburn had joined them at the centre, then as roughly as his strength allowed, pulled Lannel Thorey towards Heriot and Arden and then pushed him in the back so hard he fell onto the ground at their feet. The nativists cried out in sudden anger.

"Prefect, who is this man?" Heriot asked.

"His name is Lannel Thorey," Poloma said loudly. A

hush fell over the crowd. "He is the man who killed your friend Carder."

Poloma expected an uproar, or at least some sign of rage from the colonists and some sign of denial from the nativists, which is why he had arranged for Gos Linsedd and his dragoons to be present, but he did not expect the heavy weight of silence that followed his declaration.

Heriot pointed to the gangly man. "He killed my friend?" Anger tightened her voice.

Poloma nodded.

Heriot took a few steps towards the man. "His name is Lannel . . ."

"Lannel Thorey," Poloma said. "A man of Kydan."

Still no one spoke.

"He is yours, Heriot Fleetwood," Poloma told her, "yours to punish as you see fit."

"As I see fit," she repeated. Her gaze was fixed on Lannel Thorey's face. She hated him with a sudden intensity that made her breath quicken and her pale face flush with blood. Behind her, still with the other colonists, stood Arden, saying nothing, watching Heriot as intensely as she watched the murderer.

"As you and the colonists see fit to punish a Kydan who slew one of your own," Poloma replied.

Heriot looked up sharply. "Who killed a man of Kydan," she said.

Poloma regarded her levelly but did not reply.

Heriot went to one of the dragoons and drew his saber before the trooper could stop her. She marched back to Lannel Thorey and raised the blade high above her head. The man looked at her steadily, without remorse or hate, just a blank acceptance that made her hesitate. For the most part the colonists and nativists were too surprised by

Poloma's revelation to react, but some of the nativists started raising their voices in protest.

Arden's voice rose above the gathering. "As you said, Heriot Fleetwood, he killed one of us, a man of Kydan."

She moved to bring the sword down, but although she tried to put her whole body into the effort her arms stayed upright, the sword still pointed to the sky, as if held by some invisible bond. She remembered Carder—respectful, hardworking, gentle Carder—grunted in effort and something like pain and tried again. The saber swung down, whistling, and chinked into the soil by Lannel Thorey's hand. He blinked as dirt sprung into his eye.

Heriot said stiffly, "He killed a Kydan. Let the Assembly decide his fate."

17

COUNTRY air was losing its appeal for Lerena Kevleren. Too much of a good thing, she decided, was wearying. It was her own fault, she knew; she had declared early in the journey to Rivald that as empress she must travel by sedan, despite her advisors recommending she travel in horse-drawn carriage. Being drawn by animals would not befit her station, she told them. By the time her expedition started its ascent of the mountain range that separated Hamilay from Rivald she knew insisting on the sedan had been a big mistake.

It was the landscape, she decided. She remembered the one time she had traveled by the filthy steam carriage from Omeralt to Somah, she had seen the countryside change almost minute by minute, from the dry uplands around the capital to the verdant pastures and forests of the coast. But traveling by foot, the landscape changed too slowly to be remotely interesting. One day was much the same as the next. And every night she was lodged in a different mansion, or sometimes nothing more grand than a large house whose occupants had been chased out by her Royal Guards. And the air. It was pure enough, she granted, but it gave her hayfever, and all the animals about did their business wherever they liked without any discipline whatsoever, and as any Kevleren could tell you, without discipline there was no love.

The countryside could do with some tidying up. Perhaps, Lerena thought to herself, that was something she could turn her mind to after this Rivald business. She had by now completely dismissed from her mind any plans to build her own farm. Her ancestors had been quite right in banning all animals from Omeralt, except for those familiars belonging to members of the Kevleren family, and the thought of spending her summers amidst a lot of mooing, baying, hee-hawing, neighing, whinnying, mewling and shitting animals was an anathema. Better to stay in Yunara's lovely aviary. *My* lovely aviary, she reminded herself.

The climb up the mountains was bumpy, too, as her carriers strove to keep her sedan level despite the slope and the slippery road. She was jostled one way and then the next, and when Uilder was with her they were sometimes thrown together despite Uilder's best efforts. Lerena got tired of hearing, "I'm sorry, your Majesty" and "I beg your forgiveness, your Majesty," and very tired of saying, "It wasn't your fault" and "Never mind, dear, but could you get your elbow out of my neck?"

Lerena did, however, find some satisfaction in seeing the look on the face of the commander in charge of the patrols along the border. He had been told to expect the empress and her retinue for a state visit to Rivald, but in case of spies among his soldiers or in his camp, he was not told she was being accompanied by an army. The first thing he could think to say was, "Your Majesty, I do not have the supplies to feed such a force!"

"Close your mouth, Commander," she told him. "And don't worry yourself. We brought our own supplies, and soon enough we'll be eating off the fat of Rivald."

The commander, numbed into shocked silence, stood to attention next to Lerena's sedan as the full complement of the Royal Guards marched past in perfect time. In their great coats and dark green shakoes they looked impressive enough to make even Lerena's heart swell with pride. The effect on the locals and the frontier troops, used to wearing foraging gear and any old cap, was one of gawping astonishment. Lerena thought they looked like a line of stranded fish.

The Royal Guards were followed by her family members, pale and dark-haired, impressive and dour and escorted by their Axkevlerens. Then more Royal Guards and cavalry and line infantry and . . .

Lerena sighed. It was such a procession. Standing atop a mountain and watching her fine army march past almost made up for the journey. She looked north, silently farewelling her empire until she should return. The blue water of Horse Run Lake glistened far below, and she could dimly make out a smudge of brown smoke from the thousands of hearths that warmed the houses of Kuttle, the largest Hamilayan city before the border. North of the lake was a great forest, dark and forbidding and growing up the slopes of the mountains like a green blanket. Some Hamilayan historians suggested it was from here, rather than Hamewald on the other side of the border, that the Kevlerens originated centuries ago, spreading north and south and dominating all they met.

Then Lerena looked south, across the uplands of Rivald, and beyond to a hazy yellow expanse of grasslands. My new province, she thought to herself, just waiting to be taken. Another day or two and they should reach the border itself, situated in an easily defended pass. Once the pass was secured, though, the whole of the south was open to the army, and nothing would stop them.

Lerena drew a deep breath and boarded her sedan. She gave the commander a reassuring smile and ordered her carriers to continue the journey.

Leader of a Hundred Clave Warder drank the last gulp of wine in his mug, his mind ticking over what route to take for the day's final inspection of the guards at the border post. He took pride in his position, carried out his responsibilities with all duty and care, and had learned long ago that inspecting the line the same way every night was guaranteed to encourage soldiers of the lower ranks to figure out a way to rort the system, from bribing friends to stand in for them to catching naps when they were sure they would not be discovered slacking off. Despite their tendencies to subvert the rules, he respected the men under his command, and believed they in turn respected him.

Did not like him, though. Oh, no. Once your men liked you, it was only a quick march to them hating you. If they thought you were their friend, they would start expecting favors, and favors denied only led to bad blood.

Warder put the mug down, took a moment to make sure his dress sword hung correctly from its baldric, and walked out from his quarters into the still air. Being a lowlander, he always found evenings in the mountains to be uncomfortably cold, but he had to admit that the low temperature helped keep the guards awake.

The sun was halfway below the horizon, swollen and yellow as a ripe peach. He licked his lips. Not long now before stone fruit would be in season and sent up with the supply train from Hamewald; maybe even from one of the orchards he had bought around the city for his retirement. He glanced up. The sky was cloudless, and in the east he thought he could already see the faint glimmer of a star or two.

He walked up the northwest trail first tonight because it was the first he came across in his wandering. He nodded to guards stationed along the way, occasionally stopped for a word or two, especially if he had news for them. Sometimes he would straighten a jacket or pat a shoulder or re-arrange a cap, but mostly he nodded and went on by. By the time he reached the highest point in his route the sun was down and twilight taking over. The sky above was a smooth pearly gray, slowly giving way to a velvet night. His breath frosted when he breathed out, and he could no longer feel the tip of his nose. The air seemed to become even more still, and he distinctly heard the jangle of his sword's hilt in its sheath faintly echo off the hillsides.

Warder stopped. The echo continued for a moment, then stopped. He looked around. There was nobody in sight. Above, the stars wheeled around him. He could hear his own breathing in the way that is only possible when everything else is silent. He was thinking that where he was right now, standing with the mountains all looming around him, was the loneliest place in the world.

Then he heard a chink, like a small rock falling. He turned around, saw nothing unusual at first, then on the trail noticed a strange pale thing with feathers. He knew what it was, but his mind had been so far away it was having trouble catching up. Something stung his cheek and he automatically put his hand to his face. When he drew it away it was wet with his blood.

Another arrow whisked past his nose and hit the side of the mountain. Chink.

Without meaning to, Warder screamed. A little, pathetic sound that was almost a falsetto whimper. The sound of it was high and thin, like the cry of a distant eagle.

His brain caught up but there was no more time for thinking. He spun on his heel and ran as hard as he could back down the trail, calling the alarm all the way. By the time he reached his starting point near his quarters his company had formed a double line across the pass, firegons primed and at their shoulders. Formed up like that, he realised how small in number they were, thanks to economies made by the governor in Hamewald, that upstart Beloved called Chierma. Sixty men instead of a hundred. He hoped all they were facing was a reconnaissance party or a small section of skirmishers who had decided to try their luck. After all, they were using bows not firegons, which meant the enemy had been trying to be stealthy.

He took his position at the right of the first line and attempted to catch his breath. He wiped his brow with the back of his hand, surprised how much he was sweating. He scanned the pass ahead, desperately searching for any sign of the enemy. There was none, and except for the occasional clatter of a firegon and the shifting of feet, nor was there any sound. He dabbed his cheek with his fingers to make sure he had not imagined the whole thing. Ironically, the blood reassured him.

Someone coughed, and he looked along the line. Many of his men were looking at him curiously, wondering what all the fuss was about.

They think I panicked because I saw a bird or a rabbit or something, Warder thought, and could not help blushing. He wondered if he should say something, or if defending himself would seem a failure of leadership to them. Then again, not saying anything might make them think he *had* panicked.

Damn.

"Eyes ahead!" he ordered angrily, and all faces turned away, which he felt gave him a brief respite.

A shot rang out, echoed around the pass.

"Who fired that?" he demanded.

No one answered.

He moved in front of the line, faced his men and shouted, "Who fired their weapon?" He could hear how shrill his voice was sounding.

A man on his right moved forwards. Warder thought he was about to speak, but the man dropped his firegon, put his hands to his chest and dropped.

Another shot. A man just to Warder's left screamed in pain and dropped his weapon, shaking his hand in pain. Even in the fading twilight Warder could see that the man's hand was shattered.

Another of his soldiers gasped and pointed, and Warder turned slowly to face a whole stream of Hamilay infantry marching in close order then spreading out into a double line to match his own, but with four or five times as many men.

He moved quickly out of the way and shouted, "Fire!" His command let off a ragged volley. He coughed as he breathed in gonblack smoke. One or two of the enemy fell. As if in slow motion, he watched the Hamilayans raise their own firegons, heard a muffled command from an enemy officer, and then saw the enemy lines hidden by a pale cloud. An instant later the sound of the fusillade crashed out, echoing back and forth in the pass. It was deafening, bewildering, and at first Warder could not make sense of the world. When he did, he saw his lines had too many gaps in them. After only a single volley, his company was in tatters.

The enemy fired again. He saw the head of the man beside him jerk back as if someone had tugged at his hair, then saw the surprised eyes and the neat red hole in the forehead and a trickle of thick blood ooze from it. The man dropped without a sound.

"Oh, by the Sefid," Warder muttered, forgetting there was no longer any place for the Sefid in the life of the republic.

His men started drawing back, a step at first and then two, and three. Some turned and ran.

"Wait!" he ordered.

A third volley. Something thumped into his waist and he looked down, aghast, but the only damage was to the toggle connecting his sword's sheath to the baldric, a steel stirrup now bent out of shape. Ridiculously, the first thing he thought was that it was now going to be impossible to release the baldric.

He looked up to see he was the only man still standing in position. Everyone else was running or on the ground, dead, dying or wounded.

Without thinking about it, he turned and ran himself.

It was all so clean, Lerena thought. For the site of a battle, there was little blood and no corpses at all on the ground. Until Uilder pointed to a pyre made up of what were obviously burning bodies, the fat crackling in the night air, she doubted whether the enemy had stood here at all.

She ordered her carriers to lower the sedan and she stepped out for the first time in her life onto Rivald terri-

tory. She waited until a group of Kevleren and court officials had gathered around her and declared in a strong
voice, "I hereby claim this land for the Hamilayan empire;
it will be called the Province of Rivald."

There was scattered applause and one or two weak
cheers.

The smoke from the pyre was starting to catch at the
back of Lerena's throat. She covered her mouth and coughed
politely. The smoke now had a taste to it, and she almost
gagged on it.

"We must go on," she said.

"Your Majesty, it's night," Uilder pointed out. "The
way may not be safe, and your carriers are tired."

"Get me more carriers," Lerena said determinedly. "We
move on. Another mile at least."

The army, almost settled for the night, roused itself like
a lethargic snake and crept into the growing darkness.

Leader of a Hundred Clave Warder surveyed his fellow
survivors; he counted them, automatically assessing how
fit each of them might be for further fighting. He shook his
head. Not enough to slow a raiding party let alone an invasion. As distressing as the lack of fit soldiers was the
scarcity of weapons. Most of the firegons had been dis-
carded during the rout, and between them they had no
more than a dozen firearms and an assortment of swords,
bayonets and knives.

What he wanted to do was retreat even further, retreat
all the way back to Beferen, by choice, but he knew he
could not do that. It was not that he was a brave man—he
would never forget how he ran with his command only a
few hours before—but he was fully aware that between
his home and the invading army there stood no one else,

and although they could offer no genuine resistance to the enemy, it was important some kind of contact be maintained, otherwise the enemy would be able to maneuver freely and secretly.

As soon as night had fallen, Warder had sent two runners to Hamewald, and he hoped they might be a third of the way there by now. With luck a patrol from the city garrison might pick them up. With extra luck the governor would despatch at least some reinforcements and maybe even a troop of cavalry, mounted troops being better suited for this work.

With luck, he reminded himself, and neither he nor his command had had much of that in the last day.

He carefully checked their location. The mountain road widened and leveled here, and once the Hamilayan army reached this point there was probably no stopping them. Certainly there was no army in the north of the country that would get here in time. That probably meant Hamewald would be lost, leaving the Rivald forces with no choice but to retreat, burning, breaking and poisoning everything they left behind to deny the enemy any supplies and comforts. He could see no feature or structure that would provide his men with even the barest protection. If the enemy came all they could do was withdraw out of firegon range and see what they did.

There was a call behind him and he looked over his shoulder. There was a cloud of dust on the road to the south which caught the rising sun, and as he watched it rose higher into the sky. Someone was coming north, and judging by the amount of dust being kicked up it was probably cavalry of some description. His heart immediately lightened. He glanced northwards to make sure the enemy had still not appeared. Just a little while longer, and he may yet be able to deliver the Hamilayans a nasty surprise, at least enough to slow them down a little.

He walked into the middle of the road, straightened his uniform, sheathed his sword, crossed his arms and stood as erect and as martial as possible. A short while later a small company of horse appeared, and Warder guessed as soon as he saw the formation, with two riders in front and on flank but held close to the main body, that the cavalry were working as a bodyguard. Any troop expecting imminent action would have had the boundary riders well out in front and very wide to give as much warning as possible of the enemy; this troop was protecting someone huddled in the middle, and Warder was pretty certain he knew who it was. He wondered if this boded good or ill for him and his reduced company, or good or ill for Rivald. Were there more reinforcements coming behind? Judging by the size of the dust cloud, he doubted it.

The first riders continued past Warder, but the others pulled up and moved aside for their charge, a tall man with a beaked nose and rheumy eyes. A white wig sat not quite right on his head.

Bloody upstart, Warder thought to himself. "Your Grace. This is a surprise. I was not expecting reinforcements for some time yet."

Chierma, once Axkevleren, now Governor of Hamewald, regarded the officer with distant concern. Warder frowned; he had expected disdain at best.

"You have been roughly handled," Chierma said.

"I did not have enough men to hold them," Warder answered. "The Hamilayans," he added absently. His left hand played with the hilt of his dress sword.

Chierma nodded. "I see."

"I should have had more men," Warder blurted. He was aware that all eyes turned to him, not just the governor's.

Chierma took a deep breath and surprised Warder again by nodding. "Yes, you're quite right. You could have done nothing more. You should take what is left of your command and make for Hamewald. Report to the garrison commander there. He will assign you new duties."

For a moment Warder did nothing. His head was suddenly empty, and he felt adrift.

"We have brought some small supplies," Chierma went on after a pause. "You may have what we can spare. I suggest you make your move soon, before the Hamilayans arrive."

Warder made to look behind the governor. "You have no other soldiers?"

"Just this troop. Hamewald's defense would spare no more. Indeed, Beferen has allowed us hardly any army at all." Chierma adjusted his wig. "I suspect the Safety Committee underestimated the threat from our neighbor."

"So it seems," Warder said quietly, then turned to signal to his last ensign to gather together what was left of the company. "I have some wounded, your Grace."

"Take them with you," Chierma said, looking north to the mouth of the pass. "There is nothing I can do for them here."

Warder nodded, saluted half-heartedly, and moved off the road. Chierma returned the salute and ordered some supplies to be left behind. A short while later he and his escort were gone, swallowed by the mountains, and by the time Warder's company was ready to move off even the sound of their horses, echoing in the pass, had died away.

Chierma saw the glint of metal near a rock high up the valley to his left. He ordered the troop to halt and for the outriders to return. The troop leader tried to argue with him but Chierma shut him up with a cold stare. "Now I want you all to go back," he told the officer.

"Your Grace," the man said, laughing mirthlessly, "you jest, surely? The enemy will take you without any effort. You are the governor of Hamewald, and we are sworn to protect you."

"You cannot protect me against what is coming," Chierma said levelly. "I must face this alone. I have the authority of the Safety Committee behind me, and perhaps I can convince the enemy to hold off, or at least divert them, until Beferen sends more soldiers. Either way, your presence here will be of no assistance, and may be of some hindrance.

"Return the way we came, and render if you can what aid you might to our valiant Leader of a Hundred Clave Warder on his march back to civilization." Chierma smiled, and it was so unexpected that the officer could not help smiling back.

"Off you go," Chierma ordered. "Quickly, before the enemy comes."

As they left, some looking over their shoulder at the lone governor, Chierma said softly, "And may the Sefid be with you."

"You'll want to listen to this," Idalgo said.

Paimer, who was attempting to tie his cravat correctly by looking at his reflection in a saucepan of water, said irritably, "This is not another of your riddles, is it?"

"It concerns the empress."

That got Paimer's attention. He stopped fiddling with the cravat and looked up at his Beloved. "Who is she talking to? Not herself again, I hope. She is doing that a lot, lately."

Idalgo raised his eyebrows. "You are one to talk."

Paimer did not rise to the bait. Pointing out the obvious, that he talked with Idalgo himself, would only elicit a smart-ass reply, and Paimer thought he had suffered enough at the hands of smart-asses, starting with his late sister, the previous empress, and continuing through the female line to Lerena. Not to mention one or two of the males in his life, including those who should better know their place.

"Who is she talking to?" he asked again.

"No one now," Idalgo said with a lazy sigh. "But if you hurry, you can go with her."

"Go with her?" Paimer looked around. Most of the army was still preparing for the day's march. "Go with her to where?"

"Just up ahead," Idalgo said tightly. "You'll get such a lovely surprise."

"I don't like surprises . . ."

Paimer stopped. Idalgo had gone. Probably ahead to enjoy Paimer's expression when he found his surprise. He stood up slowly, giving his muscles time to stretch, and saw Lerena's sedan winding its way through the camp. Some of the Royal Guards were hurrying to catch up and form an escort. Without quite knowing why, Paimer felt some sense of urgency and, as quick as he might, loped after them.

Some time later, Paimer saw the empress's party stop, met by some of the army's scouts, one of whom came back to speak to Lerena directly. Paimer caught up and heard the tail end of the conversation.

"He is by himself?" Lerena asked.

The scout nodded, wringing the cap in his hand. He had

probably never seen a Kevleren before, let alone spoken to one.

"And he says he is the governor of Hamewald?"

Paimer frowned in thought. The title seemed familiar. The urgency he had felt back at camp grew inside of him, and like a small child he hopped from one foot to the other. The action caught the attention of the scout, and the man stared at Paimer. Next, Lerena's head poked out of the window to see what the scout was staring at.

"Where did you come from?" Lerena asked.

Being addressed by the empress, he automatically moved to adjust his wig, but realised he had left it behind in the camp. He opened his mouth to say something but could think of nothing that would sound sensible or convincing and simply shrugged instead.

Lerena looked cross and as if she might order him back. Then she was obviously struck by what she thought was a particularly clever idea. "Uncle, you've been this way before, haven't you?" she asked sweetly.

"As you well know, your Majesty," he said, coming up to her sedan. The scout, abashed because he did not recognise Duke Paimer Kevleren without his famous red wig, bowed and moved aside for him.

Lerena pointed to the front of the party. "Then you should be the one talking to this unexpected . . . ambassador."

Paimer looked in the indicated direction, and saw a longyard away a solitary man on a horse. Faint recognition stirred in him, but he was too far away to be sure.

"Of course, your Majesty," he said, and walked forwards.

It was the wig that gave the stranger away. Paimer would

recognise it anywhere. It sat on the head of one Chierma Axkevleren, Governor of Hamewald, like a pile of guano.

Chierma wondered who was the odd-looking man walking towards him. He was lean, sparse, with something of the maniac around the eyes. His hair, what was left of it, seemed to float above his head. The walk was oddly familiar, however, and spoke of accepted authority. More, he corrected himself. *Assumed* authority. And then he knew.

Oh, by the Sefid! Chierma thought. Not him!

He gaped as the man came closer. When he was in hearing distance he said, "It is you, isn't it, your Grace?"

"Why are you still on your horse?" the duke asked stiffly.

Without thinking, Chierma dismounted, holding the reins in his hand. Some of the guards near Lerena stiffened, and he held up his hands to show he was unarmed. Both Chierma and Paimer realised the other had been reduced in some way and they studied each other intensely, searching for some hint of what their opposite had lost.

"Your wig has gone," Chierma said, knowing even as he did that that was not it.

"Pity yours hasn't," Paimer replied.

Chierma searched among those still with the empress. "Where is your Beloved?" His nose pinched as he searched his memory. "Idalgo, yes?"

"He comes and goes," Paimer said shortly. "What is it you want?"

Chierma was about to say, but something about the duke's manner, and that look in his eyes, stopped him. "I wish to talk to Empress Lerena Kevleren about a very important matter."

"You can tell me. I will pass on your message."

Chierma slowly shook his head. "I don't think so, your

Grace. If you don't mind I will convey it directly to her majesty."

Paimer seemed to consider it, then he said, "Wait here," and abruptly turned on his heel.

Chierma breathed through his nose in frustration. He could not believe he had risked all to talk with the Hami-layan empress only to find his path being obstructed by Paimer Kevleren.

The reins in his hand jerked up and he turned to see Englay sitting astride his mount.

"She will see you," Englay said. "The duke will not be able to stop that."

"You see the future," he said, trying to be sarcastic, but he could not manage it. He was irritated that she was here.

"The future," she said gaily. "What do the dead care for the future?"

"Kill him now, your Majesty," Paimer urged Lerena.

She looked at him blankly. "Whatever for?" She poked her head out again to look at the stranger. "He seems harmless enough."

"It's *him*," he said. "The one I told you about."

Lerena frowned in puzzlement. "Him?"

"The one who overthrew the Lady Englay, his mistress."

"Our cousin Englay Kevleren?"

"He was her Beloved!" he hissed.

What clouded Lerena's face at that moment was a mixture of many emotions, but Paimer was sure hatred drove them all. It crossed her face like lightning across a dark sky.

"Now I remember," she said fiercely. And then her eyes widened and all emotion except wonder left her. "But how . . . ?"

Paimer was not sure what to make of the change. "How what, your Majesty?"

"How could he be alive?" she asked, but the question was obviously directed at herself. She reached out, grasped the lapel of Paimer's jacket and pulled him towards her. "How did *he* survive the Wielding?"

And then the same look of wonder overtook Paimer. Lerena had used the Sefid to slay every Beloved in the world, and yet here was Chierma Axkevleren, Beloved to Lady Englay Kevleren, whole and hale and cheekily demanding an audience with the empress.

"Bring him to me," she said distractedly.

Paimer shook his head. "Your Majesty, consider what you are saying. If he survived the Wielding, is it safe to have him near you? Is it safe to let him live a moment longer than necessary?"

Unexpectedly, Lerena smiled. "I will not let him live a moment longer than necessary, Uncle. You have my word. Now bring him to me."

Paimer nodded stiffly, not willing to force the issue. His respect for Lerena's prowess with the Sefid, and her willingness to use it, made him more cautious than he used to be. When he turned to the waiting governor, he thought he saw two people there. He blinked, and Chierma was alone again.

It was a tight fit in the sedan, Chierma thought, even when the girl called Uilder left them. He had always assumed that the empress would have a bigger sedan than he had ever seen before, but it seemed no larger and no more comfortable than the one Englay had used. He wondered if this spoke of her modesty or frugality. Probably something to do with tradition, he thought. The Kevlerens were very big on tradition.

The empress sat opposite him, appearing relaxed and curious, and Paimer sat on his right, as tense and rigid as a steel blade. Chierma was feeling decidedly uncomfortable, but having come this far he was no longer in a position to change direction. It was worth more than his life to turn his back on Lerena, and he had an uncomfortable feeling the empress knew he understood that. He felt outmaneuvered even before negotiations had started.

The empress and her uncle regarded him silently, waiting for him to speak. At first, despite all the mental rehearsing he had done to prepare for this moment, all he could think of saying was, "Welcome to the Republic of Rivald, your Majesty." He bit his lip when he realized what he had said—reminding the empress of the overthrow of her own family—but it was too late to unsay it, so he smiled in what he hoped was a convincingly ironic manner. To his relief, she returned the smile, minus the irony.

"What you mean, Governor, is welcome to the Hamilayan province of Rivald."

"Ah," Chierma said, and noticed that even the Royal Guards outside were dressed for fighting and not the parade ground. "A state visit, then."

"Exactly. I'm touring my lands, meeting the people. It's something I've been meaning to do for quite some time."

"I have been preparing the way for you," Chierma said carefully.

"I can imagine," Paimer scoffed.

Chierma ignored the duke and did not take his eyes off Lerena. "You met with hardly any resistance in the pass. In the last war, we held you up there for weeks. The ease of your passage was entirely my doing. I was responsible for organizing and posting the troops in my district. The way to Hamewald and south through Rivald's great plains is virtually clear. The north of the country . . . the province . . . is, for all intents and purposes, already yours."

Chierma could not see whether or not the empress was surprised by the news. Again, there was a long pause, but this time he restrained from filling the silence. He had come to say what he intended. What happened next was entirely in their hands.

"Well, is this not a turnaround?" Lerena asked eventually. Chierma was not sure if she was directing the question to him or Paimer. He was not sure he liked the term "turnaround," since it could be applied to him as easily as the situation he created for Hamilay.

Paimer nodded, reluctantly conceding the point, barely glancing at Chierma.

"We shall advance at once," Lerena continued. "And you, Governor, will stay close to me. I would seek your advice on several matters."

"Of course, your Majesty," Chierma said, bowing as low as he could in his seat to hide the blush of relief.

"I will place you in the care of my uncle, the duke. You shall consult with one another and advise me on Rivald."

Both men looked aghast at each other.

Lerena grinned, enjoying the reaction. "I'm sure you have a great deal to catch up with."

The air inside Paimer's tent was a little smoky from the two braziers, despite a draught hole in the centre of the roof, and the carpet, cushions and seats made the space seem more like a tavern than a tent. Paimer and his guest were sitting opposite each other, each being served wine from different servants. The guest did not look as if he was having a good time, and Paimer did not even pretend to enjoy playing the host.

"You look exhausted," Paimer said to Chierma.

"It's been a long day," Chierma said flatly.

"Do you recognize the wine?" Paimer asked.

"I remember," the guest said solemnly.

"Of course, from my last visit." Paimer blew air out of his cheeks. "Who would ever have guessed that one day I would be returning the favour of your hospitality, Governor Chierma?" Paimer swallowed a large mouthful of wine and hiccuped. "Actually, no, no, no. Sorry. Won't do at all. You are No Name, late Governor of Hamewald. You have nothing. Nothing at all. No master, no mistress. Not even a country."

"Her majesty says we are to consult with each other," Chierma said, changing the subject.

"That is her idea of a joke," Paimer said evenly. "She does things like that lately. She is hard to predict. Sometimes she is even hard to understand."

The duke finished his wine and held his mug out for a refill. A servant hurried to oblige. "Well, let us consult the vintage from Offra. We shall tell her majesty what wise words we receive from the vine."

Chierma looked doubtful at first. He looked around the tent as if searching for an escape route. Then he sighed heavily, shrugged, drained his mug and held it up for a refill. "Why not, your Grace. Your health."

After an hour of drinking, which included precious little conversation, Paimer dismissed the servants and did the pouring himself. After another hour, the conversation picked up for a while, covering the governance of Hamewald, the geography and the weather of Rivald, local music . . . but then their attention started wandering. They were finding it increasingly difficult to remain perched on their seats, and in the end they sat on the carpet and stretched out on it, and soon both fell asleep.

18

VELAN Lymok knew Numoya Kevleren was using his new eyes to watch from the keep, so he sat as erect as possible on his horse and resisted the temptation to slide a finger around his starched collar every few minutes to let in some air. At the same time, he tried to control his temper as the rabble in front of him slowly—oh, so slowly!—started to take on something of the discipline of real soldiers. In truth they were simple warriors, trained from childhood to fight with sword and spear as individuals; an army for them was nothing more than several hundred individual fighters, whereas for states like Rivald and Hamilay, an army was a single creature with a single mind and a single intent.

"Look sharp on the right!" he cried with as much authority and as little exasperation as possible. "You're drifting! Keep close to the man on your left!"

The members of the right-most file shuffled back into formation.

"And keep your firegons upright and close to your chest. You, man! The one with the orange shirt! Both hands on the firegon! It's not a flower for your mistress!"

Rough laughter, much blushing on the part of the fellow with the orange shirt. Quenion had promised Velan proper uniforms soon, which would help instil a sense of unity and pride. The blue and white of Rivald would certainly look better in rank and file than the present rainbow of red and yellow and green and orange, all the vegetable dye colours the locals had used for centuries and saw no need to change.

Velan sighed heavily. Quenion had also promised him real firegons. At the moment, his recruits had to practise with branches, broom handles and fence posts, anything with the rough weight and dimensions of a real firegon.

Promises. Lots of those so far, Velan thought. Not much else.

"Wheel left!" he shouted.

And wonder of wonders, the rabble, if only for a few seconds, actually performed like a real company of soldiers. The left file stepped in place while turning a quarter, while each succeeding file marched at a slightly faster pace until the whole unit had done a perfect wheel. Velan hoped his highness had seen that. His majesty, Velan corrected himself.

"That was pretty," Numoya said appreciatively. He dabbed at the sweat on his forehead with his sleeve.

"They just turned left," Quenion said.

"One hundred men *wheeled* left at the same time while keeping in formation," Numoya answered, his voice coldly neutral.

Quenion swallowed. "Yes, of course."

"Do not speak out on matters about which you have no understanding."

"Of course, your Majesty."

Numoya turned away from the window and regarded

his Beloved. She met his gaze for a moment before lowering her eyes, as befitted her position.

"You are better today?" she asked.

"You are reminding me of your service," Numoya said petulantly.

Quenion's shoulders slumped. "No, your Majesty. I was inquiring after your health. I am concerned for you."

"As is your duty."

She nodded. "Of course."

"I am feeling better," he said stiffly. "Every day I see further, and every day details are more sharp. This morning when I woke I saw that the sky was blue."

"That is wonderful news!" she said excitedly, looking up again.

"But that is the only color I can see."

"It is only the first, your Majesty. I know it! Soon you will see green and red—"

Numoya held up his hand and she stopped. "Again, I must remind you. Do not speak out on matters about which you have no understanding."

"I can expect it, surely?" she pleaded. Did he not see that she hoped for *his* sake?

"Expect nothing."

Again, she cast down her gaze. "Nothing, your Majesty?"

"Do you know what separates my kind from the rest of humanity, my Beloved?"

Quenion could hear the anger lying beneath his apparently calm voice, and she was afraid of it. "So many things, your Majesty—"

"One thing," Numoya hissed, the anger surfacing so quickly that Quenion involuntarily retreated a step. "And one thing only. Our ability to use the Sefid. Everything else—our power, our authority, our *right* to rule—stems solely from that. If not for the Sefid, the Kevlerens would not exist, and if not for the Kevlerens the Axkevlerens, the Beloveds, the Hamilayan empire and the kingdom of Rivald would never have existed."

"I know this, your Majesty—"

"Yet still, against every precept, all your training, against the Kevlerens themselves, you believed *you* could manipulate the Sefid to gain what you wanted."

"No, your Majesty!" Quenion pleaded. "Never! I helped you use it! I only wanted to help you!"

"You used me, Quenion, the way a soldier uses a firegon or an archer a bow and arrow. You drugged me, then used me."

"Only to give you back your life! To make you whole!"

"Know then, Quenion Axkevleren, that because of what you have done, because of your transgression, I will never be whole again. Through me or not, you used the Sefid to Wield, and the universe is made awry because of it."

Quenion's eyes filled with tears, and she held up her head to keep them from rolling down her cheeks. She did not want Numoya to see her cry. He would be even more ashamed of her.

"Get out of my sight," Numoya ordered her, his voice returning to a cold neutrality. "I will send for you if I need you."

After she was gone he put a hand against a wall to steady himself. He was feeling suddenly light-headed. He used his sleeve to dab at his forehead again.

Ever since reports had stopped coming down from Chierma in Hamewald, President Croft Harker had been preparing himself for the worst. Steeling himself against despair, he could not help going over the republic's short history again and again trying to identify where it had all gone wrong, and every time he came to the same conclusion: that Rivald's death warrant had been signed as soon as the Safety Committee had overthrown the ruling Kevlerens.

Indeed, not just Rivald's death warrant. He doubted Empress Lerena Kevleren would be disposed to grant clemency to many on the Safety Committee.

When the courier arrived with reports of a large Hamilayan army making its steady progress south from Hamewald, he did not in fact feel despair at all, just a sullen hatred of Lerena and her family.

He immediately called a meeting of the Safety Committee. He intentionally arrived late so the entire committee would be present, sat down without acknowledging anyone's greeting, opened a folder and without formality read the message delivered by the courier. When he finished he looked up, surprised how quietly his colleagues accepted the news. He waited, and no one said a word.

It is their fatalism, he thought, and lack of imagination. They have no conception of what has befallen Rivald.

"I believe we must confront this threat to the republic," he said.

"We shall defend Beferen," Leader of a Thousand Klyne Ferren said. He was the most senior member of the committee, and in many ways the most old-fashioned despite his support for the revolution. He sometimes reminisced about the "old days" as if they were a golden age instead of a time of tyranny and repression.

"We will set up barricades, conscript the population—"

"Barricades will not stop the Hamilayans," Harker said. Ferren blinked at the interruption. Harker usually coddled and shepherded Ferren to earn his support, but he had neither the inclination nor the time to indulge the old officer on this occasion.

Ferren looked piqued. "Then what of this Kevleren who sits in our colony of Sayenna? What has come of your attempt to lure him back to help defend the republic?"

"It is too late to expect help from that quarter. Even if Numoya Kevleren agreed to help us, he would not get here in time. I had hoped the invasion would be another year off. I was wrong." He met the gaze of every other member. "We were *all* wrong."

"Then what do you suggest?" Leader of a Thousand Marquella Montranto asked, almost as if he had been cued.

"First, I need extraordinary powers, above and beyond those the committee has already accorded the office of president. I need plenipotentiary authority to deal with the crisis."

"I will move such a motion," Montranto said.

"Wait on," Ferren said. "We don't even know what powers Harker is asking for."

"Does it matter?" Harker asked. "Do any of you have any plan for confronting the Hamilayans before they reach Beferen? And other than trying to barricade the city against the Sefid," he continued, staring down Ferren, "do any of you have any plans to defend the capital?"

There was silence, and Ferren looked away from the president, surrendering. He sighed, and seemed to take on another decade of life. "I will second the motion," he said wearily.

So overawed were the members of the committee by the invasion and by Harker's apparent decisiveness and determination, there were no other dissenting voices and the vote was carried unanimously.

Harker smiled thinly. He had not wanted any interference, but he could not help feeling that some sign of resistance would have reflected greater courage among his colleagues. Well and good, he thought, they deserved whatever fate Lerena handed out to them.

"As of this moment, then, the Safety Committee of the republic of Rivald is prorogued. You will all be assigned military functions in due course, mostly to do with the defence of Beferen."

Before any questions could be asked, he stood and left, leaving the others to reflect on what the future might hold for them. They would understand in time, Harker knew, that indeed they had little future at all.

Numoya took over one of the keep's chambers as a campaign room. He placed several tall wooden tables in it, then covered all but one of the tables with every map and chart Quenion could obtain of the New Land. On the largest table, however, he kept a master map, where all verified geographical information was recorded, together with notes about the height of hills, the depth of rivers, seasonal rainfall and anything else that might affect an army on the march and in need of supplies. Over time, a thick dark line representing the proposed route slowly wound its way from Sayenna towards Kydan, following The Wash north until it met the junction of the Elder and Younger rivers, then heading northwest directly towards the Bay of Kydan, avoiding the Frey River altogether. A thinner line followed The Wash to the Elder, from the Elder to the Frey, and then west to Kydan; the reverse of the route Numoya and Quenion had travelled in their flight to Sayenna.

The first route presented two problems: the country between the point where the army left the river system and

headed inland towards the Bay of Kydan was largely unknown, and any attack on Kydan required boats. If the
army had followed the rivers all the way, the boats only
needed to cross the small gap of land between the Elder
and the Frey, but overland they needed transport, and because of their weight the only animal that could pull the
boats the whole distance were bullocks.

"But that means slowing down the whole army," Numoya mused aloud, tapping his lips with a pen.

"Which makes it vulnerable," Quenion said cautiously.

"Obviously."

"But only if there are peoples on the route with the
courage to attack it."

Numoya stared at Quenion under heavy lids. "If you
had procured better charts and reports of the land between
The Wash and the Bay of Kydan, we would have a better
idea of that possibility." He sighed deeply. "Anyway, I'm
not concerned about an attack that would threaten the
army, but small pinprick raids that will divert its attention,
slow it down even further. I want Kydan in my hands before the end of summer, and any delay threatens that objective. If we wait until autumn, who knows how many
reinforcements Hamilay will have sent to secure the city.
We have to strike now, and block off Hamilay's main
access to the New Land. Only then will we be safe in
Sayenna."

"I tried . . ."

"You should have sent traders into this territory."

"They use the rivers, rely on them to get their
goods . . ."

"You are making excuses. You should have used your
initiative."

He saw something flicker in Quenion's eyes. "I did that

once," she said quietly, "to heal you, and seem only to have embittered you."

"That was theft," he said coldly. "You stole the life of an innocent." His voice rose as anger flared in him. "You stole the life of someone who had not been trained as an Axkevleren, who did not understand what she was doing." He flung his pen on the map. Ink splattered from its end. He rubbed his forehead with one hand. "You stole my love for you!"

Quenion gasped in shock and ran from the room. Numoya opened his mouth to order her to return, but something, some shadow of his former feelings for her, stopped him. He listened to her retreating steps on the stone stairs outside, feeling sorry for her but even sorrier for himself.

Love for Quenion had grown in him—indeed, must have been present for her manipulation of the Sefid to work—but that very deception had crushed it like a flower under a great stone. She had used him like a Kevleren using an Axkevleren, to access the Sefid for her own purpose, and using his love for her as the key. She had demeaned him, and as well had caused the death of an innocent, someone he did not know or love.

Numoya's head pulsed with a heavy ache. He went to the room's only window and looked out over his kingdom. He smiled mirthlessly at the grandiose joke. His *kingdom*. He could have walked from one end of it to the other in less time than it would take him to eat his evening meal.

He had to admit, however, that it was a pretty place. He did not know if he would ever get used to the warm sun in this part of the world, but that was more than compensated by the strong, bright colours and the clear sky and the promise of a future grander than anything offered him by Beferen and its Safety Committee.

Numoya touched his eyes. It was a miracle he could look out over Sayenna. He grimaced then, and remembered it was not a miracle of his own making.

He closed his eyes and the ache behind them slowly abated.

Velan Lymok's favourite time of day was sunset. Although the sun was stronger in the New Land than he was used to back in Beferen, he found himself acclimatizing very quickly. He liked the warmth on his face as he stood at the top of the keep and looked west back towards Rivald and Hamilay, the old lands, the old ways. He was saying goodbye to them forever, and was glad of it. A sea breeze brought the smell of ozone and tide, of a future unencumbered.

Unencumbered by anything except uncertainty, he told himself honestly, for he was unsure what the future would bring. He was no leader, not really, despite the uniform and the rank. He knew the parade-ground drill, the theory of it, but he had never expected to do more than lead small patrols out to guard Rivald's northern frontier with Hamilay. He certainly never expected to be one of those leading an invasion force.

He laughed despite himself. It was a joke, of course, played against him by fate, or the Sefid, or the Kevlerens. Perhaps all three working together to send Velan Lymok onto the battlefield as a general. All history nothing but a rehearsal for the great comedy about a man afraid of responsibility in charge of an army.

Thinking of the army, he looked north to the river plain north of Sayenna. Fields and orchards had been taken over by a great camp, and just by glancing at its ragged fringe and counting the new tents and shelters he could tell how much it had grown during the day. As many as two thousand had gathered together, recruits from all along the river and the area around Sayenna. By Hamilayan or even Rivald standards only moderate in size, but as the natives constantly told him, no armed force on this scale had ever been seen before in the New Land.

Velan had been spending every daylight hour drilling four companies, each of a hundred men. He did not think Quenion would be able to scrounge up or make that many firegons, at least not to a standard that he would put much faith in them under battlefield conditions, but the rest could still fight with their traditional weapons.

With properly drilled companies leading the way, they should have an army without peer in the New Land, and certainly one capable of taking Kydan, even if that city still had a handful of longgons, as Quenion assured him it did, or at least did up to the point she and Numoya had escaped from the city.

He heard someone climbing the steps to the tower, and Quenion appeared. For a moment their eyes met, but Velan broke the contact, coughed as if he was interrupting a private conversation and pretended to look out again at the landscape. Quenion blushed slightly and looked as if she might turn around and go back down again. Velan secretly hoped she would, but she seemed to steel herself and went to stand by him. He tried to pretend she was not there by determinedly staring at the middle distance.

"Tell me, Leader of a Thousand Velan Lymok, was it what you saw that displeases you about me, or what you think you saw?"

He was not surprised she knew how he felt, but was surprised at her directness. He wondered if all Beloveds were so blunt.

It was confidence, he realised with a shock; that was

what she possessed, that was what drove the bluntness, a willingness to confront any obstacle. She should be leading the Kevleren's army, not he. And then, with surprising intensity, he was struck by the thought that she probably *was* leading the army: after all, she was responsible for creating it, recruiting for it, arming it . . . for all he knew, she might even be creating its strategy, letting the Kevleren think it was all his idea.

"I know what I saw," he said feebly, and stepped away from her, making for the steps.

Quenion grasped him by the elbow. "Wait. What did you see?"

Velan shook his head.

"Tell me, *what* did you see?"

Velan prised open her fingers and turned away.

"What are you afraid of, Leader of a Thousand?"

He turned suddenly, fear and doubt, frustration and anger, surging through him. "What am I afraid of? For a start, how about knowing that at any time, at the slightest whim, you could take anyone you choose, including me, and turn them into a corpse so his bloody majesty can manage a spot of Wielding?

"Or how about expecting to be nothing but a courier for the Safety Committee and ending up being general of a rabble of barely trained natives on behalf of a rebellious prince—"

Velan stopped, knowing he had gone too far. The skin on his arms goosebumped, and the hair bristled on his nape. He swallowed, wiped spittle from his mouth with the back of a hand. Then a strange calm settled on him, and he waited to see what Quenion would do, half expecting her to cry for her master.

*   *   *

As soon as the committee meeting had finished—and Harker was confident there would never be another—he set in place people he knew could administer the republic and its capital for the time he expected to be away. If he succeeded in his mission, he would be back in a matter of days. If he failed, then long-term administration would soon be in the hands of the Empress Lerena.

Harker also sent the handful of officers from the Safety Committee whom he trusted implicitly to the three main military camps within a day's ride, ordering them to organize what troops they could and meet him at the headwaters of the Eskelstone, the river that eventually ran through the capital to meet the sea.

On the day he himself left Beferen with a small escort, he paused long enough to look back with mixed emotions at the city, loathing its miserable climate but not able to despise it completely. It was like a limpet, hanging onto its wet perch regardless of hazard, and about as attractive, but Harker could not help admiring it for its stolid, almost pugnacious resilience. He did not think he would ever see it again.

"President Harker, where do we go?" one of his escort asked.

"North," Harker said. "As fast as we can ride."

"I did not kill the girl, if that's what you were thinking."

Velan, still waiting for denunciation, said, "I saw you covered in her blood."

Quenion nodded. "I did not think it would be so . . . messy."

"Then you did kill her," Velan said, a voice in his mind telling him to let it go and get away from the woman. No good would come of this conversation. But she stood there, her expression almost pleading, and he found he could not leave her.

"She died because of what I did, but she did not die by my hand. That would have made her useless for his majesty's needs."

"You mean as a sacrifice." He said the word almost as a sneer.

"Of course. How else was he to be made well? What chance had we of surviving, of furthering his majesty's cause, if he was not whole again?"

"Are our survival and his majesty's cause so inextricably linked?"

Quenion blanched, and again Velan expected her to cry out, to denounce his treachery. Instead, she said, "I am his Beloved. What else can I think?"

He assumed she was being rhetorical, but a part of him wondered. What did she want from him?

"We cannot return to Beferen," she continued. "You know that."

"The despatch you sent back to the Safety Committee guarantees that," Velan said shortly.

"Even before that you knew Numoya Kevleren would not return, and you knew you would not return. You have no future in Rivald. As soon as you stepped off the ship that brought you here you knew that. I could see it in your eyes.

"We are committed to the New Land, and have only one enemy that stands in our way, the same enemy our people faced in Rivald. The Hamilayans are in Kydan, and until they are removed we will not be safe, and for us to defeat Kydan we need two things: an army and Numoya Kevleren."

Velan returned to the parapet and once again looked north, across rich fields, the camp of the gathering army, grass plains that extended all the way to distant mountains. An onshore breeze brought the smell of the sea as well, and it all made him think of limitless space, of unbounded potential. It was there for the taking, if he had the courage. Then he looked down and saw some of Numoya's household in the keep's courtyard; some were washing clothes, one sewing, another chopping off the head of a chicken. He felt suddenly repulsed by the whole idea of being a servant of the Kevlerens. But what choice had he any more? What choice did any of them have?

It occurred to him then that Quenion was not pleading for Numoya's cause but for herself. She wanted absolution for what she had done to heal her master, and as the only other witness of what had happened she was seeking it from Velan.

"Not even a great cause excuses *any* action," he said.

He was surprised when she smiled slightly. "You understand then? You understand what I am going through?" She spoke as if it was enough, as if all she needed was to know that he understood why she had done what she had done, even if he did not condone it. Who else in all of the New Land could she have turned to?

And Velan thought that a time might come in the war when he too could be compelled to carry out some order or action or perform some deed that needed not forgiveness but simple understanding.

"I do," he said truthfully.

19

I thought you were going to take off that man's head," Arden said.

Heriot Fleetwood stopped at the entrance to the Assembly. She frowned in thought and said, "I wanted to. I thought I was going to."

"What stopped you?"

"You did, as you well know."

Heriot thought Arden actually managed to look smug, a first for him.

People edged around the pair to get into the building; some brave souls muttered something about the manners of foreigners, glancing sideways at Arden.

"You helped me realise we had reached the point where we, the colonists, had to make our stand either as Hamilayans—exiles—or as Kydans. You surprised me. I thought you were quite ready to take up arms against the nativists."

"I was," Arden said darkly. "Until that moment I thought we were going to."

"And what changed *your* mind?"

"A politician," he said. "Come on, we'll be late."

To the relief of many behind them, they moved into the

Assembly and found seats high up in the gallery. Most of the councilors were already present, and standing by Poloma were Galys, Kadburn and Gos.

"You mean our illustrious prefect?" Heriot asked.

"There's more to your friend than meets the eye."

She remembered the first time she had met Poloma Malvara, in the colony's recruiting office in Omeralt. She had been very impressed by the exotic-looking man, and believed he was a prince. In a way, he was a prince, or what might pass for one in Omeralt. He had treated her with unexpected courtesy, and although he had not been able to help her, something about his manner had helped her make the decision to leave the old world. At the time she'd thought she was going to the island of Kael, the furthest limit of the Hamilayan empire, and according to rumor a place of unlimited opportunity.

Heriot smiled to herself. Unlimited, indeed. Kael was only a small province, while the New Land was a whole continent, largely unexplored and unknown, as terrifying and alluring as the future. And Poloma was a part of that. In some ways, he was the key to the New Land and the future together.

On and off, the two had met several times since their first encounter, on the voyage across the Deepening Sea and subsequently as prefect and head of the Colonists' Guild. She recognised in him a gentleness and earnestness that appealed to her, and a deep reserve of unexpected courage in someone so slight and unassuming. There was, as Arden suggested, more to him than met the eye.

When the Assembly had filled, Poloma made a signal to someone near the entrance, and Lannel Thorey was escorted in by two colonists and two nativists, his hands still bound. He held himself erect, but there was no sign of

pride or hope in his face. He was made to stand at the opposite end of the council table from Poloma, who said
something in Kydan, then repeated it in Hamilayan for the
benefit of the colonists, recounting what he had discovered
about the death of Carder. Kysor Nevri and some of his
supporters made a show of being bored by the recounting,
muttering for the prefect to hurry up. Some councilors, and
many in the galleries, told them in turn to be quiet. Heriot
was pleased to see the opinion among the nativists shift so
decidedly against Nevri.

Then Poloma told the Assembly how the prisoner had
crept into his house to kill him. On hearing this, even Nevri
and his supporters were silenced, and Heriot and Arden
exchanged surprised glances. Finally, Poloma told how
Heriot Fleetwood, a true Kydan, had passed responsibility
for Thorey's judgement and sentence to the Assembly. He
asked Heriot to stand, and when, reluctantly, she did so,
most of those in the galleries applauded her. Blushing, she
sat down again.

Still speaking first in Kydan and then in Hamilayan,
Poloma asked the Assembly to judge Thorey. Poloma nodded to Kysor Nevri, and Heriot had never before seen a
man look so divided; to his credit, he looked Thorey
square in the eyes and said, *"Amrifa."*

"Guilty," Poloma translated, and it seemed a great sigh
of relief went up from most in the gallery and not a few of
the councilors.

Poloma then nodded to the man next to Nevri.

"Amrifa."

And the man next to him.

"Amrifa."

And so it went, round the whole table. Not one councilor declared Thorey innocent of the death of Carder.

"The Assembly finds Lannel Thorey guilty of killing Carder," Poloma declared. "Now we must sentence him."

"No," Nevri interrupted, his voice unexpectedly confident. "First we must decide the status of his victim."

"What do you mean?" Poloma demanded.

"I mean, we must determine whether or not this Carder was a Kydan and so warrants the attention of the council's justice."

Poloma should have guessed that Kysor Nevri would come up with some way of defending his supporter, but too late realised his success in getting the colonists in the person of Heriot Fleetwood to accede to the authority of the Assembly had made him overconfident. He had ordered the city council to meet urgently so he could use the dramatic revelation of Thorey's crimes to force the whole city to unite behind him rather than Nevri. But his opponent was not going to give up so easily; cornered, he was fighting back, keeping open for as long as possible the division between native Kydans and colonists.

He quickly explained to Galys, Kadburn and Gos what Nevri had said. Nevri, quite content to have thrown Poloma's plans into chaos, left the next move to the prefect.

"Whether Carder is considered Kydan or not is another issue entirely, surely," Galys said to Poloma.

"Regrettably, no," Poloma said. "The Assembly can sentence Lannel Thorey for killing a Kydan, but has no jurisdiction over the slaying of a foreigner unless that foreigner was here by explicit invitation of the Assembly, such as a merchant or mercenary. Carder was here under his own impetus, or rather that of the Empress Lerena, which has no provenance in Kydan law."

"So Kysor Nevri hopes to save Lannel Thorey by get-

ting the Assembly to agree that Carder was a foreigner
without protection," Kadburn said.

"More, if I understand Poloma correctly," Galys said.
"By agreeing that Carder is without protection, the Assem-
bly in effect denies any colonist the status of Kydan.
Nevri's side will win by default."

Poloma nodded. "And Thorey will answer only the
charge of attempting to kill me."

"Does the council vote on this issue?" Kadburn asked.

"Yes."

"Can I speak to the council first?"

"On this issue?" Poloma looked skeptical. "I do not see
how this can help, except to stress your foreign origin, because I will have to translate for you."

"I wish to speak on a related issue, one that will affect
the council's decision on Carder's right to protection under
Kydan law. On the right of all of us from Hamilay to such
protection."

"As prefect, I can grant you the right to address the
council, but I am not convinced it will help."

"Do you have a plan, then, to counter Kysor Nevri's
move?"

Before Poloma could reply, Nevri himself spoke up.
"Come along, Prefect Malvara. Let the council vote on
this." He jerked his head, smirking, towards Heriot Fleetwood up in the gallery. "Or should we offer her the chance
to carry out an execution after all? A colonist slaying a
Kydan: that will help your cause, no doubt."

Poloma smiled thinly at the taunt, and said to Kadburn,
"No, my friend, I have no plan." He stood and told the
council that Kadburn Axkevleren would speak on the issue
before a vote was taken.

Nevri opened his mouth to object, but obviously

changed his mind. Something of the smirk returned and he said, "By all means. Let the servant of a Hamilayan Kevleren speak." Some of his supporters snickered appreciatively.

"For the last several days I have been gone from Kydan," Kadburn said. "I traveled secretly up the Frey River to see for myself what the villages and towns were like that served as the plutocrats' source of recruits for their attack on Kydan."

He paused slightly between phrases to let Poloma translate.

"Is this nothing more than a repeat of your warning about an attack from the Rivald Kevleren?" Nevri shouted. "We've heard the warning before and nothing came of it!"

"They are being recruited again," Kadburn said evenly, and when Poloma translated there was a sudden hush in the Assembly. "I have observed the towns and villages. Few men attend the fields. There are hardly any boats fishing on the river. I see only a handful of men in each village, and they are too old or too young for soldiering."

Poloma caught up translating and asked, "Who is recruiting?"

"I saw a band of young men leave their village on the south side of the Frey River and head inland. They were carrying weapons and enough supplies for several days travel. As they went, they were joined by other bands from other villagers, all armed as well."

"They are going away from Kydan?" Nevri cried, pretending to laugh. Poloma thought the councilor could guess where Kadburn was going and wanted to head him off. "Then what have we here in Kydan to fear? And what does this have to do with Lannel Thorey and the colonist called Carder?"

"They were not moving as a band going to attack another village or town. They had no scouts in front of them. They did not seem afraid of what the next day might bring. They are gathering somewhere far from here for a purpose. What center apart from Kydan has the resources and the need for such a number of warriors?"

"Sayenna," Poloma said for him.

"Sayenna," Kadburn confirmed. "And Numoya Kevleren rules Sayenna for Rivald, and Rivald is the enemy of all Kydans."

There was a murmur of agreement from the gallery.

"Last time Kydan was attacked, colonists and Kydans combined to defeat the enemy. Barely. With preparation and fair warning, we can defeat this new threat. The colonists will not fight for a city that does not want them. But they will fight for a home. Give them that and they will die for Kydan, as Kydans."

When Poloma had finished translating, Nevri stood up quickly, looking sullenly at Kadburn. "As I said, we have heard this argument from you before. Nothing happened. Why should we believe you now?"

"You may choose not to, of course," Kadburn said, and he sounded as if it did not matter to him one way or the other if he was believed. "But why reject us? We *want* to be Kydans, not Hamilayans."

Nevri pounded the table with a fist. "Because what need for Numoya Kevleren to attack us if none of you from Hamilay are in the city?"

"You are a fool, Kysor Nevri," Kadburn said. "We not being here did not stop Numoya Kevleren from attacking and *taking* Kydan more than two years ago."

Galys Valera knew Councilor Nevri was defeated as soon as he hesitated. Kadburn had stopped him short, and everyone on the council, and everyone in the gallery, could see that the leader of the nativists had no reply, and that whether or not the colonists were present in Kydan, Numoya Kevleren would still attack. He blustered something eventually, but no one was listening any more, and that was obvious to Nevri as much as it was to Galys. His voice trailed off, he sat down, and Poloma quickly called for a vote on Carder's status under the city's law. Every member of the council who voted, voted to accept Carder's death as equivalent to the murder of a citizen of Kydan; Nevri could not bring himself to vote for the motion, but he had the good sense to abstain rather than vote against it. When Poloma officially announced the result, the gallery applauded.

Then Poloma raised again the issue of sentencing Thorey, and this time Nevri made no interruption. Galys, watching Thorey, saw his blank expression replaced by one she had seen before on the faces of the defeated and the cornered, a kind of numb acceptance that there was no more hope, and probably never had been.

Poloma listed the three sentencing options under Kydan law: exile, execution or being bonded for servitude to the family of the victim. He then added that since Carder had no family to speak of in Kydan, that left the first two options. Another councilor pointed out it would be foolish to exile someone who could turn themselves over to Numoya Kevleren to revenge himself against the city.

"I would never do that!" Lannel Thorey cried. "If I committed any crime it was because of my love for Kydan!"

Galys found herself believing him, and could see how he might think killing Carder and even Poloma were acts of patriotism, but his words fell on deaf ears, and when the second vote was taken, he was sentenced to be hanged in the Great Quadrangle outside the Assembly at noon the following day.

Poloma then formally asked if anyone would enter a plea for Thorey's life. All eyes turned to Kysor Nevri, but the councilor stared straight ahead without saying a word. Thorey's shoulders trembled and he finally lowered his gaze, knowing he was, at the last, without any friend in the world.

"I will plead for his life," Galys said.

Now everyone in the Assembly looked at her. Even those who did not understand her words had some inkling of what she had said because of the looks on the faces of her fellow colonists.

"Strategos, did I hear you correctly?" Poloma asked.

"You did, Prefect Malvara. Translate my words for me, if you would."

"Galys, what are you thinking?" Gos said. "You are pleading for the life of a man who almost tore this city apart."

"I know what I am doing," she said, and nodded to Poloma to continue.

He dutifully translated for her, then asked on what grounds she entered the plea.

"That although Carder had no family as such in the New Land, his life belonged to the expedition that came across the Deepening Sea, and his work contributed to its success, and his labor will be missed. That being the case, Lannel Thorey should be bonded for servitude to those attempting to make a new life for themselves in Kydan. I plead for the life of Lannel Thorey because in bondage he can help secure the safety and freedom of the city."

When Poloma had finished translating, a hubbub rose in the Assembly as it seemed everyone at the same time turned to their neighbor and spoke. Galys kept her gaze on Lannel Thorey and saw his surprise that someone from among the colonists would plead for his life. Then she saw him glance up at the gallery towards Heriot Fleetwood, who before had spared his life when most expected her to take it.

Poloma asked for quiet and put Galys's plea before the council. The vote was unanimous.

"The life of Lannel Thorey has been spared," Poloma announced, "so that for the rest of his days he may serve the colonists from across the Deepening Sea."

"So that he may serve Kydan," Galys corrected. "*CanKydan*. Our city."

Kadburn was as surprised as anyone else by the way things had turned out in the Assembly, but he also understood at a very deep level the rightness of what had happened. Everything from Poloma's plan to use Lannel Thorey to discredit the nativists, his own contribution in revealing the gathering of forces against Kydan, to Galys's unexpected act of clemency, had not only ended the threat of division within the city, but united it in a way that would not have been possible otherwise. It would be almost impossible now for any of the indigenous inhabitants to doubt the commitment of the colonists to the city, nor for any of the colonists to doubt they now had a future as Kydans.

The rightness he felt, however, had a deeper current as well, something that went further back than today's events, and he pondered on it as he gathered with Galys and Gos outside the Assembly. His two friends were talking, but he was not really listening. A light shower started, the drops surprisingly warm. He glanced up at the sky and saw that heavier rain would follow soon. It would take some getting used to, this New Land weather. Back home in Omeralt it was winter that brought the rain, not summer.

No, he corrected himself. Not back home. This is my home now. Should have been Maddyn's home as well. Although grief rested heavily in his heart, he realised it had been some time, perhaps a tenday or more, since he had really thought of his late master in anything but a cursory way. He felt ashamed, and puzzled by it, because there had been a time after Maddyn's death when he thought he would never be able to think of anything else except his loss.

That was part of it, Kadburn thought, part of the rightness. Although Maddyn's expedition now looked as if it had a better than even chance of succeeding, it was partly because Maddyn himself was no longer a part of it, and never could have been if Kydan was to be a single city with one heart. Maddyn's purpose was to take Kydan for the Hamilayan empire, to be a colony that served the Kevlerens. With something like shock, because he had never considered it possible, Kadburn understood that it was in Kydan's best interests, and the best interests of all its citizens including those from Hamilay, to oppose any attempt by a Kevleren to rule the city, whether the Kevleren was from Rivald or Hamilay.

He heard Galys and Gos deep in conversation. Gos did not seem happy with the way it was going.

"I am reluctant to break them up," Gos was saying. "They have been trained to fight as a single unit."

"The city cannot pay for the maintenance of the companies as they stand now," Galys said firmly.

"You cannot let Kydan depend just on its militia. It failed them when Rivald attacked the first time. Amateur soldiers led by amateur officers who cannot tell one end of the spear from the other can only invite disaster."

"Their militia worked well enough before soldiers came from the old world," Kadburn said.

"Dealing with the petty raids of neighbouring tribes and disaffected villagers," Gos said. "I cannot imagine the New Land returning to those days."

"That is true," Galys said placatingly, "but the Kydans had some foresight. As Kadburn says, the militia were good enough in their day, and the Assembly had the foresight to build the Citadel."

"For its size it is as good a fort as I've come across," Gos agreed, "as long as an enemy does not appear with longgons. They would make short work of it."

"We still have longgons of our own," Galys pointed out, "from our transports."

"We could do with *Annglaf*'s longgons though," Kadburn said. "She might get back before the attack."

"Only if Captain Avier has been extraordinarily lucky with current and wind," Galys said. She put a hand on Gos's shoulder. "Look, the problem with our professional soldiers is that they were trained to serve an empire, an empire that was large enough and rich enough to create and maintain a full-time army. By Hamilayan standards, Kydan is not even a large city let alone what we would have called an independent state."

"But in the New Land it *is* an independent state, and needs a full-time army," Gos argued. "Surely the battles it has fought over the last few years are proof of that."

"But not one as large as Maddyn brought with him from Hamilay."

"I don't want to see the companies broken up," Gos said dourly.

"Some of the companies," Galys said. "Not all."

"Which ones would you keep?" he asked suspiciously.

"We keep the best of them: Maddyn's household guards and the dragoons. Even if Numoya Kevleren has Rivald units, they are still the best soldiers in the New Land, and certainly give us a great advantage over any native threat Kydan is likely to face."

"And the engineers," Kadburn said.

"They might be more useful dispersed," Gos said, thinking aloud. "They could pass on their skills, and we'll have need of those as the city grows."

"The same applies to our other three companies of infantry," Galys argued. "In fact, we should use them as the backbone of a new militia. We can then mix colonists and Kydans together, and arm them with firegons instead of their old spears."

"It would do much to help unify the two groups," Kadburn admitted. He saw Galys smile slightly, and wondered if he and Gos were carefully and skilfully being maneuvered into some plan Galys had long ago conceived. What of it? he thought. She is a strategos, after all, and that is her duty.

"And militia do not receive pay," Galys continued.

Gos was now nodding in silent approval. Kadburn was not surprised. Galys was letting him keep his beloved dragoons. "And dissolving the three regular companies gives us more civilian colonists to expand our farming and building projects."

"Do we reorganize now or after Numoya attacks?" Galys asked.

Gos shrugged. "How long will he be?"

"He must attack before summer is over," Kadburn said. "He cannot risk the empire reinforcing our position here."

"Then not much time," Galys said. "In that case, keep things as they are for the moment."

"Keep things as what are?" Poloma asked, looking pleased with the world as he joined them.

Galys ran through the discussion about the military. "I would not wait," Poloma said. "True, our militia are novices compared to your professional soldiers, but they understand discipline and courage. They will take to training, and I think the boost to morale would more than make up for any temporary lack of cohesion."

"And it will give us three more companies to use in the defence," Gos said. "Who will command?" he asked Poloma carefully.

"I see no reason why you should not have overall command, Commander Gos Linsedd. It is your specialty, after all."

Gos bowed slightly. "In that case, I will immediately draw up plans for the defence."

Gos and Kadburn left for Karhay, heads leaning together in conversation.

"That was well done," Poloma said to Galys.

She smiled quizzically at him. "I don't know what you mean."

"Of course you know what I mean," he said. He looked back at the Assembly. "I am ashamed to admit it, but I am surprised it worked."

"What is that?"

"The council. I was beginning to wonder if politics had destroyed what was once a noble institution. I was relieved to see that it has not."

"You are speaking ironically, of course."

Poloma started walking across the Great Quadrangle, Galys accompanying him.

"Why do you say that?"

"You yourself used politics. The whole thing with Lannel Thorey was a political masterstroke."

"I did not consider it in that light. At the time it just seemed the natural thing to do."

"You are a natural politician," Galys said.

Poloma laughed lightly. "You tease me."

"What has happened to Thorey, by the way?"

"You are changing the subject."

"You seemed uncomfortable with the last subject."

"He is being held in the Citadel. You may use him as you wish, now, Strategos. He is bonded to you."

"To the colonists," she corrected.

"Theoretically, I suppose. But technically, since the law makes no allowance for bonding to a whole community but only to an individual, he is literally *yours* to do with as you see fit."

As they left the quadrangle the Long Bridge loomed in front of them.

"How is your mother, by the way?" Galys asked. "Feeling better, I hope."

Poloma's face turned somber. "I wish it were so."

"I am sorry. Is there anything I can do?"

Poloma shook his head.

The friends parted at the Long Bridge, Galys walking down the eastern ramp to catch a ferry back to Karhay. Poloma headed straight for home, deep in thought, and only paused when he passed the basilica of Kydan. Urged by tradition and childhood memories, he wandered in and stood before the statue of Kydan, half human, half crocodile.

He bowed his head and prayed for his mother, the way she had taught him all those decades ago. It did not make him feel any more confident about her health, nor did it erode his scepticism about religion. Yet when he had finished he looked again at the statue and realised something for the first time. The god's theme was one of unity, of joining two disparate parts into a living whole, and that was just what he and his friends had managed to achieve in the Assembly that day. It seemed to him, in a strangely sacred way, that it was absolutely meant to be.

20

IF not for the circumstances, Chierma would have en-joyed the empress's progress. Summer was easily the best time of year to see Rivald, with its fields of ripening wheat and, further south, barley. The sun was warm without being harsh; most of the annoying insects had been reduced by swallows, and the air had a sparkling purity that was missing entirely when autumn and winter rolled around with their storms and snow and ice and air as heavy and gray as lead.

Chierma grimaced as yet another troop of cavalry rumbled by, flattening yet another crop in their haste. What was the rush, after all? What in Rivald could possibly stop the invader? Indeed, the rest of the army moved at a snail's pace; it was like a glacier, tumbling, grinding, crashing its way over the countryside, inexorable and destructive.

His horse farted, and he heard moans of disapproval from soldiers marching behind him. He threw an apology into the air, more from good manners than any contrition on his part—the soldiers would never have complained if he had been an officer or a Kevleren—and pulled gently on the reins to stop his mount from wandering off the road to sample the vegetation.

A runner appeared by his side.

"Your Eminence, his grace Duke Paimer requests your presence at the midday meal."

"Inform his grace that I would be honored," Chierma said, and the runner disappeared.

Well, he told himself, that's another meal taken care of. He estimated he had to cover about a hundred more before the army reached Beferen. Perhaps he should make friends with more of the Kevlerens and spread the load of hosting him. But Paimer could afford him, so why bother?

He saw a girl by the side of the road, doing her best to avoid the boots and hooves of the invader and at the same time corral her charge of ducks. She is one of mine, he thought, and here I am consorting with the enemy.

No, Chierma, don't blame yourself. You did not ask to return home in this way. It is not your fault.

And then he thought that perhaps it was his fault, at least as much as anyone else's. He had been part of the revolution that had overthrown the home-grown branch of the Kevlerens, and everything that was now happening to Rivald stemmed from that action. He felt shame and despair in equal measure.

The girl looked at the invaders not with hate, or any genuine emotion, just a cool indifference, and at that moment he felt he did not belong in Rivald after all, and he saw himself as she saw him, as a foreigner, as an outsider. He wanted to tell her the truth, but it occurred to him that truth had become an increasingly flexible commodity around Lerena Kevleren. Indeed, if Paimer was right then reality itself was becoming an increasingly flexible com-

modity around the empress. Not to mention how loose the
universe felt every time Englay appeared to him.

The girl fell behind, and he hoped she and her ducks
kept safe. And there were thousands like her, all over Rivald. He would do whatever he could, a lonely governor
returning to the capital with an invading army, to keep
them all safe.

Lerena heard birdsong and immediately stuck her head
out of her sedan, startling one of the Royal Guards. She
searched for its source but without luck. Uilder asked her
if anything was the matter. Lerena pulled her head back
into the sedan and glared at the Axkevleren.

"What makes you think anything is the matter?" she
demanded.

Uilder mumbled something.

"How long before we get there?"

"Your Majesty?"

"How long before we get to Beferen?"

"Your generals think it will be about thirty days. Maybe
more, depending on the condition of the road over the
highland in the south, and the size and location of the
enemy's army."

Lerena barked a laugh. "Their army will not be an im-
pediment, I assure you."

"No, your Majesty."

Lerena breathed through her nose. Thirty days. She
fumed. If she had known how long it would take to get
from Omeralt to Beferen she would never have undertaken
the expedition.

Yes I would have, she thought. But I would have sent
someone else to take charge of it.

Who? she asked herself. Who else but herself could

have led it? Who else could she have trusted? Not Paimer, that was for sure: he was increasingly unstable. No, there was just her. Everything depended on her. The world turned on its axis because of her.

More birdsong. Instinctively, she moved to the window again, but checked herself. She saw Uilder watching her carefully. She was a sly girl, that one. Sallow faced. Always apologizing. What did she really think?

Lerena's eyes narrowed and she thought about the bird that had been making that song. It sounded again, this time closer. And closer. Something landed with a soft thump on the roof of the sedan. Lerena smiled to herself. So easy. She extended her arm out of the window and felt two scratchy bird feet rest on her wrist. She brought her arm in and saw that she had enticed a finch. It had a yellow beak and a ring of orange feathers around the neck. It was a sweet thing.

Lerena held the bird in her hands, stroked its breast, glanced up at Uilder, who looked at her in wonder, and something like fear.

That's better, Lerena thought.

A picket appeared from behind bushes, two men in rough brown clothing with long-barreled firegons primed and raised to their shoulders. Harker and his escort stopped, and a third man appeared behind them, his weapon held casually in the crook of his arm. It was primed, too, Harker noticed with satisfaction: these men knew what they were doing. Officially they may only have been rated as militia, but they were tough mountain men, trained to fight in their own way and on their own ground.

"I am President Croft Harker," he said.

The two men with firegons at the ready did not lower their aim, but Harker saw them both swallow.

The third, gray haired with skin as tanned as old leather, approached diffidently but cautiously. He held out his hand. "Sir?"

Harker retrieved a thick, folded parchment from inside his jacket and handed it down. The soldier opened it carefully, almost reverentially. Harker knew he was unlikely to be able to read—few under the Kevlerens in Rivald had been encouraged to learn—but would recognize the seal at the top readily enough, and would be able to count the ship silhouettes underneath it, which indicated the rank of the parchment's owner.

The man handed the parchment back and saluted. The other two lowered their firegons and snapped to attention.

Harker returned the salute. "Go back to your duty," he said warmly, proud of their professionalism. They would have need of it in the days to come.

A short while later he reached the camp the pickets had been protecting. He and the escort made their way between gray tents and temporary pens, made from roughly cut branches, holding hundreds of horses. Many of the soldiers they passed, like those of the picket, were local militia, but most were troopers. When they reached the center of the camp a cluster of officers appeared from a large tent, caps under arms, and saluted Harker. The president dismounted and a trooper ran up to take his mount and lead away the escort.

One of the officers came forward and offered his hand.

Harker took it gladly. "It is good to see you again, Aland Terko. Five years ago, wasn't it? On the frontier?"

"Yes, President," Terko said, happy to have been remembered. "Your army is waiting for you, sir."

"Good work, all of you," he said to the officers. "Have we found the Hamilayan army yet?"

Terko nodded. "A tenday from here, at least. The Kevlerens travel in sedans."

"The slower the better," Harker said. "It gives Beferen more time to prepare, and us more time to prepare the ambush."

Chierma was exhausted. Paimer wanted to talk and talk and talk. He wanted to talk about the Kevlerens, about the Beloveds, about Axkevlerens generally, about history and the end of history. And he wanted to talk to Idalgo and Englay, and he could not talk to Englay unless Chierma was present because he was her anchor. At least, that was how she sometimes described him. Usually, it was "My little traitor," or "My unrequited lover," which was worse, but sometimes it was "My anchor, my sweet, rusting anchor."

Actually, come to think of it, Englay never referred to Chierma by that term when talking with Paimer, only when talking with Idalgo. And it happened to be the same word Idalgo sometimes used to describe Paimer, but only when talking with Englay.

Until then, it never occurred to Chierma how odd it was that ghosts talked to each other at all. Until meeting Paimer again, he had told himself—insisted to himself—that Englay was his personal illusion, or maybe personal demon, a way for his wounded heart to punish him for overthrowing her the year before. (Just a year? It felt like a hundred years had passed since then.) But then that first night, when Paimer and Chierma were forced together by the empress and they got drunk, he saw Idalgo Axkevleren appear from nowhere, and then Paimer started talking to someone behind Chierma and he realised the duke could see Englay.

"The universe can be a terrifying place," Englay said, sitting beside him in the duke's sedan. Chierma noticed Idalgo was now sitting beside Paimer.

Sunlight glanced through a gap in the leather curtains and shone on Idalgo's face. It looked like normal skin, and when the light touched the Beloved's eye, the pupil contracted.

"We know that better than they," Idalgo said to Englay.

"They will learn," Englay replied.

Then both were gone.

"I hate the way they do that," Chierma said.

Paimer smiled thinly. "I used to think Idalgo had just run off on some private errand, or to complete some task I'd forgotten I'd ordered him to do." He looked down as if ashamed of the admission. "In truth, I thought—I suspected— I was insane. In a way, I wish I was."

"Maybe we both are."

Paimer sighed wearily. "No. Not yet anyway."

Chierma shivered despite the warm summer day. "There's more to come, isn't there?"

"I think so. I think there's something terrible still to happen."

"They are like vultures, aren't they, our ghosts?"

"Not at all," Idalgo said, reappearing and managing to sound affronted. He spoke to Chierma with hardly any courtesy at all, much less than a Beloved usually extended to another Beloved. On the other hand, Idalgo fawned over Englay, while managing to be subservient and patronizing at the same time towards Paimer. Chierma was at the bottom of the social heap, and the others did not think twice about reminding him of the fact.

"We are more like ravens," Englay said.

"That was Yunara's favorite," Idalgo said offhandedly.

"That's true," Paimer said, remembering. He tried to remember what Yunara had looked like. She had been beautiful, but he could not picture her face, only an impression of it, like a wet footprint. He remembered her way with birds, however, a way the empress seemed to have acquired.

"Lerena is good with birds," Idalgo confirmed. "I must say, that was a surprise."

"Tell me," Chierma said, looking straight as Idalgo, "*why* are you here?"

There was stilted silence for a while. Chierma was suddenly very aware of all the sounds around him: the tramping of the army, the coughing of throats irritated by all the dust in the air, the humming of insects, Paimer's breathing.

Idalgo and Englay looked at each other, their faces terribly blank, as if there was no intelligence at all behind them, and for an instant Chierma thought he could detect a warm, yellow glow behind their eyes. The colour made him think of melted butter, of newly minted gold coins, of butterfly wings, of pure light on a summer afternoon.

Idalgo and Englay smiled at the same time, and Englay placed a hand on Chierma's knee. He flinched.

"Why are we here?" she said almost kindly. "Because you love us, that's why."

21

FOR a moment, with a heavy rain sweeping southwest along the coast from a black sky, Velan Lymok thought Sayenna almost managed to look like Beferen. But only until he saw that the choppy sea was still blue, the houses bright white and the temperature warm enough to make his stiff-collared uniform stifling. He discovered that he felt contentment, a patient reservoir of wellbeing he had not thought to ever possess, and this despite the onrushing future, a future brought more into focus on this particular morning. The army of Numoya Kevleren was arraigned in formation around the plains north of Sayenna, standing solidly in the rain while Numoya rode slowly up and down the ranks, looking forbiddingly like a pale god, his Beloved trailing behind, as solemn as judgment.

The army of twenty-three companies, standing at attention, looked formidable indeed, and prettily dressed in Rivald's traditional colours of blue and white as if defying the dead gray sky above them. The effect was spoiled somewhat by the lack of firegons, but through Quenion's efforts ten full companies were properly armed, and the rest carried their traditional weapons of swords and dag-

gers and spears and rhomphaias. Pennants, quartered with
Rivald's colors and pictograms of local animals and trees,
helped identify one company from another, and each company commander was an experienced Rivald soldier. All in
all the most powerful army yet assembled in the New
World. Numoya assured Velan it would be more than suf-
ficient to take Kydan, which only the previous spring had
almost fallen to a frontal attack by a band of untrained, uncoordinated and badly led river tribes.

Numoya and Quenion joined Velan when the inspection
was finished.

"They'll do," Numoya said to no one in particular. For
a moment he frowned as if he had a headache, then he
turned to Velan. "Well," he said, sounding distracted,
"the sooner we start, the sooner we'll take Kydan. Let's get
the army moving."

Velan nodded, glanced at Quenion who looked away,
and rode to the head of the army, riding as erect as possible because he was conscious he had to make the best impression, not only for Numoya but to fulfil the army's
expectations of what a real Rivald officer should look like.
Sweat itched under his collar, but he ignored it. His boots
chafed against his heels, but he ignored them too. His cap
was too tight, but he left it where it was, straight and level,
the peak down a tad to shade his eyes. When he got to his
position, he drew his sword, raised himself in the stirrups
and waved the sword forwards. Without looking behind
him, he prodded the horse into a walk, heading north,
keeping The Wash to his right. From the sound of tramping feet, not much dulled in the rain, he knew he was doing
something he never imagined ever doing, even in his
wildest dreams: leading an army to war.

*   *   *

Poloma Malvara had woken to the clearest skies for a week. The air was already warm, and by midday it would be stinking hot and overbearingly humid. He had not experienced a day like this for more than two years and did not look forward to it. He had become at least partly acclimatized to Omeralt's climate, which was considerably cooler and drier than Kydan's. On the other hand, he would never miss Omeralt's winters, which were bitterly cold. If he had his way, winter would be spent in Kydan and summer in Omeralt. That would be perfect.

For the moment the day was bearable, however, and after so many days of rain the blue sky lightened his spirits.

He frowned. The moment he thought of his spirits being lightened he felt his heart tighten in his chest. Although he did not consider himself remotely religious, he did not totally disregard the idea of a soul or an afterlife, unlike the Hamilayans, who seem to have been poisoned by the Kevlerens and their use of the Sefid, as if the only power that counted in life was that Wielded in the old land.

He went to his mother's room and knocked gently on the door. She was a light sleeper and would answer at any moment. He knocked again.

"Mama?"

The day, so blue and clear, was as still as night.

He put the palm of his hand flat against her door, feeling for something, some sound or sign or stirring.

"Mama?"

His hand dropped to the handle and he opened the door a crack.

"Mama? Are you awake? It is morning. Such a beautiful morning . . ."

He did not finish. His lungs emptied of air in a rush and his skin stretched around his face.

Poloma opened the door wide and stepped in. He saw Sorkro in her bed, looking as small as a cricket, lying straight on her back. He went to her side and, already knowing what he would feel, placed his wrist against her forehead. As cold as bone. Her skin, which was so thin it seemed almost translucent at times, was now opaque and creamy, as if the body within had shrunk. Only her cheeks seemed right, sharp and shiny. Her brown eyes looked up, up past the roof of the Malvara house and into the sky, up towards whatever lay beyond. Sorkro could see again.

"It's like a snake," Numoya said, speaking offhandedly to Quenion, as if she were no more than a clerk taking notes. He pointed to the marching column of men and draft animals winding its way across the broad grass plain that spread west of The Wash. "My army is like a snake that will strike at the heart—"

He stopped himself, suddenly self-conscious. He glanced sideways at his Beloved. Not that it mattered. It was not as if he was speaking to anyone who truly cared.

"To strike at the hearts of my enemy!" he half shouted. He knew he did it to spite her, and could not help feeling ashamed of it, but that only seemed to drive him on. He had discovered he was cruel, and was not as sorry for it as he would once have been. But things had changed lately: love had been perverted, the Sefid misused, his trust misplaced.

He frowned as he felt the first twinge of a new headache behind his eyes. He seemed to be getting a lot of them lately.

When the army had passed he fell in behind, his personal escort and household retinue following after. He motioned to Quenion.

"Join me, my Beloved," he said. "Ride by my side."

"It is not my place to ride by your side," she said demurely.

"By your own actions your place is by my side," he said plainly.

She spurred her horse until she rode level with him.

"How do you think our plan will go?"

"Your plan, your Majesty," Quenion replied. "I had little to do with it."

"Do I detect a hint of disquiet? Did you think you would share with me the responsibility of setting strategy? After all, why not? You certainly shared with me the responsibility of Wielding, even of making a sacrifice, whether or not I wished to share it. Surely planning a war is insignificant compared with that."

"Please, your Majesty," Quenion said plaintively. "I did it for you, from my love for you. Do not be angry with me any more."

Numoya almost gave in then, remembering the love he had once felt for her. But no. That had been a mistake. He should have followed his first instincts and not let her worm her way into his affection. How had he let that happen? How could he possibly forgive someone for using the Sefid—even if indirectly, and even if for the good of a Kevleren—something no one had ever done before outside of his family?

He reached out until he held one of her hands in his. She winced in pain as he squeezed, but said nothing.

"No, my Beloved. I am not angry with you any more, and when this war is over, which thanks to you I can now witness with my own eyes, I will prove it to you."

Quenion whimpered then, and in revulsion he threw her hand out of his and rode ahead so he did not have to see her face.

He was surprised then by feelings of self-revulsion, and pity for Quenion.

Why should I care? he asked himself. Can I truly still love her after all?

A part of him asked, Why not? He was, after all, a Kevleren still, and she his Beloved. No matter her crime, the basic nature of their relationship still existed. Stretched to breaking point through her actions, perhaps, but not yet actually broken.

A wave of nausea passed through him and he gave up thinking about it.

"Tell me, Arden, did you ever have a lover?"

Arden, who was standing near the stables keeping a lookout for Galys Valera, did not even look down at Heriot when she asked the question. The strategos was late, which he thought was probably unusual for her, and for the second time he searched the island and the channel between Karhay and Herris for any sign of her.

"No."

"Axkevlerens are not allowed to take lovers?"

"No."

"And afterwards, when your mistress died and you left the service of the Kevlerens, did you ever have a lover?"

"No."

Heriot thought for a moment and then asked, "Is this your choice, or lack of opportunity?"

This time Arden did look down at her, and under that gaze Heriot found herself blushing. "I'm just curious—" she started to say defensively.

"Neither," he said, and she heard a weary kind of puzzlement in his voice. "I have never had the desire."

Heriot looked shocked. "You're not . . ." She stopped when she remembered she had seen he had all the necessary equipment when they had bathed in the river with the other colonists.

"I don't know if it is some drug the Kevlerens give us as children in our food or drink, or the intensive training forcing us to concentrate our love on our mistress or master, or some side-effect from our closeness with the Sefid, but no Axkevleren ever marries or has children. I can think of no exception." His voice became harder. "We are drones."

"Not choice then."

"No, it is not choice." He closed his eyes for a moment. "It is never from choice."

She nodded to herself. "Good," she said, adding quickly, "that it is not through choice, I mean."

Arden nodded as well, now pretending, like the slight woman behind him, to look for Galys Valera.

"I hope my curiosity did not offend you," Heriot said.

"No."

"It seems to me you were not surprised I asked the question."

Arden grunted. "I have been expecting it."

"Well, we *are* friends," she said.

"Yes."

"And sometimes the matter does come up between friends. The air has to be cleared, now and then, to make things . . . clearer."

"We are still friends, Heriot Fleetwood. I cannot imagine a time when we will not be." She did not know if it was his imagination or not, but his voice sounded tight enough to break. Suddenly his huge neck craned forwards. "Here comes the strategos now. About time."

There was a long pause, and Heriot said, "You must truly hate the Kevlerens."

Arden rumbled like thunder. "I cannot imagine a time when I will ever be friends with one."

Soon after they were joined by Galys, breathing heavy from running from the dock to the stables. She smiled uneasily and said, "You wanted to see me?"

"Congratulations," Heriot said.

"For what?"

"I hear you have been given command of the new militia force. You will be leading both colonist and native in the new companies. That is good. It will help us all be Kydans."

"That's the plan," Galys said cautiously. "How did you hear about this, may I ask?"

Heriot smiled thinly. "The Colonists' Guild still operates for the meantime. Until we can be sure things have settled in the city. They pass all sorts of interesting tidbits on to Arden and me."

Galys's expression showed her sudden interest. "Any tidbits I should know about?"

Heriot shook her head. "I don't think so, Strategos."

Galys shrugged, understanding that the use of her title in this way was Heriot's way of maintaining the separation between them. They were allies, perhaps, but not yet friends. "Why did you ask me to meet you?"

"The companies will have firegons?" Arden asked.

"Some, I hope. There will not be enough for everyone in the militia, however."

"That is what we thought," Heriot said. "You will have need of other weapons."

"Well, we have some in the Citadel armory, and we're putting together plans for making our own weapons, but it will take time."

"I think we can help you," Heriot said, and nodded to Arden.

To Galys's surprise, Arden took two steps back until he was next to one of the stables' outside walls and slammed into it with his shoulder. Some of the stones moved inwards. She had not realised just how strong and heavy the big man was. Then her mouth opened in even greater surprise when he used his hands to literally pull stones out of the wall as if there was almost no mortar at all between them. Something clattered by his feet, then a whole swag of bright, metallic objects tumbled out of the hole he had made. Swords and daggers, and even one or two axes.

"By the Sefid!" Galys cried. "Where did all these come from?"

"From the last battle," Heriot said. "We kept them secret in case . . . well, just in case."

Galys regarded the small woman for a moment. "And now?"

"A sign of trust," Heriot said. "Between us and the natives, between us and you and the other expedition leaders. Will they be of use?"

"Invaluable," Galys said.

"I will get some of our people to help get them across to the Citadel," Arden said, leaving them.

"Better get some men to help repair the wall too," Heriot called after him, and Arden raised a hand to let her know he had heard.

"I'm sorry I was late," Galys said.

"All of us have a lot of work to do. I understand."

"I wish it had been work," she said grimly. "I was called

to Poloma Malvara's house this morning. His mother, Sorkro, died in her sleep last night."

As the army followed The Wash, Quenion watched the river flowing past as they followed it north. The further they went, the narrower it became and the faster its waters. She knew that there were several fords near Sayenna where it was safe to cross but then hardly any at all until it divided into the smaller Elder and Younger rivers. In the south she saw herons wading in reeds along the banks, casually searching for any fish that entered the shallows, and cormorants placidly swimming midstream until diving with a speed that surprised Quenion every time she saw it. Towards the end of the first day, large white-breasted eagles took over from the cormorants, swooping low over the water and only touching it when their talons dipped to catch a careless fish, and when the reeds gave way to gangly, straggly trees, kingfishers perched on their branches to leap on any unsuspecting fish or frog or lizard that came within view. Dragonflies hovered over quiet pools, while below them small beetles with long legs skated along the surface.

After a time some of the pain from her confrontation with Numoya that morning eased, and she found herself wondering if life was like a river, following a single course, with tributaries always flowing into it, never out, and adding to the current until it became so strong there was no hope of reaching safety. Or in fact did life have branches that flowed out of it, breaking the hold of the current and cutting new paths for those brave enough to follow them?

Perhaps it was best to be like the birds and insects that lived off the river, only rarely venturing into the water itself. But then Quenion saw Numoya's army again, sinuous and inexorable like the river, and she saw herself trapped in its current and being washed away.

"Is everything all right, sir?" asked the engineer.

Kadburn looked at the man without recognising him. Before him squatted a longgon on its large ship-style carriage with small wheels to reduce the travel on recoil. He remembered the last time he had been this close to one, and his master Maddyn Kevleren lighting up like a paraffin ball, disappearing in a blaze of heat and greasy black smoke, then the canvas bags of gonblack going up and the explosion hurling him and many others off the wall . . .

"Sir?"

Kadburn focused on the man's face. Ensign Lakdon. He wondered what his first name was. "What is it?"

"You asked me to report when the work on the wall was finished."

"Ah." Kadburn looked over the walkway to the inside of the Citadel. The wall he was standing on had been quickly put back together after the battle against the plutocrats in spring, but the job had been rushed and careless and the wall would have been useless against any determined offensive. Galys had set the engineers to work on reinforcing it. "It's done then?"

"Sir," the engineer said, tapping his forelock. "It can stand up to almost anything, even a few shots from enemy longgons, should they have any. Against anyone else it will last until the Sefid fades away."

"Good job," Kadburn said, nodding his approval. "What's next for your lot?"

Ensign Lakdon sighed. "Ditches, sir, and the like."

"Hot work," Kadburn sympathized.

"Well, not as hot as an enemy right in your midst, I warrant. So best get a start. If you'll excuse me, sir."

Alone again, Kadburn lost himself with the memory of the terrible day Maddyn died, but he shook his head and walked on, checking that each longgon was securely in place, its ropes properly tethered to deep-set ring bolts, and that each had close to it stores of shot arranged in small pyramids, and bags of gonblack in boxes to protect the powder from rain and stray sparks. He took his time, wanting to know where every longgon was and what was covered in its field of fire. The longgons were manned by sailors from the merchant ships that had brought the colonists across the Deepening Sea, and each piece had one of them on duty at all times, acting as guard and, taking advantage of the wall's commanding view over any approach from the east, extra lookouts. In the courtyard below, Maddyn's household troops were on permanent station in the Citadel. They were the best infantry in the city and so had the best chance of holding the fortress in any attack, and it seemed fitting to Kadburn that they should defend the place where their master had died. Whoever held the Citadel would eventually hold Kydan, and Kadburn was going to make damn sure that it was not a Kevleren.

Velan Lymok was not sure what made him do a night patrol, going by foot from one company camp to the next, talking with the commanders, saying a few words with guards and those too nervous to sleep, but it felt like the right thing to do, and unlike a lot of things he sometimes did, he did not feel the time had been wasted. By the time he returned to his own tent he was tired but strangely less worried about the days to come. A Rivald cook from Numoya's retinue had stayed around to make sure he had something to eat, and a couple of soldiers were set on guard duty. He thanked the cook and dismissed the guards, trusting to everyone's exhaustion to be left in peace. Besides, he wanted to be alone, unwatched, unnoticed, not thought about in the least. For a short while, for a single night, he wanted to be invisible.

He sat down in the dark outside his tent and ate the meal the cook had made for him, surprised how hungry he was. He watched the field of campfires in the dark, comforted by their number, and surprised by how warm the night was, and humid. The air seemed to settle even as he sat there, however, becoming clearer, and the stars became sharper and harder. He was able to recognise many constellations he knew back in Rivald, but they seemed to be in the wrong part of the sky for this time of year. The Herdsman, the Mother, the Horse and Rider. When he was a child his grandfather had told him stories about the constellations to help him remember their names and their relationship to one another. He could not remember most of the stories any more, and suddenly it seemed to him a great loss.

"Don't say anything," said Quenion's voice behind him.

He started and, despite her warning, almost demanded to know what she thought she was doing.

"Numoya is asleep," Quenion went on quickly, softly. "I should be by his feet, but I cannot sleep by him. Not tonight anyhow."

For a long while she did not say anything, and Velan thought she might have crept back to Numoya's tent, but then she said, "I have been watching you for a long time. I saw you looking up into the sky, and I remembered when I was a very small girl I used to do that all the time. I cannot remember my mother or my father. I had a sister, at least, but I cannot remember her name or what she looked like. But I remember the nights, and all the stars, and I remember thinking that under a sky that big there had to be a place for me somewhere.

"It's strange, isn't it, how the world gets smaller as you get older. It's not that the universe shrinks, I think, only that our imagination does.

"I am telling you this because I think—I know—you'll understand. I do not think Numoya Kevleren has a place for me in his imagination any more, and in a strange way that knowledge has made the world bigger for me again."

Hattie had not left Sorkro's side all day, and Poloma was worried about her. He tried to make her leave, but she was made of lead and would not move and there was nothing Poloma could do about it, so he watched her. In a way he was relieved because it meant he did not have to watch his mother all the time. Although the slight, papery thing in the bed was no longer something he could consider his mother, it still had her face.

A few hours more and it would be the second dawn since his mother had died, and she would be placed on a pyre and the pyre would be set alight and her spirit would join Kydan, half woman, half crocodile, and Poloma would be the very last of the Malvaras left alive in creation. He had thought, when he had thought about it at all, that the responsibility would weigh down on him, make life almost unbearable, but in a peculiar way it liberated him. Being a Malvara no longer depended on what Sorkro did or said, or what his dead father or any of his dead siblings had done or said. It was entirely up to him now, the new Wisdom of Malvara. He could remake the family in any way he wished.

The problem was, he admitted to himself, finding it
harder and harder to hold his grief at bay, that he had liked
the family his mother had shaped, had liked having her
wisdom and knowledge and prescience to depend on when
the path ahead divided or became hidden.

People had come in all day, briefly and respectfully, to
offer Poloma their thanks for his mother's life, and to offer
a hand rested briefly on his shoulder, each touch giving
him that little bit more strength he would need to face his
life alone. Then, towards the very end of the day, when the
sky was darkening, little Heriot Fleetwood appeared and
stood by him. He felt uplifted, given a great gift by this
simple whitesmith from far across the Deepening Sea, and
when she left, instead of putting her hand on his shoulder,
she had instead, ever so briefly, put her hand in his.

22

NOT more hills, Lerena thought despondently. She hated being transported up and down hills. Her carriers tired out more quickly and they had trouble keeping her seat level; in some consideration for their efforts, she insisted Uilder walk when the incline was steep. They did seem like a pretty series of hills, though. Green and rolling, like in a picture or a stage backdrop.

Lerena thought she could do with a play right now. If she had thought about it, she would have ordered Kashell Graythane to accompany the expedition to put on performances for her at night, and to collect first-hand material for her next play, the *Conquest of Rivald* or *Lerena Rules Supreme* or some such. Or perhaps Lerena herself would write the play and Kashell Graythane could produce it. At least that meant the facts would be straight and she could remove unnecessary characters from the story to help it run more smoothly. Lerena hated bumpy plays, with so many characters the stage looked as crowded as a steam carriage.

She poked her head out of the curtain. The hills did not seem much closer, and the sun was still very high, so no

point in ordering the army to make camp yet. If she had
known conquest was such a boring enterprise she would
have arranged more entertainment.

She decided to order Paimer and Chierma to attend her.
They made good conversation, and that would pass away
some of the time.

"They move as slowly as a mob of drunk soldiers,"
Aland Terko said, using his spyglass.

"Where is their cavalry?" Croft Harker asked, leaning
forward on his elbows to get a better view of the procession. Lerena's army had not yet reached the foothills of the
higher land where he had set up his ambush, and it was
lined out as pretty as a string of pearls.

"I've got reports of them coming in from the flanks. I
guess they'll be assigned to escort the baggage train at
the end."

"They must have at least one good general among them.
Where are their light infantry?"

Terko looked through the spyglass again. "Some skirmishers coming to the front now. They'll probably lead the
army through the hills."

"How many?"

"Looks like a battalion, at least."

"Enough to work as advance guard and protect the
flanks for the lead elements," Harker thought aloud.

"That evens the odds a lot," Terko said.

Harker grunted. "Don't let the others know."

"It's not too late to pull back."

Harker shook his head. "There is no better terrain for an
ambush between here and Beferen. If we're going to make
a difference, it has to be in these hills where we know the
geography well enough to use our cavalry."

Terko smiled grimly. "I was hoping you'd say that."

Harker spat in the direction of Lerena's army. "By the Sefid, I could have crawled to Beferen by now."

Lerena's immediate entourage stopped for a midday meal while the army kept on its way, its head now entering higher ground. The empress, Paimer and Chierma sat on blankets on thick, sweet-smelling grass some distance from the road so they would not be disturbed by the dust clouds thrown up by tramping boots, and were served pastries and strawberries freshly picked from a nearby field by her Axkevlerens.

"The last high ground before Beferen," the empress said gaily, pointing south at the hills. "Afterwards, it's downhill all the way to the capital of Rivald, and then it is all over." She glanced at Chierma, and he guessed correctly she was looking for his confirmation.

"I sincerely hope so, your Majesty," he said quickly. "Although I am surprised no army has met us yet."

"My generals tell me our scouts have seen no sign of any opposition. They are all occupying Beferen." She smiled sweetly. "Oh, we will have a surprise for them."

Chierma returned the smile, but tried to suggest a shrug with it. "Rivald has some good soldiers, your Majesty. I am sure some of them would prefer to fight before your forces reach Beferen."

Lerena picked up a strawberry and pretended to inspect it. "Have you any military experience?" she asked.

"Only in administration," Chierma said. "As governor of Hamewald I was responsible for frontier defense."

"We're not on the frontier any more, and you're not a governor any more."

Chierma took a deep breath. "That is very true."

"Then I will trust my generals' judgment on this," she said.

But have your generals actually done any fighting? he wanted to ask, but kept the question to himself.

"It is a good question, though," Englay said, sitting down next to him on the blanket.

He stared at her pale skin, her dark hair and brown eyes. All physical traits shared by the Kevlerens, but in Englay he thought they reached something close to perfection. He wanted to kiss her on the lips, press her against him.

"Pay attention," Englay warned, a smile tugging the corner of her mouth.

"What are you staring at?" Lerena demanded.

Chierma coughed into his hand. "I was just thinking, your Majesty."

Lerena regarded him with hard eyes that shone with guarded curiosity. "No, you weren't. What were you staring at?"

Chierma tried to think quickly. Could she see Englay? No, or she would not have asked him the question. But she must have sensed something. And he knew, instinctively, that if he lied about what he had been looking at she would know.

"Damn birds," Paimer cursed under his breath.

Lerena turned on her uncle like a spider onto a fly. "What did you say?" she demanded.

Paimer, puzzled, held up a strawberry with a neat round hole in it. "Damn birds got to the fruit before me."

She reached out and took the strawberry from his hand and threw it away. "Eat another," she spat. Then sweetly, "Have a pastry, Uncle." She lifted a plate of them and offered it to Paimer. Tentatively, making sure he did not select any with fruit, he chose one and nodded his thanks.

"She is not insane, if that is what you are thinking," Englay said to Chierma, "no matter what you think of her behavior. In some ways, she is the sanest person alive."

Chierma did not look at Englay this time. Instead, he concentrated on his food and hoped Lerena had forgotten her question to him.

Harker heard an eagle high above, its screeching call echoing between the tall walls of the chasm where he and the thousand cavalry under his direct command waited patiently for the attack to start. The actual timing of the attack was something he had left in the more than capable hands of Aland Terko, who as an officer on the frontier had arranged more than his fair share of ambushes, and had had to fight through a few as well. When Terko considered the enemy was at its most vulnerable, he would order the light infantry to open fire on the enemy's own light infantry, hopefully forcing them back on their own army and causing some confusion. That was when Terko would light the signal fire, and when Harker would lead the cavalry out of the chasm and into the right flank of the Hamilayans.

He tilted his head back and found the eagle, gray-breasted, soaring between thermals, its wings dipping to change direction. Waiting, just like us, Harker thought. I hope it has more luck than us, for truly most of us will not live to see this day out. He had not explained the mathematics to his troopers; they knew well enough.

With average luck, Harker thought his force might cause enough damage to the Hamilayan army to slow its progress towards Beferen, giving the garrison even more time to prepare defences. With better than average luck, they might even hurt the army enough to force it back north onto more secure lines of supply while it licked its wounds.

And if we're extremely lucky, Harker told himself, one of us will get through to slay the empress. If that happens, we may even halt the invasion altogether.

"It is a pity I do not believe in luck," he said aloud.

He did concede, however, that Rivald's chances would have been improved if Numoya Kevleren had been present. But even if the exiled Numoya agreed to return to fight for his country, by the time a ship could get him across the Deepening Sea there would probably be no country for him to return to. He found himself wondering what Numoya Kevleren was doing right now, and whether or not Leader of a Thousand Velan Lymok had even managed to reach Sayenna.

Quenion was supervising the division of supplies and boats, while Numoya went over the plan once more with Velan.

"Once you reach the Frey River, take your time moving east to Kydan. You must not start your attack before we have reached the bay from the south. I estimate it will take us eleven days to reach that position, so start your attack in the morning twelve days from now." Numoya made a point of speaking not just to Velan but to the Rivald company commanders gathered around as well.

Although Velan believed Numoya's opinion of him had improved over the tendays since he had joined the Kevleren's cause, they both understood his loyalty could be guaranteed if sixteen others knew exactly what his duties were.

"Do not slacken in the attack at any stage. Continue the assault until we take the city from the Hamilayans.

Whether you decide to attack the Citadel, or the north island, or both, is of no concern to me. You must make that decision when you see for yourself what their defenses are like."

Velan refrained from asking what he should do if Numoya's attack proved unsuccessful, knowing it would not endear him to the Kevleren. Nonetheless, he could not help asking himself the question, and trying to come up with answers.

"I will give you enough boats to carry your supplies by river, which in turn will leave more bullocks for the boats I will be taking with me directly overland. As you make your way west along the Frey, you can commandeer more boats from local communities to help transport your army once you get to Kydan."

"Yes, your Majesty," Velan said. He had no more questions and was keen to get on. For one thing, the sooner he moved off, the sooner he could put distance between himself and Numoya.

Quenion joined them. "All is done as you requested, your Majesty," she told Numoya. "The supplies have been divided."

"Well and good," Numoya said. "The next time we meet, Leader of a Thousand, shall be in Kydan's Great Quadrangle."

Chierma was learning to rely on good manners to survive awkward situations, and as the situation at the roadside picnic became increasingly tense and everyone else's behavior increasingly erratic, he relied on recently reacquired deference and courtesy to keep his head above water. He passed around plates of food, despite all the Axkevleren servants hovering over them like flies, was gracious to anyone who spoke to him, unceasingly smiled and gave the impression of a calm soul floating above a sea of troubles. Chierma managed this by keeping a large part of his mind detached from the goings-on around him, and so it was he among those gathered there who first heard the distant shouts and screams coming from the south. He stood, frowning, and looked up the road as it curved its way up into the highlands; Lerena's army was still only halfway through, and it extended north past Chierma and the others. He had never been a soldier, but he had a feeling that things were about to get very exciting. Then it occurred to him that Lerena might blame him for letting her army get into trouble, as if he had been part of some wicked Rivald plot to destroy her invasion. Although a part of him wished it was true, he quickly made the decision it would be best to be up front about his suspicions and hope she saw his surprise at developments as genuine rather than part of some elaborate ruse.

"Umm, your Majesty," he started. "I think something is happening."

She was giggling at some witticism made by Paimer, and for an instant he saw her as she must have been when she was only a girl, with long brown hair framing a sweet round face and completely innocent eyes, carefree and filled with promise. And then he saw through the illusion and realised that even when she was a girl the innocence must have been largely an act. She had been raised by the late empress and her court as the next ruler of the Hamilayan empire. She could no more afford to be innocent than he could afford to be trusting.

"Yes? Is something the matter? Sit down and have another pastry—"

"I think something is happening to your army," he said, feeling his heart beat faster.

She stood as well and looked south. "I'm sure I don't know what you mean . . ." Her voice drifted away and she closed her eyes. Even as Chierma watched, her skin darkened and her face sharpened in concentration.

"How dare they," she said in a voice so low that Chierma was surprised it came from her. "How dare they!"

Paimer was standing now, looking at Chierma with curiosity.

"I hear fighting," he told the duke. "Somewhere in the hills."

"It is an ambush," Lerena said, her eyes still closed. "Get me my sedan."

"Your Majesty, perhaps it is best for you to stay here, out of danger," Chierma said.

She opened her eyes and Chierma took a step back. Whether it was a trick of the sun, or his imagination, he was sure her irises had changed colour, a deep gold that seemed to shine from some internal light. "My sedan," she hissed. "Now."

There was no denying that voice, but there was no need for him to do anything because as soon as she had first requested her chair, Paimer had ordered it up. Chierma got the impression the duke knew to obey her without question or hesitation.

As soon as the sedan was ready she boarded, and without waiting for the others ordered her carriers to follow the road south as quickly as possible. Her Royal Guards, resting by the side of the road, immediately fell in before and behind. Her Axkevlerens and servants followed as best they could.

Chierma was left behind with Paimer, feeling lost and,

absurdly he thought, deserted. It was not as if Lerena was *his* empress.

"Should we follow?" he asked.

"I must," Paimer said. "It is my responsibility to protect my niece. You must do as you think best." With that he left.

Chierma looked around. He could run. No one would stop him, he was sure. But run where? After all, he was an ex-governor and an ex-Beloved, and there were few vacancies in Rivald for either position. He was certain that sooner or later, and probably sooner, that would mean working for Lerena. Not ideal, but it was not as if there was an alternative, something he had acknowledged when he made the decision to change sides and assist the empress's cause. His bitter loyalty, as Englay described it, had once again placed him in a situation where no choice he made could be considered an appropriately moral one. He was a natural-born servant looking for a mistress to love, a mistress who would love him back, not as a Kevleren to an Axkevleren, but as one human to another. He understood then he would probably never have that, and wondered if it was his fault, and that therefore he probably never deserved to be loved in that way.

He gathered what courage he thought he possessed and hurried to catch up with Paimer; he had nowhere else to go.

Terko's light infantry fired their first round so close together that it sounded like a single shot, the noise ringing in the hills hard and sharp. Individual enemy fired their weapons in response. For a short while afterwards there was no other sound, and Harker, like every trooper in the chasm, strained to hear any sign of what was happening. Then the shooting started again as soldiers on both sides reloaded, aimed and fired, but not in unison so it was not a single sound but a ripple, climbing and falling in volume on an almost regular basis.

Harker checked his saber was loose in its scabbard, tried his weight against the stirrups, patted his horse's neck pretending he was trying to calm it down instead of himself. Waited.

He wanted to look over his shoulder to make sure his men were all right, but he knew if he did they would take it as a sign of nervousness. In fact, he admitted to himself, he was not nervous. A little excited, perhaps, as was his right. But he knew what was going to happen to him, and that certainty meant he did not have to be nervous. He told himself that a dozen times.

The shooting stopped, and Harker looked up eagerly, expecting to see smoke from the signal fire from Aland Terko's position. Then the shooting started again and he realised he had been holding his breath and he let it out as slowly as he could so he did not startle his horse.

When the signal did come, one of the troopers had to tell him because he was looking for the eagle again. A small tendril of white smoke, clear against the blue sky. He drew his sabre, heard all the troopers behind him do the same, and kneed his mount to a walk.

Aland Terko knew Hamilay's light infantry was good, but he marvelled at how long they held on. They were surprised, outnumbered, outflanked, but they did not run, and when eventually they chose to retreat it was in good order. Some of his own light infantry thought they could force the issue and charged them, but paid for it with several dead. But at last they were moving back down the road, and Terko decided it was time to give the signal. He nodded to

an aide who set alight the dry brush under the green wood.
A short while later the brush was blazing, clear and yellow,
and the green wood was sending up tapers of white smoke.
He sighed with relief. His main job was done, and now all
that was left for him was to join his brave soldiers in pressing the attack on the enemy van.

He made his way along the slope, making sure he did
not automatically try to find the easiest path, which would
eventually have seen him at road level. When he came
across one of his own dead, he took the soldier's firegon
and made sure it was loaded and primed. He could tell
from the sound of shooting and the way his men ducked
low behind every boulder and crest that he was getting
close to the action. A ball ricocheted off the ground near
his boot, and he felt it tug at his jacket. He squatted, raised
the firegon and aimed along its barrel. At first he saw no
one, then noticed behind a wide bush the unmistakable
vertical movement of the rod used to ram a ball and charge
down a firegon barrel. He waited until the enemy soldier
appeared, peeping over the bush to aim a second shot, and
fired. It had been so long since he had used a firegon himself that the flash startled him and he did not hear his own
shot. Smoke puffed up into his face, and he blew it away
to see if he had hit his target. But no. The Hamilayan soldier was retreating without difficulty, which meant Terko
had probably not even winged him.

He moved on, starting to recognize the crescent line his
infantry had formed in their advance. This was not on purpose but a result of the soldiers higher up the slope who
were less vulnerable to enemy fire advancing faster than
their companions lower down. But then the line stopped altogether, and Terko knew he had reached the Hamilayan
vanguard. He squatted again and, ignoring his aged joints,

moved to the nearest crest. He lay down flat and took off his cap, crawled forward and peered over the rise. He was reasonably pleased by what he saw. A cavalry troop was struggling to control their horses against the confusion caused by the retreating light infantry and their growing casualties from the accurate firing of his men. Some of the troopers were dismounting and loading their carbines, others were trying to organize a charge. A regular line company was trying to deploy behind them, but the space was too narrow, and some of their ensigns were shouting for them to stay in column and to fix bayonets. He quickly loaded his firegon and aimed for one of the horses still bearing a rider. His shot killed the horse outright, and it fell sideways against another mount, which also went down. Neither of the riders got up again.

The whole thing was going better than expected, he told himself. As ambushes go, this was one of the better ones he had been involved in. Now if only President Harker had seen the signal they might even be able to make the vanguard rout. That would be a sight to see.

He started loading his weapon again, breathing hard with the exertion. He thought when all this was over he would resume an exercise regime, get fit again, maybe even apply for duty back on the frontier. His breath frosted. Strange, part of his mind thought. Then he saw the faint blue glow around his firegon's barrel.

"Oh," he said.

He peeked over the crest again, but could not see any Kevlerens. Who was doing this? If he saw him, he just might be able to put a ball into his brain. There was a scattering of confused figures in the middle of the regular infantry, completely disrupting their formation. Camp follower, he immediately thought, seeing the short, round

young woman forcing her way through soldiers and troopers alike. Probably been told her husband has been killed
and is out for revenge. Terko had heard of such things.
Well, if she picked up a firegon, he would kill her despite
any qualms . . .

She had long black hair, and although her lips were
moving he could not hear a woman's voice. Some very
tough-looking soldiers were trying to catch up with her.
One or two even tried to grab her arm, but she slapped
them away. Terko was not sure, but he thought he saw her
eyes actually *glowing*.

"By the Sefid, let me through!" Paimer shouted, but the
mass of soldiers in front of him could not have moved even
if they had wanted to, so choked now was the road through
the hills. Officers were trying to force some sort of order
on the mess, and Paimer was only making everything
worse. One brave commander decided that enough was
enough and ordered a cadre of his men to hold the duke
and his companions safe and out of the way.

Paimer could not believe it. Did they not recognize
him? Why would they not let him through to protect his
niece? He lifted his hand to grab his red wig and throw it
to the ground, but it was not there.

"See, that is why they have not recognized you," Idalgo
said. "They think you are just a madman."

"But I'm not a madman," he said plaintively.

The soldiers in the cadre eyed him with wary respect.

Chierma said, "Well, there is nothing for it. I'm sitting
down."

He did exactly that. Paimer remained standing, raising
and lowering his arms in frustration, but he said nothing
more.

"This is going to be interesting," Idalgo said.

Paimer frowned at him. "What?"

"Absolutely," Lady Englay said. "It's going to be terrible." She glanced down at Chierma. "Good idea. Sit down, everyone. It will be easier for you if you are closer to the ground."

Idalgo nodded encouragement to Paimer. "You might as well. The soldiers aren't going to let you through. Get comfortable, your Grace."

Paimer slumped to the ground. He noticed that Idalgo and Englay remained standing. "So why don't you sit?"

"We don't want to miss anything," Englay said distantly.

The walk down the chasm had increased to a trot where the floor widened. Harker saw the white cloth attached to the pole he himself had placed three hundred yards from the mouth of the chasm and he ordered the charge. He had never experienced anything as exhilarating as that last ride, the wild gallop between towering red walls, the sound of the beating of thousands of hooves magnified and reflected down to the road. No wonder that when they burst out of the chasm the enemy they confronted looked more terrified than any enemy Harker had ever seen. They ran from him, ran for their lives, dropping their firegons, careening into each other like fish in a closing net. He slashed at every face that came within reach as he tried to guide his horse north to pursue the enemy, but his mount wanted to avoid any collision and was almost impossible to control. Not that it mattered. The enemy was in flight. The Hamilayans were going to run all the way back to the border. He twisted in his saddle and saw his troopers scything their way through rank and file of Hamilayan infantry, some then heading north to follow him if they could, others heading south to relieve Aland Terko.

He was getting carried away, he knew, but he also knew he no longer had the luxury to think clearly and logically. He was in the midst of the enemy and they numbered in the thousands; all he could do for his country, for his beloved republic, was spur his horse towards them.

Terko took aim at the witch, but as he was squeezing the trigger something exploded beside him. He was pushed flat to the ground and lost his firegon. His face was wet and he could not see. He tasted blood in his mouth and knew he had been wounded, but he felt no pain yet and so did not know where or how badly. He scrabbled for his firegon, got his hand around its barrel and then threw it away, screaming in shock because the metal had been too cold to touch. He wiped the blood away from his eyes and tried to crawl back down the crest away from the enemy. Still he felt no pain, and he wondered what was happening to him.

Someone bounded over the crest towards him. One of his light infantry, his mouth and eyes opened so wide they looked distorted. Then the man disappeared and in his place was an expanding cloud of blood. Pieces of bone hissed past Terko's ear, and one shard lanced through his calf. He screamed again in horror. He kept on scrabbling backwards, trying to get away, ignoring the pain in his calf and the growing, burning pain in his heart.

"Oh, sweet Sefid," Lady Englay said. "It is almost more than I can bear!"

Chierma looked up and saw his love sway on her feet. She seemed delirious, and then he saw that Idalgo was exactly the same.

"She is drinking it up," the Beloved said.

Chierma shivered then, suddenly cold, and glanced at Paimer, who was rubbing his arms vigorously and breathing out in puffy clouds.

"The empress," he said under his breath.

"But who is she sacrificing for us to feel the effect this far away?" Chierma asked, looking at Paimer for an answer. "Would it be Uilder?"

The duke looked suddenly weary, and said, "She has no need, I think, for sacrifice any more."

And Chierma understood what Paimer meant. The knowledge made him feel completely insignificant. If he had known he would never have gone over to Lerena. He would have deserted his post in Hamewald and run as far as he could away from Rivald.

Englay smiled down on him. "You only understand some of it," she said.

"My master has known all along," Idalgo said proudly.

"That's because he helped start the whole thing," Englay said, but not at all reprovingly. Chierma was surprised to see her lean over and kiss Paimer's bald head. Stupidly, he felt jealous rather than curious. Paimer did not seem to appreciate the gift, though, and scratched the spot as if he had been bitten by a mosquito.

Harker was the last one. He slipped off his exhausted horse and ran back to the mouth of the chasm, but it was no good. Some of the enemy cavalry, lancers, had got there before him and blocked the way. He turned and saw the carnage he and his men had caused, and then fallen prey to. The road was jammed with heaps of the dying and the dead, but that horror was nothing compared to what he had seen happen to so many of his troopers, exploding as if someone had set off a sack of gonblack inside them. He

had seen the blue flame licking off all the firegons and
swords and lance heads and knew what was causing it. For
a while he crazily rode up and down the road, pushing
aside friend and foe alike in his desperate search for the
Kevleren doing the Wielding, but without luck. At the end,
his horse simply refused to move and its head hung down
between its forelegs.

There was a commotion south of him, and a woman
emerged among the carnage, bloodied and terrible to see.
She saw him. Without thinking he ran towards the lancers.
They raised their weapons. His heart started to burn as if
someone had set it alight. He ran faster, caught the gaze of
one of the lancers, pleaded with his eyes, ran faster still. As
if in slow motion the lancer prodded his mount and trotted
forwards. Harker screamed with the pain. He focused on
the tip of the advancing lance, and with only yards to go he
lifted his sword arm to stretch his ribs and give the point a
clean entry straight to his lungs and aorta, and threw himself against it.

When the birds started wheeling in from all over the
sky, Paimer knew it was over. Lerena was offering her familiars a special feast. He was afraid it would not be the
last of its kind.

"It will be difficult for her to do this again," Idalgo said.
"She Wielded with such strength that most of the free Sefid
has gone."

"How strong was the Wielding?" he asked timidly,
wondering for the first time if perhaps he should be more
afraid of Idalgo and Englay than Lerena. There was something about his Beloved that was no longer quite Axkevleren.

"Dig a hole," Idalgo said.

"What?"

"With your fingers, your Grace. Dig a little hole. You will not have to go far."

Paimer did not question again. He cupped his hand and scraped away some dirt near his feet, and when the soil became more compact he used his fingers to dig deeper. Soon after, he could dig no further. Something hard and slippery stopped him. He scraped more soil away, and without being asked Chierma joined him. When they saw what they had uncovered they sat back on their haunches, amazed, then dug another hole and another. After three, they stopped. They were both covered in dirt.

"What is it, your Grace?" Chierma asked.

"Glass," Paimer said. "Just a handspan down, everything has melted into glass."

23

AT first Kydan was a disappointment. Velan Lymok had expected a great river city, a splendid metropolis that dominated the landscape. Instead, it was barely larger than a Rivald town with only a single noticeable landmark, the Citadel. But then, over the next day while he studied every aspect of the way Kydan sat on just three islands, and the way its inhabitants had taken advantage of its considerable geographic advantages for defense, his opinion did not so much change as evolve.

Kydan *was* a small city, but any larger and it would have been as difficult to defend as any other, since an increase in size could only have been achieved by spreading to the mainland either side of the Frey River. And the reason the eye was drawn constantly to the Citadel was because it was, in every sense, a true fortress, magnificently built; and, as one of his levy companies had discovered when it wandered too far west, armed to the teeth. When Velan heard the sound of the booming longgon he almost jumped out of his saddle in fright, and when he turned to find the source of the sound he saw a small cloud of black smoke over the Citadel wall, and then saw a small black dot arcing high over the Frey River that grew larger and larger until it bounced on the ground with a soft thud about twenty yards from the levies, then rose in the air for a short distance before bouncing again into the company, flinging aside people like broken toys, and bouncing again, and again, before rolling to a stop. When the company retreated in something like panic, it left a dozen men behind, mangled beyond help.

Velan, like almost everyone else under his command, had never heard a longgon fired in anger, let alone witnessed the destructive result a longgon ball could have on densely packed infantry. He imagined the effect on a unit of cavalry would be even more horrifying. When one of his men recovered the ball and brought it to him he was able to heft it in a single hand. He found it hard to believe that such a small thing, no matter how heavy, could cause so much destruction.

"Good shooting," Kadburn said, clapping the chief of the longgon crew on the shoulder. "That was as fine a shot as I've ever seen."

The chief pushed out his chest. "Aye, sir, but I wish you'd let us fire earlier. I'm sure we could hit them close to a mile from this elevation."

"I admire your enthusiasm," Kadburn said. "But let them think they know our range."

The chief grinned as if he had just been let in on some diabolical secret. "I understand, sir."

Poloma joined Kadburn on the wall. The Beloved saw a man who was not only hiding a great deal of personal grief, but who at the same time was trying to demonstrate calm and confidence in the face of the latest threat to Kydan's independence. Kadburn had to admit that Poloma

Malvara was a stronger man than he, and Maddyn for that matter, had believed. If Maddyn had lived he would have found it difficult turning Kydan into anything more than a colony of Hamilay while letting Poloma live. In a way Kadburn was glad Maddyn would never have to face that. He was equally glad that he had made the decision to help keep Kevlerens out of the city, making him Poloma's ally.

They stood side by side, and with a look from Kadburn, the longgon crews along that section retreated a decent space to let the two leaders talk in private.

"How strong is the enemy force?" Poloma asked.

"It's not numbers that count in a siege," Kadburn said authoritatively. "The defender's advantage is counted in stone as well as soldiers."

Poloma said nothing. He waited patiently.

Kadburn sighed. "Between a thousand and fifteen hundred."

"So they outnumber us at least two to one."

"You want more for a siege," Kadburn argued. "At least three to one. More likely five to one. And a good number of the enemy is made up of levies."

"Like our militia," Poloma observed. "And we have three islands to cover."

"Two, really. Kayned is not important."

"Tactically, perhaps, but strategically it is very important. Imagine the effect on morale if the enemy captures a third of Kydan's territory."

"Then we will retake it," Kadburn said simply.

"I assume the advantage of an attacker is the choice of where to make the assault."

"And the advantage of the defender is that we can shift forces where they are needed."

"Except we have not one continuous land mass but

three islands, so shifting forces becomes as much a logistical exercise for us as it does for the enemy."

Kadburn swallowed. Everything Poloma was saying was true. But he had the same intrinsic faith in the city's cause as he once did in Maddyn's destiny. He could not believe Kydan would fall to Numoya Kevleren. He trusted Poloma Malvara and Strategos Galys Valera and Commander Gos Linsedd to bring them through if he and everyone else just did their part.

"No one will take the Citadel from me, Prefect," Kadburn said solemnly.

"Apparently crocodiles can be a problem," Quenion said.

Numoya, fighting lethargy, nodded vaguely. He was looking out over the Bay of Kydan, a much bigger expanse of water than he expected. From his time in Kydan, looking west to the bay, he had assumed it widened gradually until merging with the Deepening Sea, but in fact it was a large body of water in its own right, separated from the ocean by two curving headlands that rose precipitously from the land on either side. He was surprised geography could be so deceptive. He remembered when he was a boy he and his cousins and all their Beloveds would sometimes explore the hills north of Beferen. They would climb one hill only to be surprised by another bigger one over the rise.

While in Kydan he had seen maps of the area, of course, but on a map the bay had always been the size of a coin.

"Do you think our boats will be big enough?" he asked.

"Your Majesty?"

He motioned towards the bay. "Can they cross such open water?"

"Our crews say the only problem will be the crocodiles at the other end."

"Crocodiles? Yes. In the swamps. They can be quite big, you know."

"Yes," Quenion said uneasily. "I know."

Numoya touched his lips with the side of his hand. "Yes, of course you do. You were with me in Kydan. Well, someone armed with a firegon in the prow of each boat should solve the problem."

"Forgive me, your Majesty, but would not a pike be better? A firegon going off might give away our attack, and not guarantee killing the beasts. They have very tough skin. At least with a pike it can be pushed away, if not injured."

Numoya nodded. "Very good. Yes. See to it."

Quenion made to move off, but hesitated. "Your Majesty, are you feeling well? You seem distracted."

It was disillusion, he thought. *I am always expecting things to be different from the way they really are. I am absurdly optimistic. I think the world is shaped to my needs. Perhaps all my family think like that.*

"Are you sure you're not feeling ill?" Quenion persisted.

Numoya rubbed his temples with his fingers. His skull seemed too small for his brain.

I was disappointed by the Kydans, how ungrateful they were to me and my people. I was disappointed by the officers who overthrew my family in Beferen. I was disappointed by my Beloved who deceived me into sacrificing an innocent. And I was devoted to the Kydans, although they did not know it. And I was proud of the officers before the revolution, though they did not know it. And I loved Quenion. And she knew it.

And I still love her.

That was the problem, he realized.

Some of his lethargy slipped away from him.

Yes, I still love Quenion.

So how does love work? Chierma wondered. He tried to keep the thought to himself, because he did not want Englay to answer. He did not trust her anyway, any more than he had trusted her when she was alive. But he had to think of something, and when he was not concentrating all he saw in his mind's eye was the slaughter of Rivald's last hope in the highlands and the terrible charred remains of soldiers and horses massed in smoldering heaps.

So did I ever truly love her? Is trust a kind of love?

"It's possible to trust someone you don't love," Englay said.

"I wish you wouldn't listen in all the time."

"But you were shouting," Englay said. She was standing by him on the rising ground before Beferen. He had expected to see it the way it was the last time he left the city, the way it was most days: clouded over, dark and oppressive. Instead, the sun was shining brilliantly and Beferen actually seemed as if it could be a halfway attractive place to live.

"Well, if the city survives the next day or two," Englay said, "perhaps she will give you an apartment near the palace."

"We're talking about Lerena?"

"She will be mistress of Beferen, have no doubt."

"Of that I do not have any doubt at all," he said, shivering with the memory of what he had seen in the highlands.

"You were talking about love," Englay said, almost wistfully.

"I was questioning it, I think."

"Before Lerena killed me, I knew you loved me, and not just the way a Beloved had to love his Kevleren. I knew what you felt was a passion. I liked that about you then, and I like that about you now. In a way I regret I could not return your love in the same fashion. But you were an Axkevleren, and it wasn't possible."

Chierma realized his eyes were brimming with tears. It was not fair. He should not have to listen to this.

"And that made you want to hurt me," Englay said. "You always hurt the ones you love because they are the most vulnerable. I understand that at last."

Chierma felt hot tears on his cheeks. He touched them almost in wonder.

The black tide of Lerena's army crept over the rise, and to Chierma it seemed to match the black spread of Beferen, like a misshapen twin.

"You were never good for me," he said bitterly.

"Of course I was good for you," Englay said. "I gave you purpose."

He studied her carefully, seeing Englay and Lerena and even parts of Paimer in her face.

"I would have liked to find my own purpose, I think."

Galys Valera ordered her six militia companies, training in the Saddle, to quick march again. Lannel Thorey, standing just behind her, translated for the benefit of the native Kydans. Since being released from the Citadel by Galys and conscripted to help train the militia, he had slowly come out of his depression. He never smiled, and refused to look Galys in the eye, but he did what he was asked without hesitation and was obviously a quick learner. Galys thought he could make a useful member of the militia.

There were some groans after the order, some unkind curses that she was undoubtedly meant to hear, but they would have been surprised to learn she was heartened because the curses were coming in two languages.

She had arranged the companies so that the half comprising the Hamilayan regulars could keep their firegons, but at the same time lend their discipline and experience, while the native contingent armed with swords, and some with spears, could act as a mobile defence to protect those with firegons from an enemy charge when they were reloading. What resentment existed between the two groups effectively was flattened by Galys's hard training regime, which had them working day and night until they were too exhausted to resent anyone except Galys.

Now all the hard work was bearing fruit. Not only were they starting to work together, but the soldiers were picking up one another's patois and slang and opinions of leaders. And they were looking out for one another in training, and taking pride in their new units. Galys encouraged a friendly rivalry between the six new companies, and a fiercer rivalry between the militia and the preserved professional units.

But today of all days she wanted them so tired they did not have enough strength left to think about the enemy who had arrived outside the city that morning. Today was also the last day they would get any training before they experienced their first fight as militia companies. Although they would ideally stay together, Kydan did not have the military strength to let her do that. Some would have to be ready to go to Karhay if needed, some kept as reserve on Herris, and at least one sent to the third and most southerly island, Kayned, to stop the enemy from landing a few men and a flag to claim it, and hopefully dissuading a more serious attempt to take it.

One of the longgons fired, and everyone in the Saddle stopped what they were doing. Even Galys paused long enough to look over her shoulder back at the Citadel. She had not thought the enemy would attack on the same day they arrived, and was relieved when no more shots were heard. It was just Kadburn sending the enemy a message: if you reach out your hand to take us, we will bite it.

She turned her attention back to the militia and ordered them to resume the march. This time there was not a single curse. All the training and exercising suddenly seemed insufficient, despite their earlier complaints.

The world was empty. Lerena, watching her army file past to deploy around Beferen, was extending her senses looking for any trace of that great ocean of Sefid she had been swimming in since she had killed her sister Yunara. There was nothing. She had used it all in her great Wielding in the highlands. Her heart beat faster when she thought on it, remembered the great river of rage that had driven her like a log in a flood, reveled in the memory of her enemies being rent asunder like paper sacks. Then, like the Sefid itself, the joy drained from her when she looked out and saw no blue haloes, no tendrils of power.

Lerena consoled herself with the thought that soon all of Rivald would be in her hands. She would have achieved what no Kevleren had ever achieved: the unification of the continent under a single throne. She felt a thrill of anticipation when she thought of what she might be able to do then. Better, when this was over she could return to her aviary, to her lovely birds, to Omeralt on its high plateau, and she would never leave again.

She lightly gripped Paimer by the elbow. "Uncle, I want you and the other members of our family to stay close to me during the siege. I want you all to be safe. My Royal Guards will form a cordon around us."

Paimer nodded weakly. He was looking more frail than ever, but as devoted to her service as ever. In all the world there was no one she loved as much as her uncle.

When night fell, the boats that usually ferried between Karhay and Herris carried Gos Linsedd, Ames Westaway and all the dragoons south of the Frey River. There were not enough ferries to carry all the troopers and horses in one wave, so Gos went first with half the troop while Ames waited impatiently by the docks with the other half, peering into the darkness for any sign of the boats' return. He and the troopers constantly tended their horses and kept them as quiet as possible. Sounds travelled much further along the river at night, and they wanted to give no hint to the enemy of what they were about.

When the ferries did return they came like ghostly shapes, hardly visible under the moonless sky. A gentle northwesterly blew which countered the current and made the surface of the river itself as flat as an iron sheet.

Ames was the last to board, and their progress was so smooth around the islands to the mainland that he almost felt as if he was stationary and the world itself was floating by, turned by some invisible hand. He looked overhead for the stars, but they were hidden behind cloud. He wished he could hide his apprehension as easily. Knowing he would soon be in battle made him afraid. And tired, he realised, as if his body was punishing him in advance for the stress and trauma he was going to put it through.

Disembarking at the end was harder than boarding because there was no dock to ease the way. The horses had to be coaxed into the shallows and then led by hand to the shore. Once in the water it was not too arduous an experience for the horses, but for the troopers, often waist high in water, it was a different story. Ames noticed that Gos had sent a few troopers west along the bank to rescue anyone who might lose their footing and get taken by a current. As it happened, there were no emergencies, but they emerged from the river sodden and tired, with their boots caked in rich sticky silt.

Most of Gos's half-troop was already arranged in column, and Ames organized his men behind them as soon as they emerged from the river.

"Well done, Ensign," Gos told Ames when he reported all were ready. "All across without a single incident. Now we head south as far as possible for what's left of the night."

Ames took one last look behind him and saw the boats making for Herris. In the still darkness they were like parts of a dream, not quite real at all.

"They head for Herris now," Gos told him. "They must hide from the bigger enemy boats."

"I hope the militia are up to it," Ames said with the casual disdain of a professional, already forgetting that half the militia's number had been professionals themselves.

"Never underestimate Galys Valera," Gos said. "She is the best of us, Ensign. The very best of us."

Gos gave the word and the long column set off. For the first hour they went by foot, moving as silently as possible. When the river was far behind them, they mounted their horses and rode over the grasslands at a steady trot. They had a lot of ground to cover and not much time in which to do it.

*   *   *

Velan Lymok had studied the eastern approach to Kydan until it was too dark to see much more than a long-yard. He could have gone closer, he supposed, but did not want to tempt any of the longgonners to take a pot shot at him. The thought of being hit by one of those iron balls made a shiver pass up his spine.

At any rate, by nightfall he had made up his mind where and how to attack. At first it had been a fine puzzle, but considering all the facts, the mission set him by Numoya Kevleren, the best chance of any real success and with due regard for the soldiers placed under his command, a solution had finally emerged. Now he had to set about devising a plan to implement the solution, and that was a harder task. Unfortunately he only had until morning, because at some point during that day, Numoya Kevleren would make his attack.

He returned to his tent and made maps, then asked some of the local river people to tell him about currents and sandbanks and shallows. Some of those had fought in the last battle, under the plutocrats, and could also tell him where and how the defences had been improved. He worked late into the night, and by the time he was finished he had a plan. He knew it was not perfect, but with the time given him and the limited intelligence of what things were now like on the northernmost island of Karhay, it was the best he was going to come up with.

Velan stood outside his tent, and as he did every night now he made a tour of the camp, always ensuring he moved slowly and near firelight to avoid being accidentally shot or stabbed by one of the pickets. He talked with his company commanders, many of them veterans, and listened to their advice. He talked encouragingly to those soldiers who were still awake, Rivald and native, trying not to be too patronizing or too aloof. Then he returned to his tent, undressed and set out his uniform and inspected it. Tomorrow was going to be his first ever major battle, and he was going to do his best to look immaculate.

He suspected Numoya was using him because he looked the part rather than from any confidence in his ability, and had given him command mainly of levies and the least trained soldiers, but Velan was determined to do better than simply look the part. He was going to behave with determination and fortitude, and military stoicism. He was going to behave like an officer.

"What's it feel like now that you're an officer?" Heriot asked Arden.

He grunted.

"I mean, you've come a long way, haven't you? From Axkevleren to homeless vagabond to pressed colonist to Grim Arden, Master of Horse and commander of all the armed forces on the island of Karhay."

"Every damn one," he said, waving at the collection of colonists that were manning the walls. Galys had given them a handful of firegons, the ones taken from dead Rivald soldiers when the city was first taken by the Hamilayans, since the caliber was different from the Hamilayan weapon and would not take the same weight ball. But otherwise they were armed mainly with scythes, pole arms, hammers, carpenters' spikes and long knives. And courage. A great deal of courage.

"I think Strategos Galys Valera likes you," she said.

"I think Strategos Galys Valera had no one else to turn to. The commander is off with his dragoons, Kadburn Axkevleren is responsible for the Citadel and Poloma Malvara for the rest of Herris, and she herself is in charge of the militia."

"And you look impressive swinging an axe . . ."

"You are exaggerating."

". . . lopping off limbs . . ."

"You stick close to me, Heriot Fleetwood. I don't want to see any harm come to you."

Heriot touched his arm lightly. "I know. And I'll protect your back."

Arden actually smiled slightly. "You going to use that hammer again, like last time?"

"No, I could hardly lift that bloody thing." She pulled a dirk from her belt. "But I reckon I could stick one or two enemy using this without much trouble."

He sized up the dirk and looked dubious.

"When this is over, we must discuss the Colonists' Guild," she said.

"With what in mind?"

"I think it is time we dissolved it; it has served its purpose. If we win this battle, defeat Sayenna, we should concentrate on making Kydan one city with one people."

"I hope you are right. You don't think Councilor Kysor Nevri and his supporters will pick up where they left off if they feel they no longer need us colonists to defend Kydan?"

"Not with any right on their side, and in the end that will defeat them."

Arden nodded slowly. "I knew making you head of the guild was the right decision."

"Your Majesty, everything is ready," Quenion said. "The boats are waiting."

"You know this is a turning point, don't you?" Numoya Kevleren said.

Quenion paused before answering. After everything she had been through in the last few months, it seemed to her that every day was a turning point of one kind or another. "Yes, your Majesty," she said.

"If we succeed in the morning, we can re-establish Rivald in the New Land."

Quenion thought Numoya looked tense, like a drawn bow. His hands trembled and his skin looked drawn over his new face. She wondered what he really saw with his eyes, whether the world he saw now was the same world he had seen before his injuries.

"I want you to know, Quenion Axkevleren, that you are forgiven."

Quenion started. "Your Majesty?"

"You are my Beloved, and I love you the way a Kevleren should. You are forgiven."

Quenion, unsure what to say, bowed her head.

"It is time for us to go," Numoya said.

They walked down to the boat assigned for them, already crowded with Rivald soldiers, and Quenion helped Numoya board. A soldier leaned over to help her over the gunwale, and she took her place behind her master in the bow. As the boats slipped away from the shore, Quenion tried to sort through the conflicting emotions whirling in her brain. She had longed desperately ever since the night she had deceived him with the servant girl to find his forgiveness, but now that she had it she found she resented the blessing. She had done what needed to be done to heal Numoya, to make him whole again, which was clearly her duty, but to have done so by sacrificing her own life would have left him without a Beloved, left him without the one

person who could help organize the preservation of a Rivald presence in the New Land. Without her, none of this
would be happening. Instead of forgiving her, why was he
not asking for her forgiveness for treating her like a traitor
instead of a Beloved?

What right did he have?

She knew the answer already, and it pushed into her
mind. She resisted it, but in the end she had neither the
strength nor the history to deny what she knew for a simple fact of existence.

Numoya was a Kevleren. He spoke the truth. It was his
place to offer forgiveness and not to seek it.

She gripped the gunwale with one hand and looked at
Numoya, proudly standing in the bow with his long black
hair and long lean limbs and long history of power and authority. And as the boat glided into the future, the sky
above still dark, she acknowledged that he loved her as a
Kevleren must love, but could no longer be sure she loved
him in return.

24

"IRE!"
Paimer winced as the combined companies making up the first assault wave on Beferen shot their firegons as one. The sound reverberated like a thunderclap and echoed over the landscape.

"That would've loosened a few bowels in the city," Idalgo said cheerfully.

But Paimer knew no one in Beferen had anything to fear from the volley. It was more to start things with a bang and to clear the infantry's barrels so they would be forced to close and use the bayonet to attack.

"Advance!"

The order, starting with an officer on the extreme right of the columns, was repeated along the line, and the companies marched forward, the ground rumbling beneath their marching feet, their firegons, fixed with bayonet, held in front, and each unit accompanied by engineers carrying scaling ladders and ropes. Even as they moved off, the second wave moved forward to occupy their starting positions. When the first wave was far enough in front, the second wave started their march as well, and in turn was followed by a third. After that went a couple of troops of cavalry, a hopeful move on the part of Lerena's generals, since they would not be much use unless the walls of the city fell in the first attack.

"Not entirely impossible," Idalgo said. "The walls are new."

"And surmounted by spike and well defended," Paimer pointed out.

Idalgo shrugged. "Nonetheless, Beferen will fall."

"You sound very keen," Paimer observed.

"And your wig is askew."

Paimer adjusted his head-wear. "This is bloody war, Idalgo. You never liked it before."

Idalgo grinned but did not answer, so Paimer returned his attention to the attack. The first wave was halfway to the city walls. He heard the distant cough of longgons, saw small specks arch over the battlefield and land among the massed columns of the Hamilayan infantry. Bodies disintegrated and gaps appeared in the columns but they marched on. A longyard from the wall the officers called the charge, and the soldiers let out one long yell and ran flat out. Soon they were inside the firing arc of the enemy's longgons, but then the enemy infantry on the walls could fire on them, and from where Paimer stood the rattle of their first volley sounded like coins shaken in a can. Up close it must have been terrifying, although nowhere near as terrifying as the hundreds of balls scything through the infantry body and limb.

While the first wave carried out their assault, the second wave held back long enough to raise their firegons and fire at the defenders. Then they, too, made their charge.

"Things are going well," Idalgo said.

"I don't think they are going to take the wall," Paimer said.

"That isn't what I meant," Idalgo said, more to himself than to the duke.

Because Kadburn knew the enemy had to attack by boat, he had most of the longgons set to fire in a long line that stitched the Frey, starting a longyard from the end of Herris and ending about half a mile upriver. He was on the wall before dawn, in time to greet the rain that swept in from the northwest. The rain was warm and soaking and made the air smell of dust. Then, just before sunrise, he saw the dark shapes of boats heading towards Kydan and he gave the alarm. Bells and gongs echoed the alarm throughout the three islands of the city, and soldiers, militia and citizens ran to their posts to await orders or to repel the enemy, whichever came to them first. As the light improved he noticed that the banks of the river next to the boats seemed to be waving, as if they were bringing their own private breeze. Then he made out the dull clunk of metal against metal and realised they were soldiers.

"Clever bastard," Kadburn thought aloud.

"Sir?" asked one of the longgon chiefs.

"He can't fit all his soldiers into the boats, so instead of ferrying one lot down and then sailing back to get reinforcements, he's bringing them as far as he can by foot." He felt like groaning, because it also meant the plan for Gos to attack the enemy's reserves while they were still on the mainland would probably fail.

"All the more targets for us, surely?"

"Depends on how long it takes him to transfer soldiers to the islands." Kadburn bit his lip. "Or island."

"They're almost in range, sir."

Then Kadburn received his second shock. The boats were not coming down in single file, but four or five abreast, so they would all the quicker come under the shadow of the longgons' firing arc.

"Shoot!" he shouted. "Now! Get as many of the boats as you can!"

Klyne Ferren concentrated on slowing his writing. As the sounds of battle wafted up to the palace from the wall, his first instinct was to hurry writing his orders and then rush to the battle, but as military governor of Beferen, he must be the last to rush, to show any concern or anxiety about the attack. Clerks bustled about him in their normal way, taking his lead as an example.

When the last order sheet was signed and powdered, he gave it to a courier. "To the commander of the Offra light infantry company stationed near the east docks. There will be no reply, so when you have done that please report for duty to the commander of the reserve here at the palace." The courier, only a boy, saluted, took the order and walked out of the governor's office; as soon as he was out of sight he broke into a run, his boots clicking on the polished hardwood floors.

"Well," Ferren said, standing up slowly so his knees did not creak. "That is that. All I can do here is done."

"You will be joining the reserves now, sir?" one of the clerks asked. The man was being solicitous, Ferren knew, but he still found the insinuation irritating.

"No. The commander of reserves will need no help from this old man. I only have one duty left to me now."

He nodded to all the clerks who had helped him during his brief stint as military governor, doffed his cap and walked out of the palace for the last time.

The streets were empty and the sun was shining. Ferren thought this might be the first time in the history of the city that both had happened at the same time. For the briefest of moments he could almost believe there was nothing wrong at all, then he caught a whiff of gonblack in the air and, despite the sun, the day became gray and solemn. He straightened his uniform and walked in the direction of the fighting, smiling confidently whenever he passed groups of soldiers waiting their turn to go on the wall. He reached a point fifty yards from the main gate when he saw his first wounded. They had been wrapped in coarse blankets and left on the side of the street. A physic was slowly making his way among them, doing what he could. Blood trickled down the gutter and then down the drains; from there the blood would find its way to the cold waters of Beferen's harbor.

He took a firegon and ammunition belt from an unconscious soldier, walked up the ancient stone steps to the barely adequate wall defending the capital of what once had been the world's second most powerful state, and waited for the enemy to come to him.

It was worse than Velan Lymok had imagined. The destruction caused among his soldiers by the longgons made him want to retreat, to save as many lives as possible. Instead he struggled to remain calm while directing what forces had survived the first landing to attack the newly built wall in front of them, and ordering the few boats he had left to ferry across the rest of his soldiers.

It did not take him long to realize he had not suffered as many casualties as he had feared. Many survived the destruction of the boats and swam either onto one of the islands or back to the mainland. Those boats that had reached Karhay had unloaded their passengers quickly and efficiently, and fortunately the defenders here had only a few firegons, quickly suppressed when Velan ordered covering fire. Soon after he had a large enough force to start the attack proper. He gave instructions to the most senior company commander, then set about organizing the reinforcements as they arrived from the mainland by boat, or from the river under their own power.

His soldiers, despite the rain and slippery ground and the ordeal they had already suffered under the Citadel's longgons, kept a tight formation and advanced against the enemy wall, a long, strongly built barrier that gave plenty of cover for those behind it but in most places was no more than two yards high.

There was a great cry from both sides as the first assault hit the wall, the soldiers trying to clamber over. Defenders, armed mostly with modified farming tools as far as Velan could make out, fought valiantly, but his troops, greater in number and better armed, managed to get onto the wall quicker than he had thought possible, and then over it. Behind them streamed yet more soldiers, and he quickly sent reinforcements with strict instructions to hold the section of captured wall and go no further to ensure his men could not be cut off from behind.

Velan Lymok and his diversionary force had accomplished their task and drawn the attention of the defenders to the northeast of the city, to Karhay. If Numoya Kevleren had been able to stick to his own plan, then he should already be starting his assault on the southwest of the city.

"Repelled!" Lerena cried. "What do you mean 'repelled'? I sent twelve of my best companies against that piddling fence they call a wall, and you're telling me they were 'repelled'?"

The general receiving all of Lerena's attention visibly wilted. "Your Majesty, the enemy defended with great vigor, with great courage."

"And what about my bloody soldiers? Did they not show great vigor and courage as well?"

"Yes, your Majesty—as did your generals!—but there was nothing more we could do. Our losses were too high, and they had enough reinforcements to repel every attack."

"Who ordered my soldiers to retreat?" she demanded.

The general looked as if he would keel over from a heart attack. "I did, your Majesty."

Lerena closed her eyes and calmed her breathing. When she opened her eyes again the general was sweating profusely. He had seen what Lerena had done to the enemy in the highlands, and half expected to blow up at any moment. She smiled sweetly at him. "Then you will lead the next attack."

The general almost fainted with relief. He could handle that.

"Prepare the next assault for an hour's time," she ordered, and he hurried off. Lerena turned to Uilder. "Order my family to ready itself. Each member is to come here with one of their Axkevlerens." Uilder bowed and quickly walked away so the empress could not see her terrified face.

"Can you hear it?" Numoya asked Quenion eagerly.

Her master's voice broke her reverie. She listened. "Firegons. The battle has already joined."

The rain, which had started just before dawn, had soaked everyone through to the skin, making their clothes heavy to wear. As well, visibility was reduced, and for some time Quenion had wondered if they might even be heading in the wrong direction, perhaps north across the bay, and would miss Kydan entirely. But the boat crews knew what they were doing, and soon the dim mound of an island loomed in the middle distance.

Their boat was the first to make landfall. Well, the first to hit the swamp. Quenion looked uncertainly over the side. The water here smelled rank, a mixture of brine and decomposing vegetation. Small white crabs scuttled around the exposed roots of mangrove trees.

Numoya did not seem to care. He leaped over the gunwale and started moving east through the mangroves, ignoring the multitude of bugs, crustaceans and snails. He did not even check to see if anyone was following him. He knew everyone would, because that was the way it was when you were a Kevleren: where you led, others followed. Quenion shuddered and followed him over the side, shivering when she felt her boots sinking into the mud below. Something nipped her forearm and she slapped at it. Numoya was already several yards ahead of her, and she hurried to catch up. She heard soldiers drop into the swamp and some soon overtook her so they could be near their leader. By the time Quenion had placed herself behind Numoya, the water level had dropped noticeably. Twice she slipped and resurfaced covered in mud, but in this case the rain was a mercy and soon managed to clean away most of the muck.

"Not far now," Numoya was saying, his voice sounding almost feverish. "Not far now and we will have won."

Quenion staggered between mangrove trees, tripping over roots, fighting mud and weariness and insects, but she knew she had to keep Numoya in sight. She was his

Beloved. She had duties and responsibilities. And by the Sefid so did he but never saw it.

Stop it, she told herself. You're not doing yourself any good thinking like this. He's forgiven you. You have what you wanted.

She kept repeating it, needing to believe it was what she wanted, needing to believe it was what she had always wanted.

The enemy soldier appeared over the edge of the wall, clear-skinned, round face red from exertion, firegon in one hand. He got one leg over, then saw Klyne Ferren standing there with a firegon. The soldier gave a strange expression that was halfway between smile and surprise. Ferren raised his weapon and fired point blank. There was a spray of blood, and a red cloud of it expanding over the wall, and the face seemed to be sucked in by the hole where the nose had been. The body fell backwards over the wall and was gone.

"Reload your weapon, you fool!" the soldier next to him cried out while also shooting at an enemy soldier almost over the wall.

It had been so many years since Ferren had reloaded a firegon that he fumbled with the gonblack dispenser, putting too much down the barrel. He finished loading just as the head of an enemy soldier peeked over the rim of the wall, calculating whether or not he could slip through the gap between the stonework and the hurriedly made barricade above it. Ferren aimed and fired, and he was hurled onto his back with the recoil. When he got to his feet he noticed a swathe of blood where the head had appeared.

"On your right!" someone shouted, and Ferren spun around. While he had been dealing with one enemy, another had managed to reach the walkway. He growled at Ferren and charged with his bayonet. Ferren instinctively brought up the firegon and squeezed the trigger. Click.

There was a shot from behind him, and a puff of gonblack smoke drifted past his head. The attacking soldier screamed in pain, grasping his left shoulder. Ferren swung out with the butt of his firegon, hitting the man so hard both his jaw and the firegon butt were broken. The man screamed in pain a second time, and Ferren, without thinking, stabbed him in the stomach with the splintered end of his firegon, and he went down.

Ferren searched around for another weapon, found only a sword. He picked it up and hefted it for weight, tried a few practice swings and returned to his station. There were no more enemy to kill. Feeling vaguely disappointed, he dared peer over the wall. They were still there, but holding back, waiting for something.

Arden had been organizing a courier to the mainland to let Galys and Poloma know the strength of the attack on Karhay and his belief that this was shaping up to be the major assault, when he noticed a trickle of retreating colonists who were not wounded. He sent the courier off and, with Heriot in tow, moved to intercept them. By then the trickle was becoming a flood. Arden ordered Heriot to halt and reorganize the retreating colonists while he ran up to investigate.

"Wait, Arden!" Heriot called after him, but he ignored her.

He did not have to go far before seeing the blue and white dressed infantry spilling over the wall and forming a perimeter, behind which more of their fellows were quickly forming a column; he knew that once that got moving, the colonists, for all their courage and determination, would not be able to stop its momentum.

As it was, some colonists were already pulling back in disorganized haste, and others were getting shot or bayoneted because they were making uncoordinated attacks. Arden realised the enemy had to be thrown back now while their numbers were still relatively small.

He ran to some of the retreating colonists and ordered them to form a line. Given an instruction, most were happy to fall in, and soon he had two ranks. Then Heriot joined him with the colonists she had organized, and he had the force he needed. He raised his hand to order the charge when Heriot, who was watching the enemy closely, said "Wait! They're preparing a volley!"

Arden could see the Rivald soldiers raising their firegons, checking with each other that all were loaded and ready. Then an officer on the right of the perimeter raised his hand. For an instant the two leaders met each other's gaze, both with their hands in the air.

"Down!" Arden boomed, and as one, almost every colonist dropped to the ground.

The enemy salvo crashed out over the island.

"Now, while they reload!" Arden shouted.

The colonists needed no more prompting. They screamed as they leaped to their feet and ran towards the enemy. "Stay behind me!" he told Heriot.

Arden charged in, swinging his axe with all his strength. Soldiers in blue and white uniforms scattered before him if they were fast enough. If not, they went down. Heriot scrabbled after him, jabbing at any who came too close to Arden from behind, although she never actually stabbed anyone because no one came within striking distance of the giant. By the time the enemy figured they had to get rid of Heriot before they could deal with Arden, other colonists had followed in the wake of the pair.

Arden noticed all the firegons lying around and grabbed the shirt of one colonist, ordering her to get others to help pick up as many firegons as they could, together with ammunition and gonblack, and distribute them among colonists. That done he charged in again, zigzagging his way through the partly formed enemy column. One brave Rivald soldier went at him with his bayonet, but Arden brushed the firegon aside and split the man from neck to waist with his axe. The blade stuck in the body and pulled down Arden's arm. Another soldier saw his opportunity and raised his firegon over his arm for a strike against Arden's back, but Heriot was there first and her dirk sank into the soldier's thigh. He screamed, fell, and Heriot stabbed him in the throat.

All was confusion. Arden wanted to pull back a few yards and see what was happening so he could give orders and coordinate the effort, but the melee was too general, the fighters too dispersed. Then it all stopped, and there was no one in Rivald's uniform still standing west of the defensive wall.

Arden told Heriot to make sure enemy reinforcements did not retake the breach, then formed all the colonists who had been given firegons or found one themselves into a party that stood back from the wall.

"You are not to attack anyone, or move anywhere, until I give the explicit order to do so," he told them. "You are our plug. Whenever the enemy puts a hole in our defences, you fill it."

They gave him a ragged cheer, but by then he was already gone and organizing another group of colonists to sort among their fallen comrades, the dead to be taken out of sight, the wounded who could not walk to be taken up to the stables where the physic station had been placed. That done, he returned to the site of the battle and gave command of that sector of the wall to an older woman who seemed the calmest and most collected of the colonists there. He and Heriot then returned to his newly formed mobile defence and waited to see what the enemy did next.

In the end, Lerena had to use soldiers to force her family to cooperate. Some begged her to let them be, to count their Axkevlerens out of the sacrifice, to spare them after the terrible loss of their Beloveds only months before, but she would not listen to them. She ordered troopers to the scene, and threatened them, her own cousins, with execution if they did not cooperate. When they heard that, most of the Axkevlerens pleaded to be sacrificed to save the lives of their masters and mistresses.

In the end, willing or not, the Kevlerens and their intended sacrifice stood in a line before Lerena, looking down on Beferen. Behind each Kevleren stood a trooper with saber in hand. The ground that swept before them was littered with bodies and dark stains, becoming so thick near the walls of the city that they seemed to cover the ground entirely.

Paimer, shivering like a reed in a wind, stood next to his niece. He wanted to close his eyes, but he could not turn away, could not hide from it. At heart he was a Kevleren, and as limited as his own ability with the Sefid may have been, he was drawn to sacrifice and Wielding like a fly to a cadaver.

Lerena said, gently, "You are not to Wield yourselves; I would not force that on you. I will do it alone. If you try to Wield you will be slain." She sighed deeply. "Now."

Every Kevleren reached out and gently grasped their chosen Axkevlerens around the neck. The styluses under the nails of their little fingers unerringly found jugulars, and the sacrifice started.

At first nothing, then the temperature started to drop. Paimer noticed the breath of his cousins clouding in the air. Blue flame licked off the sabers of the troopers. Eddies stirred between them, whipping up hair, carrying with them the moaning of the dying and the soft whimpering of their killers. Blood seeped around his feet, and the smell of it filled his nostrils. His skin prickled with the cold.

Idalgo should be here, he thought.

"I have been here all the time," Idalgo said.

"That brings me comfort," Paimer said. He glanced sideways at Lerena, saw her lips moving as she started to Wield, and wondered with terrible curiosity what she would make.

Gos Linsedd felt his stomach sink when he realized the enemy were not where he expected them to be. He had been so sure that the Rivald reserves would be upriver and out of reach of the Citadel's longgons that he had brought his entire troop with him. Now a significant portion of Kydan's military had been rendered next to useless.

"There's fighting at Karhay," Ames Westaway said slowly, looking through his spyglass while standing in his stirrups.

"Has all the enemy crossed over?" Gos demanded. "Is there none at all for us?"

Westaway did not answer right away, and Gos forced himself to be patient.

"They've lost many of their boats," Ames said, "but I'll wager not as many as Kadburn Axkevleren was hoping."

"And the enemy soldiers?"

"Most are across, Commander, but there is still a size-able force waiting to be transported, and they are on our side of the river. The boats are doing the best they can." The ensign shut his spyglass and slumped back in the saddle. "We have not much time."

Gos did not hesitate. The troop moved out, four abreast, and headed north. They kept to a walk despite the need for haste, but after the long night's ride their horses had only enough strength for one charge at the very end. He wished he believed in something more than the Sefid, and to his surprise found himself asking the goddess Kydan to intervene on his behalf. He thought Poloma would think it very strange, and probably very wonderful.

Klyne Ferren sniffed the air. He was smelling more than gonblack. His scalp was warming. He looked up and gasped. The barricade above the wall was on fire. He opened his mouth to give the alarm, but as he watched the fire seemed to follow one of the branches with a strange, almost intelligent purpose, and his voice died in his throat. Fire did not do that, his brain told him. The flame crept along until it reached another part of the barricade and suddenly expanded with a sigh of heat that breathed against his face.

"By the Sefid," he said hoarsely, and not as an exclamation.

The whole barricade caught fire. It went up in a sheet of almost white flame, burned so intensely that Ferren had to turn his head away and shield his face with his arms. The fire made a single roaring sound; there was a brilliant flash that he could see even through his closed eyelids. Some of the defenders on the wall shouted as they involuntarily took a step back and fell off the wall. And then nothing. He

opened his eyes, slowly parted his arms and peeked between them. The barricade was gone.

A ladder appeared at the top of the wall, then two grap-
pling hooks. He ran to the wall, sword in hand, and looked
over. How could there still be so many of the enemy? They
had already slain so many—

Something whacked into his jaw, blood speckled his
face, and he reeled back. He did not know what had happened, then a surge of pain started with his jaw and spread
all around his head as if it had been put in a vice.

Poloma and Galys were together on the Long Bridge,
with Lannel Thorey patiently waiting a few paces back.
They ignored the rain and concentrated on trying to hear
the tempo of the fighting on Karhay. They were waiting for
word from Arden before deciding whether or not to send
reinforcements. They had boats ready to go, although they
also had to be ready to flee if the Rivald decided to hunt
them down with their own vessels instead of using them as
transports. Poloma had suggested using their boats in that
way themselves, but Galys pointed out how few fighters
they had to spare and how big the enemy boats were.

"I remember the first time I saw the Long Bridge,"
Galys said, patting the stone railing. "I was with you then,
and we were marching to take the Citadel."

Poloma grimaced. "That seems like years ago now."

"It was only a season."

"If we win today—"

"We will win today," Galys said definitely.

"If we win today," Poloma persisted, "I don't ever want
to fight a battle in Kydan again."

Galys said nothing. She knew no such thing could be
guaranteed, not in the dangerous world they lived in.

"Do you remember the conversation we had on the *Hannemah* on our way across the Deepening Sea?"

Galys laughed lightly. "Which one? We must have talked for hours."

"About Kydan being strong enough to never be picked on again by Rivald. Or Hamilay."

"Yes, I remember. And I remember you saying you did not want Kydan to be a big fish, but a little invisible fish."

"I've decided there are no such things as little invisible fish," Poloma said. "The sea is divided into big fish and their food."

"You want Kydan to be strong?"

"I will tell you, Strategos, what I want for Kydan. I want a university. I want a steam carriage and bridges. I want to unite all the people along the Frey so they are our friends and not our enemies. I want to build a proper commercial dock for merchant ships from all over the world to come here and help us get rich.

"Yes, I want Kydan to be strong, strong enough to have all of those things. I want you to know this."

"Then I will make you a promise, Prefect Poloma Malvara. If we survive this, I will help you build that city."

It was Poloma's turn to laugh. "I already knew *that*."

When he saw the barricade go up in flames, Chierma turned away from the scene and vomited. When his stomach emptied he wiped his mouth with the back of his hand. He was too ashamed to look up.

"That wasn't your finest moment," Lady Englay said.

"Go away," Chierma replied.

Chierma watched Beferen's last moments of independence. The Hamilayan infantry had managed to climb the wall in greater numbers than before, although at terrible cost. It seemed to him that the companies in the attack had paid the price for this moderate success with half their numbers. Then he remembered the empire at Lerena's back. She could replace the losses in a single season, whereas Rivald would never recover, even if somehow, miraculously, Beferen survived the assault.

And maybe, just maybe, it might survive the assault, he thought, seeing the Hamilayan forces repulsed for the second bloody time. Soldiers were running away from the wall, many throwing away their firegons. Rivald soldiers on the wall were cheering, waving their weapons in the air.

"I do not think Lerena has finished yet," Englay said.

Chierma wondered what else the empress could do. Englay looked at him with something like pity and, for the first time, something like fear. He remembered what she had said to him not long before, about Lerena killing her.

"She will slay her own," he said under his breath. "She will sacrifice Kevlerens."

Numoya took the time to put his companies into formation before breaking into open ground. He was on the far right of the lead column as they started their march, and could not help his chest swelling in pride as the core of his new army stepped in almost perfect time towards the completely undefended western end of the city. In the excitement he no longer felt the throbbing pain in his head.

As the soldiers encountered the first few scattered houses and other structures they flowed around them like sand, joining again on the other side. In the distance was the Citadel, and before that, Numoya knew, was the Long Bridge. It was the bridge where the enemy would first try to hold him back, given enough warning to prepare, but he could hear very distantly the sound of combat and knew

their attention was focused on Velan Lymok and his forces.
The popinjay had done his duty.

At first they met few civilians, and those disappeared
inside their homes without making trouble, but soon they
reached the start of what would become the main street,
the east-west axis that joined the most expensive housing
with the Long Bridge in the west of Herris, and the Great
Quadrangle, the Assembly and the Citadel in the east.
More and more people fled, alerting any Kydans further
ahead. As the Rivald progressed the road surface improved, increasing their pace in the heavy rain, but buildings closed in on either side, forcing the files of the
columns closer and closer together.

Eventually houses gave way to shops and stalls and the
road started its incline towards the Long Bridge. On either
side spread the Saddle and beyond the islands of Karhay
and Kayned, and although he looked for signs of Velan
Lymok's detachment on Karhay, they were out of sight.
The sounds of fighting there had quelled, but he could still
hear sporadic fire. Closer to hand, at the far northern end
of the Saddle, he saw a clump of what looked suspiciously
like organized units, but they were in the wrong place at
the wrong time and they would not get to the Citadel before him.

Numoya and the head of the column reached the apex
of the bridge. Before them lay the heart of Kydan and,
waiting for them at the end of the bridge, several hundred
more enemy soldiers.

Ferren cursed his own weakness as the pain in his jaw
made his vision blur and dim. A chip of granite flicked into
his cheek. Mortar dust blew into his eyes. He heard the
sound of a heavy stone scraping. The wall trembled, then

lurched forwards, then back, and Ferren was thrown from his feet. He looked around and saw that no one had been left standing. He pulled himself up by gripping the top of the wall and leaned over to see what was happening. There were no enemy soldiers nearby; they were all fleeing back towards their own lines. Behind them he could see other companies starting to form, and several troops of cavalry. He did not like that sign of confidence.

Another chip of stone ricocheted off his face, as sharp as a razor, adding to his pain, and he swore under his breath. Something tugged at his jacket, then his pants, then the back of his hand was cut. He was surrounded by a gray cloud, and he could just make out that all the other defenders on the wall and the gatehouse seemed shrouded by something similar.

He did not have time to be afraid. The cuts were coming more frequently. A sliver of granite pierced his cheek. He swatted at the cloud as if it was made from mosquitoes. An entire block from the wall scraped loose and clunked onto the walkway. A crack appeared along its length and it exploded. Shrapnel shredded Ferren's left leg. He could not help screaming. He tottered towards the stairs to get away. He heard a longgon crash through the walkway to his right and fall on the soldiers below.

He put his right foot on the first step, dragged his second over. Then the next step. The rise pushed out, hitting him in the calf. A large chunk of stone slammed into the back of his head and he heard his skull crack. He started to fall, tried to balance himself but missed his footing. He fell sideways against the wall of the gatehouse, bending his arm the wrong way under the weight of his own body. His consciousness fluttered like the wings of a butterfly and

started slipping away. More stones hit him, breaking ribs
and a kneecap.

Ferren fell, bouncing on the stairs. He landed in a heap
at the bottom, the gray cloud tightening and tightening
around him.

The first sign Galys and Poloma had that they were in
serious trouble was when they saw civilians fleeing from
the west and running across the Long Bridge and down the
ramp to the Saddle. One of the first to cross the bridge
rushed up to them, his hair sodden and sticking to his ears,
and said Rivald infantry were marching straight for them.

"That isn't possible," Poloma said flatly. "Kadburn
Axkevleren has been watching their boats from the
Citadel. If any had gone around the island he would have
told us."

The civilian stared wide-eyed at the prefect. "Six companies, at least. And many are Rivald troops, like the ones
who came two years ago. They are pale-skinned," he
added, nodding at Galys, "like the strategos."

The man ran on, and was followed by a thickening
stream of refugees.

Galys swallowed. Behind her, on the east side of the
bridge, were two militia companies, a third was waiting on
the western side, and another two companies were down in
the Saddle in case they had to be ferried quickly to Karhay.
The sixth company she had sent to Kayned, and she
wished now she had kept it closer to hand.

"Do you think it is true?" Poloma asked her.

"We cannot let them reach the Citadel," Galys said in
reply. Poloma paled. She turned to Lannel. "Go over the
bridge and order the company there to join me here." Lannel nodded and ran off.

"Poloma, go down to the Saddle and get the other two companies and bring them up as well. Arden and Heriot will just have to manage on their own. I'll prepare a line of defense here. We'll be able to deploy in line, and the Rivald crossing the bridge will have to stay in column."

"That gives us an advantage?" Poloma asked, sounding doubtful.

"As long as the enemy doesn't charge," she said.

Poloma hurried off and Galys started organizing the two companies already at hand. When Lannel arrived with the third, marching double time, she ordered it to the left of the line she had created. Those armed with firegons she placed in two ranks, and behind them placed those armed with spears and swords, with strict instructions to keep their weapons out of sight. She had time to glance over the bridge to check on Poloma's progress. He had reached the bottom of the ramp and was running towards the dock at the northern end of the Saddle and the companies that were stationed there. She wished he could run faster.

Galys heard the tramping of marching infantry. The sound vibrated through the stone of the Long Bridge. Little swirls of stone dust fell from the railing.

"Do not fire until I give the command!" she ordered.

One of the militia pointed back to the bridge.

Galys turned and saw a line of caps broach the bridge's crest, then faces under the caps, then rank and rank of Rivald infantry. With a shock, because she had not expected to see him so close to the action, she recognised Numoya Kevleren at the head of the column. In a surge of panic she herself almost ordered the militia to fire, but the enemy was still too far away for her to be sure the Kevleren would be hit. But if she waited too long he might Wield. Poloma had told her stories of the last time Rivald troops had invaded Kydan, and Numoya had sacrificed his Beloved then to destroy the few militia that had dared resist them.

Unexpectedly, the Rivald lowered their firegons, shouted a war cry and charged. Before she or Lannel could stop them, the first two ranks of militia instinctively raised their weapons to their shoulders and fired. The enemy was too far away for the salvo to slow the charge. A scattering of the enemy fell, but their fellows just rolled over them and kept on coming.

The Sefid had been renewed and was even stronger than before. Lerena felt as if she could have floated on it all the way back to Omeralt. The sky glowed with it, reflecting off the great sea of blood that washed around her feet. Every nerve in her body seemed to be on fire, but she was not harmed by it. She could see stars beyond the sky, and deep into the seas that girdled the world, and in the hearts of caverns that lay beneath the earth. She could hear every mind in creation, feel every pang of hunger, every spasm of fear, every coil of love.

Lerena also saw the two ghosts that hovered nearby. They were reveling in her sacrifice, and she was happy for them, but also curious. But first things first. She turned her attention to Beferen and saw that her army, with her help, had at last managed to get past the wall. Even from here she could hear the wailing of its people, and she was both elated that victory was hers and struck by pity for the suffering of her Beferen subjects, for that is now what they were.

She would help them. She would help all of those who owed her allegiance. And they would love her the way Axkevlerens always loved Kevlerens, for in a world where she was the greatest of her kind, all must naturally turn to her for love.

She looked down and saw Paimer. He was curled at her feet, like a small child. He most of all she would protect. After all, she could not see into the future, although the possibility of doing so was something she was keen to investigate, and a time may come when she might need him.

She ordered the troopers to gather together the bodies of her dead relatives and their Axkevlerens and to make a funeral pyre for them.

"The smoke will rise over the whole world," she told Paimer.

Numoya had stayed at the top of the Long Bridge when he ordered his infantry to charge. He watched the battle keenly, and almost clapped for joy when the enemy militia fired far too soon to have any effect. Then he received the first of three surprises. The front two ranks of the enemy quickly and in good order retreated to the back of their line, and those who took their place were not armed with firegons but spears and swords. His troops had too much momentum to stop, and anyway could not deploy to use their firegons effectively while they were on the bridge, so they charged on, ploughing into the militia. The enemy line bent backwards but did not break, and with their specialty melee weapons had a distinct advantage over their opponents armed only with a bayonet atop a long and clumsy firegon. Those Rivald soldiers at the very front were able to shoot, and several enemy fell, but not enough.

The second surprise was the militia commander, who Numoya saw shouting orders from the right of her line. It was the blonde strategos who had taken him prisoner when the expedition from Hamilay had taken Kydan from him.

She was one of his special foes, one of those he wanted to slay with his own hands.

But first he had to destroy the militia in front of him.

He had the numbers, but while in column they could not be put to best use. His soldiers had to force the militia away from the bridge so his companies could deploy in line and outflank the enemy. Eventually the weight of numbers would tell in the center and he would get that space, but he may not have the luxury of time. Who knew what reinforcements the Kydans could call on?

The strategos was signaling a new command. Before his men could do anything, the front ranks of the enemy who were armed with swords and spears dropped to their knees, revealing the re-formed ranks of militia armed with reloaded firegons. With one smooth movement they raised their weapons and fired. A cloud of black smoke billowed out and temporarily obscured his view of the struggle, but when it cleared he saw the devastation it had caused. Virtually half of the first of the Rivald companies had been mown down, and those behind wavered. He expected the strategos to order her own troops to charge then, but she did not. Instead, the first ranks stood up and readied to receive the Rivald if they should charge a second time. She was a fool, Numoya decided, to throw away that opportunity, and he would not give the woman a second chance to cause so much carnage among his troops.

The third surprise was an alarm from his last column. He ordered Quenion to take charge of the van and ran back to the end of his column. Several soldiers were pointing down to the Saddle. He looked over the rail and saw two companies of infantry, probably those he had seen earlier at the far end of the Saddle, jogging towards the western ramp to take his force from behind. He had been delayed longer than he thought, and they were moving faster than any militia had a right to.

There was only one solution. His stomach cramped at the idea of it, and his headache returned twice as strong. He had to destroy the militia companies in front of him so he could turn in time to destroy those rushing to come behind him. If he did that, then Kydan would be his again, and all would be the way it should be.

He ran back to the van and Quenion, his Beloved.

Velan Lymok had lost his best troops in his several assaults on the wall around the settlement on Herris. Even when he knew he no longer had the numbers to take advantage of any breakthrough, he kept on, doing everything he could to give Numoya Kevleren the chance he needed for final victory. As the day wore on, however, and the Citadel showed no Rivald flag, he knew there was little to be gained by continuing the attacks. His duty now was to pull his people back from the island and get them safely to the mainland. If he saved enough of them he might even be able to dissuade any pursuit. But first he needed the boats to stop bringing reinforcements to a lost cause and start taking his troops back to the mainland instead.

He had a company armed with firegons who had been badly mauled in the first assault, and these he set up in a defensive line between the enemy-held wall and the shoreline. Then he arranged his remaining companies as if he was organizing another assault. Finally, he told a runner to tell the next boat master to come back empty, and to pass the word to the other masters as well.

He looked one last time to the Citadel. No Rivald flag. No victory. Something had gone wrong, and he could no longer wait. The enemy behind the wall showed no inclination to attack him, for which he was grateful, although the longgons in the Citadel were firing again. He quickly watched some of the shot to make sure his infantry on the mainland had not wandered into range, but they were completely safe. He was puzzled by the waste of ammunition, and could only assume the longgon chiefs or whoever was commanding them was hoping they would get lucky. Perhaps they were trying different amounts of gonblack to see if they could make the balls drop short. As far as he could see, however, the longgons posed no threat to his forces at the moment, and the more ammunition they used up now the less they would have to shoot at his retreating companies later on.

All he needed to do was wait for the boats to return so he could withdraw his force, and then gather the courage he would need to face Numoya Kevleren to explain why he had ordered the retreat.

A moan of despair from his own troops startled him, especially since their position was still comparatively strong, but a glimpse of flame out of the corner of his eye made him turn, and there on the mainland south of the Frey, he saw most of his boats drawn up on the bank and burning down to their keels.

Gos Linsedd led his dragoons as close as possible to the river in the hope that the one way the Rivald troops would not look for trouble would be the way they themselves had come. When he had halved the distance he heard the distant booming of the Citadel's longgons, and hoped Kadburn had not mistaken him for Rivald cavalry coming late to the assault. But the shot were flying northwards, well over the heads of the enemy. In fact, the enemy were watching the shot as well and hooting as they hurtled harmlessly overhead.

Gos grinned. The enemy were very busy looking everywhere but east. Clever Kadburn.

When he was two longyards from the enemy position he raised his sabre to his shoulder. Immediately his troop fanned out to his left, forming two lines, Gos in charge of the first and Ensign Ames Westaway in charge of the second. Now they were spread out it was only a matter of time before they were sighted. As soon as he saw an enemy soldier raise the alarm, he lowered the saber and pointed its tip straight at the Rivald on the south bank and, as if it was one beast, the troop moved to a gallop. A moment later their beautiful line became ragged, with some horses managing the pace better than others after the long ride, but when they slammed into the enemy there was not enough of a gap between them to make any difference to the effect of the charge. The infantry scattered, screaming in fear, and many of his troopers pursued them.

Gos reined in so he could get a better idea of the situation. That's when he saw the boats on the bank; obviously they had been in the process of either loading or unloading infantry, and were now trying to push away from the bank. Some of the infantry in the shallows tried to hold the boats back until they could get on, and the crews hacked at them with small axes.

Gos gathered his half-troop and charged again, clearing away the foreshore, then they drew their short-barreled carbines and fired at the crew. One master surrendered, then another, and soon most of the boats were in his hands. He did not have enough men to look after so many prisoners, and rather than risk them freeing themselves and recapturing their boats, he ordered the vessels burned.

The fire raised cheers in the Citadel and a salute from the longgons.

Quenion did not know what to do with the van except keep her post and make sure the pressure was kept on the militia blocking their way. One thing she decided to do was copy one of the enemy's tactics by organizing two ranks that did nothing but use their firegons. Because their frontage, restricted by the span of the Long Bridge, was so much narrower than their opponents', the effect was not as dramatic, but it did slow the enemy's fire which gave more opportunity for the Rivald soldiers to wear away the militia.

Suddenly Numoya was by her side again, and she looked at him with relief in her face. He was looking at her with a grim intensity that confused her. She was wondering what she had done wrong now.

"The enemy will soon be behind us as well," he said.

"Then we must break through here quickly," she replied.

"Yes." His voice was feverish, flushed, and then he said, "My Beloved," and all the emotion she knew he possessed seemed to fill the words. She could not help the feeling of joy that swelled through her, but just as quickly her mind, as clear and sharp as a Sayenna dawn, drained the joy away.

He was going to sacrifice her to save his army, as he had done once before with his first Beloved. Numoya Kevleren was going to slay her.

Quenion had time to realize the irony: the man she once thought she loved more than her own life was at last talking to her with fierce, unbridled passion, but only to pass on her a death sentence.

His hand reached and she recoiled. He frowned, confused.

"Quenion, my Beloved, this is necessary. To save our cause, for the Kevlerens, for Rivald. I need a great sacrifice. I need to sacrifice what I love more than anything else in the world."

His words almost seduced her all over again, and for the briefest of moments she was again a true Axkevleren, with but one purpose and that to serve Numoya. Then his hand stroked her hair, then her cheek, and the spell was broken. She remembered what she had done for him already, what her predecessor had done for him, what Beloveds all through history had done for that family, and she realized she did not want to die.

His hand finally rested around her neck, and she could feel his little finger with its sharp stylus running over the rise in her throat that showed her artery. Without hesitation she grasped the dagger from his own belt and with all her strength drove it straight up into his jaw, and screamed in his face that she did not love him.

CAPTAIN Avier of the *Annglaf*, escorting the *Hannemah*, the *Grayling*, the *Zarim* and the *Laxton*, returned to the colony expecting a mild welcome, without a great deal of effusion, but was certainly not expecting to find a city in the throes of recovering from another battle. Smoke from funeral pyres lifted high into the sky, smoke he had seen from some distance and which had given him some premonition that not all had gone so smoothly during his absence.

When he landed, however, he found the mood of the people to be almost festive, and he was surprised to find himself being officially greeted by Poloma Malvara, affirmed Prefect of Kydan; together with Galys Valera, affirmed Strategos for Kydan; Heriot Fleetwood, affirmed Advisor to the Prefect on Unity; Gos Linsedd, affirmed Commander of the Kydan Army; Kadburn Axkevleren, affirmed Warden of the Citadel; and a strange, tall man who was introduced as Lannel Thorey, Probationary Ensign in the Kydan Militia. Most of all, he was startled to learn that in his absence he had been affirmed as Commodore of the Kydan Navy, with a grand fleet of one schooner, four ex-grain ships and a dozen or so boats used to ferry passengers and cargo between islands.

He was flattered, and certainly thought commodore sounded better than captain, then wondered if it came with extra braid for his jacket.

"I am moved and gratified by the honor I am being paid," he said to Poloma, who was quite obviously now the man in charge. The others all stayed at least a step back from him. Avier studied the prefect closely and saw a great deal had changed in him: he was more confident than before and, if possible, even more somber. But the smile and handshake he offered when Avier first stepped on land was genuine and touching.

Avier cleared his throat and said, "I wish my news was as grand and promising."

They all gathered at Poloma's house. As soon as food and drink had been set out by the servants, Avier quickly related what he had discovered in Hamilay.

"I was told that one night in spring the Sefid rang so true and pure that everything made of metal in Omeralt and for hundreds of miles around shone blue. The next morning, so the story goes, there was not a single Beloved left anywhere in the empire." Avier glanced at Kadburn, swallowed. "It was hard to believe, and I said so. I was told off for a fool. Then I asked when this was supposed to have happened, and making allowances for the fact that we in Kydan were halfway round the world, it was about the same time General Third Prince Maddyn was killed."

His audience said nothing at first, so remarkable was the news. Kadburn stood up stiffly and walked around the room, his eyes downcast.

"At first we thought it was Numoya Kevleren who had done it . . ." Galys started, but could not finish.

Kadburn came behind her and put his hands on her shoulders. "Killed the prince, and Grammarian Kitayra Albyn. We learned before your return, Captain, that it could not have been Numoya, but until now it remained a mystery." Kadburn smiled thinly. "Sorry. Commodore."

"It must have been done by whoever it was who Wielded in Omeralt that night," Galys continued. She caught Avier's gaze. "Was it Yunara?"

"That's the other amazing thing about that night," Avier said slowly. "Not just every Beloved in the empire died, but so did the Duchess Yunara."

There was a surprised silence. Yunara had been recognised as the most powerful Wielder for several generations of Kevlerens. Perhaps the most powerful ever.

"I don't believe it," Gos said, then quickly, "No reflection on you, Commodore . . . but . . . what could possibly slay Yunara?"

Galys said, "What you really mean is *who* could slay Yunara?"

Avier shrugged. "There are rumors, of course, but no one really knows. All that anyone can say is that Lerena is the only one in court who did not seem seriously affected by the events of that night, even though her own Beloved had died with the others."

Galys and Kadburn exchanged glances. "Lerena?" Kadburn asked. "The empress? But she was never known for her ability with the Sefid . . ."

"As I understand it from those who have been to the court, many now regard Lerena the same way everyone once regarded the Duchess Yunara. People are afraid of her."

"But she . . . liked . . . Maddyn," Kadburn said.

"Yunara tried to kill Maddyn, once, and the duchess

thought she *loved* him," Galys pointed out. "What more, then, would the empress be capable of doing?"

They all fell silent, until eventually Galys said, "There is much for us to think on. The situation back in Hamilay is not what we thought it would be, and many things we believed we knew and understood have proven wrong. It seems to me that Hamilay has suffered its own revolution, and the world is changing on both sides of the Deepening Sea."

Velan Lymok and Quenion Axkevleren were called before Poloma Malvara. Quenion recognized his companion as the blonde woman who had held the Long Bridge so capably against Numoya.

"You have a choice," Poloma said.

"That's heartening," Velan said dryly. Although they had been treated as well as could be expected for prisoners of an invading army, no one in Kydan had shown them any kindness or generosity beyond the basics of food and water. He was not expecting that to change in the near future.

"In fact, you each have different choices," Poloma continued, ignoring Velan. "You, Quenion Axkevleren, are free. Your choice is simply to stay if that is your preference, or to leave for wherever you wish."

"But I was the Beloved of this city's great enemy."

"We will remember you for being the destroyer of this city's great enemy," the woman by his side said. "You have earned your freedom."

Quenion said nothing, obviously not expecting such clemency. Working all her life with the Kevlerens had not taught her anything about mercy.

"And you, Leader of a Thousand, Velan Lymok, have two choices."

"You are not freeing me, I gather."

"Not yet," Poloma said. "You can wait here for a ship from Rivald and thence return to that state and never come to the New Land again. You will be kept under close watch while you stay here, but not be imprisoned."

"And the second choice?"

"Assist us in our expedition against Sayenna."

Velan blinked. "You are not serious."

"Absolutely," the woman said. "This city has been invaded four times in the last two years, and three of those times either originated from or were supported by the city of Sayenna. Kydan, obviously, cannot be free until Sayenna is captured, incorporated or destroyed. And now would seem an ideal time, considering that most of its garrison is either dead or captured."

"How would I assist you exactly?"

"Show us where it is," Poloma said simply.

Galys returned one more time to Kitayra's room in the Citadel. All of the grammarian's possessions had been sorted, packed and bound. All of Kitayra's possessions except two, that is. The grammarian's papers, which Galys intended to study, and Kitayra's mysterious birth chain. The next time one of Kydan's merchant ships made for Hamilay it would take with it Kitayra's possessions and hand them over to some appropriate authority who would then make sure they reached her family somewhere in the empire. Lerena's empire, Galys reminded herself. Even though she believed now that Lerena had been responsible for so much of the destruction and heartbreak of the last few months, she found it hard to come to terms with it. She had grown up believing in the *rightness* of empire, in its moral as well as practical value, and believing that all that was good about the empire was embodied in its ruler.

Now that she believed Lerena Kevleren was corrupt and immoral, what did it mean for the empire itself? Did it diminish entirely the goodwill and noble efforts of all those who strived within its borders?

It was a problem for which Galys had not yet found a solution, and was not confident she ever would.

At least she had Kydan now, a home apart from Hamilay and Lerena and all the other Kevlerens, a home that would help her cut ties with her own past and help her start, at last, a life of her own.

She pulled the imperial birth chain from her pocket. Much of its brilliant, scintillating colour seemed to have gone, but there was still something indefinably strange and threatening about the stones. She was convinced the birth chain was somehow involved in Kitayra's death, and that Kitayra's death was somehow involved with Lerena's sudden and unexpected supremacy with the Sefid. She did not yet have all the answers, but the path to those answers seemed clearer now.

She put the birth chain away and looked out over her home. She could already see where she would site Poloma's university, and where the tracks for the steam carriage would be laid to connect all three islands, and eventually all the settlements between Kydan and Sayenna.

A beetle scurried along the windowsill. She watched it trying to find a way out, then helped it by pushing it gently in the right direction. A nudge here and there is all it takes, she told herself, to set a life on a new course, to reveal new horizons.

Galys sighed deeply and left the room, closing the door

behind her. She had a life that was worth living, and she was going to make sure that was exactly what she did.

A flash of memory, of another life lived so long ago it could have been another age.

A flash of pain, of dying, and then, strangely, of killing.

A flash of hunger.

The creature moved one limb, and then another, and stumbled from its hiding place. A night sky, velvet blue, wrapped the world. Stars. It remembered, vaguely, the stars at sea, and the white foam at a ship's bow. It remembered peace and contentment, and desired it.

But first it needed food.

It sniffed the air, scented something nearby. It turned and saw in the distance a yellow glimmer. A house, it remembered. Yes, there would be food there. When it was no longer hungry, maybe then it would find peace.

It shambled off into the night, leaving behind the headland and the sea, the stars dancing high overhead.